Flowers of Chivalry

Nigel Tranter

CORONET BOOKS
Hodder and Stoughton

FLOWERS OF CHIVALRY

The young man who sat at the table, quill in hand was extraordinarily like his brother, and yet so very different. In feature and build and colouring they were not far from identical; but in expression, demeanour and bearing there was no similarity. Where Alexander was keen-eyed, firm-mouthed and strong-chinned, yet with laughter lines apt to qualify any aspect of sternness, William looked gentle, studious, diffident almost, and apt to be abstracted, not weak but passive, as though habitually suspending judgment. Two years the younger, despite his reflective air, he managed to look more junior.

"Still poring over papers, Will! On my soul, your eyes will drop out, one of these days! Can you not find something better to do, this fine July afternoon?" He said that affably, however, smiling, and tramped over the papers to clap his brother on the bent shoulders. They were good friends, these two.

Principal Characters, in Order of Appearance

Sir Alexander Ramsay of Dalwolsey: A Lothian lord.

Sir William Douglas of Liddesdale: Borders lord, known as The Flower of Chivalry.

Donald, Earl of Mar: Great noble, now Regent of Scotland.

Ramsay of Redheuch: Vassal laird of Sir Alexander.

Pate Ramsay of Cockpen: Cousin and esquire to Sir Alexander.

William Ramsay: Sir Alexander's younger brother.

Patrick, Earl of Dunbar and March: Great Borders noble.

Andrew Murray of Tullibardine: Perthshire laird.

Sir Andrew Murray, Lord of Bothwell and Avoch: Guardian of the boy King of Scots.

John Randolph, Earl of Moray: Second son of the late Regent.

Queen Joan, or Joanna, Plantagenet: Child wife of David the Second.

David the Second, King of Scots: Son of Robert the Bruce.

Bishop Bernard de Linton: Chancellor of Scotland.

Wattie Kerr: Groom to Ramsay.

Lady Mariot Randolph: Daughter of the late Regent, younger sister of Moray.

Bishop Maurice of Dunblane: Friend of the late King Robert.

Robert Stewart, High Steward of Scotland: Grandson of the late King.

Bishop John of St Andrews: Primate.

Sir Archibald Douglas, Lord of Galloway: Chief of that great house.

Edward Balliol: Usurper. Son of the late King John Balliol.

Scott of Rankilburn: Borders chief. Ancestor of Buccleuch.

Sir Alexander Seton of that Ilk: Lothian lord.

Lady Agnes Randolph, Countess of Dunbar and March: Sister to John and Mariot.

Sir Simon Fraser: Borders chief and veteran fighter.

William de Montague, Earl of Salisbury: Great English noble.

Edward the Third: King of England.

Sir William Keith: Knight Marischal of Scotland.

Sir Alexander de Mowbray of Barnbougle: A disinherited lord.

Sir Henry de Beaumont: Disinherited lord of English extraction.

John Plantagenet, Earl of Cornwall: Brother of Edward the Third.

Lord Robert Manners: English commander. Friend of King Edward.

Part One

1

The men who stood by the bedside eyed each other and shook their heads. It would not be long now was their unspoken assessment. The Earl's breathing was growing irregular and shallower.

The youngest there, Alexander Ramsay, biting his lip, moved over to the window and looked out and down to the street. The wide market-place of the old town of Musselburgh was packed with folk, standing amongst the stalls and booths, men and women, even children. Most were staring up at these windows, silent, waiting, an extraordinary sight. They had been there almost since first light, as indeed they had been the day before, and the day before that. Ramsay wagged his head at them and over them helplessly – and he was not a helpless man by nature, nor any head-shaker.

He was joined by another man, not much older but compared with the slender, fair-haired Ramsay seeming so, tall, massively built with great breadth of shoulder, dark, swarthy enough to be known as the Black, the Black Knight of Liddesdale. Suitable enough to be thus dark, for he was the son, even though illegitimate, of the late and legendary Black Douglas himself, the Good Sir James, closest of all the Bruce's close friends and lieutenants: Sir William Douglas, also known as The Flower of Chivalry.

Douglas did not look down at the waiting crowd but peered sideways and upwards through the window, to the right, to where he could just see the Tolbooth tower rising high above the roofs of the town. Up there on that precarious platform, two men-at-arms stood, clutching whatever they could for support and gazing seawards. They had a flag to wave but were not waving it.

"Nothing!" Douglas growled, but low-voiced for him. "Still no word. This is damnable! This idle waiting, when all hangs in the balance."

Ramsay did not answer. For three days and nights they had been facing this grievous situation and problem.

"Mar will heed me nothing," the dark man went on, almost below his breath, which sounded the odder in a man whose voice normally rang out loud and clear and vehement. "We ought to be on our way. All could be lost. Moray himself would be the first to order it – were he able to speak, to command."

The other nodded, but at the same time made a little cancelling motion of his hand, as though he both agreed and disagreed. "Soon, now," he murmured. "And there is no signal. It seems the enemy waits also."

"But *they* have the choice, man! The ships can land where they will. *We* are hamstrung! We . . ."

A choking sound from behind them turned them about, and they moved back to the others around the bed. The figure thereon was in some sort of convulsion now, feeble enough but the first real movement for long hours. All there feared that it was the last, the end; but out of its so evident hurt the man opened eyes which had been closed for days and nights. Panting, lips moving soundlessly, he looked up, but blankly. Then the eyelids closed again, and the watchers held their breaths. But the fine eyes reopened, and this time they slowly focussed on the faces around him, pausing at each for a moment or two, until they reached Donald, Earl of Mar. There they lingered.

The lips moved again, in more than the fluttering breathing, and after a false start, formed words, faint, laboured but clear. "Cousin . . . it now . . . is for you. The . . . task. Go. God . . . help you! And . . . and . . . go!"

However uncertain the message intended by those penultimate words, the last was sufficiently positive, a command. And there was no more. The effort had exhausted the remaining tiny vestige of strength, the final effort on this earth of a man whose life had been all effort. The body on the bed heaved up and then subsided, still.

Thomas Randolph, Earl of Moray, nephew of the Bruce and Regent of Scotland, was gone to join his hero and friend, the late King.

For long the group round the bed gazed down at the man who had led them since the hero-king's death three years before, Moray the just and good, a man loved as well as

10

respected, and feared by evil-doers. It was the end of an era, they all recognised, as well as of a ruler and tower of strength. This was the last of that most renowned band of Bruce's devoted paladins, who had helped him to save and free Scotland. Sir Neil Campbell of Lochawe had died before the King. The Good Sir James Douglas had fallen carrying Bruce's heart on crusade. Angus Og MacDonald, Lord of Islay and the Isles, had perished in a Hebridean storm the year after his king. And now Sir Thomas Randolph of Moray, to whom Bruce had entrusted his five-year-old son David, Prince of Scotland, as Regent and Governor. None of them had made old bones, like their master; too many wounds, too many huge exertions, too many nights spent wet and cold in caves or under the stars. Not that Moray had died of his many wounds or worn out by fatigue; he had long suffered the painful affliction of the stone, refusing to let it restrict his running of the child-king's realm – but it had won in the end.

As usual it was the urgent and impatient Sir William Douglas who spoke first. "God rest his soul!" he exclaimed. "We shall not see his like again. But – we must be doing! We have delayed already too long. Balliol and the English lie but a mile or two off, in their ships. They could land at any time. And any place. We must catch them then, at their landing, when they are weakest."

"Yes, yes. To be sure, Douglas. But we must needs pay our respects to our leader and Governor first, surely. My good cousin, Moray. And the people must be told." That was Donald, Earl of Mar, the only other earl present, another nephew of the Bruce, his sister Christian's son, but no great warrior this one, a man of moods and tempers, able enough but erratic.

"The people can wait!" the dark man declared shortly. "The realm's safety can not, my lord. You heard him, the Regent? He said to go. Go now, to your task. *He* knew. The best respects to pay are to do what he said, commanded!"

They all looked at Mar, all soldiers, campaigners, leaders of men, except himself – yet they all accepted that it was Mar's decision, one of the great earls of Scotland and kin to the monarch, however much they might doubt his military qualities.

Frowning, he glanced towards the window. "Is there any word from the watchers? Any sign?"

"None, my lord," Sir Alexander Ramsay answered him. "They keep good look-out, but the flag is not raised. So the English must still remain undecided, their ships beating up and down the Forth."

"Then there is no great haste. They are undecided because they cannot see our army, what it does and just where it is. This town hides our men. Move out from this Musselburgh and they will see us, see where we go. And our strength. They can then move, decide where to land, up-firth or down. We are well enough here. No need for haste yet, Douglas."

There was sense in what the Earl said, but not enough for Will Douglas. "An army, my lord, takes a deal of time to make move from camp. In especial when at a town. This is our fourth day here. The men have settled in. Gone drinking in the town. Found women. If Balliol decided to make for Leith, to disembark there and try to capture Edinburgh, he could be landed and marching before we could marshal our force to assail him. Or the same at Dunbar behind us. The army should have been kept standing to arms, not encamped. The Lord Regent would never have allowed that."

"Watch how you speak, sir! I do not require your preachings! The men were weary, the horses also, after our forced march from Colbrandspath. They required rest and sustenance if they were to fight."

More tactfully, Ramsay came to his friend's assistance. "True, my lord. But they are well rested now. They should perhaps be readied, at least sufficient of the horse to ride at short notice."

There was a murmur of agreement from some of the others, especially Sir Colin Campbell, son of the great Sir Neil, who tended to find the Douglas too strong meat.

"Very well," Mar acceded. "Go you and ready the horse. I will down and tell the good folk of this honest town of the loss they, and we all, have suffered. They must have loved him well to wait there, these days . . ."

Distinctly doubtful about having this dispute over the body of their respected leader, and the propriety of leaving him there to go about their duties, the group broke up, some touching the still-warm hands in a sort of homage, others bowing the head.

Douglas and Ramsay hurried downstairs and slipped out by the back door, to avoid the crowd. The former was heading for the open area of Pinkie Braes, a little way to the south, where most of the Scots army was encamped, to order immediate readiness to move; but Ramsay said that he would climb the Tolbooth tower to see for himself the situation as to the English fleet.

Musselburgh's Tolbooth, comprising the townhouse, burgh court-room and jail, was no noble edifice, but it did possess a quite lofty bell-tower, the highest viewpoint of the ancient town. Pushing his way through the throng around the door, Ramsay mounted the twisting turnpike stair to the narrow ledge at its summit, to join the two watchers and stare seawards across the mouth of the River Esk.

The enemy position was reasonably clear, at least. A sizeable fleet of large sea-going vessels – he counted twenty-seven ships in all – were tacking about in the ten-mile-wide firth perhaps some two miles from this shore, obviously waiting there, but not anchored and under partly furled sails. The look-outs informed that there had been no change in the situation during their tour of duty, except that two vessels had detached themselves from the main fleet some hours previously and sailed off almost directly northwards, across Forth for the Fife coast opposite. Sir Alexander would just see their white sails against the loom of the Fife land, if he looked. They seemed to be beating up and down that other seaboard. Why, who could tell? Seeking provisioning, it might be?

Ramsay, shading his eyes in the July sunshine, gazed, pondering. Two ships only, out of twenty-nine . . .?

That fleet represented not only dire menace but grievous disappointment and resentment for the Scots. Since Bannockburn, eighteen years before, there had been no major English invasion of Scotland; the Bruce had seen to that. Indeed, since 1328, the year before King Robert died, there had been actual peace, signed and sealed at Edinburgh and confirmed at Northampton the following year. But now, with Bruce gone and a five-year-old on his throne, Edward the Third of England, having reached man's estate, and militarily ambitious, like his grandsire, had torn up that peace treaty, on the ridiculous pretext that he had been under full age when he had signed it, and the clauses returning the lands in Scotland of certain disinherited English lords had not been complied with. Using as convenient cat's-paw Edward Balliol, son of the late and unlamented King John Balliol – the Toom Tabard of Scotland's shame, whom Edward the First had caused to be made King of Scots and then scornfully dethroned and banished to France when he proved less co-operative, and whom Bruce had succeeded on the throne – this third Edward had given Balliol an army, plus the levies of the said disinherited lords, and sent him north to win back his father's kingdom, on condition that he swore fealty for it to the King of England and made it a vassal state. On hearing of this dastardly about-face, the Regent Moray, although sick, had promptly assembled a Scots army and marched south for the Border to offer suitable opposition to invasion. They had reached Colbrandspath, where the Lammermuir Hills came down close to the cliff-girt shore, offering the best defensive site in the East March north of Berwick. Waiting there, they had learned the alarming news that, presumably hearing of the Scots defensive move, Balliol and his force had embarked in a fleet of ships provided by King Edward, at Holderness in Yorkshire, and were sailing north to attack from the sea. Hastily the Regent, leaving only the small party of Borderers to hold the Pease Dean passes, in case of a subsidiary land attack, had turned back and forced-marched northwards, to try to be in a position to confront the invaders before they disembarked in, presumably, the Edinburgh or Stirling vicinity. Both English and Scots had arrived in the Firth of Forth area about the same time. But the horseback haste had been too much for the pain-racked Earl of Moray. And now Scotland was direly threatened, and without a ruler.

Ramsay turned from eyeing the seaward situation to look down into the market-place below, where he could see Donald of Mar addressing the Musselburgh citizenry, informing them of the death of their good Regent, so admired and trusted by the people. Who would succeed Moray was uncertain; but unfortunately this Mar looked the most likely candidate, that rather than choice, as nephew of Bruce and cousin of the child-monarch. Moray had a son, but he was not yet twenty years, too young and inexperienced to be Regent. Mar clearly was assuming the responsibility already.

Descending to street level, Ramsay made his way through the sorrowing throng and past the houses of the newest part of the town, called the Newbigging, for the open ground of Pinkie. Here, below the minor ridge of Inveresk, the army was encamped, some five thousand strong, a great concourse, stirring and colourful, with innumerable infantry cantonments, horse-lines, a few lords' and knights' pavilions and tents, flags, banners and pennons fluttering everywhere and cooking-fires sending up their blue smokes into the summer air.

Making for the section of the main cavalry lines where his own troop of eighty Dalwolsey men were settled, he found them already astir and preparing to move, so urgently authoritative had been Will Douglas. All around, the horsemen were seeing to their mounts and saddling up. He doubted whether quite so much haste was necessary, with the enemy still evidently undecided as to procedure. Already the grim news of the Regent's death, although expected, was casting its shadow over all.

Douglas was not hard to find, his blue and white banner with the scarlet Bruce's heart in the centre larger than most and on a higher staff. He was not chief of the Douglasses, there being a young earl thereof, but as tutor of Douglas he acted as though he was. Ramsay was telling him of the two ships which had left the fleet and made for the Fife coast, and conjecturing whether they could be scouting for a possible landing-place there, seeking provisions, or what, when a man came at a run through the camp, shouting breathlessly for Sir Alexander Ramsay. It was one of the Tolbooth watchers.

"They sail, sir – they sail!" he panted. "They're awa'. The hale fleet o' them. They're off."

"Off where, man? Which way?"

"North. Ower the Forth. After yon other twa . . ."

"Fife! Making for Fife?" Ramsay turned to Douglas, but that man was already in action. He strode to grab the nearest horse, and vaulting up shouted down, "The Tolbooth!" and was off.

Ramsay found another mount and clattered after.

Cleaving a way through the alarmed crowd, they dismounted and hurried up the Tolbooth stair. On the summit ledge, they stared seawards. There was no doubt about it. The entire fleet was heading due northwards, under full sail, the leading ships already nearly halfway across the ten-mile firth.

"Fife – they have decided on Fife!" Douglas cried. "A landing there, and we are left here! We cannot reach them over there, with this host, in under three days. God's curse on them; they have us outwitted!"

15

"Or . . . it could be but a ruse?" Ramsay suggested. "To head over there, so that we go from here, chasing round by Stirling, eighty, ninety miles. And then they turn and sail back when we are gone. To land on this side."

The other gazed at him, nibbling his lip. "Aye – it could be, it could be so. With those devil-damned ships they are able to fox us! It could be either: a ruse or a Fife landing, unopposed. What to do? What to do?" He banged clenched fist on the stonework. It was not often that that man was at a loss.

"We can wait," the younger man said. "Wait here, until we know what they intend. Send fishing craft from this Mussel-burgh haven to watch them. Balliol can do no great harm in Fife, save harry the Fifers!"

"He can drive west for Stirling. Or north for Perth. East for St Andrews would serve him little. But Perth, now . . .? The Highlands? Atholl? David of Atholl is in England, Bruce's enemy. Or *was*. He may well be with Balliol, and with the other dispossessed lords. Aye, it could be Perth. Based there, with the southern Highlands and Atholl at his back . . .?"

"Or no more than a device, a ruse."

"Come . . ."

They ran down the twisting stairs and back to the house, the best in that town, where the dead Regent lay and where Mar and some of the other lords and knights were lodging. Bursting in on these as they sat at wine discussing the future, the two young men announced their news, without ceremony.

Its effect was dramatic. All there rose to their feet exclaiming, gesticulating, questioning. Most, Mar included, dismissed the notion of a ruse. It could be a Fife landing, and thence to the north to capture Perth. If Balliol had been for Stirling, he could have sailed up Forth in those ships to near the town. Perth. And Atholl – aye, Atholl, that traitor. And Angus – English d' Umfraville was Earl of Angus, through his mother. Another of the disinherited.

So the talk went to and fro, with Douglas, as usual, growing impatient. If it *was* Fife, he shouted above the din, they should be on the move, not blethering here.

The need for an accepted leader was never more apparent. Douglas would have led, nothing surer; but he was only a knight, however distinguished a one, and the lords present would be loth indeed to follow him.

Donald, Earl of Mar did not fail to see the need, nor the

opportunity. He rapped on the table. "Sir William is right," he declared. "We must be doing. We move, forthwith. I will take the cavalry and ride fast, by Stirling, for St John's Town of Perth. My lord Constable, you will bring on the foot, so swiftly as you may, by forced-march. It will take some time for the English to land their men and be fit to march, after days cooped up in their ships. They will carry no horses aboard, so they will require to scour Fife for mounts. That will take more time. We could get between them and Perth, I say."

"If you hasten!" Douglas growled. "But – what if all this is but a ruse? And the ships turn and come back to this side?"

"I judge that to be unlikely. But, if so, then let Dunbar see to it. Send to Patrick, Earl of Dunbar and March, on the Middle March. He could be here in a day, with his moss-troopers."

"If he *will*!" Hay, the Constable demurred. "That one is not to be trusted, any more than was his father. The Regent had little faith in him, nor did King Robert, even though he is now wed to Moray's daughter."

"An old story," Mar said. "Dunbar has got over his weakness for the English, since he wed! Black Agnes wears the breeks now in that house, I swear! Forby, he accepted the duty of Chief Warden of the March. He has some thousands of men watching the Tweed crossings. Douglas, you are a Middle March man. Ride you south to the Earl of Dunbar and command him to come here to Lothian, with much of his strength and at his best speed, to counter any English landing here, if such there should be. And if not, to come on to me at Perth."

"*Command*, my lord? On whose authority?"

"On mine, Douglas, on mine! Until the Council can meet and appoint a new Regent, I will bear that burden. As is my duty, I think – aye, and my right. Will any gainsay that?"

None there did, although there was no cheering nor acclaim either.

"I could do better, I think, than run courier for Dunbar!" Douglas objected.

Having established his position, Mar was prepared to be patient. "It must be someone goes whom Dunbar will heed and respect," he asserted, tactfully. "One who can advise him, with some standing. Who better? If there is to be fighting

17

here, on this coast, Douglas's aid will serve well. Forby, Dunbar's Border mosstroopers will respect the Knight of Liddesdale."

Mollified, Douglas accepted all that as his due, although Ramsay, for one, suspected that Mar's main aim was to rid himself of his awkward critic.

As Douglas led a move towards the door, Ramsay spoke up. "My lords, two matters which might serve," he suggested. "A small fast force to ride at once for Queen Margaret's Ferry. To cross Forth there and hasten up the other shore. Such could much hinder any English landing, harass and delay. Even four score horse, not over-difficult to ferry across, could make much trouble for Balliol over there. By the ferry, they could be at Aberdour or Kinghorn by midnight. A dozen miles, or thirteen, to the Queen's Ferry from here; two hours. The same on the other side. Two hours crossing in the ferry-scows. Six or seven hours in all."

Men paused, nodding.

"The other, have Musselburgh fishermen sail their craft across to keep watch on the English. Many small boats, to send back word."

There was general agreement. Ramsay offered himself for the former task, with his Dalwolsey contingent.

But Mar had other plans for him than leading a sortie to Fife. Another could do that. Sir Alexander Seton perhaps – older and more experienced a captain. Ramsay of Dalwolsey was a great laird in these parts of Lothian. The Esk valleys and around could produce many more men than Ramsay's and Seton's troops of horse. All were going to be needed. Let Ramsay see to it. Quickly gather more men, especially horsed men. Bring them here, to this Lothian coast, in case Balliol turned back. If he did not, join Dunbar and Douglas and march north.

There was obvious sense in that, although Ramsay, like Douglas, would have relished a more active role.

There was no more delay, as all headed for the camp. The dead Regent must be left meantime in the Musselburgh folk's care.

Leaving his troop of horse in the care of one of his small lairds, Ramsay of Redheuch, Sir Alexander bade farewell to Douglas and rode off up Eskside with his esquire and cousin,

Pate Ramsay of Cockpen, a cheerful youth of eighteen. They had only seven miles to go up the fertile valley, halfway to the town of Dalkeith where the river branched into two, and thereafter up the South Esk's windings to Dalwolsey. At Dalkeith he left Pate to summon the town's magistrates to collect, arm and horse the couple of score of men it was their feudal duty as a burgh of barony to provide, and thereafter to go on to Newbattle Abbey and demand the churchmen's dozen of the Abbot's guard. He himself pressed on for his castle.

Dalwolsey was a fair heritage to have been left. Although the castle had been savaged more than once by the occupying English during the late Wars of Independence, his father, Sir William, in the years of freedom from invasion which had followed Bannockburn, had repaired and restored and extended it, so that now it was one of the finest fortalices in all Lothian. Sir William, like so many of the Bruce's active supporters, had not lived long after signing the famous Declaration of Independence at Arbroath in 1320, another victim to long years of campaigning. Alexander, the elder son, had inherited at the age of seventeen. Now it looked as though he too might have to fight to defend his birthright. Hitherto he had won his spurs, and knighthood, only in minor paramilitary duties for the Regent, in keeping order in the unruly Borders and on the Highland Line; also in tourneys and joustings, where he had made quite notable mark.

As always he was apt to do, he reined in his horse at the sharp bend in the gut of the green valley, which gave the place its name in the Gaelic, *dal-a'-h'oisinn*, the dale at the corner, where suddenly the castle came into view, although that was but a poor description of its impact. Soaring proudly high, massive and dominant on a thrusting rock-base round which the river circled protectively, its rich redstone towers, battlements, bastions and curtain walls, punctuated with arrow-slits and shot-holes, seemed to challenge all comers. Below, on a slight widening of the valley floor, almost a meadow before the steep rock-face and close-running river, the castleton crouched, its cot-houses and cabins humble, yet assured, in the fortalice's protection.

Cantering past the little houses, scattering poultry, pigs and barking dogs and waving to the women and bairns who came to the doorways to stare and smile, he rode up the sharp ascent to the castle forecourt. The drawbridge was down and the portcullis up, this summer late afternoon, and he drummed in across the timbers over the moat, between the twin drum-towers and under the carven arms of a black eagle displayed on blue, through the gatehouse pend and into the inner courtyard.

A guard from the gatehouse came hurrying to take his horse, but Ramsay told him not to stable the beast for he would be requiring it again shortly. Greeting the servitors who appeared at the arched doorway of the great L-shaped keep, he enquired for his brother William. He need scarcely have asked. Yes, his brother was up in his own room in the Well-tower, writing and studying books as usual. That was announced with a sort of patient compassion.

Grinning, he returned to cross the courtyard to the substantial round tower at the north-east angle of the parapetted curtain wall, which stood apart from the keep and gave strong flanking protection to the only approach to the castle, up which Ramsay had ridden. This almost detached tower was an unusual feature, containing the deep castle draw-well in its vaulted basement, and with a curious stairway, not the normal turnpike, winding its way up within the thickness of the walling, round and round, to give access to the two upper storeys and parapet-walk of what was almost a separate establishment, and William Ramsay's private domain.

Clanking his way up this spiral ascent in his half-armour, Ramsay came to the topmost floor and flung open the door. The circular chamber, lit by narrow slit-windows facing all quarters, was nevertheless additionally illuminated by two oil-lamps on a great table so covered in papers and parchments, quills and ink-horns and the like, as to be itself hidden. The floor likewise was littered with paper, books and documents, so that it was barely possible to enter without treading on them; a strange apartment to find in so martial and defensive a fortalice.

The young man who sat at the table, quill in hand, was extraordinarily like his brother, and yet so very different. In feature and build and colouring they were not far from identical; but in expression, demeanour and bearing there was no similarity. Where Alexander was keen-eyed, firm-mouthed and strong-chinned, yet with laughter-lines apt to qualify any aspect of sternness, William looked gentle, studious, diffident almost, and apt to be abstracted, not weak but passive, as though habitually suspending judgment. Two years the younger, despite his reflective air, he managed to look still more junior.

"Still poring over papers, Will! On my soul, your eyes will drop out, one of these days! Can you not find something better to do, this fine July afternoon?" He said that affably, however, smiling, and tramped over the papers to clap his brother on the bent shoulders. They were good friends, these two.

"Better than what, Sandy? Better than dashing around the land in uncomfortable chain-mail, waving sword and lance? To what end?" the other asked mildly. "For all your flourished steel, you have never yet in fact slain anyone, I think? Whereas I, now, am reading and writing of our ancestors the Norsemen and the Picts, or Cruithne, who, I would have you to know, slew by the thousand! At least the Norsemen did. Are you aware that the Vikings, when they had despatched their enemies, used to cut off their heads, wash their faces and trim their hair and beards, to hang up in neat rows to be smoked and decently preserved, like kippered herrings? And we, as of our Norman blood, are their descendants."

"Lord! Is that what you are at now? Here's a fine way for a supporter of Holy Church to spend his day!" William Ramsay had wanted to be a priest, but their father, with only the two sons, and anxious that in dangerous times the Ramsay line should survive, had forbidden it, since churchmen might not marry.

"I am more interested in the Cruithne, our maternal ancestors, in truth. They were an extraordinary people, and admirable, although we think and know so little of them. Less bloodthirsty than the Norse or the Scots. They worshipped the Unknown God, through the sun – hence the stone circles, their temples. Did you know, Sandy, that *cruithne*, in the Gaelic, means wheat-growers?"

"No. But, see you, such splendid tidings must wait, I fear. Since they have waited near a thousand years already! Today we have less worthy but more pressing problems: Edward Balliol and the English!" He launched into an account of the military situation.

Will Ramsay listened, shaking his fair head.

"So today and tomorrow we must raise as many men as we may. We have little time. I wish to be back at Musselburgh by tomorrow night at latest, with a fair tail. Pate is seeing to Dalkeith and Newbattle. There are near-at-hand holdings and villages where we can go tonight. *We* must go to them; I have no time for them to come to me. There is Masterton and Lingerwood, Gowkshill and Newlandburn, Carrington and the Templar lands. I want you to go to the several outlying granges of Newbattle Abbey, Newton, D'Arcy, Whitehill, Burnbrae if you have time – these should be good for another score of men. You are good with the churchmen! Tomorrow we will move further afield."

His brother looked unenthusiastic, but, sighing, rose and laid down his pen. "You will need some refreshment, Sandy . . .?"

"A beaker of wine and some oatcakes and honey will serve, meantime . . ."

Some twenty-four hours later, Alexander Ramsay rode away northwards again from Dalwolsey, under the eagle-on-blue standard of his house, with one hundred and twenty mounted and armed men behind him, from beardless youths to greyheads, the Ramsay barrel all but scraped. William waved them off, wishing them God-speed. There was no suggestion that he should accompany them; no warrior, he would be of more use at the castle to send on additional recruits as they might arrive from far-out properties of the barony. The women and children of the castleton watched them jingle off with just a trace of foreboding.

Back at Musselburgh, Ramsay found the situation unchanged. There was no sign of the English fleet, so presumably Balliol had in fact landed in Fife. Leaving his men at the now empty camping-place, he rode down to the harbour, where he soon found fishermen to confirm an English landing at Kinghorn, almost directly across Forth. The landing had been opposed, they reported, but had proceeded, with some fighting – so evidently Seton and his party had reached there in time to achieve something.

After all the haste, there was nothing now for Ramsay to do but await the arrival of Dunbar and Douglas. Seeing his men settled at Pinkie, he and Pate returned to the house in the market-place where they had lodged before. They found the dead Regent's body still there, but now prepared for burial, interment to be the next day. The Provost of the burgh, who was fussing about, was obviously glad to see such a person as Sir Alexander Ramsay with whom to share responsibility for arrangements. For his part, that young man was less happy. He had few notions as to how the funeral of a realm's Regent should be conducted, and certainly did not seek the position of chief mourner, much as he admired the late Moray. However, this would be only a temporary interment, presumably, for the great Randolph would surely not be left to lie in Musselburgh's kirkyard.

So next noontide the Ramsay contingent formed a guard-of-honour for Bruce's nephew and friend, with Sir Alexander walking behind the cart bearing the flag-covered coffin, with the Provost and magistrates. All the town turned out to watch and pay respects and crowds followed the cortège to the parish church, where the local priest, no more confident than anyone else about dealing with such an eventuality, offered up only a fairly brief and normal service and got all over as expeditiously as possible. To Ramsay's relief, nothing more appeared to be expected of him than being first to move to the newly-dug grave and throw a handful of soil on the coffin, head lowered. He felt that it seemed a very inadequate leave-taking of one of Scotland's paladins and a hero of Bannockburn.

In the late afternoon, Sir William Douglas turned up, with a small personal escort. He had left the East and Middle March force at Soutra, at the head of Lauderdale, to hasten ahead to discover the situation. Yes, Dunbar had agreed to leave Tweed and march north, reluctantly, and his cavalry was now entering Lothian, the foot God only knew how far behind. He had some seventeen hundred horse, mainly mosstroopers, and three thousand foot.

Douglas was not sorry to have missed the funeral.

It took another day for the March cavalry to arrive at Musselburgh, under the Earl of Dunbar and March. A heavy man in his late thirties, short of neck as he was of temper, he had blunt features but sharp, wary eyes, which seemed amiss in someone so powerful-looking and influential. No doubt he was well aware that few in the land trusted him. Yet he was perhaps the noble of the most distinguished lineage in all the land, directly descended from the ancient Celtic royal house, even to the extent of not having a surname. Indubitably, he, like his father, considered that he had more right to be sitting on the Scots throne than any son of Bruce or Balliol. Unfortunately for such pretensions, his sire had taken the English side in the Wars of Independence. His attitude to the two young knights, Douglas and Ramsay, was condescending, almost resentful. Clearly he had not wanted to come on this expedition northwards and did not consider Donald of Mar as suitable as himself to be Regent, and was reluctant therefore to obey the commands transmitted by Douglas. It was indeed something of a triumph for the latter to have got Dunbar thus far. But now, finding no English on the south shore of Forth, he deemed duty, if that was what it might be, to be done.

It took all of the younger men's efforts, Douglas's typically forceful, Ramsay's more tactful and persuasive, to convince the Earl that a further move north to Perth was necessary for the realm's safety and well-being. He eventually acceded but would not hear of the infantry slowly following on all that way; they should turn and go back to the borderline. This was agreed and was probably sensible.

2

Next morning the wholly mounted company of almost two thousand set off westwards up Forth. As the crow flew they had no more than some thirty-five miles to go; but as they must ride, to get across Forth at its first bridge, at Stirling, it was nearer eighty miles, two days' hard riding for a host, even seasoned Border mosstroopers. They followed, necessarily, in the tracks of Mar's army. The pity that the Scots had never developed a navy, unlike the English – not that ships could have transported all the horses.

They reached Stirling the first night, and camped by what was now the River Forth, below the mighty fortress-castle on its towering rock. Three days before, Donald of Mar had passed this way.

Now the green rolling ranges of the Ochil Hills lay between them and Perth, thirty-odd miles long by some seven wide. They could ride along the northern foothills, by Dunblane and Sheriffmuir and Auchterarder, or on the southern side by Alva, Dollar and Glenfarg, the former somewhat the shorter, both routes joining where Earn met Tay. They learned that Mar's force had taken the northern option and it seemed wise to follow that.

When, by the following late afternoon they had covered over twenty of the thirty-five miles, at Aberuthven, just beyond Auchterarder in Strathearn, they halted. They learned from local people that Mar's army, after reaching Perth, had received word that the English under Balliol, after landing in Fife, had marched north and were now in the Forteviot area, the ancient capital of the Celtic kings, now no more than a village on the south bank of Earn. Mar had moved out from Perth, therefore, in strength, and was now on the *north* side of Earn, on the high ground of Dupplin Muir. What his plans were, of course, they could not tell; but it seemed reasonable to assume that he was threatening Balliol's position below, on the boggy meadows of the winding river.

A hasty conference of Dunbar's leaders decided that their force should stand where it was meantime, until they at least knew Mar's plans and dispositions. Information was obviously essential, and Douglas, his usual vehement self, proposed that he should take a small scouting party forthwith to spy out, if he could, the English positions, whilst someone else went forward to find Mar and learn his intentions. Ramsay was about to volunteer for this duty when another of the lairds, Andrew Murray of Tullibardine, announced that he would do it. This South Perthshire was his country and he knew the terrain like the palm of his hand. This was accepted. Ramsay said that he would accompany Douglas.

It was evening now, and threatening rain, and darkness would be upon them soon – or as much of darkness as was to be looked for in a Scottish summer. They rode off eastwards with a mere half-dozen men-at-arms, after questioning Murray as to directions. They circled the village of Dunning, with its ancient towered Celtic church, and then down into the lower ground, towards where the Water of May met the larger River Earn. Here, in the woodlands of Invermay, they gained the cover they required to move on unseen to Forteviot, where Balliol was reported to have halted. Whether he was merely camping there for the night or intending to fight Mar from there, was what they sought to discover, if possible.

In fact, when they cautiously reached the edge of the trees above the river haughlands, even in the half-dark, it was not difficult to conclude that the English force had in fact chosen a strong defensive position rather than any mere convenient camp-site. No cooking-fires burned, no tents, much less pavilions, appeared to have been erected. The army was occupying a very strategic site in the wedge of land where the Water of May reached the Earn, protected on three sides by river, marsh and steep banks.

"They know what they are at, those English carles!" Douglas said. "A well-chosen position. They bide meantime."

They raised their eyes to where, northwards, on the higher ground which slanted up to Dupplin Muir, the glow of camp-fires, many fires, lit the lowering clouds, barely a couple of miles away.

"*Mar* does not seek to hide his position," Ramsay observed.

"If they would come to the fight, one will have to move, to abandon their advantage – the English in their secure position between the rivers, or Mar the benefit of high ground. This Earn ensures that neither could cross that deep river unopposed."

"How many, think you, has Balliol there?"

"Three thousand, four thousand – no more, I would say."

"Mar may well have three times that number."

"Aye, but does he know how to use them?"

They rode back to Aberuthven, in thin rain, with their report, to find Murray of Tullibardine already returned, with the information that Mar's army was encamped over quite a large area of Dupplin Muir, in the Cairnie vicinity, opposite Forteviot. Apart from his own force he had collected large reinforcements from Perth, so that he now numbered almost twenty thousand men, most of them foot, admittedly.

"He does not need our help, then," Dunbar commented. "We have wasted our time and strength in coming all this way." Criticism of Douglas and Ramsay was implicit.

"What does Mar intend?" Douglas demanded of Murray.

"He will attack, he says, in the morning."

"Balliol's position is strong. At Mill of Forteviot, protected by the Water of May and the Earn. How does Mar plan his assault?"

"He did not inform me!" Murray said shortly. He gave impression of neither knowing nor caring. Dunbar's faction in general had little love for Mar's, any more than the late Regent's.

The Earl did not appear to think it necessary to set guards before retiring for the night; but Douglas and Ramsay did, using their own men.

It was Ramsay who was awakened first, in the barn of a farmery, in the early hours of the morning, by one of his Dalwolsey troopers, sent by a sergeant of the guard. It was to report that there was some large movement of men, in the low ground of the Earn valley, to the east. A Douglas scout well forward had sent back word.

"Which way?" Ramsay demanded, immediately alert. "Movement which way?"

"This way, sir, from the east. Many men, moving quietly."

"From Forteviot, then? *This* side of Earn." Ramsay rose and hurried out. He did not go to waken Douglas yet, but went to check the scout's report. What he heard confirmed his perturbation. He called for horses and sent a man to rouse Sir William Douglas, to tell him that he, Ramsay, was riding north-eastwards to the Earn valley. He would go as far as the Dalreoch ford, the main crossing-place on the road to Perth. If it was the English making some night manoeuvre, either they were retiring southwards, which seemed unlikely; or else they were seeking to get round behind Mar's force, whether to reach Perth avoiding a fight or even intending some assault in darkness. This might even be on their own camp here, if the enemy had word of it, or on Mar's. If it was the latter, or Perth, they would have to get across Earn – which meant the Dalreoch ford, for elsewhere the river was uncrossable. Without knowing the district well, he could not assess the situation better than that.

So he and his little group trotted through the night the two miles to the Dalreoch ford, on the main route to Perth. Every now and again they reined up to listen, but heard nothing save the hooting of owls, sighing wind in trees and the murmurs of

27

running water. Nothing gave hint of large-scale movement, either in front or on their right. The scout, when contacted, said that he had been more than a mile further east when he had heard the sounds.

Cautiously they approached the river at Dalreoch, annoyed when a dog barked at them from a wayside cottage. Still no indication of movement. Dismounting, Ramsay and the scout moved down to the ford. There was nothing to be seen there save the dark running waters, no sign of any large body of men or horses crossing recently.

Beginning to judge that it was all a false alarm, despite the scout's assurances, Ramsay, about to turn back, thought of that barking dog. If it had barked at them it would undoubtedly have done so at any large party earlier. They retraced their steps to the cottage and hammered on the door.

A frightened man opened, holding a large, growling cattle-hound. Reassuring him that no harm was intended, Ramsay asked if any group of men, large or small, had recently come this way, adding significantly that they would almost certainly be English. The man declared that he had seen and heard nothing, before the lord's own coming. He had heard of the English army at Forteviot, hence his alarm.

Ramsay told the cottager of the large movement the scout had heard, further east, but coming this way. If they had not crossed here, and had not proceeded further west towards Aberuthven, where had they gone?

At first the man shook his head doubtfully. Then he said, "The English, lord – they wouldna ken the bit ford at Inverdunning?"

"Is there another ford? I thought that this Dalreoch was the only one, hereabout."

"It's no' a right ford, lord. Most times you'd no' win across it. But now, at the top o' summer, you can. Wi' the watter low. They could get ower, there. But the English wouldna ken o't."

"Where is this, man?"

"Inverdunning. Where the Dunning Watter joints Earn. Above a mile downstream frae here."

"Then let us try there. Come you with us, friend. We are of the good Regent's army. Mount you up behind one of these. Lead us . . ."

Less than eagerly the man did as he was bidden and they

rode on, down Earn, picking their way in the darkness. The rain had stopped.

It did not take long to reach the Dunning Water, a somewhat lesser stream than the May. Rising out of higher ground in the Ochils, however, it brought down a deal more silt and gravel, and some of this it deposited in the main river just below its confluence, to form something of an underwater causeway. This was not to be seen in darkness but the guide assured them that it was there, stretching across perhaps twenty feet wide and under some three feet of water. Ramsay did not have to dismount to perceive the traces of recent passage of a large number of horses: droppings and churned-up sand and mud. Also, as they peered, the cottager pointed out a couple of stakes projecting above the surface. He had never seen those before, he assured; they must have been erected to mark the passage for the strangers.

The enemy had crossed here, undoubtedly. Somebody must have guided them. It could only be to get behind Mar's force, in darkness.

What to do? Mar must be warned, if possible. Ramsay sent two of his men back, with the cottager, to inform Douglas, and with the scout and one other, rode carefully in, to cross the Earn.

The water, in fact, did not reach up to the horses' bellies, in this season, but it would be very different at other seasons. Reaching the other side without difficulty, they climbed the quite steep bank. There was no problem in following the tracks of the Englishmen, even through woodland; several hundred horses leave no lack of traces, darkness notwithstanding. Ramsay reckoned that they were here less than two miles west of Mar's position. He went warily, since they might come up with the English at any time. He kept wondering how the enemy had learned of that more or less secret ford.

Such questioning was relegated to the back of his mind, for suddenly they heard the unmistakable sounds of battle, or at least struggle and fighting, ahead, distant but clear enough, shouts, screams and the clash of steel. Attack, then – night attack! Not any mere outflanking manoeuvre.

Again, decision. Clearly there was nothing that three men could do in this situation, of any avail. They could go on and observe. But better, probably, to ride back for help.

So it was back to that Inverdunning ford, with all the speed they could make in the darkness. Across it, they were halfway back to Aberuthven when they met Douglas.

He had nearly two hundred men, his own and Ramsay's, and was in no very amiable frame of mind, not knowing what went on and doubting whether all this alarm was necessary. On hearing of the night attack on Mar, however, he became a different man, all decision and action. They would go to Mar's aid forthwith.

Ramsay was for returning to their own camp and collecting a larger party. He had no idea as to the English force's strength, but he reckoned that they would not have sought to assail a major army's encampment in any small numbers. But Douglas declared that a small-scale counter-attack *now* would be much more valuable than any larger effort later. Nothing was more sure than that it would take some considerable time to convince Dunbar that Mar needed and warranted help, and then to rouse and ready any major body of his sleeping troops.

So they turned and headed eastwards once more, riding fast, to splash across that ford – with Ramsay shouting to his friend his surprise that the enemy should have learned of it.

They had not gone much further than Ramsay had reached previously, on the edge of Dupplin Muir, when they not only heard the shouting and clash ahead, above the drumming of their hooves, but something different, at least to Ramsay's ears. Urgently he called on Douglas to draw up. Reluctant, impatient, that man signalled their followers to do so.

"Listen!" Ramsay cried. "They are coming!"

Quickly all recognised that there was a large body of horsemen approaching, the thunder of hooves causing an actual trembling of the ground – which had communicated itself to Ramsay. There was yelling and shouting too, but this was something other than the bawling and fury of battle; there was elation in it, triumph rather.

Even Douglas accepted that message. Fortunately there was fairly close scrub woodland hereabouts, providing ample cover even for their largish company. Hastily the two leaders urged their men aside into the trees, right and left, for safety or perhaps ambush.

They were only just in time. Down the broad track – it was scarcely a road – came a lengthy column of mounted men, five or six abreast, laughing, shouting, swinging weapons, trophies, even banners. They were anything but on the alert, and their English voices proclaimed them to be the enemy; but any notion of an ambush could quickly be forgotten, for clearly there were very large numbers here, many hundreds, as the column clattered by; no attack, however unexpected, could hope to succeed, especially unco-ordinated as it would have to be. This was Balliol's night force returning, and obviously in triumph. There were double riders on some of the horses – presumably captives.

When, at length, the column was past, and there was no pursuit, the hidden Scots emerged. Douglas was in a state of mixed rage and frustration.

"We might have taken them, had we but known!" he cried. "Even so many. Cut them up. Done *something*. They were heeding nothing. A plague on it – to have to stand by and watch!" He glared at Ramsay, as though it was all his fault.

That man was more concerned with what this enemy elation signified. "Riding back like that, exulting. Not followed, nor fearing to be. They must have gained some sort of victory. Achieved what they set out to do . . ."

"Aye. We had better go see. Mar was ever a fool. With the numbers of men he has, these English should have been swallowed up, even in a surprise attack. And if he could not trounce them, he should never have left them to ride off. He has no notion of war. Yet thinks to be Regent! I swear that we will find only confusion when we get there."

They found much worse than confusion when, a mile or so further, on the highest Cairnie area of Dupplin Muir, they reached the encamped Scots army. All was panic, dismay, disarray, sheer chaos; so much so that they themselves created a new panic, some men fleeing wildly, others seeking to attack them, as wildly, despite their shouted slogans of "A Douglas!" and "A Ramsay!" Clearly there was no effective central command at work. Equally clear, despite the darkness, paling now towards dawn, were the bodies strewn around, dead and wounded, the latter screaming, moaning, beseeching. There were many reeling about, too, drunk apparently.

Cursing, Douglas headed his company, in almost defensive formation, for the centre of the camp area, causing more alarm all the way. They shouted for Mar, Menteith, Fraser,

Campbell. None informed, none heeded, perhaps none knew.

Eventually they came across a group in some sort of order, under a young man who proved to be none other than young Randolph, the late Regent's son, now the new Earl of Moray. His relief at learning their identity was obvious, and significant. He had not been with his father on the Border expedition, so must have joined Mar at Perth.

Excitedly he told them of the attack, of the complete surprise – seemingly no guards or sentries had been posted, and there had been much drinking – of the great numbers of the enemy, their riding down of the sleeping camp, their effective tactics and ruthless killing, their picking out and capture of the high-born and leaders, clearly under the guidance of someone who knew all these. He himself had only escaped by a hair's breadth . . .

If the young man – he was little more than a youth – expected sympathy and understanding, he did not get it from Douglas.

"Are you all purblind fools?" that man demanded. "No watch set. No plan of defence. No leadership! No pursuit, even . . . !"

"Pursuit?" the other repeated. "How could we pursue? They had us, unready, at their mercy, scattered. And their large numbers . . ."

"Numbers! Lord – how many are *you*? Fifteen thousand? Sixteen? There were not more than eight hundred to a thousand of them. We watched them pass. Numbers, by the Mass! You outnumbered them by six to one! But – where is Mar? Is he fallen? Taken?"

"I know not . . ."

Muttering his opinion of all such feeble leadership, Douglas led them all off in search of the said leaders, or such as might have survived. They found them quite quickly, Mar, with some other notables, including the Earl of Fife who, like young Moray, had been at Perth collecting more troops to aid the late Regent. They were all in a state of agitation, needless to say, bemused and angry, but not revealing any obvious guilt over unpreparedness, however undisguised Douglas's strictures.

Mar's main preoccupation appeared to be how the English had got there from the other side of Earn. He had sent a party

32

to guard the ford near Broombarns, the next one to the east, but there had been no word of an attempt to cross there. And there were scouts watching the approach from the Dalreoch ford, to the west. He had considered their position was secure . . .

Ramsay spoke up. "They used a little-known ford at Inverdunning, as did we, my lord. Impassable, save in dry weather. So – they must have been informed. *We* knew naught of it."

"God, what dastard would tell the English of that?"

None could answer him. But Robert Bruce, Earl of Carrick, an illegitimate son of the late King Robert's brother Edward, spoke. "I have an Englishman. Captive. Wounded and left behind when they fled." Douglas snorted at that word 'fled'. He thought nothing of *this* Robert Bruce. "He says that he is squire to Umfraville of Angus, one of the disinherited English. *He* might tell us something of this."

"Fetch him, " Mar directed.

"What matters that, now?" Douglas demanded. "You should be readying for a counter-attack, not bewailing treachery. You cannot have lost over-many men. Out of your thousands." Only the Flower of Chivalry would have got away with addressing Mar, Regent and earl, like that.

"What does the bold Douglas suggest?" Fife asked sourly. "In darkness. And lacking any possibility of surprise."

"An attack on two fronts. You from the east, crossing at two fords down, for this first one you spoke of will be well guarded, you may be sure. And ourselves – that is, Dunbar's force – from the west. We should have them. They will be hopelessly outnumbered. Even *you* still much outnumber them! And after this, this folly, they will scarcely look for so swift a recovery."

Stung, Mar pointed an angry finger. "By God, sirrah, keep you a civil tongue in your head! You may be the Black Douglas's bastard, but you will not speak your betters so and not rue it! We require not *your* instruction in warfare!"

"I think that you do, by this night's showing . . ."

Ramsay intervened hurriedly. "My lord Regent, no doubt you have already considered a joint assault. With my lord of Dunbar. His force, from whence we have come, is at Aberuthven, five miles to the west. He can reach Forteviot, where are the English, without having to cross Earn. If we can convey your orders, I am sure that the enemy can be trapped and made to pay for this dastardly deed."

This more judicious approach failed to mollify Mar. "If I need your advice, Ramsay, and Dunbar's aid, I will command it," he said stiffly. "Because we were assailed in cowardly fashion when asleep does not mean that we are incapable of upholding the realm's cause. Nor craven, as this Douglas as good as suggests! I will inform the Earl of Dunbar and March of my decisions in due course. Meantime, I have more to do than stand here and receive your guidance!"

"Dammit, man . . . !" Douglas began again. But fortunately or otherwise, the Earl of Carrick then turned up, pushing a reeling figure in good half-armour but helmet missing, little more than a beardless youth, who was obviously in much pain, one shoulder held awkwardly lower than the other, probably suffering from a broken collar-bone.

"This is the English esquire to Umfraville," Carrick said, giving the unfortunate an extra jolting push.

Douglas switched his verbal assault to the prisoner, without waiting for Mar, Moray or anybody else to question him. "You – how did you, your people, learn of that little-known ford at Inverdunning? Where you crossed Earn?" he demanded. "*We* did not know of it, so how did you English?"

The youth hesitated, biting his lip, but not for long, when he was dealt a buffet to the head which all but felled him. Choking, he almost babbled.

"Sire . . . my lords . . . it was a Scotchman. He came to us, in the night. Seeking my lord Edward – my lord Balliol. Told him of the Earl of Dunbar's army. Said that he had come from it. Said that he knew of a secret ford . . ."

"Came from *Dunbar's* force! Guidsakes, boy, watch what you say!"

"It is true, my lord. He was a well-spoken man, on a fine horse. In rich clothing. Murray, I heard him called, by Sir Gilbert . . ."

"Murray, by the Mass! Murray, you say . . . ?"

"Aye, my lord, Murray of, of . . . Tol, Till . . . of some such . . ."

"Murray of Tullibardine?" Ramsay put to him.

"Yes, that is it. That is the place."

The Scots stared at each other, appalled. Murray of Tullibardine it was who had come earlier to find out Mar's situation, one of Dunbar's lieutenants, a Perthshire laird of broad acres – and one who would undoubtedly know this area well, with lands not ten miles away.

"Dear God – Murray!" Douglas cried, and smashed fist on breastplate in a characteristic gesture. "For this, he will die!"

"So that is the quality of Dunbar's aid!" Mar jerked. "Spare us more of it, I say!"

"My lord Regent, the Earl of Dunbar will know naught of this, I swear!" Ramsay exclaimed. "He would never . . ."

But none heeded him now. Mar had turned away dismissively, and Douglas himself was striding off for his horse. Unhappily the younger man went after him.

Summoning their troopers, without farewells or other exchanges, they set off back for Aberuthven, with mixed feelings.

At that encampment, stirring with first light, they went straight to Dunbar's quarters in the largest house of the village, the vicarage, and found the Earl just risen and, with his leaders and knights, demanding breakfast. Both newcomers' eyes searched the group for Andrew Murray. He was not there.

"Tullibardine!" Douglas grated. "Where is he?"

"Andrew?" Dunbar answered, shrugging. "I know not. Probably not risen. He will be here, no doubt. Why?"

"We would ask him how he spent the night!"

"Not ranging the country as you two appear to have done, I wager! What have you learned? If anything?"

Douglas and Ramsay exchanged glances.

"A sufficiency," the former said levelly. "*You* did not send Murray on any mission then, my lord?"

"Send Murray? After he returned from Mar? No – why should I? He will be here, in camp, somewhere. What is this?"

Again the mutual glances. Dunbar at least sounded genuinely mystified.

"If not in *this* camp, he will be in another!" Douglas asserted grimly.

"Another . . . ? You mean, you think that he has gone back to Mar's?"

"Not Mar's – Balliol's!"

Breaths were caught, as all stared.

"What folly is this?" the Earl demanded.

"Folly, aye, but worse than folly, my lord! Treachery. Murray has turned traitor, we believe. Balliol and his English attacked Mar's camp this night, in darkness, and made great havoc there. Led over a secret ford of Earn, by a Scot. And that Scot, Murray of Tullibardine, according to an English prisoner."

"God's Wounds – I'll not believe it, sir! Andrew Murray? Never! You rant, man, you haver!"

"Then fetch him, my lord. And see how he denies it."

"Aye. Scott, find me Tullibardine and bring him. We'll put an end to this nonsense."

"You say that Mar has suffered havoc, defeat," Home of that Ilk put in, distant kin of Dunbar's. "An attack in darkness?"

They related their experiences that night and the present situation, to a hail of questions. There was astonishment, almost incredulity, although scorn for Mar's leadership appeared to be Dunbar's principal reaction. They were still at it when Scott of Rankilburn came back, to report that there was no sign of Murray of Tullibardine nor his esquire in the camp, and some said that they had seen them riding off early in the night.

That information stilled the chatter.

"Why would he do this?" Ramsay demanded of them all. "Betray his country?"

Dunbar shrugged. "Perhaps he did not consider it betrayal. Perhaps he considers Edward Balliol to have a better right to the throne than Bruce's bairn! King John Balliol's son and a grown man, not a child."

"It would still be treachery," Douglas averred. "Balliol is here only as Edward of England's puppet, with an English army."

"It is a point of view, man. A child-king is of no use to Scotland. Nor is a Regent like this Mar! Balliol might indeed serve better. And could spare us English invasion."

"Is that *your* point of view, my lord?" That was steely.

"Not so. I did not say that, sirrah. But it could be Tullibardine's."

They left it at that meantime. Douglas and Ramsay returned to their own people, to put all in readiness for a full-scale move against the English at Forteviot, in conjunction with Mar's army.

Nothing of the sort eventuated, however, no call from Mar arriving. When, by mid-forenoon there were no orders nor messages for Dunbar to move, Douglas in particular grew impatient and apprehensive. He proposed a move eastwards on their own, with messengers sent to Mar to discover the situation and to urge prompt assault. Dunbar was less keen. If Mar was in no hurry to attack, or feared to do so, why should *he* rush in? Mar was apparently the Regent – let him act the part.

No progress forthcoming on that front, Ramsay suggested to his friend that they ride over again to Dupplin Muir to discover Mar's intentions and seek to instigate a co-ordinated attack on the English. Douglas acceded.

With only a small party the two knights once again took the now familiar road by Inverdunning and its ford and on to the higher ground beyond. Well before they reached the Cairnie area, they came to realise that events there had not stood still as they had imagined. The unmistakable din of battle, a major clash of arms, sounded from afar.

"Lord, they are attacked again!" Douglas exclaimed. "This Balliol is no shrinking milksop, as was his father! If he it is who commands the English."

"That noise is from further over," Ramsay declared, keen-eared. "Not where they were camped. Beyond some distance, eastwards."

They reined up, the better to listen. It became apparent that there was large-scale fighting, but that it was taking place at a considerable distance, the sounds muted and muffled by intervening terrain. Mystified, they rode on.

When they reached the camp area it was to find only a few men there, servitors, baggage-minders and the wounded from the night's affray. The newcomers' demands as to what had happened elicited the information that the Earl of Mar was attacking the English. An assault from the east, using the ford near Broombarns. To avenge the night's dastardly surprise.

Douglas swore. "The fool! To attack alone. Not to call us in. And to use that nearest ford. The abject bungler! He does not love Dunbar – and Dunbar hates him – but this is sheerest folly . . . !"

"They still will much outnumber the English."

"No doubt. But Mar is no commander. I fear for him – or, at least, for his people."

"They are doing battle. We can hear that. Let us see how they fare . . ."

Spurring on eastwards they found themselves skirting the steep drop, almost cliff-like, where the heathy levels of the moor fell to the flats of the winding Earn. Here they could soon look down on the English camp area, across the water; but like Mar's, there were few people to be seen there, only gear and some horses. The shouting, screaming and pandemonium of war was now not far ahead, loud, daunting even to seasoned fighters.

Round a major bend in the river, beyond quite a bluff of the high north banking, they were confronted by an extraordinary and appalling sight. Quarter of a mile away, battle raged, or perhaps massacre would better describe it. Down the steep slope to the Earn vast numbers of men, mounted and on foot, were pouring, to the ford area opposite the Broombarns farmery. Not that the ford itself was visible as such, for the river was entirely blocked by a solid mass of men and horses. As the newcomers reined up to stare, they perceived that this shoal of bodies, human and animal, was in fact fallen, down, inert, save for flailing limbs and hooves; and over it, on top, were struggling, staggering, floundering more men and beasts, striving to cross on this wide bridge of their prostrate fellows, and being pressed on by the weight of their down-charging compatriots descending the hillside behind. And despatching them as they reached the south bank were the English, drawn up in a solid front, smiting and thrusting methodically, cutting down, killing, their front ranks standing on a wide wall of slain, taller than man-height, the better to stem the flood.

"Lord – the Gadarene swine!" Ramsay gasped. He knew his Bible. What Douglas said was unrepeatable.

Horrified, they watched as this terrible folly went on, more and more Scots plunging on down the hill to add to the shambles beneath, riding down those before them and then themselves being overwhelmed by those behind, none with any least hope of reaching, much less defeating, the enemy, who had merely to stand firm and weary not in slaying. The river was clear west of that dire bridge of bodies, running bright red beyond.

"Come!" Douglas yelled. "On! We must halt this madness. The fools, the utter purblind fools!"

38

They dashed on along the bank-top to that ghastly scene, shouting at the top of their lungs, to stop, to wait, to hold back. Not that there were a great many left to heed; most of the army was already gone, lost, submerged under its own weight, determinedly crazed, in self-immolation. Fortunately there was one wiser head there, in some lesser degree of leadership, a veteran of the Bruce campaigns, who recognised Douglas and Ramsay as they rode up. He hailed them thankfully, crying that he had been trying to halt the flood of this insane attack but that the Earl of Fife, commanding the rearguard, had been ordering them on and on. Fife himself had ridden down now, but the men would not heed *him*, a mere captain . . .

The Douglas's stentorian bellow, his innate authority and no doubt his reputation as a commander and the Flower of Chivalry, had its effect, reinforcing almost certainly some reluctance of the remaining rank and file to throw away their lives uselessly in the obscene carnage and indescribable mêlée below. The suicidal surge dwindled and halted. Everywhere along the lip of that decline, men stood and stared instead of rushing downwards.

The sight was scarcely able to be comprehended, even to seasoned warriors. The low ground presented such a scene of disaster as the mind all but refused to take in. It was not only the river which was piled high with bodies: the level area between the foot of the slope and the water was equally covered with the fallen, these not felled by the enemy but by their own fellows pounding down the hill on top of them as they sought to hold back from adding to the heaps in the Earn's ford, burying more hundreds under the weight of horses, men and armour. With the heaving mass of lashing hooves, flailing limbs, broken lances and jagged spears producing the shrieks and wailing of the damned, it all made as graphic a representation of hell as man could have conceived.

Horrified, those above gazed, helpless to aid their comrades. Douglas had his trumpeter blow the recall time and time again, and a few on the upper fringes below did turn to make their way back up the slope. But it was a pitifully small number who could disentangle themselves. The watchers could see nothing else that they might usefully do. Clearly they could by no means reach the English. And no descent of that hillside would help those already down. Douglas and

Ramsay reluctantly decided, presently, that the only practical course was to return to Aberuthven with the news and to persuade Dunbar to attack Balliol in the rear. It would be too late to save any large number here, but at least they could seek to wipe out some of the shame.

Turning away to leave that holocaust, they could not but feel guilty of a sort of desertion, foolish as this might be, seeming to abandon their fellow-Scots. They rode off from Dupplin Muir set-faced.

But back at Aberuthven, Dunbar's reaction to their tidings was wholly negative. He would not mount any attack. Mar had not sought his aid, so he and his people would have to extricate themselves from their own bungling incompetence. The English knew of his presence here, since Murray must have informed them. They would be prepared for any assault from the west. He was not going to throw away *his* strength in any wild and useless gesture. He had barely two thousand men. He needed them for the defence of the Border. He should never have come north on this crazy mission. He was Warden of the Marches, not any sort of whipping-boy for Mar – who ought never to have been appointed Regent. He had had enough of folly.

Demand, plead, even accuse, as Douglas would, the Earl was adamant. They would ride for Lothian and the Merse forthwith.

It was Ramsay who managed to persuade the Earl to at least postpone this programme, by convincing him that it would be prudent to remain in the vicinity for a little while, to learn what Balliol's next move would be after his victory over Mar. If the English now turned south again, for Stirling or Edinburgh – as seemed probable, since they were not likely to head north into the Highlands – it would be wise, surely, to be aware of this, warned. They might well be on Dunbar's heels. Although forced to admit the sense of this, the Earl countered by suggesting that Ramsay, and Douglas too, since they were so concerned, should go forward again and discover the situation for him.

Weary as they were with all this toing and froing over the same ground, the two friends could scarcely refuse – and indeed were the obvious choice for the task. So it was to horse once more, this time with only a score or so as escort, and back whence they had so recently come.

When, in mid-afternoon now, they reached the vantage-point on the high ground at Dupplin where they could look down on the Forteviot area, it was to perceive that the English camp was in fact now altogether deserted. And the din of battle no longer sounded from ahead. They pressed on.

The battlefield, if such it could be called, when they could see it, proved likewise to be abandoned – save for the dead, wounded and scavengers; at least there was no fighting now, no armies save of the fallen, nor any sign of the victors, as far afield as they could see. Astonished, they wondered what had transpired, and decided that, few as they were, they could risk going down there to enquire of the many busy searchers and looters and the wounded and incapacitated.

Descending the slope was as though entering the pit of the damned. The yelling and screaming had died away to a comprehensive moaning and groaning which seemed to rise and fall like the surge of a tide on a shore, punctuated by the intermittent shriek, or whinny of a horse in agony. The heaps of the fallen covered all the level ground and some way up the bank, as well as the area of the ford itself, and seemed to heave and quiver still. The smell of blood and ordure permeated the August air.

The sight of a disciplined party of armed and mounted men descending upon the scene, even only a score, clearly alarmed those nearby, at least on the north side of the river, whether they were aiding the wounded, robbing the dead or gathering arms and armour. However, faced with the scale of the catastrophe and horror, the newcomers did not attempt to interfere, display authority or even offer succour. That was not what they were here for, as Douglas announced grimly. What they required was information.

Wounded were everywhere, sitting about or lying dazed and lost in pain and misery. Douglas and Ramsay questioned a few on the outskirts of the piles of slain but could get little coherent out of them – save appeals for help, to which they had to turn deaf ears, however unhappily. But presently they did find one who could tell them something, who indeed called to Douglas by name, presumably recognising the red heart on blue and white heraldry on his breastplate: a Fife laird, Wardlaw of Pitreavie, one of the Earl of Fife's rearguard. With a broken arm and split brow he was in a poor way, but able at least to speak rationally. He panted out enough to give them some idea as to the situation.

The disaster was utter and complete, he declared. All had been mishandled, from start to finish. And the bunglers had paid for it, most of them with their own lives. Mar was dead. As were the Earls of Menteith and Carrick. The new young Moray also. Sir Alexander Fraser, the Chamberlain. These he knew of. How many others, God alone could tell. Many were taken prisoner, his own lord, Duncan, Earl of Fife amongst them. All was lost, lost . . .

Douglas interrupted to demand where were the English? What had happened after the battle?

They had marched eastwards, down Earn, Wardlaw said. Soon after the fighting ended there had been much blowing of trumpets and marshalling into formation. They did not go back to their camp but hastened off in formations along the riverside, leaving all this, and only a small rearguard, behind. It seemed that they had lost very few men . . .

"Eastwards? Down Earn?" Douglas exclaimed. "Why? Where do they head? In such haste."

"I know not . . ."

"Perhaps to their ships?" Ramsay suggested. "These could have sailed north, from Kinghorn, around Fife Ness, to the Tay near here."

"But why the haste? After so great a victory. They would not need the ships. Not so soon . . ."

"Having defeated Mar, they might wish to return south, quickly. To grasp the entire realm, with the fortresses of Edinburgh and Stirling and Dumbarton. They could do that more swiftly by sea. Reach the Forth again more quickly than by marching, and get behind this force of Dunbar's."

"It could be. But – I do not see it. They have defeated the main Scots army, slain the Regent and the most important lords. Why this haste? They will know that Dunbar has no great host here. Murray will have told them that the foot has returned to the Border." Douglas turned on Wardlaw again. "Were they perhaps but chasing the remnants of Mar's army? Following them, to cut them off from Perth, where they had come from?"

The other shook his bloody head. "I think not. No large numbers fled. The Earl Duncan saw to that. He commanded the rear. And the English were still on the wrong side of Earn for chase . . ."

Mystified by the English behaviour yet only too appreciative of their ability and initiative, the two knights decided that
their first duty was to report to Dunbar as quickly as
possible. They would take this Wardlaw with them; he could
ride behind one of the troopers, wounded as he was. They
might still gain further information from him.

So it was back up Earnside once more, with their rescued
Fifer mounted behind one of the Dalwolsey men, tied to him
with a belt lest he swoon away with the pain and jolting.

At Aberuthven, their tidings resulted in a hasty council of
war in the vicarage. Dunbar was not impressed by the ships
theory. As he pointed out, Balliol would have captured a
great number of Mar's horses, in which he had inevitably
hitherto been notably short because of the impossibility of
transporting them by sea. Was he likely to throw away that
important advantage by re-embarking in the Tay? Much
more probably he was pressing on to Perth. It was a strong
city, with walls, and he might wish to capture it, as a base.

This found general acceptance.

Ramsay had a new suggestion. Might not this English move
eastwards be only a clever device? To cross Earn further
down and then turn north-abouts and come back this way?
Having defeated Mar, might they not think to do the same
here? To destroy this force likewise. Another night attack,
perhaps, on this Aberuthven?

That gave all there pause. After Dupplin Muir, none
scoffed at it as impossible.

Out of much discussion it was decided that at least this
possibility could be countered by themselves making a move
forthwith. Since they would be better to know the English
intentions anyway, if possible, they would shift camp to
Balliol's former strong position at Forteviot. They would stop
there overnight, leaving guards at the Dalreoch, Inverdunning and Broombarns fords, and so should be secure from
attack across Earn at least. Tomorrow they could decide on
their further course, once Balliol's whereabouts were established.

Orders to pack up camp were issued, and a move eastwards
along the south side of Earn made, as evening settled on the
land.

Still with no certainty of the English position, but witn
scouts out ahead and parties at the fords, they took over the

former English encampment where the Water of May joined the larger river, and settled for the night. This time Dunbar left no lack of sentries awake.

They had an undisturbed night.

In the morning, Dunbar was persuaded to proceed on cautiously down the Earn's meandering course, following in the still obvious tracks of Balliol's forces, scouts ahead and on the flanks. They had no difficulty in discovering where the English had crossed the river, at the Bootmill ford some three miles east of the battlefield, the miller there confirming that they had thereafter headed almost due north, on the way to Perth town, which was less than three miles away. A ridge of low hill lay between the Earn valley and the city here, known as Kirkton Craigs, rising to twin summits with something of a pass between them. Up and through this pass the English had marched, to disappear beyond, the miller said. They had not reappeared.

It was Perth, then; it could not be anything else. Dunbar's leaders conferred and decided that they had little option but to go on and try to discover Balliol's position and probable intentions – although the Earl's own reluctance was entirely evident. It looked as though there would be no fighting if Dunbar had his way, Douglas muttered to his friend.

All recognised that just to follow up and through that pass on Kirkton Craigs would be folly, since it would present an ideal ambush-place where even a small number could hold up an army. To the east, the main road to Perth threaded a lower but still dangerous pass, at Moncreiffe Hill; but west-about Kirkton Craigs sank to a long, grassy escarpment of no great height, above Aberdalgie, over which they could cross without danger of ambush. They would be observed from the city, to be sure; but that was inevitable whichever way they went.

So the move was made across the Bootmill ford and north-west thereafter, following up the Aberdalgie Burn for the higher ground. There was much woodland here, and as they rode through it out from its cover emerged men, singly and in groups, mainly small but some quite large: the remnants of Mar's defeated army, thankful to see a Scots force to which they could attach themselves. Not that Dunbar welcomed such uninvited adherents; quite the reverse. But they came along behind, just the same, in ever increasing numbers, for the Aberdalgie woods proved to be full of them. They were all on foot, of course, whereas Dunbar's host was all mounted. So they formed a long straggling tail.

Up on the summit of the long Lamberkine escarpment Dunbar drew up. The view from here was extensive in all directions. The walled city of Perth was plainly visible just two miles to the north-east. Even at that range the activity going on just outside the walls and gates was plain, large numbers of men busy erecting palisades of timber and digging ditches for defence, others using horses to drag felled trees from the nearby woodland.

"So – Balliol settles in at Perth!" Douglas said. "He prepares for siege. Why here? This is strange. What means it?"

None could answer that. Perth, on the edge of the Highlands, was important as a gateway to those northern and mountainous regions. But as far as Lowland Scotland was concerned, the significant part for any English invaders, it was on the perimeter, comparatively unimportant.

They waited there on the ridge, debating the meaning of what they saw. Ramsay put forward the suggestion that it might be because of the so-called disinherited lords, who were known to be with Balliol. These were Englishmen, or the sons of Englishmen, who had wed or been born to Scots heiresses during the period of English domination before Bruce had freed Scotland. These had, of course, taken the English side in the Wars of Independence, and been forfeited thereafter. But at the final peace treaty of three years before, their claims to the forfeited lands had been put forward. Nothing had been done about this, officially, by the Scots authorities. And now they marched with Balliol. It so happened that some of the most important of these lands lay in the North, this because the great Comyn estates were largely there – and Balliol was kin to the Comyns, who had been the richest and most powerful family in the land. Henry de Beaumont claimed the earldom of Buchan, as husband of the Comyn heiress thereof. Gilbert d'Umfraville, Scots only on the female side, was Earl of Angus. David Earl of Atholl had taken the English side and was with Balliol, his mother another Comyn. And so on. Might all this not have something to do with this occupation of the northern city?

Mulling over this, they were joined by ever increasing

45

numbers of the stragglers from Mar's host, an accession of numerical strength which was but an embarrassment to the Earl of Dunbar, whose most evident wish was to be elsewhere. But he could scarcely turn and ride away now, southwards, in the face of the invaders, without at least making some gesture – especially with Sir William Douglas making his opinion vehemently felt, and others with him. It was decided that they should move down and forward, nearer to the town and there take up some threatening posture. The fact that Balliol had shut himself up in Perth instead of making an attack on Dunbar looked as though he was now unsure of himself for some reason. Perhaps he had suffered more at Dupplin than the reports suggested. He might even have been wounded. Or it might be that some of his supporters were reluctant for further warfare meantime. It might even have something to do with his shipping, which the watchers could now see lying in the Tay near the city.

Dunbar's much augmented host moved slowly down, almost due eastwards, to a foothill area called the Buckie Braes, less than a mile from the south gate of Perth. This was as near as the Earl would venture. There amongst whin bushes and thorn trees they camped. They would appear a large and menacing army of mixed horse and foot, from the town. At Douglas's urging, with evening falling, Dunbar sent forward Scott of Rankilburn and a trumpeter to demand the surrender of the city. Also the yielding up of the traitor, Murray of Tullibardine.

In due course Scott returned from Perth's South Port to announce that his summons and message had been ignored. None were surprised.

They settled down where they were for the night, building huge fires all round the perimeter of the camp and setting strong guards in case of any possible attacks from the town.

The situation was unchanged in the morning. The enemy were still working at erecting palisades and strengthening the walling. Dunbar, for his part, appeared to be quite content to watch and do nothing more – for of course he had no cannon or other siege-machinery; but even his own Border lairds felt that something must be done. Douglas suggested that they should at least have men to cut bundles of sticks and faggots for filling in the defensive ditches, as indication to the enemy of a proposed assault on the town – even if the present leadership was too delicate to contemplate such course. Without waiting for agreement, he set his own and Ramsay's men to faggot-cutting; and soon they were joined by others.

For how long this waiting game might have gone on there was no knowing; but soon after mid-day there was an unexpected development, unexpected equally by both sides. This was the appearance in the narrowed Tay, off Moncreiffe Island, of a new squadron of ships, which promptly opened fire on the English vessels already anchored off the town walls, these last as promptly answering back with their own cannon. Suddenly there was a naval battle going on, entirely visible from the Buckie Braes, to the astonishment of the less active land-based forces.

However surprised they might be, the Scots at least knew who these aggressive newcomers were, in especial William Douglas, who crowed with glee. This undoubtedly was John Crabb and his Flemings, from Berwick-on-Tweed, with their armed merchant ships. Apparently Douglas, when he had been sent to the Border to enlist Dunbar in this campaign, had met Crabb at the Earl's headquarters at Coldstream, near Berwick, where that individual was superintending the supply of the Warden's force, and there had found the Berwicker a man after his own heart. He had suggested to him there and then that there was a part for him and his shipping friends to play in the present conflict. Crabb was a quite famous character, chief of the powerful and wealthy Flemish merchant community who had helped to make Berwick the chief port of Scotland, dealing largely in the export of wool from the great sheep-runs of the Lammermuir area, also salted fish from the Merse coast, and the import of cloths, arms, wines and other goods. Crabb it was who had so greatly helped the Good Sir James Douglas, Will's father, in the recapture of the town and port from the English in 1318. Now here undoubtedly was John Crabb with his merchanters, following up the younger Douglas's suggestions about taking a hand in getting rid of Edward Balliol – the Scots trading ships, of course, always having to be well armed to defend themselves from English pirates.

Unfortunately for this fine initiative, however, it fairly soon became apparent that the English warships were still better armed with heavier and longer-ranged cannon, so that they could hit back more than effectively. Also the narrow channel of Tay, constricted by Moncreiffe Island, did not allow space for manoeuvre, and the merchant ships were thereby disadvantaged, whereas the enemy were partly protected behind piers and dock-works. When three of the dozen Berwickers were ablaze and one aground on the island, it was obvious that this attack could not be sustained, and Crabb's squadron had no option but to withdraw. Quickly sails were hoisted on the English ships, and with rowing-boats towing them out into the river, they set off after the retiring vessels. Both groups thereafter disappeared from view behind the Tarsappie and Elcho ridge, cannon still firing, although growing muffled by distance.

If the appearance of the Berwick ships had been unexpected, so was the effect on the situation at Perth. For instead of encouraging the Scots to greater efforts against the occupied town, the opposite resulted. Dunbar was angry. This was folly, he declared. These wretched merchants ought never to have come seeking battle and leaving Berwick endangered. For the English forces on the Border would quickly learn that much of the port's strength had sailed away northwards and would almost certainly take advantage of it to attack that coveted and vital fortress-town. Berwick was infinitely more important to Scotland than was this Perth; and he, Dunbar and March, was Warden of the Borders and responsible for their defence. Also, of course, his own lands in the Merse and Lothian were the more endangered, although he did not require to spell that out. He had had enough of this wretched adventure into which Douglas had led him. He was going to return to the Borderland forthwith, and no argument about it. If those English warships pursued Crabb's vessels to Berwick, only seventy or eighty miles by sea, which they could cover in under two days, then Scotland's main port could fall and the Border be wide open to invasion.

The orders to pack up and march were issued there and then.

Nothing that Douglas and Ramsay might say was of any avail, retiral it was. Reluctantly, since there could be no sense in their own small company remaining outside Perth, they had to go along with the rest, even though they certainly were not going to return with Dunbar to Tweedside.

From the summit of the Lamberkine ridge, presently, they

looked back on Perth and its environs sadly. The ships could be seen, in the other direction, now far down the estuary of Tay, still firing at each other, but clearly the Berwickers heading for the open sea and safety. It seemed one more sorry day for Scotland. Robert the Bruce must be turning in his grave.

3

The two friends were as glad to part from Dunbar and his people, at Stirling, as the Earl was to see them go, relations between them having reached a new low. Ramsay's suggestion that Dunbar might wish to call in at Stirling Castle, and pay his respects to the child-monarch there, had been ignored.

They rode up through the steeply-climbing streets of the town to the wide tourney-ground and forecourt of the mighty castle on its rock, the strongest fortress in the land, their two hundred followers somehow seeming much more impressive than heretofore, in the narrow wynds, their horses' hooves striking sparks from the cobblestones. Up at the raised drawbridge before the frowning gatehouse, they reined up, and shouted that here was Sir William Douglas of Liddesdale and Sir Alexander Ramsay of Dalwolsey, seeking audience with the King's Grace. Those names, it seemed, were sufficient warrant for the captain of the guard to admit the visitors without seeking higher authority, and the drawbridge was lowered for them; but the troopers behind them were ordered to remain in the tourney-ground. The two knights dismounted and entered the castle.

Led up through the outer and inner baileys and past various ranges of battlements, to the high palace block, they found two men awaiting them, who apparently had perceived their arrival; or rather a man and a youth, standing in the doorway, both richly dressed, the man tall, slender and finely-featured, of early middle years and wearing an air of authority; the younger good-looking, fresh-faced, eager.

"Ha – Douglas! And Ramsay!" the man addressed them. "So it is you. We wondered what host that was which we could see passing by His Grace's house without pause – a strange behaviour. Earlier we had assumed that it was my lord of Mar, the new Regent, come to take his duty to the King. But seemingly not . . . ?"

"No, Sir Andrew," Douglas answered shortly. "Not Mar. Dunbar it is who rides past. We greet you. And you, my lord John. Or . . ." Even Douglas hesitated. Not only had this youth to learn of the death of his brother, but the Earl of Dunbar and March was in fact his brother-in-law.

"*I* am not Moray, sir," John Randolph said. "That is my elder brother."

"I fear not, my lord. *You* are Earl of Moray now . . ."

The other drew a quick breath, and Ramsay, who felt that this was hardly the way to inform someone of his brother's death, was about to speak when the older man intervened.

"What is this, Douglas?" he demanded. "This of Moray. And of Dunbar? You mean my lord of Dunbar and March, the Warden, our friend's goodbrother? Do not speak in riddles, man." That was rapped out.

Douglas would not have accepted that tone of voice from many. But this individual was rather exceptional: Sir Andrew Murray, Lord of Bothwell and Avoch and Petty and much else, son of Wallace's great co-victor at Stirling Bridge thirty-five years before, guardian of his wife's nephew the boy-king and husband of Christian Bruce the late monarch's sister.

"You have not heard, then? Of Dupplin Muir? And Mar? And what has happened?"

"Mar I left at Perth, five days ago. After voting him in to the regency. Dupplin? That is near to Perth, near the mouth of Strathearn, is it not?"

"Aye. A place that we shall not forget for long! There Mar met Edward Balliol – and threw all away in blind folly! Utter rout, disaster. Now Balliol sits in Perth town. And Mar is dead . . ."

"Mar dead! The Regent! Defeated? God in Heaven . . . !"

Ramsay spoke up, concerned for the youth. "There were two actions to the battle, if battle it could be called. A night attack by the English. Therein, my lord, your brother did well, one of the few who did. We spoke with him. But in the

Scots attack later, mismanaged grievously, many lost their lives. Not only the Regent himself, the Earls of Menteith and Carrick, Sir Alexander Fraser – and your brother. I am sorry . . ."

John Randolph, biting his lip, turned away.

Andrew Murray shook his head wordlessly and led the way within.

In an upper room of the palace the visitors recounted the main details of the happenings at Dupplin and Perth, to the hearers' dismay and distress. Young Randolph soon left them, with Sir Andrew pacing up and down the chamber.

"What now, then?" he demanded, of himself, clearly, as much as of the newcomers. "What will Balliol and the English do? Who is to lead the realm? To govern? There must be a new Regent. Yet, so many are dead, you say. Who, then? And Dunbar? He plays a doubtful part – but then, he ever did. How much trust can we place in him now? Here is a broil, indeed!"

"Dunbar will play his own game, you may be sure," Douglas said. "He was in haste to get back to the Border. I would not put it beyond him to make his own terms with the English, so long as they leave *his* lands untouched! He is no sound Warden of the Marches. As for Balliol, God knows! He is no seasoned fighter, yet that night attack at Dupplin was a shrewd stroke, ably carried out. I say that he may have men with him who *are* able commanders. Some of these disinherited lords, perhaps. Umfraville of Angus fought long for the Plantagenet. So did Beaumont. David of Atholl is but feebler fowl. But others are not. They could steer Balliol to good effect."

"No doubt. But how? In what direction now? Will he come here, seeking to grasp young David? Besiege this castle? Or Edinburgh's, first? He would require heavy cannon to seek take this strength. He might surprise Edinburgh and win them there. We must send and warn Edinburgh. And ready all here."

"Why did Balliol go to Perth?" Ramsay asked. "That was not by chance, after Dupplin, for his ships sailed there, after landing him at Kinghorn. He must have intended that from the start. Why? What can Perth do for him? Unless he intends to raise the North against us. Perth could serve for that, the door to the Highlands. He has Angus and Atholl with him.

Beaumont married to a Comyn – and all the Comyn lands leaderless. Mar, too, now lacking its earl. And . . ." He glanced towards the door out of which John Randolph had passed, ". . . the earldom of Moray too, now deprived. You, my lord, are from the North. Might not that be Balliol's aim?"

"Aye – the North is in sorry state. Always was. But the Highland West, the clan chiefs, keep the eastern earls looking over their shoulders. If they march south, the clans march east!"

"If Balliol could win over the clan chiefs. Not John of the Isles, but . . ."

"Let us hope that may be his intention," Douglas interrupted. "For it would take time. And time we need. We have to rouse the land, raise a new army. Warn Edinburgh Castle, and the others, Dumbarton in especial. Send someone to watch Dunbar. Sakes – we need time indeed!"

"We need more than time," Andrew Murray pointed out. "We need a new Regent. And quickly. To give authority for the rest. The realm must have a leader."

"*You* are the King's guardian here," Douglas said. "You could issue the orders in the King's royal name. None could fault that, in this present trouble."

"I am not the Regent. Only a Regent has the necessary authority to raise and lead the crown's forces. To order mustering. To appoint commanders . . ."

"You *could* be," Douglas asserted. "Who better as Regent than Sir Andrew Murray, the King's uncle, the good-brother of the Bruce!"

Ramsay nodded. "Indeed, my lord – who better?"

Murray rubbed his chin, silent.

"Who else, then?" Douglas insisted. "None of the earls will serve. Menteith and Carrick are dead. Mar leaves only a child. Angus and Atholl are Balliol's friends. Ross is little known outside his own lands. Strathearn and Moray are under age. Dunbar none could trust."

"Fife? He is premier earl."

"He is a prisoner of Balliol, after Dupplin. None of Bruce's old lieutenants survive, now that Sir Alexander Fraser, the Chamberlain, is slain . . ."

"Save your own uncle, Sir Archibald Douglas, your father's brother."

"Aye, Uncle Archie is well enough. Good to lead a charge

of cavalry! But no commander. I would make a better Regent my own self!"

The other two rather blinked at that.

"Well – *you* cannot appoint me Regent! Nothing surer than that," Murray said. "It requires the Council's decision. But – how many of the Council still live? How to call a meeting . . . ?"

He was interrupted, not this time by the ever brash Douglas but by two children. A rather striking, dark-eyed and vivacious girl of ten or eleven years burst into the room, flinging the door wide, followed by a boy, perhaps three years younger, fair but slight, and being largely dragged in by a deer-hound almost as tall as himself.

"My lord, my lord," the girl cried. "David says that you are going to take him hawking. And not me. To the Fords of Frew. It is not true? You would not do that? You would not leave me? It is a lie, a lie!"

"She should not *always* come!" the boy blurted. He had a very slight impediment in his speech. "She always wants to be first, to fly the best hawks, to ride fastest. Girls should not be so . . ."

"If I ride better than you do and fly better hawks, is that *my* fault?"

"It is, it is . . . !"

"Your Graces! Your Graces, hush you!" Sir Andrew said, bowing however, to each in turn. "Here is no way to greet these two good knights, come to your house. Here is Sir William Douglas of Liddesdale, of whom I have told you, a famous jouster, known to all as the Flower of Chivalry. And this is Sir Alexander Ramsay of Dalwolsey, a stout fighter also, and son of another."

The children stared, the girl interestedly, the boy doubtfully.

The two visitors bowed deeply.

"You, Sire, come and receive Sir William and Sir Alexander," Murray urged. "They are your good and loyal friends."

David Bruce, letting go of the dog reluctantly, edged forward hesitantly, and, scowling, held out a not-over-clean hand. Douglas, grinning, dropped on one knee and reached out to take that small palm between his own, upright, in the time-honoured gesture of fealty.

53

"My lord King," he said, "yours to command." And rose.

Ramsay did the same, smiling to the boy. "Your Grace's leal servant," he assured.

Joanna Plantagenet pointed at her husband. "Say something," she told him.

Turning away, the King of Scots said, "No!" He grasped the hound's collar again.

"*I* have heard of Sir William Douglas," the Queen declared. "You have unseated more knights, at tournaments, than anyone else. Have you ever killed any?"

"No, Your Grace. Not at tourneys. Elsewhere, perhaps!"

"One does not kill people at tourneys," David said scornfully. "Everyone knows that."

Murray looked from one to the other. "Yes. So be it. See now, these good knights and myself have matters to discuss. Important matters for Your Graces' realm. Perhaps you will graciously permit this, this audience to end, for the present? I fear that there can be no hawking this day. Another day . . ."

"Come, David," Joanna said.

These two had been wed for three years. It was one of the last acts of the ailing Robert Bruce's reign, to try to ensure peace with England thereafter and give a helpful start for his little son when he mounted the throne, to marry him to Edward the Third's young sister; this, one of the terms of the long-sought peace treaty of 1329. Alas, the desired peace did not seem to have resulted, too much to hope for in the ages-old bedevilled relationship between the two realms.

"Her Grace appears to wear the breeks in this marriage!" Douglas commented. "She is the elder, to be sure. But . . . !" He left the rest unsaid.

"Aye, David is . . . difficult," Sir Andrew acceded. "I fear that there is not much of his father's strong character there. Strange, for his mother, Elizabeth de Burgh, was a fine woman, nowise lacking in strength."

"He is but a bairn," Ramsay said. "And was not his royal sire himself scarcely a hero, when young? From all I have heard."

Douglas dismissed their liege-lord with a wave of the hand, anxious to revert to more important matters. "This of the regency," he declared. "It must be settled swiftly. Can you produce a Privy Council meeting, however small, to effect it?"

"I do not know which lords of council still live, man! Dunbar will not help us, it seems. The bishops, yes, I can get a few of them quickly, I think. Your uncle, Sir Archibald, is on the Council . . ."

"Never mind Uncle Archie! He is down in Galloway – too far away. *I* will speak for him! He will vote for you! Two or three bishops will serve well enough, in this pass. With ourselves . . ."

"You are neither of you councillors!"

"Bernard de Linton, the Chancellor, can swear us in – on the King's command! That is, yourself!"

Embarrassed by this abrupt assumption of promotion, Ramsay hastily intervened. "Not necessary, surely? Some lords remain who were not with Mar. Or Dunbar. Some bide too far away to be brought here in time. But Sir David Hay, the new Constable, lives only at Errol, in the Carse of Gowrie. He is of age, now. Sir David de Lindsay is Keeper of Edinburgh Castle. He will be there. Sir Michael Wemyss, Sheriff of Fife, was not with the Earl of Fife. He should be at Wemyss. Sir Alexander Leslie will also be in Fife, at Ballinbreich. And what of the Lord Robert? The High Steward, the Bruce's grandson. He will be but seventeen years, but he is next heir to the throne, as well as Steward. Should he not be here . . . ?"

"These, yes. If we can bring them here, in time. With a clutch of bishops. That would serve for a Council meeting," Murray agreed. "How soon can it be achieved, think you?"

"Speedy it must be, or all may be lost," Douglas asserted. "We may have only a few days, if that. And Edinburgh must be warned. Balliol may move swiftly, as he has done hitherto . . ."

Out of further discussion it was decided that, since these important lords and bishops could not just be summoned casually to Stirling lacking a Regent's authority, and without understanding of what was involved, they must be informed not by any mere messengers but by informants whom they would accept and respect. Bernard de Linton, Bishop of Man and Abbot of Arbroath, the realm's Chancellor, was nearby fortunately, lodging in Cambuskenneth Abbey; so Murray himself could tell him. He would send young Randolph to Glasgow, to Bishop John de Lindsay there, and then to take boat for Rothesay Castle, on Bute, where lived Robert the

Steward. Douglas would go to Edinburgh to inform Lindsay of Crawford and Luffness, then hasten on southwards to order a major muster of the Douglas manpower, in the name of his uncle and himself. And Ramsay would go north-eastwards, to Errol in Gowrie and then to Fife, to St Andrews, Ballanbreich and Wemyss, or possibly best in reverse order, leaving the Primate, Bishop Bennet of St Andrews, to summon the other privy-councillor bishops who were, as it were, within range. They would set off on their errands in the morning, the meeting to be called for ten days hence.

They prayed that it would all be in time to be effective.

It took six days for Alexander Ramsay to complete his mission, the delay being partly occasioned by his difficulty in running to earth young Sir David Hay, the High Constable, who was not at his castle of Errol in the Carse of Gowrie, across Tay. This being only some ten miles east of Perth, the word of the happenings there had reached him quickly, and recognising danger he had prudently departed further east still. The trouble was, where? He had many remote prop-erties in the Sidlaw Hills to the north and might have retired to any of these. Eventually Ramsay found him in his townhouse in Dundee, a worried young man. He had been Constable of Scotland for only two years, since the death of his heroic father, another of Bruce's band of paladins, and was in doubt as to his responsibilities in that office and his abilities to carry them out. But he agreed to attend the Council meeting. Then it had been back across the Tay ferry to Ferryport-on-Craig and so to St Andrews, where Bishop Bennet, the Primate, had undertaken to see that his col-leagues of Dunblane, Dunkeld and Brechin were informed. The earlier calls on Sir Michael Wemyss and Sir Andrew Leslie had not presented any problems.

Delay or none, Ramsay was the first of the envoys to return to Stirling. He found Sir Andrew Murray closeted with the famous Bernard de Linton, now Bishop of Man and Chancel-lor, or chief minister, of the realm. This able cleric had succeeded Nicholas Balmyle as Bruce's secretary and chap-lain, and gone on to become Abbot of Arbroath and author of the celebrated Declaration of Independence, signed at that abbey in 1320 by the nobility of Scotland, and endorsed wholeheartedly by the King. Middle-aged now but lacking nothing in keen intelligence and quiet vigour he, like Murray, was clearly much concerned over the present situation.

Although no major developments had been reported in the interim, and Balliol appeared to be still in Perth, there were ominous rumours circulating of serious defections to his cause. It was said that even the Bishop of Dunkeld, William de St Clair, one of those to be bidden to the Council meeting, had joined the English at Perth. And John of the Isles, son of Bruce's friend Angus Og, it was alleged, was on his way to support Balliol; although this was less unexpected, since after his father's death he had been rebellious and difficult. It was worrying that Balliol appeared to be attracting favour like this, after Murray of Tullibardine's defection. Was there any likelihood of a major secession developing in Scotland in favour of the invader? It was, of course, inevitable that many should look apprehensively at the reign of a child-monarch, and a dozen years at least of regency, with all the problems, weakness and stresses that must involve; and it was a truism that Scotland always needed a strong king to rule it. Would Edward Balliol, son of Bruce's predecessor King John, seem to offer to some a better and stronger kingship than that of the boy David? Surely, backed by England as he was, and indeed with an English army, Balliol would be seen to be no more than a Plantagenet puppet? And yet, Tullibardine . . . ?

Bishop de Linton cross-questioned Ramsay shrewdly on the Dupplin disaster, his views about Balliol and Perth, on Dunbar, and on his recent mission. The younger man was thankful that they had got someone of this calibre as Chancellor. Murray was a splendid soldier and leader of men, but no statesman such as was so evidently required in this crisis.

The Bishop seemed to take it for granted that Murray would be the new Regent, with no very obvious alternative, and did not foresee any major opposition at the Council meeting. Meantime, what was needed was information about Balliol and his intentions; that and the assembling of a large Scots army, just as quickly as possible. Only a regent could actually *command* this, in the King's name; but some forces could be raised voluntarily from loyal supporters, the burghs and Holy Church, and calls for this were already sent out. With four days still to go until the all-important meeting, it was suggested that Ramsay should now ride off secretly northwards once more, for the Perth area, to try to discover Balliol's position and plans, and to return in time to inform the Council.

Sandy Ramsay was possessed of a fair fount of energy and could not refuse this second mission, although he scarcely relished the task. On a fresh and less notable horse than his own, dressed in the good homespun of a small laird, and with only the one attendant, the Dalwolsey groom Wattie Kerr, neither wearing any armour or carrying arms other than small sword and dirk, he set off again that very evening, over Stirling Bridge and the long causeway beyond, into the late-August dusk.

They rode quietly all night, taking turns to doze in the saddle, up the Allan Water and over the bare slopes of Sheriffmuir below the northern flanks of the Ochils. By daylight they were not far from Aberuthven, where they had encamped with Dunbar.

It occurred to Ramsay to go call on the cottager who had led them to the little-known Inverdunning ford that dire night. He might have the local gossip as to what went on at Perth. They found the man already cutting his rig of thin oats. He made no comment on the visitor's changed dress and style but was able to tell them something of the invaders' activities. The English were still occupying Perth; but there was much coming and going northwards into Atholl and north-eastwards to Angus. This was only to be expected, with the disinherited lords of these parts seeking to muster men therefrom. But there was also considerable visiting of Scone and Dunkeld, it was said, so it looked as though the churchmen were being pressed and drawn in. And there were hordes of wild Hielandmen camped on the North Inch of Perth, plaguing the countryside around, worse than the English.

This interested Ramsay, since it might confirm the fears about the Lord of the Isles. He was particularly concerned about the Bishop of Dunkeld, since he was a Privy Councillor. Yet William St Clair, of the Roslin, Orkney and Caithness family, was not the sort of man to be readily intimidated. He had been a loyal supporter of the Bruce, who had indeed always called him 'my bishop', and had once heroically raised a force and personally driven the English out of Fife at the lance-point.

Ramsay could scarcely risk trying to enter Perth itself, for all gates would certainly be guarded; also, once in they might not easily get out. But he could go round it and seek to gain confirmation of these stories; west-about necessarily, since the Tay bounded the town on the east. So they rode on, heedfully, up on to the higher ground skirting the Aberdalgie and Lamberkine ridges again, and down on to the levels of the Burghmuir, west of Perth.

Here they had to make a further detour westwards, almost to Ruthvenfield village, to avoid the large force encamped on the Burghmuir, not Highlanders and therefore presumably Balliol's English army, no longer pent up in the walled city. They were not challenged and were able to swing eastwards again thereafter, to reach the Tay just above the North Inch parkland. Here indeed was to be seen another great camp, with many cooking-fires but few horses, and therefore presumably the Highland host of John of the Isles. They kept their distance.

From there they could look across Tay to the Scone area, a bare mile away, where amongst woodlands rose the famous abbey and the Boot or Moot Hill, scene of Scotland's coronations and resting-place, until 1296, of the Stone of Destiny. Because of the trees, it was difficult to see what went on there, but there was clearly considerable activity, horsemen coming and going and what looked like pavilions being erected. What this might represent was anybody's guess, but Ramsay thought that it might mean that Edward Balliol was intending to move personally out of the confines of the town and into more comfortable and spacious quarters in the abbey. Which would imply a stay of some time, rather than any swift sally southwards with his army. If this was so, it was an important indication, and ought to give the loyal Scots leadership a breathing-space, time to make their dispositions and gather strength.

There was no means by which they could cross Tay, save by the town bridge, or by the nearby Derders ford where the River Almond joined the greater stream; and almost certainly both would be well guarded and too great a risk to attempt. Ramsay decided that his best course now was to proceed northwards up Tay to Dunkeld, another fourteen miles or so, to try to discover the position of the Bishop thereof and if in truth he was being intimidated by Balliol. He was an important man and very influential in the Church, the ecclesiastical leader of a vast area of the Southern Highlands. If he defected, it could be a serious blow.

So they journeyed on, weary now after their all-night ride, and were glad to turn aside, in the late afternoon, to the Greyfriars monkish hospice for travellers at Luncarty, where not only could they obtain food and shelter but possibly news – for the monks were renowned always for their ability to gain information, their wandering friars famous carriers of gossip.

At Luncarty, without seeming to press the good brothers too closely – and by making a generous offering to St Francis – Ramsay learned that their lord Bishop William was indeed with Edward Balliol at Perth, not as any sort of hostage or prisoner they thought but of his own free will and good judgment. They understood that the Abbot of Scone was there also, likewise the Abbots of Coupar-Angus and Inch-affray. They revealed also that the Earl of Fife had passed this way a few days earlier, in company with the disinherited David de Strathbogie, Earl of Atholl, likewise not seeming any sort of prisoner, going north openly to raise Atholl for Balliol.

This information, if accurate, worried Ramsay seriously. It seemed to imply a grievous trend of support for Balliol's cause on the part of powerful men who should have been upholding their child-monarch and his regency. If many others did the same . . .

He decided that there was no point in going on to Dunkeld now. They would return southwards with their findings, but go via Inchaffray Abbey in Strathearn. If it was true that that abbot had also joined Balliol, and voluntarily, it would be ominous, for Inchaffray had been one of Bruce's favourite foundations, its former Abbot Maurice, now Bishop of Dunblane, carrying the arm-bone of St Fillan, for blessing, before the Scots army at Bannockburn.

Next morning, then, their horses well rested, which was as important as their own state, they took the drove-road westwards to Moneydie and so to the Almond ford at Dalcrue thereafter, and over the hill to Methven in Strathearn, nine miles. From there it was only another six, up the strath, to Inchaffray, set on a sort of island in the level marshlands, a fair place however remote.

At the abbey, although not unkindly received, they gained no comfort. The Abbot was absent and indeed gone to Perth, they were told. A messenger had come for him. When, taking a chance, Ramsay asked from whom the messenger had come, to cause a mitred abbot to hurry off to an embattled town, he was informed that it had been from the Lord Bishop of Dunkeld, no less. This sounded strange, for although Ramsay was no expert in matters ecclesiastical, he knew enough to be aware that Strathearn and Inchaffray were in the diocese of Dunblane, not Dunkeld, and therefore the Abbot's superior was Bishop Maurice of Dunblane, not Bishop William de St Clair. However, as a mere caller, he could hardly cross-question the sub-Prior, his informant. They took their leave, the more perturbed.

It seemed to Ramsay that since he could as well return to Stirling by Dunblane as by the way they had come, it might be as well to call on Bishop Maurice there, for guidance. He surely, of all men, would remain loyal to Bruce's memory and his son's support. He might already have left for the Council meeting, of course.

They pressed on, therefore, south by west, across the wide and water-logged levels of mid-Strathearn, making for the Innerpeffrey ford over the great river, and so by Muthill and the Muir of Orchill's high ground to the Allan Water again at Braco, and so to Dunblane.

It was late in the afternoon before they reached the fine cathedral, built by David the First, which towered over the little market-town, only to find Bishop Maurice gone, not directly to Stirling as yet but westwards to Doune apparently, to Doune Castle, a seat of the Randolphs, Earls of Moray. For what reason was not given. Ramsay, who could reveal his true identity now, decided to ride on to Doune, only another four miles and not greatly out of his way.

Doune lay amongst low green hills on the north bank of the River Teith, a village which was really only the castleton of the massive stronghold which reared high above the riverside on its rocky mound, on the site of what had once been a Pictish fort; hence its name, a form of *dun* meaning a fortified place. It was dusk before the travellers rode up to the frowning pile and presented themselves at the gatehouse, where the portcullis was already down for the night although the drawbridge was not raised. The assertion that Sir

Alexander Ramsay of Dalwolsey came seeking the Lord Bishop of Dunblane, however, gained them quite speedy entry.

This was an earl's establishment and things were done accordingly. A chamberlain received them and Wattie Kerr was sent to the servants' quarters while Ramsay was conducted upstairs to the private hall, a lofty and handsome vaulted apartment on the first floor, with two great fireplaces, a dais, and walls hung with tapestries. Therein, spacious and grand as it was, only two people sat, and not on the dais: a man in late middle years clad in ecclesiastical black and crimson, and a young woman simply but effectively dressed in a short-skirted over-gown of olive-green homespun above white linen. The chamberlain announced him with a flourish. Deer-hounds came to sniff at him.

It was the young woman who rose and moved forward. She was slenderly well-built and graceful, darkly good-looking with fine grey eyes which seemed to contrast almost dramatically with her plentiful black hair and colouring. She smiled kindly. At a guess the visitor would put her age at about eighteen.

"Welcome to Doune, Sir Alexander," she said. "I do not think that you have honoured us previously? But I have heard you spoken of, and well. I am Mariot Randolph."

Ramsay bowed over her hand. "You are kind as you are fair, Lady Mariot," he declared, with an attempt at gallantry. Then he bit his lip, remembering that this was the recently bereaved sister of the young Earl slain at Dupplin and the daughter of the Regent who had died at Musselburgh; so gallantry was probably out of place meantime. Also, of course, lovely as she might be, *fair* was scarcely an apt description of her beauty. He changed his tack. "I pray that you forgive this, this intrusion, at this time – especially as I am unkempt with long riding. I came seeking a word with my lord Bishop, whom I was told was here."

"Then here he is, sir. It is good that my lord has brought you to our door."

Bishop Maurice stood, a heavily-built man of iron-grey head and strong features. "Greetings, my son," he said, strong-voiced. "I knew your father, Sir William. I am the more pleased to meet his son. You come seeking me?"

"Yes, my lord. I come from Dunblane. And before that from Inchaffray. After Perth and Scone . . ."

"Ah! Then your errand is unlikely to be a spiritual one!" the prelate commented, almost grimly. But then, he had a rather grim expression anyway. "I would have thought that you would come from Stirling?"

"I left Stirling three days back. On a, a mission. Of enquiry." Ramsay glanced at the girl, who took the hint.

"I will go find you some refreshment, Sir Alexander. After all that riding you will be requiring it. Sit you." Gesturing, she left them alone.

"You have been spying out the land, my friend?" the Bishop said. "To no great joy, I fear?"

"No. I was sent to discover what I could of Edward Balliol's dispositions and intentions. By Sir Andrew Murray. And I have not learned much of these, save that he does not appear to be planning any swift march from Perth, but settling there, rather. Joined there by John of the Isles, in treachery. But, there is worse treachery than that, I think, for the Isleman was never to be trusted. It is the churchmen, my lord, whose loyalty I now doubt."

The Bishop waited, unspeaking.

"Your colleague, my lord Bishop of Dunkeld, it seems is with Balliol. And of his own will, it is believed, not as any prisoner. As is the Abbot of Scone; although he, so near to Perth, could have been constrained. But the Abbot of Coupar-Angus is said to have joined Balliol also. And, when I called at Inchaffray, your own abbey, I learned that its abbot had likewise gone to Perth, sent for by Bishop William! What means this, my lord? Is Holy Church deserting King David, the Bruce's son, in his hour of need? Only three years after his father's death?"

The other shook his head. "Not Holy Church, my friend – of that you may rest assured. But some may . . . mistake their duty, sorry as I am to say it. This of Bishop William, who is my friend, I much deplore his views in this. I know that he considers Scotland to require no child-king but a strong man to lead the realm . . ."

"That must be a regent, in these circumstances. Young David *is* the King, crowned and anointed."

"To be sure. *I* say that, also. But there is the argument that so long as a child is monarch, whomsoever the Regent, there will be division and internal warfare in the realm, power-hungry men seeking to grasp the King into their own hands to rule in his name, factions seeking to change the regency, intrigues and anarchy. And the kingdom suffering, Holy Church with it. That is Bishop William's contention."

"You knew of this, then?"

"I knew that he thought in such fashion. But not that he would go so far as to support Balliol and his English master. That is grievous news, if true. And I knew naught of these others. Nothing of this of Inchaffray, which comes under *my* authority. I shall certainly deal with that . . ."

The young woman brought in a servitor, with cold meats and wine for the visitor. Bishop Maurice changed the subject.

"I am here to offer my respects, sympathy and what little comfort I can give, to the Lady Mariot in her sorrow and loss," he said. "To be bereft of father and brother in so short a time is a sore blow indeed. But the good God is giving her the courage and strength to bear it."

The girl inclined her dark head, unspeaking.

Ramsay cleared his throat, "I am sorry," he said. "It is hard, afflicting. What can one say?"

"There *is* nothing to be said," she answered simply. "I have sought to dry my tears. My father was a sick man, I knew. But this of Thomas . . ."

"Strange that I should have been with them both, so near the end. I was at my lord Regent's bedside at Musselburgh; with him all the way from the Border, a hard journey. And later at his graveside. He was a noble man . . ."

"John told me of that. He was here before he journeyed to the West. To call the Bishop of Glasgow and the High Steward to this meeting. But, eat, Sir Alexander. *We* have already fed . . ."

"This meeting – who will be there?" the Bishop asked. "There must be great gaps in the Council now."

"There can only be few there, yes. And the need for haste means that those far off cannot be reached in time. Balliol does not seem to be moving as swiftly as we feared. But a new Regent must be appointed without delay."

"That should be Sir Andrew Murray. Thank God that we have him! None will oppose him, I think – save perhaps my lord of Dunbar and March!" And he glanced over at their hostess. "He might deem *himself* a candidate. He is of the ancient royal house. And goodson to our late Regent, to be sure."

"That Earl will not be at the meeting," Ramsay said, he too looking at the girl. "He, he rode on. On to the Border, passing by Stirling. He would not come with us to the castle there, to the King. He esteems his place . . . elsewhere!"

The Bishop stroked his chin thoughtfully.

"Patrick, my goodbrother is . . . Patrick!" the young woman said, and left it at that.

"*I* married him to Agnes," the older man observed, almost apologetically. "I fear that it was a doubtful choice . . ." He paused, as a commotion sounded from outside, the clatter of hooves and shouting.

The girl went to a window, to peer out into the half-dark. "Here is John returned," she reported. "Sooner than he thought . . ." She went to greet her brother.

"That is a fine young woman," the Bishop declared. "I have known her all her life, watched her grow to womanhood. I pray that she makes a better marriage than did her sister!"

Ramsay had nothing to say to that.

"Young John Randolph – or my lord Earl, as we must now name him – will not have found Bishop John of Glasgow," the older man went on. "For he has gone to France, two weeks past. I could have told him that, had I known. One less for the Council . . ."

Mariot Randolph reappeared, with her brother and another young man, little more than a youth likewise. "Here is John, and the High Steward," she announced.

Ramsay had not had occasion to meet Robert Stewart for a few years, and then he had been a mere boy. Now, at seventeen, he was fully grown, stocky and well built, and would have been quite good-looking had it not been for his eyes, which inevitably drew attention and kept retaining it however involuntarily. They were, in fact, extraordinary, embarrassingly so, appearing to be out of focus, what should have been white red and bloodshot, and watering as though permanently in tears. He had been born that way, for this was Robert the Bruce's grandson and namesake, son of his daughter Marjorie Bruce, who had been thrown from her horse at Paisley and produced this child before dying, damaged in her womb. His mind was sound enough, as was his body; only the eyes told the sad story of Marjorie, victim of Edward of England's spleen after 1306, held captive for years as a child and suffering continual indignities, before eventually winning home and being married to Walter, the Steward, and then dying within the year. Walter Stewart, a stout fighter if less successful as a husband, had himself died in 1326, the eleven-year-old succeeding to the high office. So this was Robert, High Steward of Scotland and heir presumptive to the throne, known behind his back as Rob Bleary.

The Bishop and Ramsay bowed.

Mariot, seeing the young man peering short-sightedly, hastened to add, "My lord Robert, here is the Lord Bishop of Dunblane and Sir Alexander Ramsay of Dalwolsey. Sir Alexander is just come. From the North. After much travel."

"I believed you to be in Fife and Gowrie," John Randolph put in. "Summoning the Constable and others to this meeting?"

"I did so. When I returned to Stirling, Sir Andrew sent me back to as near to Perth as I could win, in safety, for news of Balliol . . ."

"And that news, sir . . . ?"

"He remains at Perth, as yet. Sadly, some are rallying to his cause, against their allegiance to His Grace. Your neighbour, my lord Robert, the Lord John of the Isles. And . . . others."

"John MacDonald may be my neighbour, at Rothesay, but he is no friend," the young Steward said shortly.

The girl sent the chamberlain for more food and wine. She made a very competent hostess and clearly was used to being mistress of this large establishment, which she had been for over two years. Her mother, the Countess, was still alive, but preferred to live up at Darnaway Castle in Moray, the main seat of the earldom, where her youngest daughter, Isabella, stayed with her. The Regent had required quarters near to Stirling and Edinburgh, in the cause of government, and had installed his second daughter as chatelaine at Doune. Although there could have been only a year or so of difference in ages, she seemed much more mature than her brother, Ramsay noted.

The Earl John explained that he had found the Bishop of Glasgow gone abroad when he reached that city; proceeding on to Dumbarton he had taken ferry to Bute and on to Rothesay, to reach the Steward. They had not delayed their return to the mainland and had ridden directly here, all taking less time than he had calculated.

All agreed that they would travel together to Stirling next day.

When the newcomers were finished their repast, Mariot produced a harp, and entertained them to a selection of songs and ballads, in both Scots and the Gaelic, in a clear and tuneful voice, her brother and the prelate egging her on; evidently this was her custom of an evening. Ramsay was the more impressed. So, most obviously, was the Steward. Bishop Maurice's rather stern features softened as he watched and listened.

But much riding had made the young men heavy-eyed, and noting it, the girl urged them bedwards before long. She had an escort of three to her own bedchamber door that night.

In the morning they made an early start, for although it was only a dozen miles to Stirling, the Bishop was past the stage of hard riding and moreover wanted to call in at his palace at Dunblane in passing. They took leave of the Lady Mariot appreciatively, Alexander Ramsay and Robert Stewart vying with each other in their expressed approval.

That Privy Council meeting at Stirling was small in attendance but vital in importance. There were only nine of the original councillors present: the Chancellor himself, Sir Andrew Murray, the Bishops of St Andrews and Dunblane, Hay the High Constable, Sir Michael Wemyss, Sir Alexander Leslie and Sir Simon Fraser, brother of the late High Chamberlain, who had happened to be visiting Touch-Fraser nearby, from Kincardine, of which he was Sheriff. But Bernard de Linton, by general consent, had sworn in four new members, in the presence of the child-king to make it look more official: the High Steward and the new Earl of Moray, under-age as they both were, Sir William Douglas just returned from the Douglas country, and Sir Alexander Ramsay. So, a dozen strong, after bowing out the young David, they sat down round a table in the palace hall, and the Primate, Bishop Bennet of St Andrews, opened the meeting with prayer – a shaky prayer, for he was a sick and ageing man and even the journey from the East Neuk of Fife had taxed him.

Bernard de Linton, level-voiced and businesslike, started with a brief review of the dire situation confronting them, not exactly playing down the dangers but giving the general impression that all could be handled, given wise decisions, determination and courage. He paid tribute to their dead colleagues, in especial their late and good Regent Moray and the High Chamberlain, and condoled with the son of one and the brother of the other, here present. Also, to be sure, the High Steward's cousin, the Earl of Carrick. Their first priority, however, was to appoint a new Regent for His Grace, that the rule of his realm should be sustained and directed. He, as Chancellor, had no hesitation in proposing Sir Andrew Murray for that all-important position, the King's guardian and uncle by marriage, a close supporter and friend of their late beloved monarch King Robert, son of Wallace's heroic partner, and a notable warrior himself; which none could deny was essential as an attribute in the present circumstances, as the disaster at Dupplin had so grievously demonstrated. Was it agreed?

Put that way, with Sir Andrew present, it would have demanded a determined opponent to say otherwise, especially when William Douglas vehemently added his support, indeed asserting that any other choice would be folly or worse.

No alternative name was put forward, and the appointment was made, with acclaim.

Now, in the King's name as Regent, Murray in theory presided over the meeting, although the Bishop in effect still managed it. He suggested that the Regent called on Sir Alexander Ramsay to give his account of the situation as far as his recent enquiries had revealed it.

Ramsay recounted briefly the Dupplin tragedy and its aftermath, Douglas interspersing his own comments. Then dealt with Balliol's remaining at Perth, his apparent interest in Scone, his reinforcement by John of the Isles and, glancing almost apologetically at the three bishops, the apparent adherence of prominent churchmen to the Balliol cause – this last drawing snorts from Douglas, who had no love for the clergy.

Bishop Maurice spoke up, pointing out that deplorable as this defection was, there could be a certain reason and excuse behind it, which they were as well to recognise since others might well think the same way. He emphasised the problems and dangers inherent in a child-monarchy, and how some would see Edward Balliol, son of the sad King John, the

Toom Tabard, as possibly making a more effective king. This, of course, would be a violation of the oaths of allegiance to young David sworn at his coronation, but some might hold that lightly.

"Churchmen? Sworn in an abbey, before all?" Douglas demanded.

The other shrugged.

Bishop John of St Andrews raised his quavering voice to declare his distress at this. And not only at the episcopal defection but his anxiety at what it might lead to, in Church as well as state. They all knew that the English Archbishop of York had the effrontery to claim spiritual hegemony over the northern realm, on the grounds that since there was no archbishop north of York *he* must be the Metropolitan of Scotland. If William of Dunkeld had gone over to Balliol, which meant in effect to the English, then he could be used to further such claims. Indeed, one of the most senior bishops as he was, he could possibly aspire to St Andrews and the Primacy himself, with Balliol's backing, and in return admit the spiritual authority of York.

These fears came forth in fits and starts, the old voice choking with emotion at times.

Some there, notably Douglas, were impatient over such mere clerical worries, anxious to get on to the more important matter, the military situation. But the Chancellor saw it otherwise, stilling their murmurs.

"My lords, this could be a vital issue," he said in his quietly authoritative fashion. "Edward of England, like his father and grandsire before him, has the similar audacity to call himself Lord Paramount of Scotland. This insolent claim is based on two factors. One, that the first Edward chose John Balliol as King of Scots at the competition for the throne, and this was accepted; and two, York should have archiepiscopal dominion over the northern kingdom, since Scotland did not have its own archbishop, and York pays tribute to the English crown. So now, if Edward Balliol gains power here, and an admission of York's hegemony could be gained from Scots churchmen of standing, then Edward Plantagenet is in a position to establish his claim, and gain the Pope's approval. And that of other princes of Christendom."

Silence greeted this, as Bishop Maurice nodded agreement.

"What to do, then?" Murray demanded. "How can we affect this issue?"

"With the sword!" Douglas barked. "You priests can say your prayers! I say our steel will speak louder than clerks' orisons! That is what we must be at – raising an army."

"A moment, Sir William," Bishop de Linton requested. "My lord Regent – we shall fight the better if our backs are protected. This issue affects the realm as much as the Church. And I think that we might take steps to counter it. An envoy to the Pope, at Avignon. Before the Plantagenet may think to do the like. To gain a clear papal pronouncement as to the Scots Church's independence and autonomy. The envoy to take a suitable gift! Holy Church could produce such, my lord Primate?"

"Oh, ah – to be sure . . ."

"Who should be sent?" Murray asked. "Yourself . . . ?"

"No, no. I fear that I may be needed here! Who better than my lord of St Andrews himself? He can speak with the due authority. And it would have other advantage. If the Primate is furth of the country he is safe from Balliol and the English. They might assail St Andrews and capture him. Then claim that they have his acceptance. Such has been done in the past. If the Primate has gone to the Pope, they are held, no?"

Bishop John gabbled a mixture of alarm and agreement.

"Well said, my lord Chancellor," the new Regent commended. "Does this Council agree that the Lord Bishop of St Andrews sails forthwith for France?"

With none disputing it, Douglas thumped the table.

"Now – to what signifies!" he exclaimed. "We shall not defeat the invaders with papal bulls and suchlike! Armed men, well led, will do that – and only men. I have two thousand Douglases marching north from Liddesdale and Douglasdale. And I have sent messengers to my Uncle Archie in Galloway to muster his fullest strength. He should raise another two thousand in a week or two. Will others do the like?" That was a blunt challenge, as he gazed round the table.

There were frowns and grunts. None other there could produce men in such numbers, yet none liked to admit it.

"I can field three hundred," the young High Constable said, rather diffidently. "Or . . . perhaps more."

"Given time, I can do the same," Leslie growled.

"Of my own folk, I can bring only one hundred," Sir Michael Wemyss said. "Of the sheriffdom of Fife, I know not how many. My lord Earl of Fife is prisoner with Balliol. He took many men with him, to join Mar. So, many are gone. Probably many died at Dupplin. I know not the Earl's wishes in this . . ."

"From what Sandy Ramsay says, your Earl was not unhappy with Balliol!" Douglas asserted. "*You* muster Fife's manpower."

"Yes. You have this Council's authority so to do," Murray agreed. "For myself, from Bothwell I can raise five hundred. Many more from my northern lands, but that will take time, which we may not have. The same will apply to you, my lord of Moray? But you have other lands, nearer. Doune. And some on the West March, I think?"

"Morton, yes, was my father's. So now is mine, I suppose. I . . . I do not know what numbers Morton can produce – Armstrongs, Johnstones and the like. Or other lands. I have never had to do this," the youthful Randolph conceded. "I could find one hundred at Doune, I think . . ."

"And I three hundred from Touch and Gargunnock," Sir Simon Fraser nodded. "More from Peebles and the Forest . . ."

"These are but scantlings, handfuls!" Douglas broke in. "We need thousands, many thousands. The entire realm must be raised and marshalled."

"Now that I am appointed Regent I can so order," Murray acceded. "But a great muster cannot be achieved in a day or so."

Ramsay spoke up. "A great many were lost at Dupplin Muir. But many must have survived. Some stragglers joined Dunbar as we approached Perth. There could be broken men thereabouts. If these could be gathered . . ."

He paused, as the captain of the castle guard knocked and entered the chamber, apologising for interrupting, and going to murmur to Murray. That man's eyes widened and he half rose from his seat. Then he sat again and pointed a finger at the captain.

"Tell all," he directed. "God in His Heaven – all must hear this!"

The officer hesitated, clearing his throat. "My lords," he said, "a messenger is just come. From the Provost of Perth.

71

With tidings. Strange tidings. As to the Lord Balliol. He, he is now crowned king. At Scone . . ."

He got no further, the outcry drowning his words, as men jumped up crying their astonishment, disbelief, fury. At the Regent's direction the captain went back to the door and brought in the travel-stained courier from Perth, a young man looking distinctly alarmed at the company he was to keep.

When Murray could gain approximate silence, he ordered the newcomer to give them his message, to tell all.

Haltingly at first, after a number of false starts, the courier gave them the gist of it. The previous day, St Finnbar's Eve, Edward Balliol had ridden to Scone and there gone through a coronation ceremony, the Abbot of Scone celebrating, the Bishop of Dunkeld performing the anointing, the Earl of Fife placing the crown on his head, or *a* crown. Now he was proclaiming himself King of Scots and calling on all true men to rally to his standard.

Appalled, his hearers sat, all but bereft of speech, shaken, bewildered. But not William Douglas. He smashed a fist on the table and hooted.

"Mummery! Play-acting!" he shouted. "This is an antic, to delude fools, no more. There cannot be any such coronation, since we already have a King of Scots, duly crowned and anointed. Young David. This impudent impostor cannot claim a throne which is already occupied. Here is folly, bairns'-play!"

"It is more than that, Sir William," the Chancellor said gravely. "It is almost beyond belief, yes – but dangerous. This will confuse and subvert many, I fear. Make our task the more difficult . . ."

"All must know that it is false, man! Laugh it to scorn."

"All, my friend? Not, it seems, the Abbot of Scone, William of Dunkeld and the Earl of Fife! If these go along with it, indeed aid in it, how many others, and lesser men, may think alike?"

"Aye," Bishop Maurice agreed. "This is serious indeed. Many who are unhappy with a child-monarch will now have excuse to reconsider their allegiance."

"None can fail to know that it is false. That King David is their rightful liege-lord, and this merest mummery."

"If these three had not assisted, it would have been less grievous. But the Abbot of Scone is always the coronation celebrant, the Earl of Fife, heir of the MacDuffs, hereditary crown-bearer, and William of Dunkeld an important and respected prelate, our late King's friend. This could sway many."

"Then the sooner that we are up and doing, not talking here, the better!" Douglas rose.

"We all share your impatience, Sir William," Murray said. "But we must plan our actions to best effect. Each must know his due task if our fullest strength is to be marshalled. This mustering of forces requires much thought. A host of messengers will require to go out to all landed men. Where shall we assemble? This Stirling is too close to Perth for safety; we could be attacked by Balliol's army while we mustered. The Burgh Muir of Edinburgh is by tradition the realm's rallying-place . . ."

"Aye, make it there," Douglas acceded. "Seven days from this."

"Too soon, man. Your Douglases could be there by then. Ramsay's people. Perhaps Fraser's. But others, no. With the messengers not yet gone out . . ."

"Balliol may strike quickly now."

"I think not," the Chancellor put in. "Not his main thrust. Having gone through this coronation gesture, he will wish to use it to greatest effect. To let all know of it. So *his* messengers will be going out, likewise. I would say that he will delay, therefore, to see what numbers come to his call."

"That is sound reasoning," Bishop Maurice nodded. "Say two weeks, then, at Edinburgh? But, there is another matter to consider. The King's safety. Having gone so far Balliol will almost certainly try to capture young David. He may well send a force here to Stirling, and soon. This is a strong fortress and he might not be able to take it. But even if he could besiege it and wall up the young monarch inside – aye, and his Regent too – that could tell in his favour. I say David should be moved . . ."

"Where do you suggest, my lord?" Murray asked. "Where is safer than Stirling Castle?"

"Rothesay, perhaps? A royal castle, and the High Steward's seat. On the Isle of Bute. Or, Dumbarton first? If he was pursued there, he could be taken out by boat, at night. To Bute or deeper into the Highland West."

"Aye, that is best. My lord Robert, will you see to that?

73

When you go to raise your forces in the West. Take His Grace and the young Queen. Likewise, I think, my wife, the Lady Christian Bruce, with you. To Dumbarton meantime. I shall be elsewhere, mustering. Leslie, at Ballinbreich you are nearest to the Dupplin area. Will you seek to gather stragglers from Mar's army, as Ramsay suggests, and bring them with your people to Edinburgh? Ramsay, you will do your utmost to rally Lothian. I will send to Dunbar to join us – but God alone knows whether he will! Douglas, you will command at the Burgh Muir of Edinburgh until I arrive; and if you can, send to raise more men in the Borders. Wemyss, you will raise Fife, declaring in the King's name that your Earl is traitor! And you, my lords Spiritual, such Church levies as you may command, send me. And, of your goodness, moneys to pay for the arms, horses and food which we are going to need . . ."

Heartened by this sudden assumption of decision and authority by the new Regent, the meeting broke up.

Within an hour or so Douglas and Ramsay were riding southwards.

4

On the lofty Burgh Muir above the hill-girt city of Edinburgh all was activity, bustle and impatience. Far and wide over the common-grazing's green undulations the encampments spread, colourful tents and pavilions erected for the lords, chiefs and great ones, banners fluttering in the October breeze, cooking-fires smoking, horse-lines being watered, smiths busy shoeing and beating out iron for spear and axe heads, troops and squadrons practising formation riding, infantry deploying to form squares, hedgehogs and wheelings-in-line, trumpets and horns sounding, captains shouting commands – and half the citizenry and dogs of Edinburgh out to watch and add to the din.

At the central Borestone mound round which the most important pavilions were pitched, a group of leaders conferred, and it was here that the impatience was manifested –

especially by Sir William Douglas. That was his way, of course, always; but on this occasion he had some cause for it. Already the muster was a week late; and there were not a few contingents still to come in, including the Regent's own. It was 17th October and Balliol was known to be on the move. Just where he was now and where he was heading was uncertain, this possibly having much to do with the non-arrival of Murray and the Steward, since both would be coming from the West Country and Balliol was thought to be marching southwards down the middle of the land.

The debate amongst the leaders was mainly concerned with that important question. They had spies out, to be sure, but so far no definite reports had come in other than that Balliol and the English army, now unfortunately reinforced by the Highland and other Scots adherents, had left Perth ten days before, cavalry and foot marching southwards by Auchter-arder and the Allan Water, to cross Teith by the Ford of Keir and Forth by the Fords of Frew, presumably to avoid any opposition at the vulnerable Stirling Bridge; which conjecture had set Alexander Ramsay worrying about Doune Castle and Mariot Randolph, not to mention her brother raising his levies thereabouts. However the Earl John had duly turned up at Edinburgh, with one hundred and fifty men and the information that the enemy had passed well to the east of Doune.

There were various suggestions as to Balliol's intentions in this southwards move: that his aim was first to divide the west from the east, then to work round and isolate Edinburgh; that he knew of Sir Archibald Douglas's mustering of his Gallo-way vassals and sought to keep this force from joining the main Scots array; that perhaps he was expecting further English reinforcements from Carlisle and the West March; and so on. Sir William Douglas, who was in command here until the Regent arrived, held the opinion that Galloway itself was the first objective. The Balliols, through Devorgilla, heiress of the vast lands of the ancient Lords of Galloway, had inherited most of these; and the Comyns, their kin, had also major properties there. They could raise between them up to ten thousand men in that great remote province; and at the same time assail the western Douglas strength.

There was another question to trouble them – Dunbar. What would that strange man do? Few there had any faith in

75

him, nor expected him actively to aid them. But might he actually side with Balliol now, if he deemed his cause in the ascendant? Or would he cautiously hold his hand, there in the East March, as he had done before Perth, until he saw which side seemed to be winning, and then join it?

Ramsay, who found himself at the head of nearly a thousand men of Lothian, largely Lindsays – whose chief, Sir David, Keeper of Edinburgh Castle, was sick and so not present – Setons, Hepburns, Sinclairs, Keiths and other lesser clans, as well as his own men, offered to ride fast for the Borderland, to join Scott of Rankilburn whom Douglas had alerted to watch Dunbar; together they would make up a force large enough to give that Earl pause. But Douglas, concerned about numbers, was against any diminution of their main assembly which might at any time be faced with confronting Balliol's entire army. If only the Regent would come, from the West . . .

It was the Steward, however, who arrived from those parts, in the late afternoon, with over five hundred from Bute and his Renfrew and Paisley lordships. He could tell them little about the enemy, save that his party, coming here, had crossed the tracks of a great host in the Kilsyth area of Strathkelvin, by the horse-droppings at least a day old. Which seemed to imply that Balliol had crossed the Fintry and Campsie Fells and was still heading southwards, presumably for the Clyde valley. This was worrying, for it could mean that he was on a collision course with the Regent, who was raising the Bothwell and Airdrie areas.

Anxieties were temporarily forgotten when a cheerful contingent arrived from the North. This proved to be Sir Simon Fraser and Sir Robert Keith. Fraser was Sheriff of Kincardine, and with Keith from Dunottar, marching south, had heard that Balliol had left Perth, appointing the Earl of Fife to command there in his absence. Not thinking much of Fife's soldierly abilities, and judging him in need of a lesson for his crowning of the usurper, he and Keith had attacked Perth town, and found it surprisingly easy to take. They had captured the Earl and taken him to Stirling Castle; also Murray of Tullibardine, and him they had promptly hanged, for his betrayal at Dupplin.

The news much cheered the waiting assembly. And when, just before dark, the Regent himself put in an appearance, with a larger than anticipated company, spirits rose further. He reported that he had had to wait, hidden in the Murdostoun woodland, whilst Balliol's army marched southwards across his front, hence the delay. His scouts had assessed that the enemy numbers would reach around twenty thousand, and were moving fairly fast, a mounted host save for the Islesmen and Highlanders who, trained to proceed long distances at the run, and lightly clad, did not hold up the horse to any extent. Their destination could only be guessed at, but by their line of march through upper Clydesdale it looked as though they were heading for the West March, possibly even Galloway.

This projection coincided with Douglas's. It was decided that unless they got word of a change in direction from the scouts the Regent had sent to follow the enemy's route, the Scots host, now numbering some thirteen thousand, would set off at first light, south-westwards, on a converging course.

They made a gallant array next morning as they marched off from the Burgh Muir in great companies, cavalry and infantry, banners and standards waving, heraldic surcoats colourful, armour glinting in the early morning sunlight, trumpets blowing; but Ramsay reminded himself that Mar's army had looked fully as fine and had marched only to disaster. This time, however, they were under commanders who were soldiers, not just high-born magnates, and were not underestimating their foes.

Their foot were not in the main Highlandmen – although they had some of these, from upland Perthshire and the Glens of Angus – and so could not travel so fast and far each day. But Murray was determined that the knightly chivalry should not ride far ahead, as so often happened, and so endanger both. He aimed at fifteen miles a day, and they would march down the southern flanks of the Pentland Hills, to Biggar and Broughton and thence by Tweedsmuir to Moffat, at the head of Annandale, some sixty miles. Four days. From there they ought to be able to gain a better notion of Balliol's intentions. Also, hopefully, link up with Sir Archibald Douglas and his Galloway host.

They reached The Carlops that first evening, to camp on the moorland to the east, although Douglas would have pressed on further. There was no word from the Regent's scouts as yet.

By next night they were at Skirling, near Broughton, and here trouble broke out between Douglases and Hamiltons of the Regent's contingent, ever a danger in Scottish feudal hosts where clan loyalties and feuds often created tensions. Sir William dealt with this in his own typical fashion, hanging three Douglas ringleaders there and then, but demanding a like example to be made of the Hamiltons, which was scarcely equitable, since the Douglases had started it all and were three times as numerous as their hereditary foes.

The weather broke down thereafter, and in driving chill rain tempers were cooled. Unfortunately these conditions also much reduced their rate of march and they got only as far as Polmood, for they were now in the high uplands of the infant Tweed and the going difficult at the best of times. It was a much less gallant-seeming host which eventually reached the town of Moffat in upper Annandale, where three waters met to form the Annan.

Here they found Sir Archibald Douglas awaiting them, his Galloway levies, to the number of almost two thousand, hidden in a great declivity of the hills to the north-east. This Sir William's uncle was a genial and uncomplicated individual of middle years, lacking his late brother's energy and drive but considerably easier to deal with than his nephew, indeed seeming to find most of life much to his taste. His news for them as to the enemy was as anticipated, but with an unexpected postscript. The usurper's army had indeed proceeded on down Annandale, almost certainly to link up with another large Galloway force collected by Sir Walter Comyn and Henry Balliol, Edward's brother, from their estates in that province, many thousands strong, the reason why Sir Archibald had not risked coming on to Edinburgh. The unexpected news, however, was that Edward Balliol himself had here, for some unknown reason, left his army and with only a comparatively small escort of possibly five hundred men, struck off north-eastwards into the Ettrick Forest hills in the direction of St Mary's Loch and Selkirk. Intrigued, there was much discussion about the reasons for this strange development. Suggestions were that it was to rendezvous with another English force crossing into the Middle March; or to meet up with Dunbar on the East March and convince him to join Balliol actively.

Whatever it was, the Regent saw it as an unlooked-for

opportunity. Here was Balliol detached from his army and so comparatively vulnerable personally. If he could be captured and dealt with, much of the danger for Scotland would be dispersed and his Scots support would dissolve. Murray decided that he himself would go after the usurper, as was suitable, the lawful Regent after the false king, with perhaps one thousand hard-riding Border mosstroopers who knew the country, whilst the rest of the Scots army went on down Annandale after the main enemy force.

There was some demurring at this, especially from William Douglas, who thought it dangerous. Defeat the enemy first, was his advice, and deal with the wretched Balliol afterwards. But Murray was determined, and eager to be off eastwards without delay, for Balliol had already had two days' lead.

There was something of a problem as to whom to appoint in command of the army whilst the Regent was absent. William Douglas was the obvious choice militarily; but with Scotland's High Steward and High Constable now present, not to mention the Earl of Moray and Douglas's uncle, and even Sir Simon Fraser older and more senior, that would not do. Yet the Steward and Moray were only youths and the Constable not much more, and inexperienced, with Sir Archibald scarcely a renowned warrior. Murray got over the difficulty by appointing a triumvirate in command: Steward, Constable and Sir Archibald, with the Flower of Chivalry as specific military adviser. For himself, he would take Sir Alexander Ramsay with him, since he knew the Borderland intimately, and hoped to rejoin the main army in three or four days' time, God willing with Balliol either prisoner or dead.

By no means to everyone's satisfaction, they parted company.

The deliberately chosen Border mosstroopers, Johnstones, Elliots, Turnbulls and the like, were at home in this country and expert at following Balliol's party's trail, even at two days old. Ramsay himself did not know this Ettrick Forest area so well as the main Middle and East Marches; but from the route the usurper had taken from Moffat, it looked as though he was heading either for the mid-Tweed or Teviot dales – although he could have reached the former more easily by turning off in the Broughton area of Tweedsmuir. Mystified, they rode eastwards at a great pace, Ramsay for one not ungrateful to be done with the restraints of keeping to the pace of marching men.

They got as far as Eldinhope at the head of St Mary's Loch before the early November dark made following the tracks of even five hundred difficult; and the Regent and Ramsay spent the night in that remote peel-tower of a Scott laird. He was not the most welcoming of hosts, alarmed at the thought of what one thousand men and horses could do to his winter's supplies and forage; but at least he could tell them that a large mounted party had indeed passed this way two days previously and had turned off out of this main Yarrow valley southwards, to climb by Altrieve to the high pass of Tushielaw, which would take them to the Ettrick valley.

In the morning they left Scott of Eldinhope in rather better mood, the Regent being at pains to pay for benefits received, which clearly the laird had not expected. He told them that by turning off here, the company they were following would almost certainly be heading for upper Teviotdale, by Rankilburn, Buccleuch and Bellenden, since the Ettrick valley would merely bring them back to its junction with Yarrow again.

This sent them on their way without having to trouble too much over casting about for tracks. In somewhat better weather conditions they climbed the five-mile drove-road to the lofty Tushielaw pass, and down to Tushielaw itself, with its bridge across Ettrick, making good time, although the burns and streams were running high and making fording a problem in places. Enquiries at Tushielaw confirmed that Balliol's people had indeed proceeded on southwards, up Rankilburn towards Buccleuch, still Scott country. There could be no other objective than Teviotdale, in that direction. Will Douglas should have been with them, for he was Sheriff of Teviotdale.

Not having to pick their way carefully now they were able to cover some thirty hilly miles that day, good going for so large a party of horse, even mosstroopers. This brought them to Teviot, in the Hawick area, where they learned that the Balliol company had passed there, avoiding the town, the morning before, having apparently camped at Goldielands just to the west. So they, the pursuers, were catching up somewhat.

On the well-defined Teviotdale road they proceeded next

morning, and now were able to check at the villages and communities they passed that they were still on Balliol's route, without the time-consuming searching for tracks.

They were past Jedburgh by noon, and Ramsay, who now was in country he knew fairly intimately, pointed out that in another ten miles they would be out of Teviotdale, with Teviot joining Tweed at Roxburgh and Kelso. Thereafter they would be into the East March, and following the enemy would be less straightforward, with the country opening out and various routes possible – into the Merse, down the Scots side of Tweed, down the English side, or southwards into the Till valley of Northumberland. Where was Balliol heading, and why?

They learned part of the answer as dusk was falling and they came to the tower and castleton of Heiton, beyond Kale Water. Their quarry was at Roxburgh, three miles ahead, Heiton of that Ilk informed them. He had arrived there the previous day and was still at the castle.

This news had them puzzled. Roxburgh was a royal castle and its associated township, both quite large, situated within the narrow point of land where Teviot joined Tweed; a strong position where King David the First, son of Malcolm Canmore and Saint Margaret, had established his headquarters on accession to the throne, and from which he had in effect ruled Scotland. It was only six miles from the English Border, but in his day England was friendly, and as well as an English wife he had a great many links with the southern kingdom, in which he owned large lands and from which he had brought so many sprigs of the Norman and Flemish nobility to settle in Scotland. So Roxburgh made sense for that King David. But hardly for his present namesake. With England now the enemy, this was inevitably one of the most vulnerable places in the northern kingdom – and indeed had been captured early in the Wars of Independence by Edward Plantagenet and remained in English hands ever since, its garrison readily supplied and reinforced from over the nearby Border. The English used it as a convenient base for raids into the Scots East and Middle Marches, and as a permanent threat, its strong position on the rocky spine at the junction of the two rivers making it a very difficult nut to crack. Needless to say, the Earl of Dunbar, as chief Scots Warden, had never attempted to retake it.

What, then, brought Edward Balliol all this way to Roxburgh? To meet Dunbar? Surely not. If a meeting with that strange character was important, the usurper could have summoned Dunbar to himself, not had to ride eighty miles to see him. Was it to meet someone else? From England perhaps? Something fairly vital must have occasioned this visit. Andrew Heiton could offer no suggestions.

Whatever the reason, the Regent was no less determined to try to capture Balliol while he was thus detached from his main force. How to attempt this? It was out of the question to consider attacking or besieging Roxburgh Castle, of course, without heavy cannon. Would it be best to wait, hidden, and seek to ambush Balliol's party on their return to their main army – as surely they must intend? The difficulty there would be to achieve surprise. One thousand men could not enter and remain in the vicinity for any time without being discovered. Balliol would undoubtedly soon learn of their presence, however heedfully they hid. And when he learned their numbers, he could seek reinforcements for his five hundred from over the Border, from the castle garrison, even from Dunbar.

Ramsay suggested a ruse. Detach say two hundred, and use these to make a gesture at Roxburgh, some sort of sally towards the castle, hiding the remainder away, if necessary in groups. If only two hundred were to be seen, then the chances were that Balliol would assume that this was their full strength. So either he would be confident enough to set out westwards again with nearly three times that number; or else he might attempt a sortie against them. In which case they would try to decoy the enemy towards some of the hidden groups, where they would be outnumbered and beaten.

Murray judged this a sound scheme. But it might *not* provoke Balliol into action. He might just sit tight inside the castle. How to ensure that he came out? Some enticement? Suppose he learned that it was the Regent himself who was there. That might bring him out. But how to get that information to him?

The royal standard, Ramsay suggested. If the decoy party displayed the Lion Rampant of Scotland, that would surely indicate high authority, for only the King or his Regent were entitled to fly that flag. Murray was doubtful as to whether this would be enough; but Heiton declared that he could send a couple of men into the Roxburgh township, to the alehouses and howffs, to spread the word that the Regent himself was in the vicinity. Undoubtedly someone would carry this important news to the castle. That, with the standard idea, was accepted as worth trying.

The rest of that evening was occupied in selecting suitable hiding-places for the eight hundred horsemen towards which the enemy hopefully could be lured. The right area for this was all-important. It must be to the south, across Teviot, for the Tweed, to the north, was the greater river, with no fords nor bridges available for a considerable distance upstream; and downstream, at Kelso, the Scots could be trapped too easily. So the hiding-places must be reasonably near a suitable ford of Teviot. Fortunately, of course, Heiton knew every inch of the ground hereabouts, much of it his own property, and so could advise. The ford at Sunlaws Mill, he told them. Cross there. Broken ground this side of it. Some men could hide there, where he had a small tower. Not sufficient, but a couple of hundred perhaps. Decoy the enemy past there and on southwards for Kalemouth, another long mile. Then up the Kale Water. Plenty of cover in its narrow, winding valley. The Sunlaws people to come on after, to Kalemouth, and so closing the valley behind. The enemy bottled up, trapped . . .

This sounded an excellent strategy, and all plans were made for the morrow. Although Ramsay proposed that he should lead the decoy party, under the royal standard, Murray insisted that he himself must do that, as was suitable. None would accept a young man as the Regent. Ramsay should command at Sunlaws and close the trap at Kalemouth.

So next morning the thousand mosstroopers divided into three sections, two hundred to go with the Regent as decoys, two hundred to hide near Sunlaws ford and the remainder, six hundred, with a score or two of Heiton's own men, to head for the Kale Water valley where Heiton would place them in position from which they could ambush the pursuit once Murray's fleeing party was past. It would all be wasted effort, of course, if Balliol refused to be enticed out from Roxburgh Castle.

Murray and Ramsay rode together as far as the ford at Sunlaws, a wooded terrain of bluffs and hillocks, another Heiton peel-tower and the riverside mill. Here they parted company, wishing each other good fortune, and the Regent splashed off across Teviot, unfurling the proud Lion Rampant standard.

Ramsay spent a busy hour placing his two hundred in the available cover amongst the hummocks and wooded hollows. They were over two miles from Roxburgh Castle here, it hidden by the lie of the land. Timing was hard to calculate. It would not take the Regent long to ride there, but the displaying of himself and party in the quite large township and before the castle itself could take time; and coaxing Balliol and his people out, if successful, might take longer still. So it was a case of waiting and readiness.

It seemed a long wait. Ramsay ensconced himself in the upper storey of the mill building, where he could gain as wide a view as possible. Even so, he could not see more than half a mile in the Roxburgh direction owing to a slight ridge of grass and whins. He debated whether it would be worth sending a scout out to that ridge, to give him better warning, but decided against it.

It was almost two hours before he saw movement – and then it was fast and furious. The group of horsemen, wide-scattered, not in any formation, appeared silhouetted on the ridge and came streaming on towards the ford. At that range it was impossible to distinguish details – but the royal standard should have been visible and was not. More horsemen came into sight but in twos and threes, riding their hardest obviously. But they totalled nothing like two hundred, not much more than half that probably. Biting his lip anxiously, Ramsay prepared to hurry down to alert his men.

Then the Lion Rampant did appear over the rising ground, perhaps three hundred yards behind those first riders, but it rose above a fairly compact party, and this was backed by a still larger body of men. Suddenly it dawned on Ramsay that this flag was considerably larger than that flown by the Regent.

Something was wrong, direly wrong, he had to conclude. That would be Balliol's standard, proclaiming his usurped kingship. And the people in front were obviously fleeing rather than decoying: Murray's men. So, it was failure – and they had lost their standard.

He had only a few moments to decide on what he should do. Move his two hundred in behind those fleeing ones, to confront the enemy? There were many more than two hundred behind that large banner, so was it the wisest move? It could lead to a second defeat. Better to abide by the original plan. Let decoys and pursuers past, and then follow on, so that the enemy would be trapped in the Kale valley and their own full strength of six hundred more could be brought to bear, surely much outnumbering Balliol's company.

Hurrying down to his men, he readied them. He did not mention what he feared had happened to the Regent's party; they would guess that soon enough. He had just time to form them up and move a little way forward himself from their hiding-place, to where he could see the ford and its approaches on either side, when the first fleeing riders came pounding down, splashing over and racing on. Anxiously he watched. Turnbull of Bedrule was there and Johnstone of Lochwood, but no Regent.

However appalled, Ramsay could do nothing more at this stage than try to carry out the original plan. In only moments the pursuers were in turn coming down to the ford, and in much more disciplined order, professional English cavalry-men, not mosstroopers. But although they might be better mounted, by normal standards, they were not so well horsed for rough riding as were the Borderers on their tough, sure-footed hill ponies; on this terrain the fleeing men ought to be able to keep ahead. As the pursuit thundered past, Ramsay saw, under the great royal standard, a richly armoured knight who wore a golden circlet round his helmet – Balliol himself.

Ramsay waited impatiently after the last riders had passed out of sight. He would have liked to hurry off eastwards, towards Roxburgh, to endeavour to see what had happened to Murray, and to do what he could to help. But the first priority undoubtedly was to defeat Balliol, if possible. So, when he judged that the enemy would be sufficiently far ahead not to perceive that they were being followed, he ordered his company into pursuit.

They had a mile and a half to go to Kalemouth, and owing to the broken and wooded nature of the country, only occasionally did they glimpse the enemy ahead, Ramsay deliberately holding his men in. Clearly Balliol had not caught up with the decimated decoy party.

Fording the Kale Water, they turned up its far bank into the quickly narrow shallow valley. They did not have far to go before they heard the din of conflict ahead. So the trap was already sprung.

Rounding one of the many bends in that valley, less than a mile up, they came upon a widening, almost an amphitheatre, where two small streams joined Kale through high banks. In these declivities the ambushers must have hidden, for here battle raged amid yells and screams and the clash of steel. It seemed at first sight to be a chaos of struggling men and horses, a wild mêlée; but soon it became apparent to the newcomers that it was in fact more like a whirlpool of activity, with the ambushed English, above whom the royal standard wavered uncertainly, in the centre, whilst their more numerous attackers circled round them, smiting and thrusting but apparently making only moderate impact.

Although his first impulse would have sent Alexander Ramsay spurring to join in this process, he restrained himself and his men. These English were trained soldiers, and their reaction to the ambush was that of the cavalry equivalent of an infantry hedgehog or square. The Scots' encircling assault, however spectacular, was not likely to break that tight formation and overwhelm the enemy. Something more effective was required.

Ramsay made a swift decision – and it demanded some resolution, since it would entail cost. Reining round, he shouted to his two hundred to form themselves into an arrowhead. This was more easily commanded than achieved, for these mosstroopers were excellent horsemen and guerrilla fighters but unused to disciplined formation warfare. Urgently Ramsay directed them, all but physically pushing and prodding them into the approximate shape of a great wedge. Then, snatching a lance from one of them, he placed himself at the apex and, couching the lance, shouted to charge.

They had only about one hundred and fifty yards to gather speed and could not achieve a full gallop in the time. But at a drumming canter they bore down on the mass of men and beasts ahead, the circling Scots and the stationary English. "A Ramsay! A Ramsay!" he shouted, and the slogan was taken up by those behind in yelling threat.

Inevitably this assault had to mean trouble for some of their own folk, since they must drive through the outer ring of Scots to get at the enemy – the cost which had caused Ramsay momentarily to hesitate. But he calculated that it had to be worth it, that such casualties would be minor compared with those which would result from a prolonged, slogging, hand-to-hand battle. It was the sort of price any commander had to pay for hoped-for victory.

The charging wedge's impact on the circling horsemen was sufficiently drastic. Men and horses went down like ninepins before them, in a tangle of waving limbs, flailing hooves and broken lances. In front, Ramsay's own mount tripped over a fallen beast and rider and all but threw its own, but recovered. Impetus and the driving weight told, and the wedge, only a little misshapen now, crashed through and bore down the few extra yards upon the waiting English.

This was a very different impact, head-on against all but stationary horsemen, solid in their ranks and having seen the approach. The shock of it was breath-taking, shattering. Ramsay's lance snapped off, broken, and left his right arm and hand too numb to draw his sword. Horses reared high and screamed their terror, men, open-mouthed, fell from their saddles. But it was the horses which decided the issue, as Ramsay had calculated they would. Stationary beasts will never withstand charging ones. Whatever their riders might desire, those English mounts broke, reared, panicked, cannoned into one another to get out of the way, and doing so caused utter confusion and collapse amongst the enemy. The tight ranks wavered and melted before the driving spearhead, even though it was now sadly deformed and its speed slackened. Pounding his beast with his left fist to try to maintain the momentum, Ramsay sought to head into the press for that Lion Rampant banner.

But the enemy leadership, Balliol or other, recognised realities. Their coherence broken and morale likewise, outnumbered and with the rest of the Scots now rallying to exploit the new situation, a tight group at the centre of the company formed their own small wedge and spurred from inactive watching to furious activity – not towards Ramsay's threat but in the opposite direction. This was flight, obvious and through their own men. Lashing their horses and beating aside all in their way with the flats of their swords, Balliol and his immediate lieutenants drove off, through and away. The royal standard fell in the trampling rush and was left behind.

Ramsay would have followed on, to try to capture the

usurper, but still in the midst of the heaving crush of men and beasts he was hampered and held up. By the time that he had battled through it was too late. Balliol's party had gained enough of a start to almost ensure their escape. Besides, Ramsay's wedge was now attenuated, scarcely recognisable as such, and their mounts wearied.

Everywhere the English were now fleeing, singly and in groups, pursued by mosstroopers. It was victory, of a sort.

Panting, dizzy with reaction, and seeking to ease his all but dislocated arm and shoulder, Ramsay surveyed the scene. Then, riding on, he stiffly dismounted, avoiding the kicking of disabled horses, and stooped to pick up the now trampled and muddied Lion Rampant standard of Scotland. Some of the Scots around him cheered as he raised it. He however shook his head. It was but a poor trophy for the day – a flag in exchange for a Regent, and Balliol still at large.

Casualties on both sides proved to be fairly light, the horses having suffered the most. While these were being put out of their misery, wounded men succoured and prisoners rounded up, Ramsay went to demand of Johnstone of Lochwood and Turnbull of Bedrule what had happened to Sir Andrew Murray. They told him that all had gone well until, between Roxburgh town and the castle, before which they were demonstrating, seeking to decoy Balliol, by chance an English party had come up behind them, presumably having ridden over the Border and by Kelso ford, and they had been trapped. It was the Devil's own luck. They had to fight their way out and back, and in the midst Balliol himself and these others had issued out from the castle. Murray had turned to face them, and had his horse shot under him. And when his standard-bearer went to give him his own beast, that too was slain beneath him. The Regent was surrounded and captured. There was nothing any of them could do to save him, scattered and outnumbered now as they were. It was desperate ill-fortune, but . . .

So Scotland's new Regent was a prisoner in Roxburgh Castle, and the land was leaderless once more.

Ramsay had barely digested this sorry information when he learned more. Amongst the casualties left on the field by the fleeing enemy was a Northumberland squire named Foster, who had been stunned when his horse toppled on him but not seriously injured. This prisoner, from Coquetdale, disgusted at the way Balliol and his group had abandoned the struggle and left himself and others to their fate, was prepared to talk, no doubt in the hope of improving his own position. Brought before Ramsay and questioned, he explained the mystery of why Balliol had left his army at Moffat and ridden all this way eastwards to Roxburgh. It was because he had been summoned to do so, by no less than his paymaster, Edward, King of England. Now that he was crowned King of Scots, he was to pay homage for his kingdom to the English monarch as Lord Paramount. He was a vassal, as indeed his father had been forty years earlier. Thomas Beauchamp, Earl of Warwick, was sent to Roxburgh to receive that formal fealty on behalf of his sovereign-lord, and to state the price of English help in the matter. Balliol had formally signed documents conceding that Scotland was a subordinate kingdom under the English crown. The King of Scots would hereafter be liable on request to provide an army to aid the King of England in any of his campaigns. The Scottish castles of Berwick-on-Tweed and Roxburgh, hitherto only occupied by the English, were now ceded to England for all time coming. Two thousand librates of prime tillable land, that is one hundred thousand acres, convenient to the Border, of the Plantagenet's choice, were to be handed over as free gift, with all the folk thereupon. And the Princess Joanna's marriage to David Stewart was to be declared null and void, since both had been mere infants at its celebration, and the princess free to marry whomsoever her royal brother selected, Balliol himself being glad and privileged to wed her if this was his Lord Edward's will and choice.

Scarcely able to believe his ears, Ramsay listened to this shameful catalogue. So much for Edward Balliol, the Toom Tabard's son! Robert the Bruce must be tossing in his grave at Dunfermline Abbey!

Ramsay now found himself to be in command of this detachment, the only knight present. What to do now? Much as he would have liked to try to rescue Murray, he recognised that to be out of the question. Roxburgh Castle was proof against all but prolonged siege and heavy artillery. But Balliol himself? Presumably he would now return to his army in the west. In which case might he not still be vulnerable to capture? The trouble was, he was now warned that there was a sizeable force in the vicinity to challenge him, and would no doubt hereafter take all possible precautions. He might even elect to ride westwards across the borderline on English ground, to Carlisle and then north. And the Earl of Warwick might well provide him with additional escort. Weighing it all up, Ramsay came to the conclusion that the chances of capturing the usurper at this stage were all but non-existent, and that their wisest course was to return at once with his dire news to the main Scots array in Annandale or wherever it had reached by now.

They need not return all the way as they had come but could strike southwards up Jed Water and over to Hobkirk and so by the Note o' the Gate pass into Liddesdale. Then west by Hermitage Water to Ewesdale and Langholm and so over to Annandale in the Lockerbie area, rough going but saving much in distance. Sixty to sixty-five miles, he reckoned. Less than two days' hard riding. They would take the prisoner Foster with them. Their own wounded could be attended to at the nearby village of Eckford, and then disappear into these their own Border hills. The enemy prisoners and hurt could be left to find their way back to Roxburgh as best they could, stripped of their arms, armour and anything else worth having – although some of the mosstroopers were for slaying them out of hand.

The move was made, back up Teviot, for the Jed Water valley.

Ramsay's company had no difficulty in finding the Scots army once they reached lower Annandale, for any large host leaves ample tracks behind. Moving at the pace of the infantry, they had not covered any great distance in the interim and were in fact only half a day's march ahead when Ramsay reached Lockerbie in the Johnstone country.

They saw the camp-fires lighting up the winter dusk well before they reached the Hoddom area, near where the Water of Milk joined Annan, which meant, of course, that the enemy ahead presumably would be apt to see them also; but it was practically impossible to hide the presence of a major army anyway. Their arrival, without the Regent, created no little stir and consternation.

Presently in the great hall of Hoddom Castle, which the leaders had taken over, Ramsay made his report and handed over Balliol's royal flag, eating hungrily as he spoke. Most there listened in grim silence although Will Douglas inserted a host of interjections and questions. There was no doubting the seriousness with which all viewed the situation.

Douglas inevitably took the lead in the decision-making called for. He declared that, in this situation, it was a case of first things first. No use beating their breasts and bewailing the loss of Murray. Until he could be restored to them, as Regent, they required an *acting* Regent. Without that the royal authority could not be exercised, and the realm would be like a ship lacking a rudder. Even here, in this host, since Murray's departure, there had been difficulties of command. Some lords considered themselves to be *above* command – and he glared round the company. An acting Regent was necessary, and in the circumstances would have to be appointed here and now, from this assembly.

There were indrawn breaths at such plain speaking, but no actual rebuttals. Ramsay, accepting the need, wondered whether even Douglas would have the presumption to propose himself for the position.

The Flower of Chivalry did not go quite so far as that. Eyeing the magnates one by one, he nodded his head.

"We have here not a few whose high office would make them suitable for the position," he said. "The High Steward. The High Constable. The Knight Marischal. The Earl of Moray. All sound and excellent lords. But, all young. Too young to be Regent, I say. Lacking in experience, necessarily. They will none, I swear, contest that? The realm will better heed an older man to represent the child-king. And one who has the power to enforce his decisions, if need be, with armed might! And we have such a one here."

There was silence round that table, amidst darting glances, as men waited.

"I propose Sir Archibald Douglas of Douglasdale, Lord of Galloway, who commands more men than any other here. Who better? Brother to the Good Sir James, the Bruce's closest friend. Companion-in-arms of the heroes who saved this kingdom in the late wars. I name you, Archibald Douglas, as Regent!"

For a few moments there was little apparent reaction. All there were taken by surprise; by his expression, Archibald Douglas himself. That man was scarcely a heroic figure, however genial and powerful in manpower, but never ambitious

91

to lead. Always he had been overshadowed by his elder brother, the famous Black Douglas – and never wished it otherwise. On the other hand, he could field more men than any other lord south of the Highlands, and the Douglas power would be invaluable to the regency; indeed lacking it or opposed by it, any other Regent would be in difficulties. He was one of the very few left of the Bruce's close company, even if no paladin. And he was no man's enemy. Likewise he was Sir William's uncle, with all that implied.

Alexander Ramsay marvelled. Here was shrewd reckoning. Will Douglas was more cunning than he had thought. This way he would largely control the regency without the drawbacks of office, paper-work, jealousy. It was clever. Many who would have opposed his outspoken and disputatious self would accept his uncle.

"I agree." Young Bleary, the Steward, was first to speak. "I propose Sir Archibald Douglas, Lord of Galloway, as Regent – until we have the good Sir Andrew back."

"I also," Moray said.

"Likewise," Hay the Constable added briefly, always a young man of few words.

After these three had given their approval, it would have demanded considerable determination to have put forward an alternative nomination. None did. Oddly, it was left to Alexander Ramsay to express the only doubt.

"My lords," he said, "excellent as this is, can we so appoint? Is the appointment of Regent, or acting Regent, not the responsibility of the Privy Council?"

There was some murmured agreement at that – but not from William Douglas.

"There are sufficient of the Council here present to serve!" he asserted. "Only the clerks absent. They can confirm later." His contempt for churchmen was undisguised. "This is the army of the King of Scots. We require the royal authority now, not when priests find it convenient to be present! Is it agreed?"

There was no cheering nor acclaim, but no counter-motion either.

Will Douglas rose from his seat, and bowed to his uncle – and perforce all others must do likewise.

Sir Archibald looked embarrassed. He spread his hands. "This is . . . surprise," he said. "I do not desire the position. I doubt my ability for it. But, if it is the wish of you all, I will do what I can. With the help of you all. Until the true Regent is restored to us."

"Well said," his nephew commended, resuming his seat. "Now – to business." Nothing could more clearly have demonstrated the realities of the situation than those three words, and the tone in which they were said.

Ramsay smiled inwardly.

Will Douglas leaned forward. "Informants tell us that the enemy has halted at Annan town. Sir Eustace Maxwell has turned traitor, as I knew he would, and has joined Balliol's host there, with his own people from Caerlaverock and Dumfries and also the Comyn and Balliol levies from Galloway. Henry Balliol, Edward's brother, and Sir Walter Comyn, are with him. The word is that the usurper, or those acting in his name, have sent out a call for all Scots lords and landed men to repair there, to Annan, to do homage to him. Give him their oaths of fealty – God damn him! Which must mean that he intends to be there for some time. It is only ten miles to the English border, twenty from Carlisle. So he could be reinforced from England swiftly. He has over twenty-five thousand there already. I say that we should strike now, before he gathers more."

There were murmurs for and against such action. Sir Michael Wemyss pointed out that they were much outnumbered already; also that Annan was a defendable town with a fairly strong castle, the Bruce's former main seat.

"Annan Castle is part in ruins," Douglas said. "King Robert never rebuilt it fully after the English wrecked it and he went to Lochmaben and Turnberry. Forby, I say that they will not wait in the town to let themselves be besieged. Since they outnumber us, they will come out to challenge us. But if *we* choose the battle-ground, and with surprise . . ."

"Maxwell is a good soldier," Sir Simon Fraser said. "I have campaigned with him. Do not underestimate Maxwell. And Balliol must have some good commanders to have done what he has done."

"No doubt. But we have come here to fight, have we not? We have not marched all this way to sit and wait! And the longer we wait, the stronger Balliol will get, I judge."

Ramsay spoke. "We should not wait for long, no. But wait for a little, I say. For what *is* our aim here? Is it to win a great

93

victory? Over largely our own countrymen, who see this usurper as a stronger king than young David can be? Or is it to bring down the usurper himself? That, surely. So Sir Andrew Murray was right, although he failed. Our prime task is to capture or destroy Edward Balliol, who has sold our realm to the English. We have failed once, but we can try again."

"How?" barked Douglas.

"Not by attacking Annan when he is not yet there, to be sure! If we do, and win, will he not merely flee over the Border, and come back with *more* English? For this is now Edward of England's cause. I say, wait until he has had time to return from Roxburgh – as surely he will. Then a surprise raid, probably by night. Not any full battle. He will be lodged in the castle, awaiting his homage-makers. I know the castle, as will others here. It is not in the midst of the town, but a little way to the west, on the river-bank. And there is a good ford below it. A strong company of horse, in the night, could reach that ford undiscovered, cross, cut off the castle from the town and the enemy's main encampment, enter the half-ruined castle and capture Balliol, and away. It is not like Roxburgh, a strong fortress in good order . . ."

He got no further, his words lost in cries of acclaim and agreement. Even Will Douglas looked interested.

"How long until Balliol returns, then?" that man demanded, when he could make himself heard.

"Not long, I should think. It took us a day and a half to come, riding fast. Even if he is in less haste he will not delay, I think. This homage-taking. Give him two more days. You spoke of informants from Annan? Let them send us word when Balliol returns . . ."

"I say this makes good sense," Sir Archibald put in. "Let us so plan, Will." This was his first decision as Regent.

His nephew was not one to yield the initiative readily. "A surprise attack by night would require to be in strength. Once the enemy camp was roused, thousands would move in on the castle. We would need a large number to hold these off, form a barrier. A thousand, at least. And a thousand horse crossing a ford, in darkness . . ."

"I have crossed that ford times without number," Johnstone of Lochwood put in. "The Annan there is broad and shallow. There is a causeway. Men could cross it a score abreast."

"Will it be guarded, then?"

"That we shall have to discover. Scouts out . . ."

So the discussion got down to practicalities and planning, a new keenness evident. When, weary, Alexander Ramsay sought his couch, it was to leave an animated company still at it, Will Douglas now as involved as any, indeed automatically assuming the leadership.

That impatient man did not have so long to wait as he had feared, for the very next evening a young townsman arrived at Hoddom from Annan, ten miles distant, with the news that Edward Balliol had indeed returned to his army. The messenger had been sent by a group of Annan citizens loyal to the Bruce connection; after all, the late King Robert had been the sixth Bruce Lord of Annandale. But as well as indicating strong loyalist sympathies in the town, he had to inform that these were evidently not shared by Bruce's own nephew, the new Earl of Carrick, Edward Bruce's second son, who was lord there now and had handed over the castle, with his allegiance, to the usurper. There had always been bad blood between Robert and Edward Bruce; now this was transmitted to the next generation apparently.

It was decided to make the raid on Annan Castle the following night; and the messenger was sent back to inform his fellow-supporters of the attempt, in strictest secrecy. He was to have them arouse the citizenry, when they heard the attack develop, so as to cause panic and alarm behind the enemy forces when these were roused to counter-attack.

The numbers to be employed in the raid provided something of a problem. Sufficient they must take; but too many would be counter-productive and would militate against surprise and secrecy. It was decided that about one thousand was right, three hundred to storm the castle itself and the remainder to seal off the approaches thereto for long enough to allow the raiders to achieve their ends and retire back across the ford, it was to be hoped with Edward Balliol dead or alive. Another problem, unexpected, was that practically everyone amongst the Scots leadership wanted to be involved. But they could not all go, for if the attempt failed, there must be those left to command the main army. Nevertheless it was apparent that there was going to be a greater preponderance of lords and knights in this affair than Will Douglas, for one, desired; but his uncle was reluctant to refuse any. As a sort of consolation for the others, it was agreed that a second force of cavalry, somewhat larger, perhaps two thousand, should come along behind, as support, but to keep their distance for the sake of secrecy and only move if called for.

So the next evening the two forces were readied. It had been a wet and unpleasant day, with sleet threatening, but none the worse for their purposes perhaps. They would wait until complete darkness, necessarily, longer indeed, and then ride behind Johnstone guides who knew the terrain intimately, not by the main riverside road, which might well be guarded, or at least watched, but by little-used tracks and byways, with Johnstone scouts out ahead, under Lochwood.

A start was delayed until about eight o'clock. Although it was only ten miles direct, it would be fully half that again by the route planned; and they would be able to go only very slowly, in the darkness. Midnight for the attack, then, no earlier.

Although in theory under the personal command of the new Regent, in fact Will Douglas led, grumbling at having to carry so many lofty ones along when what was needed for this attempt was the toughest of mosstroopers. Their guides took them by a route well to the west of the main Annandale road, round the hill of Trailtrow, although they did not see it, avoiding the Brydekirk area, and on down the winding valley of a small stream running south-eastwards. Only the Johnstones knew where they were in all this, the night being as dark as it was wet, and the going unpleasant to say the least. And slow, slower even than anticipated, for moving a thousand horsemen through narrow and all but trackless unknown country by night is no easy manoeuvre. Inevitably the column became grievously extended, and Ramsay and others of the leadership were occupied throughout in riding up and down the line trying to keep the various groups together and in touch. Oddly enough, some of the young lords seemed to enjoy this, despite the conditions, John Randolph and the Steward in especial finding it almost a sporting activity.

It was after midnight before they passed a dimly discerned height called, apparently, Spittalridding Hill, where there was a monastic hospice; and there was still a couple of miles to go to the Annan ford, they were told. Will Douglas, at the front, cursed as he rode.

However, presently they were heartened by a subdued glow in the night ahead, which would be the camp-fires of Balliol's army, being kept alight through the night. The great encampment, they had been informed, was on the level ground to the east of the town, its common indeed, the opposite side from castle and river – which was a blessing.

Scouts came back to them to tell that the ford was unguarded.

They heard the river before they saw it, if seeing is the word; and although this was daunting to most, sounding as though it was running high with the rain, the scouts assured that the noise was actually caused by the shallows of the ford area, where the water was more disturbed. They would cross without difficulty.

At the river's edge, whilst the party was reassembling and being marshalled behind them, the leaders went to peer across. Their vision was by now more adapted to the darkness, and silhouetted against the glow of the fires, they could make out the black bulk of the castle. From this angle at least no light showed therein, at this hour, an encouraging sign, although undoubtedly there would be guards on duty.

A decision fell to be made here – whether the castle party should cross first, or the larger group which was to form the barrier? The latter had further to go and should be in place when the raid on the castle began; but if, by chance, their crossing and arrival was discovered and the enemy alerted, then the main objective could be aborted. Douglas held that they dare not risk this, Ramsay agreeing, and they persuaded his uncle to so rule. The castle group would go over first, dismount and take up their preliminary positions. When they were ready, send a messenger back to bring over the remainder, who would endeavour to ride on and past as silently as possible and form the barrier between town and castle.

With urgent commands for quiet, Douglas himself led the way into the river, glad enough now of its noises. They rode slowly to avoid splashing, although the horses' instinct clearly was to hurry over.

In the event, they found the crossing reasonably easy, the water never reaching as high as the beasts' bellies. By testing, they found the ford, cobbled like a causeway, was indeed wide enough to accommodate as many as a score of riders abreast, so that the seventy-yard crossing did not take long. There was some unavoidable noise, but not much.

Once over, and dismounted, the three hundred of the assault party moved quickly into their prearranged positions. Many of the leaders knew the castle fairly well, it being a Bruce seat. The entrance-front and gatehouse faced the town. It was hoped that, in present circumstances, the drawbridge would not be up nor the portcullis down, with the enemy army camped so close at hand, and its leaders no doubt either in the castle or lodged in houses in the town. So two-thirds of the attackers moved round, as silently as they could, under the high perimeter walling, to the front of the establishment, whilst the remainder, leaving a small guard on the horses, went in the other direction, west-about, to the area of the broken-down curtain walls, nearer at hand. These, under the Steward and Moray, were not to attempt ingress until they received a signal from the front party.

As Douglas and Ramsay stationed their people about one hundred yards out from the gateway, peering to see if the drawbridge was indeed down, they were startled by two figures who materialised out of the gloom from behind a low wall of the forecourt – and were almost leapt upon there and then. But one proved to be the young courier who had come to Hoddom, the other his father, a magistrate of the town. These whispered that so far all was well. The bridge was not up, the portcullis raised and the guard in the gatehouse evidently keeping warm before a fire therein. None seemed to be patrolling the curtain walls. Many of the townsfolk were waiting, ready to move out and make trouble for the enemy when the camp was roused.

Nodding their thanks, Douglas sent two messengers, one to tell the barrier party, under his uncle, to move across and into position; the other to inform the Steward's group that he, Douglas, was moving in, and to do likewise, but quietly. Then, passing the word back, he and Ramsay led the way forward, pacing heedfully.

They reached the drawbridge, and were careful to tread even more softly, for heavy footfalls on its timbers above a void could echo hollowly. Almost tip-toeing, indeed all but holding their breaths, the two hundred crept over.

No challenge rang out as the leaders entered the deeper gloom of the gatehouse-pend, under its vault.

Doorways opened off this stone passage right and left, one to give access to the porter's lodge, the other to a stairway leading up to the gatehouse itself, above the pend, from which the drawbridge and portcullis were managed. Both doors were presently shut against the winter's night. Setting men to guard both, Douglas and Ramsay moved on into the outer bailey, hardly able to believe their good fortune thus far.

In the cobbled enclosure of the outer bailey they were aware of a vague stirring and sound. But it did not trouble the invaders, for with it was the smell of horses. Round this yard was a lining of lean-to stabling; it was the slight movement of scores of horses they were hearing. From here they could see a light from an inner window of the gatehouse.

There was a second guard-chamber between the outer and inner baileys, but it was unlikely to be on the alert at night when the main gate was manned. The leaders approached it cautiously nevertheless. No challenge was forthcoming.

The inner bailey, instead of stabling, was lined with the barrack accommodation for the men-at-arms and garrison. How many might be therein, in present circumstances, there was no knowing. Ramsay counted four doorways, and stationed guards on each.

Ahead now reared the dark mass of the main keep of the establishment, wherein would surely be found Balliol and his close associates. There might well be a guard at its door also, but, it was to be hoped, no more alert than the rest. Douglas was forming up a tight group to tackle this entrance, and another to proceed round to the rear to block any back-door escape, when the night's wet quiet was suddenly disturbed. Shouts and yells erupted from nearby, to the west. The Steward's group had presumably been discovered entering the semi-ruinous domestic quarters of kitchens, bakehouse, larders and so on, at that side.

Cursing furiously, Douglas ordered the main keep entrance to be rushed, silence no longer essential.

Swords and dirks drawn, they ran up, threw open the great door, and flung themselves within.

There was little real resistance. Heavy-eyed, yawning and bewildered men appeared in doorways, and were promptly cut down by the attackers. Leaving Fraser to deal with the occupants of the vaulted basement chambers Douglas and Ramsay raced up the twisting turnpike stairway to the first floor, where would be the great hall, followed by fifty or so mosstroopers.

Bursting into this, the main apartment of the castle, lit still by the flickerings of two large log fires, they were into a scene of confusion. Some men, awakened by the shouting, were on their feet, demanding what was to do, peering from windows, reaching for weapons. More were still on the floor asleep, part-drunken no doubt, for the long tables were littered with wine-flagons and beakers and broken meats. Shouting to Wemyss to cope with this situation, Douglas wasted no time. Edward Balliol would not be couched down there, but upstairs in one of the principal bedchambers, for sure. With Ramsay and many others he ran on, up the turnpike.

There were two apartments on the next floor, intercommunicating. Douglas burst open the door into the first, where somebody had lit a lamp. Men here, in various stages of undress, were pulling on outer clothing and armour. Some had time to grab weapons before the intruders were upon them. Ramsay found himself attacking Sir John Moubray, whom he knew slightly. Sword against mere dagger, he felled the older man without difficulty. Turning to deal with the next, his glance went to the intercommunicating doorway. This door had now been opened and a man stood therein, staring. It was Edward Balliol himself, clad only in shirt and breeches. Shouting, Ramsay flung himself thither.

But he was just too late. He tripped over a fallen body and this gave Balliol sufficient time to jump back and slam the door shut behind him. As Ramsay reached it, he could hear the draw-bar within click into place. That door would not give way without some sort of battering-ram.

Yelling the news to Douglas, who was swording with Sir Walter Comyn, Ramsay dashed through the struggling mass of men back for the stairway, Down he raced, two steps at a time, and out again into the night. Almost certainly there would be a second stair leading down from that inner bed-chamber. He must reach that. He was vaguely aware of some of his own Dalwolsey men, led by Wattie Kerr, at his back.

Hastening round the keep they came up against unexpected obstruction. The Steward's party, having cleared out the domestic quarters, arrived at that side of the keep, driving before them a crowd of servitors and general retainers, women amongst them, many only partially clad. Confusion reigned.

It was Ramsay's turn to curse. Seeking to push through this terrified and bewailing throng and their attackers, making for that rear door, he recognised that this might well ruin all. If Balliol was already down a back stair, he could mingle with this crowd of panic-stricken servants and nowise stand out, in his shirt and breeches, since others were in approximately the same state. No amount of authoritative shouting would prevail in that uproar. Furiously he elbowed his way through the crush, his men behind him.

When at length they reached the expected doorway it was to find the door open. So his quarry could be already out. Swinging round there, on the step, he stared back into the throng; but in that darkness and chaos it was impossible to distinguish individuals. Turning, he ran inside into a vaulted lobby, empty. Up a narrow circular stair therefrom he went, and in the almost pitch darkness cannoned into somebody coming down. Who this might be he could not tell, but if it was Balliol he had donned more clothing, which seemed unlikely, in the rush. Pushing this individual bodily round and down, into Wattie Kerr's arms, he shouted to hold him, and raced on up the stairs.

Blessed light showed faintly at the second-floor landing, coming from an open door. Into this chamber he went, to discover a woman standing beside a great canopied bed, who screamed at the sight of him, armoured and sword drawn. Clutching a blanket partly around her, she was obviously naked. She was alone. Ramsay paused, bowed mockingly to her, and turned back.

There were two more floors above this in the keep, but the chances of Balliol having gone upstairs rather than down were remote. Ramsay left the upper floors to others, and ran downstairs again.

In the courtyard, frustrated, he gazed about him. Someone had lit a torch, but its smoky, wavering light only emphasised the hopelessness of trying to pick out individuals in the seething turmoil. The attackers could be identified by their armour and helmets, but in that confined space that was all.

Pushing his way back to the keep's main entrance, Ramsay

found Douglas emerging. To him he shouted his tidings, to that man's hot anger. They agreed that they must seal off this inner courtyard and all within it, and sift through the trapped folk. But Balliol might well have already escaped. It was maddening to have achieved so much and yet to have lost the object of it all.

They had other problems now to occupy their minds, as well as Balliol's whereabouts. The enemy army could be upon them at any time, in however disorganised a state. What of the Regent's seven hundred? And the town? Had the alarm yet roused the camp? How quickly must they organise their own retiral?

Douglas said that he would see to the situation in the castle. Ramsay should go out and discover the position outside. Inform Sir Archibald, if possible, and arrange a signal for the retiral to the ford.

Hurrying out with his little band through the inner and outer baileys, at the gatehouse their guards told them that they had heard rather than seen the Regent's force riding between castle and town some time before. They had however heard no sounds of disturbance from the encampment area beyond the town, and there was no observable brightening of the fireglow from there.

Certainly, as he stared out eastwards, Ramsay could perceive no signs of alarm or even movement in town or beyond. He was surprised, assuming that all the uproar at the castle must have been heard. But possibly not; the rain, and the town between, might have to some extent blanketed the noise, from the camp. The same might apply in reverse, of course, and the enemy army's arousal not be heard from here.

He hurried out into the forecourt, and on. Soon he came upon the first of the Regent's horsemen, Douglases to a man, riding back and forward, to form a cordon cutting off the castle. He asked for Sir Archibald, and was directed further.

He found the Regent dismounted and talking to the magistrate-father of the messenger. They both were astonished that so far no indication of trouble had come from the town common; but reckoned that it would not be long now before it did, for a few escapers from the castle had been glimpsed running in that direction. They had tried to head these off, but because they could slip into the lanes and wynds of the town, this had proved difficult. Ramsay interrupted to demand whether one of these fugitives had been a tall man in shirt and breeches; but they said that in the darkness they could not tell. When the Regent heard about Balliol, he was much put out.

There was nothing that Ramsay could do now save return to the castle. He did suggest that Sir Archibald send out a couple of scouts to as close as they could get to the enemy camp without being noticed, to send back word of any development there. As this was being arranged, they were interrupted. The sound and beat of hooves, many hooves, halted their talk – but coming from the west, not the east.

Alarmed, the Regent hastily mounted, ready for trouble. But when the first horsemen loomed close, they proved to be Sir Andrew Leslie and his lieutenants, leading the two thousand reserve force. Contrary to instructions and tired of inactive waiting, they had decided to come and see what went on.

It was not Ramsay's place to rebuke them, and Sir Archibald did not do so – for in the circumstances it looked as though no harm was done. But it would complicate the withdrawal, with three thousand men to get back across that ford, instead of one-third of that number. He said that he would return and inform Will Douglas.

Back at the castle he found that man efficiently commanding all. Douglas was annoyed at this arrival of Leslie's contingent but changed his tune suddenly when he heard that there was still no sign of the enemy encampment being alarmed. Drawing a deep breath, he abruptly beat a steel-clad fist on Ramsay's breastplate.

"By the Mass!" he exclaimed. "Here's a ploy! Man, we have three thousand horse here now. If the enemy are not roused and ready, three thousand could ride through their camp and cut it to tatters! It could be God's gift . . ."

Ramsay grinned. "I wondered whether that would come to your mind," he said.

"Quickly, then. Leave a small guard here, on the prisoners. Send for our horses. Bring them to the forecourt. Hurry, Sandy!"

It did not take long to fetch the horses round. There was some confusion as to who was to be left behind, as ever all wanting to be in at the action, the Steward and Moray flatly refusing to stay. In the end, Hay the Constable and Sir

Michael Wemyss were left in charge of castle and prisoners, and the rest hurried out to the forecourt and mounted.

There was now a great congestion of horsemen milling around in the area between town and castle. Douglas and Ramsay drove through the throng, to where the Regent and Leslie were still conferring as to what to do now. Will Douglas took charge without any pretence of consulting his uncle. Three columns of one thousand each, he ordered, under himself, Ramsay and Fraser. Ramsay to ride north of the town, Fraser south, and he would ride through the streets themselves. Wait at the edge of the common until he blew his horn. Then advance at the charge, in line abreast, and ride down the usurper's camp. Through it, turn and back again. Cut them to pieces . . .

Ramsay interrupted to ask what should be their plan if they found the camp roused – even though there was still no indication of this? Douglas said, having got that far, they would go ahead. If there was organised resistance, on their return charge, they would seek to carry on right back to the ford and over, picking up Hay, Wemyss and the prisoners on the way. But with most of the enemy leaders undoubtedly caught in the castle, he did not think that the surprised army would be in a position to counter-attack swiftly.

Time being of the essence, they delayed no longer. Breaking up the confused concourse of horsemen into three echelons of a sort, in the darkness and without much noise and shouting, was a problem, and no very exact division resulted. But that was not vitally important. Ramsay was the first to ride off, with an unknown but substantial following, north-about round the town's broken-down walling.

It was not difficult to find their way, for the faint glow of the many camp-fires guided them and showed up the loom of the burgh's buildings. Annan was not a large town, and getting into their appointed position did not take long.

Once there, with the common area open before them, it was obvious that some disturbance now prevailed in the camp; but not as yet any general alarm apparently. There was some activity, and the fires were clearly being stoked up with fresh wood to give more light; and lit lamps were moving here and there. But there was no indication of a great army of over twenty thousand being roused or in the process of marshalling.

Ramsay, forming his men into a lengthy line four deep, had not long to wait before the high wailing of a hunting-horn sounded in the windy gloom, for his group had probably had furthest to ride. Stationing himself approximately in the centre of his front, he raised his sword high and ordered the charge.

It could be only a very moderate charge, in the darkness, since any gallop could have put them into dire trouble over unseen obstacles, whinbushes, ditches and the like. So no more than a canter was practicable, and even so Ramsay, peering urgently, was much concerned with possible upset and consequent break-up of the formation, if not worse. Surely seldom had a cavalry commander led a charge with less preoccupation with the enemy ahead.

They had perhaps three hundred yards to cover to the edge of the encampment; and as they neared this it dawned on Ramsay that, of all things, the enemy had placed their horse-lines here at this western rim of their cantonment. So this is what he would reach first, thousands of tethered horses. It was on a par with the rest of their good fortune that night – save the missing of Balliol himself – for nothing could more assist their project than to drive hosts of panic-stricken and riderless horses before them through the sleeping camp.

Before they reached these lines, their right wing merged with the left of Douglas's front. No need now for quiet. Yelling "A Ramsay! A Ramsay!" he led straight into the ranks of stationary horses.

For moments, of course, it was utter pandemonium, as the neighing, screaming beasts staggered and reared, their own mounts contributing. Then the tethered horses broke loose and began to stream away. Inevitably it was into the long rows of tents, pavilions and blanketed men that they plunged. Hell broke loose on Annan Common.

What followed was as indescribable as it was chaotic. Admittedly the attacking Scots had a planned assault to carry out, but in the circumstances keeping to the plan was all but impossible. The fleeing horses in front certainly had no plans, and the riders behind were thereby constrained. But the impact on the camp lacked nothing in effect on that account. Whatever warning might have been given earlier, little arousal seemed to have resulted. Most of the enemy still seemed to be asleep as the avalanche of horses and riders bore down upon them in pounding fury. There was no resistance. Men were trampled on where they lay or tried to rise, pavilions were trodden down, tentage swept aside, stacks of arms tumbled. The noise and clamour did tend to warn those on the far side of the encampment that something was very much amiss, but this did not produce any organised stand or opposition, only flight.

Ramsay did what he could to try to keep his men in some sort of order, or at least in touch with each other and himself, but this proved to be scarcely feasible. His objective had to be to drive on through the tumult and horror as best they could, not to get involved with individuals or groups, not to be sidetracked, so as to reach that further side, there to turn and repeat the dire process, difficult as this must be. Before they started, he had warned his people on this, pointing out that if they allowed themselves to be delayed, they themselves would be in grave danger of being ridden down by their own fellows on the return charge.

In the event it was a very ragged company which won through to the east end of the common, to rein up and turn. Ramsay delayed the return for as long as he dared, to allow stragglers to come up. There was no way that he could tell what proportion of his command had managed to get thus far, but undoubtedly all had not. In the darkness he could not see what went on further down the line, but obviously the same problems would prevail there. He shouted to his riders, at least those near enough to hear, to try not to ride down any mounted men in their way, as those would likely be their own folk, it being improbable that the enemy would have been able to catch any of the fleeing horses.

Then he ordered the second charge.

Inevitably it was even more chaotic than the first, with no sort of line possible to be kept by the attackers, and what was left of the encampment now a shambles. As far as beating down and killing went, nothing very much was achieved, for the enemy were now everywhere in flight, such as could run, none staying to fight, not in Ramsay's sector at any rate.

Through on the town side of the common again, he pulled up, to take stock. Only a small proportion of his men were actually with him now, others coming in singly and in groups as they could disentangle themselves from the embroilment. It seemed pointless to repeat the process. Ramsay decided to leave Johnstone of Lochwood, who was in his party, in command meantime, and go seek Will Douglas.

He found that man more easily than he had anticipated, quite near at hand, indeed, having himself just completed his return charge and now wondering what to do next. Hailing each other, they found that they had come to the same conclusion: that so far as they could tell, in the gloom and confusion, the night was theirs, the camp completely broken up, the enemy scattered and leaderless and unlikely to rally now. Despite their preponderance in numbers still – for probably not a great many had been slain – fleeing in all directions as they had done, horseless and with few if any senior commanders, it was all but inconceivable that they could re-form and offer any coherent opposition. Likewise, for themselves to go chasing after the dispersed fleeing men in the darkness would be a waste of effort. It was sufficient.

So Douglas's horn was blown time and again in the recall.

It took some time to reassemble their people, so much so that presently Douglas, growing impatient, left some of his lesser commanders to round up the stragglers, attend to the wounded and collect the booty from the camp. Then he led the way back to the castle.

There, presently, sustained by appropriated wines and provision in the great hall, steaming before replenished fires, the victors considered the situation. Nobody had seen Edward Balliol unfortunately, but apart from that it seemed to be success all the way. The enemy dead proved to include Balliol's own brother Henry; also Sir Walter Comyn, Sir John Moubray, Sir Richard Kirkby, one of the English leaders, and other notables. And there were many prominent captives, including none other than their involuntary host, Alexander Bruce, the new Earl of Carrick. Many there were for executing this weak nephew of their late King there and then; but Moray, who was his kinsman, pleaded for his life with the Regent, and promised to stand surety for his better behaviour in the future.

It was decided that there was no point in returning to Hoddom, so messengers were sent to acquaint the main Scots army of the position and to bring them on here to Annan in the morning. Then, weary but triumphant, with sufficient guards set and scouting parties out to ensure that no possible rallying of the enemy endangered them, the victors were given one final item of news before they couched down to sleep. Amongst new captives brought in were a Maxwell laird and an English under-officer, both of whom testified that they had seen King Edward Balliol riding off eastwards from the camp area, alone, still only in shirt and breeches, presumably making for the Border and Carlisle. There was no doubt about the identity, for it was the English officer's horse which the fugitive had commandeered, by royal command.

So, it seemed that Scotland had got rid of her usurper, after a bare three months. God save King David!

5

Alexander Ramsay was back in his own house of Dalwolsey for Yuletide, and glad to be, for apart from the festive season's celebrations, which he always enjoyed, there was much that required his attention as chief of a great lordship of many baronies, many manors and wide lands. His brother William made a good deputy in most respects and could deal with much of the day-to-day management of the properties; but he was very much a stay-at-home character, immersed in his books and studies, and the more distant affairs tended to get neglected. Moreover there were functions which only the lord himself could carry out, particularly in matters of justice, for as a baron of Scotland, Ramsay had the power of pit and gallows, conferring on him the right and duty to adjudicate in most issues not reserved to the crown, a grave responsibility for a man who took his obligations seriously, and one in which his brother could not replace him. Also there were major repairs to property to decide on, as well as seasonal considerations, and orders to transmit, with regard to land use of many thousands of acres, the annual survey of cattle and horse stock and especially the great sheep-hirsels in the Lammermuir Hills, the wool from which, largely exported to Flanders and the Low Countries from Berwick-on-Tweed, constituted the lordship's principal source of wealth.

So time did not hang heavily during the weeks which

followed the victory at Annan and Balliol's flight. Nevertheless there were times when Alexander Ramsay had to admit to himself that he found all this, essential and worth while as it certainly was, somehow less than satisfying after all the excitements of the recent past; a feeling of being understretched as it were, less than fully challenged. And this, oddly enough, tended to be linked, at the back of his mind, with thoughts of Mariot Randolph.

He often thought of her. He had had his ventures and connections with young women in the past, enjoying them usually whilst remaining heart-whole. Not that he was now smitten with Moray's sister in any serious fashion, he could assure himself; but he had been much impressed by her at Doune that time, her looks, her manner and behaviour, her quiet competence – and probably the fact that the young Steward was so evidently captivated, something which might hold its own challenge.

So Yule and January passed, and the lord of Dalwolsey quite frequently caught himself wondering how he might contrive an excuse to pay another visit to the Doune of Menteith.

It was in early February that such preoccupations were abruptly, if not dispelled, at least pushed to the back of his mind, by the arrival of a messenger from the Black Knight of Liddesdale. Would Sir Alexander Ramsay, of his goodness and in his leal duty to the King's Grace and his Regent, come to Lochmaben Castle in Annandale at his earliest convenience, bringing with him such armed and horsed supporters as he could raise at short notice? With all due greetings . . .

Ramsay did not exactly cheer, but Will noticed a certain lightening in his brother's step thereafter, as he set about the business of summoning men.

The very next day he was on his way, with some fifty of a tail, including his cousin Pate, Ramsay of Redheuch and Wattie Kerr, matters of justice, building repairs, sheep and even young women relegated meantime for future consideration.

It had been a wet, raw winter, with the ground waterlogged and streams running high; but at least there had been little snow and the hill passes were open, which was just as well for a journey to mid-Annandale. They rode almost due south, by the Morthwaite foothills and the Eddleston Water to Peebles, then westwards up Tweed to that river's great bend southwards at Broughton, and so on towards its source on Tweedsmuir, darkness halting them at Oliver, where they learned that its lord, Sir Simon Fraser, had already departed likewise for Lochmaben, in strength. So it looked like a fairly major muster.

The following day, in more dismal rain, they crossed the dreary high watershed moorland where Tweed, Clyde and Annan all were born, to accompany the latter river down to Moffat. Here they met up with Scott of Rankilburn, and a couple of hundred of his mosstroopers, going in the same direction. He told Ramsay that he understood that the Regent — which meant Will Douglas — was planning an invasion of England, no less. Since the Scotts, like so many other Borderers, more or less lived by making raids into the North of England in search of cattle, women and other benefits, Rankilburn was entirely in favour. Ramsay was more moderate in his enthusiasm.

Lochmaben lay some fifteen miles down Annandale, its fortalice a former Bruce stronghold, now a royal castle, of which it appeared, since the present Earl of Carrick's shame and declension, Douglas had had himself appointed Keeper, by the Regent. It was one of the strongest holds in the land, built at the extreme tip of a narrow peninsula jutting far into the loch, and well nigh impregnable. They found Lochmaben town full of armed men and anticipatory excitement rife. At the castle Douglas received Ramsay, cheerfully masterful, his uncle amiable in the background.

The situation was explained. Edward Plantagenet of England, disgusted at his minion Balliol's miserable failure at Annan, had announced that he himself would now take over the subjugation of Scotland, despite the Treaty of Northampton, and was presently assembling a great army to bring north with him. He would invade in the east, making no secret of his intention, from Northumberland; and Balliol, necessarily stiffened by Lord Dacre and Sir Anthony Lucy, the English Middle and West March Wardens respectively, was to march in from Carlisle and Cumbria. So something had to be done, and swiftly.

Was actual invasion of England the answer, Ramsay wondered? Was that not overly ambitious?

It was a raid rather than an invasion, he was told; a raid with a purpose. Balliol, after flight to Carlisle, had passed Yule at Gilsland with Lord Dacre. He was reported to be still there. Gilsland, near Lanercost Abbey, was only fifteen miles from the borderline at Kirkandrews. Cross there, by night, and they might with luck even capture the man. But at least they could frighten him, show him that the Scots would never forget nor forgive what he had done, that he would never be safe anywhere near Scotland. And give warning to Dacre that if he led a force into Scotland hereafter, as reputedly planned, he would suffer at his house of Gilsland. It was all a gesture towards Edward Plantagenet likewise. He was not the only one who could break signed treaties.

Douglas, ever impatient, decided to wait only one more day – for there could be some Balliol supporters even now in Annandale who might send word into England of this muster. He had asked Moray, Lindsay, Leslie and others, but they had further to come, and could follow on later if they had not come by the morrow. He had now three thousand, all horsed, which should serve . . .

Next afternoon, then, they set off, a cheerful host, for this was the sort of venture that appealed to most, not any long campaign or set warfare but a raid, a dash into enemy territory, a showing of the flag, a swift paying off of old scores – and with the prospect of booty. It was as good as a holiday.

Johnstone of Lochwood and Jardine of Applegirth led the way, in their element, for this was just their accustomed Border reiving on a larger scale, and they knew all the hidden ways to go, darkness hereafter no trouble, since that was normal for the business. It was, they assessed, about forty-five miles to Gilsland by the way they would go. Ride to Langholm in Eskdale this first night, then lie up there over the morrow. Then on in darkness down to where Liddel joined Esk, cross into England at Kirkandrews and, avoiding Kirklinton and Brampton, populous areas, cross the Lyne valley and the moorlands of Bolton and Walton Mosses to the Roman Wall at Birdoswald. Then Gilsland, before dawn.

So they rode up the Water of Milk, Jardine country, and through the empty Tundergarth Hills to Eskdale, Armstrong territory. The Armstrongs were a lawless lot, paying little more allegiance to Scotland than they did to England, for they straddled the borderline; so they were not to be trusted, but Johnstone and Jardine assured the Regent that on this

111

occasion they would not cause trouble, for although they would care nothing about Balliol one way or the other, they hated Dacre, who as English Middle March Warden had recently hanged some of their people. Indeed when they heard that Gilsland was the objective, they might well be glad to join the venture.

This in fact was what happened. Despite the darkness and unannounced approach, the raiding party found the Armstrong chiefs, Mangerton, Gilnockie, Whithaugh and the rest, awaiting their arrival at Langholm, their 'capital', with some hundreds of their very tough riders assembled, a significant indication of their excellent information system in this wild Border country; and when they heard of the descent on Dacre's castle of Gilsland, they appeared to take it for granted that they would go along. Will Douglas, who as Knight of Liddesdale, and Keeper of that unruly area, looked on all Armstrongs as eminently hangable, was doubtful, to say the least, but recognised that to refuse to take them would be considered a grievous insult and could endanger them all thereafter.

The next day was spent at Langholm in a sort of wary amity, much new-killed beef being provided for the troops – they were assured, all English-bred. A further advantage was forthcoming. Armstrong of Mangerton offered to send a messenger to Graham of Netherby – his wife was a Graham – to ensure that there would be no trouble with that warlike English clan. All fords of the Esk, including Kirkandrews, were guarded on the English side by Graham peel-towers; and though these would not be strong enough to hold up three thousand from crossing for long they could send warning back to the English authorities if so inclined. This service was appreciated.

The following dusk, then, they rode down Eskside, a reinforced company. They passed the mouth of Liddesdale, and soon after came to the Kirkandrews ford. Actual guides were waiting for them on the Scots side, from the Graham tower, producing a grim smile from Douglas, for one of his principal headaches as Keeper of Liddesdale was apt to be the inroads and cross-border raiding of these same Grahams, Kirkandrews prominent.

The laird there himself, a brother of Netherby the chief, gave them God-speed most civilly, once across, the fact that they were Scots invading English soil seemingly holding no significance for him, Borderers keeping an open mind on such matters. He did not go so far as to offer to guide them onward to Gilsland, by night, since that would have been to insult the Armstrongs, Jardines and Johnstones. It was gathered that Lord Dacre was not a popular warden – if wardens were ever popular.

They made good time thereafter, considering the darkness, encountering no problems. Presumably the passing of over three thousand horsemen could not have gone entirely unnoticed, even of a winter's night, but discretion in such situations was another and necessary Border virtue, and no alarm was raised in the hamlets and farm-touns which they could not avoid, however many dogs barked. Across the next south-flowing river, the Lyne, they went without difficulty, for it was comparatively shallow, and then over the commons of Bolton and Walton beyond.

So they came to the great Roman Wall, at Birdoswald, built to keep out their Pictish ancestors a thousand years before. No patrols paced its grass-grown ramparts now. But they went warily, for Gilsland was only a couple of miles ahead.

Douglas hoped to surprise the castle sufficiently to gain access; but he recognised that however much of a surprise, this might not be possible, for it was a fairly strong place, not a major fortalice but moated and walled, with drawbridge, gatehouse, portcullis and the rest. In which case they would have to content themselves with making a demonstration, burning the castleton and village and driving off Dacre's and his people's cattle and horses. The main objective, if they could not in fact capture Balliol, was to frighten him, give him warning to keep away from Scotland in future, and show Dacre and the North of England generally that if they aided Edward Plantagenet, they were vulnerable to dire reprisals.

In the event this last had to satisfy them, for although they reached Gilsland village unannounced, they found its castle effectively beyond their reach, its gatehouse guarded, its drawbridge up and its portcullis down, Dacre presumably a man of caution. Ramsay was not surprised, having anticipated no less. Douglas, disappointed, had of course been prepared for this also, and wasted little time in cursing. He divided his force into three, one division under Fraser to sack the village and set it on fire; one under the Border chiefs to

round up all the cattle and stock they could find in the vicinity
– they were the experts at this; and his own grouping to
encircle the castle and at least present Dacre and Balliol with
a challenge.

In pursuance of this last, they waited until the first yells and
screams sounded from the unhappy village, followed quickly
by the glow of fire. Then Douglas sent his thousand horsemen
to ride round and round the perimeter of the castle, on its
slight mound, shouting. They could not get very close under
the walls because of the moat. He led his leadership group to
the drawbridge-end, and had his horn blown loud and long.

From the gatehouse there were answering shouts. Declaring his identity, and announcing that here was the Regent of
His Grace David, King of Scots, he demanded the presence of
the Lord Dacre. He had a fine carrying voice for this sort of
thing.

There was no reply from the gatehouse.

Douglas repeated his demand. Now the growing fires from
Gilsland village and castleton were beginning to cast a lurid
glow over the scene and to show up the encircling horsemen, a
menacing sight.

When there was still no evident reaction from the castle,
the Regent himself took a hand. He urged his horse forward
to the very edge of the moat, for he had not so loud a voice as
his nephew.

"I am Archibald Douglas, Lord of Galloway and Regent of
Scotland," he called. "I understand that the Lord Dacre
entertains within this hold the man Edward Balliol, who seeks
to usurp the throne of our liege-lord David. Deliver him up to
me and I will withdraw my forces from this place and return to
Scotland."

With all the background noise now prevailing, it was
doubtful whether all that would be heard in the castle. No
answer was forthcoming, at any rate.

Will Douglas took over again. There was little doubt that
his bellow would reach them. He repeated his uncle's
announcement and added peremptorily that swift compliance
was required or it would be the worse for Gilsland.

That elicited no response either. What was going on in the
castle they could only guess at. Lights were visible now in
sundry windows, but that was as far as reactions seemed to go.

This situation could not, of course, be allowed to drag on.

114

They could not storm the castle, and there was no time for siegery. Will Douglas ordered Scott of Rankilburn to go back to the now blazing village, the cottage thatches burning readily, and round up a crowd of men, women and children. Bring them here, in torchlight.

Ramsay for one did not like the sound of that, and said so, but Douglas cut him short, assuring that it was only a gesture. After all, did he not bear the title of the Flower of Chivalry?

There was still no acknowledgment from the castle, even when a wailing, sorry concourse was driven up in terror, children screaming, women sobbing, men beseeching, frantic as they were forced to penetrate that shouting ring of circling horsemen. They were brought up to the drawbridge-end.

Douglas had his horn blown again and cried out that the Lord Dacre must hand over Balliol, or these, his people, would pay the penalty. He left that penalty unspecified.

Even this produced no evident response. Disgusted, Douglas shouted that there were plenty of trees on the village green to hang all these, and ordered the sad crew to be herded back to their burning homes.

There was, it seemed, nothing more that they could do here, in the face of this masterly inactivity. The leaders turned and rode back to the inferno of a village.

Fraser's men had spared nothing. Even the church was ablaze. Most of the inhabitants had probably escaped into the night, and there had been little killing, although a number of women undoubtedly had been caught and forced to pay the price of conquest. The scene was a terrible one.

The Regent was concerned about the time. It would be dawn in less than three hours. They were a bare score of miles from Carlisle, where there was always a large English garrison. Less from Brampton. This burning, lighting up the sky, would be seen from afar. They had fifteen miles to go to get to the Esk, and would be delayed by the cattle. Time that they were gone.

His nephew reluctantly acceded. They might well prevail in any skirmish with the local forces, but in the circumstances that would be of little profit.

The horn was sounded for the recall.

This took some little time to effect, with no sign of the cattle-lifters evident. However, presently a rider appeared, from Jardine, saying that they had heard the horn. They had

115

rounded up an excellent spoil of beasts, and would drive them to meet the main host at Birdoswald or thereabouts, in a short time.

So the move was made, leaving behind a silently defiant castle, a devastated village and a terrified population. A fair amount of booty went with them, but no prisoners.

Most of the Border contingent were in fact awaiting them, with a large herd of cattle and horses, at Birdoswald, although there was no sign of the Armstrongs. Jardine and Johnstone guessed that they had decided to strike out on their own now, no doubt reluctant to have to share any of their gleanings with others. This sounded entirely in character, and believing that the said Armstrongs were well able to find their own way back to Eskdale and look after themselves, Douglas ordered onward progress.

That progress was now direly slow, with many hundreds of cattle to herd, however expert some of the herders. The leaders, men-at-arms and levies of the lords and knights chafed sorely at this delay, none more so than Will Douglas. Nevertheless he insisted that, at least until they were over Esk, they must all stay together; they owed that to the Border men and indeed all who looked for a share in the spoil.

Dawn overtook them long before they reached the Esk, or even the Lyne. However, no pursuit was in evidence, although they maintained patrols behind them as well as on the flanks to ensure early warning.

It was broad daylight when they crossed at Kirkandrews – and here there was a surprise development: John Randolph, Earl of Moray, in process of fording the river with a couple of hundred men, come late to the venture.

Moray, it transpired, was not grievously disappointed in having missed the Gilsland affair. His mind was, in fact, preoccupied with a very different problem. Just before leaving Doune he had heard from his elder sister Agnes, Countess of Dunbar and March, that her peculiar husband had now entered into a treasonable arrangement with Edward of England, not only to hand over Dunbar Castle to the English but actually to strengthen it first, at the Plantagenet's expense. Also to assist Edward in capturing the great castle at Berwick-on-Tweed. Black Agnes was outraged, declaring that she would never yield up Dunbar Castle to the English, despite her traitor husband, and she was now seeking help.

This news, needless to say, greatly concerned them all, Douglas and the Regent in especial. With the Earl of Dunbar in outright co-operation with King Edward, invasion of Scotland on the east would be greatly facilitated. Something had to be done, and quickly. Not only must Dunbar Castle, of much strategic importance, be denied to the invader, but Berwick Castle, where Sir Alexander Seton was Governor, must be warned that the Scots Chief Warden of the Marches was in league with the enemy.

While the slow business of getting the reluctant cattle across Esk was in process, a Council was hurriedly held at Kirkandrews, resulting in the decision to send Moray, and Ramsay with him, directly to Berwick-on-Tweed, to inform Seton of the dangers; and then on to Dunbar itself, to assist Black Agnes. They would have to avoid the Warden's forces, in these circumstances, so would require to plan their approaches carefully, keeping away as far as possible from Teviotdale and Tweeddale.

Tired as he was, Ramsay was glad enough to leave the slow and wearisome convoying of cattle for swift riding and positive action. Detaching his fifty Dalwolsey men to add to Moray's two hundred, he said farewell to the Regent, Douglas and the others, and set off north by east, up Liddesdale.

Going this way, up the twenty-mile-long Liddesdale and over the high Note o' the Gate pass of Wauchope to Hobkirk, and so down Rule Water to the Jedburgh area, was around thirty-five rough miles, and halfway to Berwick. They covered that without difficulty before dark, their only delay a meeting-up with their late fellow-invaders, the Armstrongs, whom they came across at the Kershopefoot crossing of Liddel Water, driving an even larger drove of cattle from Gilsland than the main body had collected, and taking a more northerly course home. These evinced no embarrassment at the encounter.

In order to avoid any trouble with the Warden's forces, they decided to give Jedburgh itself a wide berth, so followed Rule Water down to its junction with Teviot at Menslaws, where they camped the night. Thereafter they crossed the greater river at that ford and proceeded eastwards by Ancrum and over the low Fairnington hills to the Makerstoun ford of

Tweed. This brought them into the Merse by the fairly empty country of Nenthorn and Stichill. This area Ramsay knew well. Into the Home territory beyond they had to go fairly warily, but less so than if they had been a weaker company, not because of fears that the Homes would betray them to Dunbar but in that they were always jealous of their declared rights to decide who should enter their country and what they should pay for the privilege; but two hundred and fifty well-armed men in tight formation carried their own safe-conduct, and they rode through without challenge. Still, they avoided the near vicinity of Home Castle, Purves, Blackadder, Paxton and other strongholds of the clan.

They eventually approached Berwick from the north-west, rounding the skirts of Halidon Hill, and from there able to look down on the grey town at the wide mouth of Tweed, two miles off. The castle towered high above the northern limits of the burgh, outside the massive walls. All looked peaceful, with the harbour busy with shipping, for this was the foremost port of Scotland.

They had no difficulty in gaining access to the castle, where Sir Alexander Seton greeted Ramsay warmly. They were friends and neighbours, Seton's lands in Lothian being near Dalwolsey. Ramsay had not seen him since that day at Musselburgh when the good Regent Moray died and Seton had been sent off to Fife to try to hamper Balliol's landing at Kinghorn, a gallant but unsuccessful endeavour in which Seton had been wounded.

Now he was much perturbed to hear of Dunbar's treachery. Like most others, he had never really trusted that Earl; but this throwing in his lot with the English, while still Scots Chief Warden of the Marches, was a dire betrayal by any standards, and most menacing for Berwick, since as Warden he had overall authority for the town and port, if not the castle.

The big question was, how much support was he likely to have, in the East March generally and in Berwick itself in particular? He was overlord of vast lands hereabouts, the only earl south-east of Forth, feudal superior over many lordships and baronies. Even though most of his vassals might disagree with his policies, it would demand brave men indeed actually to outface him. The Homes might well do so, but the lesser East Border clans, the Kerrs, Turnbulls, Olivers, Rutherfords, Cranstouns and the like were unlikely to feel

118

sufficiently strong to do so. As for Berwick itself, strongly-walled as it was, its inhabitants were merchants, traders, shipmen, artificers and so on, not soldiers, looking to the Warden to marshall and direct them. And they had suffered a great loss when John Crabb, their notable leader, had been captured by the English on his return from his ill-fated venture to the Tay and Perth in support of Mar. Seton, warned, would now of course do what he could to help the townsmen, but his actual authority was limited to this royal castle.

For his part, Seton was able to give his visitors some information. Edward of England had ordered an advance headquarters to be set up at Bamborough in Northumberland, with levies from all over the North of England to assemble there; he himself was expected to arrive there in late March or early April, to lead his assault on Scotland in person.

Next day they left Seton to his problems and set off northwards up the coast for Dunbar, thirty miles. They encountered no diffculties *en route*, although they had to traverse one of the most dangerous ambush points in all South Scotland, at Pease Dean, where the Lammermuirs came directly down to the coast in steep wooded slopes cut up by deep ravines, and round which travellers had to wend their narrow, devious way. However, there were no opposers there today. Necessarily strung out at no more than three abreast, the column threaded the mile or so cautiously, Ramsay for one, keen-eyed to note danger-spots and ambush possibilities for future reference. When Edward Plantagenet invaded, such knowledge might be valuable.

Only a mile on, they passed the last of the Home outposts, at Dunglass, in a strong position above another of these precipitous deans; and soon thereafter Dunbar came in sight, town and castle jutting into the Norse Sea, the eastern gateway to the fertile Lothians, red in blood to match the now prevailing redness in soil and stone. Those new to the area were always astonished at the vivid crimson of the earth and buildings. Closer at hand they were apt to be still more astonished at the castle they saw, for this was different from any other in the land. Instead of being built on a mound, natural or artificial, and surrounded by a moat, Dunbar's rose in lofty towers on a series of pointed rock-stacks which thrust out of the sea, these linked ingeniously by covered stone bridges. There was no need for a water-filled moat, although there was a drawbridge, for the nearest stack to land was separated therefrom by a deep tidal creek with beetling walls. Added to all this, to keep cannon, mangonels, battering-rams and other siege-engines at a safe distance from the first or gatehouse tower, an artificial trench had been excavated across the approach headland. A further refinement was that the entrance to the town's harbour was under the furthest-out of the bridges, so that entry and exit thereto could be denied at any time by the castle's occupants, with a great boom to be lowered.

This extraordinary stronghold, flying the banners of two earldoms, stretched out to sea, the waves boiling around the bases of its soaring stacks. Ramsay had seen it before, but had never been inside. They were halted at the outer guardhouse at the aforementioned trench, to identify themselves. Here they had to part with their horses, for of course there could be accommodation for only a few animals in this castle itself. Dismounted, the leaders crossed over the first and second drawbridges on foot, leaving their men to take the horses down a long ramp to barracks-quarters and stabling at harbour level.

In the main gatehouse tower on the first stack, Moray was asking of the guard-captain whether the Countess was at home when the door from the first of the bridge-corridors was flung open and a young woman came in at the run, hair blown, laughing-eyed, skirts kilted up the better to run, fine bosom tumultuous – as unusual a Countess of Dunbar and March as was the castle of which she was chatelaine.

"Johnnie! Johnnie!" she cried, "How good! How good! Where have you come from? Mariot said that you were gone to Annandale, bent on battle?"

She made a striking picture, dark, vivacious, impulsive, well built, with masses of black hair, not actually beautiful but very attractive, arresting of appearance indeed: Black Agnes of Dunbar, an unlikely wife for the strange, sour and introverted Earl Patrick.

Ramsay knew her by repute only and had been looking forward to seeing her in person. Nevertheless his reaction now was less than might have been expected, for he was an impressionable man where women were concerned. This because, behind the Countess, another young woman had appeared, the Lady Mariot Randolph, her sister. Unexpected, this affected him strongly, indeed left him for the moment in a strange turmoil emotionally. He had been tending, of late, to think a lot about this girl, not always in the most correct of contexts, as lusty young men will. Now he stared at her in a mixture of surprise, guilt, appreciation and gladness.

He found himself being introduced to Agnes, and managed to withdraw his gaze from one sister to the other and to make some rather incoherent answers to the Countess's greetings. These were sufficiently warm and outspoken, even flattering, for apparently she had heard much of Sir Alexander Ramsay and, by the sound of her, to his credit. He sought to respond suitably.

Mariot came to kiss her brother, then turned to Ramsay. "We meet again, Sir Alexander," she said. "An unexpected pleasure. I well recollect that night at Doune."

"Yes," he agreed, inadequately. Then he realised that, after kissing her hand he was still holding it. He dropped it hurriedly. "I do also, lady."

They eyed each other, with nothing else to say meantime.

"How came you here, Mariot?" Moray asked. "When I left you at Doune there was no word of this."

"Why, after your call to arms in Annandale and the news about, about Patrick, I felt that Agnes might be glad of company here . . ."

"And I am," her sister declared strongly. "I need all the help and support that I can get in this latest folly. And so the happier to see you, Johnnie. And Sir Alexander. I despair for Patrick. I can do with some men to advise me – and you are a man now, Johnnie, I see!" And she gave her young brother a hug.

Embarrassed, he turned to Ramsay. "I think that *Agnes* was always the man of our family! I mean . . ." He grinned. "You know what I mean. She always took the lead, played the master . . ."

A playful but quite vigorous slap on the ear was his reward for that. "I'll thank you to watch your words, my new lord of Moray!" she exclaimed.

Mariot smiled. "It does not take these two long to trade endearments!" she informed Ramsay. "Thomas was different. Poor Thomas!"

121

For a moment or two there was silence, as they considered the brother so recently slain, and no doubt the beloved father who had died.

"Yes," Ramsay said again.

He found himself considering how different were these two sisters, Agnes vehement, voluble, exclamatory; Mariot quiet, with a sort of serenity to her, but warm somehow he felt – where the other might be hot.

Changing the subject, Black Agnes announced that the men must be hungry, if not tired, and led the way over the next bridge-corridor, through the vaulted basement of a second tower and over yet another bridge to the main keep of the castle. There, in an upper hall a great log fire blazed and all was comfort and warmth, with attractive furnishings, colourful wall-hangings and tapestries, cushioned benches, skin rugs on the floor and the feminine touch everywhere evident. All this in such dramatic contrast to the scene outside, for the windows showed only white-capped seas, spray and blown spume and wheeling, screaming gulls. It was like being on a ship, but a steady, secure and snugly protective ship.

While servitors were bringing food and wine, the visitors accounted for themselves, where they had come from and what had transpired, the situation at Berwick and over on the West March. Themselves, they learned the Countess's attitudes and intentions regarding Dunbar Castle.

"Patrick may intend to deliver this house to English Edward," she told them. "But *I* do not!"

"Can you prevent it?" her brother asked.

"I believe that I can. I must at least *try*. It is a strong place, and will be stronger. Patrick has given orders for it to be strengthened further, at Edward's expense. So be it – but not for England. Against!"

"You mean . . . ?"

"I mean, Johnnie, that defences are defences. Against whomsoever. Even he who may be paying for them! It is unlikely that Patrick will come here and wait for the Plantagenet. He will join him before then, before Berwick probably, with his men. And when they both come to Dunbar, chapping on this door, they will find it locked and barred. I am my father's daughter enough for that!"

They stared at her, wondering.

"Agnes has it all planned," Mariot said. "She will aid in this strengthening and building, which the English desire, encourage it indeed. Then fill the place with our own folk. And when King Edward comes, defy him. *And* her husband."

Moray hooted delighted laughter.

Ramsay was less amused. "You are brave, lady. Gallant. To be congratulated on your spirit. But, have you sufficiently considered? Edward will be at the head of a great army, thousands of men. He may not bring siege-engines when first he comes, balista and cannon. But he can get them. He will need them, if he tries to capture Berwick. This Dunbar is a most notable stronghold. But against the might of England . . ."

"That is why we must strengthen it, in every way possible."

"Even so. Cannon-fire. Great rocks, thrown by mangonels. And not only from the land. Edward has his fleets of warships. Strong as this is from the land, it could be battered from the sea."

"Then we must strengthen our defences seaward also, Sir Alexander."

Hating to resemble a wet blanket he held his peace. But his expression was eloquent enough.

"You do not think it possible?" Mariot asked.

"I do not say that. But . . . perhaps you do not know – how could you? – what cannon and mangonels can do to even the stoutest walling. I fear . . ."

"Then if *you* do, you can show me what must be done. If King Edward thinks that Dunbar is worth the strengthening, presumably to withstand assault, then he must have reason. It must be possible."

Against such feminine logic Ramsay could make no adequate response. He switched to asking what extra works Earl Patrick was planning. It appeared that these were mainly concerned with strengthening the outer landward defences, in especial the far guardhouse building, the approach from the harbour area, and the excavation of an extra moat or ditch, work due to start any day now.

This led to some discussion on the Earl's attitudes and behaviour. Agnes was very frank. She said that admittedly he was a strange man, always had been, difficult and unapproachable. But it would be a mistake to think of him merely as an errant traitor. He looked on the national position, and his own part therein, differently from others, his blood and background accounting for that. He did not look on the house of Bruce as the true monarchy for the realm. *His* line, directly descended from Bethoc, daughter of Malcolm the Second, in legitimate succession – whereas Malcolm the Third, Canmore, was illegitimate, by the miller of Forteviot's daughter – was the true representer of the ancient Celtic royal house, and the succession belonged to him, he claimed. His grandfather had been one of the Competitors for the Throne; but Edward the First had chosen John Balliol, as sufficiently weak to accept him as overlord. So Patrick had no use for Edward Balliol; but, by aiding Edward the Third, almost certainly saw himself as in a position to displace the unsuccessful Balliol and himself take over as King of Scots, with English support. He might well have made some bargain with the Plantagenet – after all, this Edward owed something, for it was here, to Dunbar Castle, that his father, Edward the Second, had fled for refuge after the disaster of Bannockburn when Patrick, as a young man, had received him kindly and provided him passage by sea to England. Once on the Scots throne, whether he would be content to remain a vassal of England, as was Balliol, was another matter; his wife thought probably not, for whatever else he was, Patrick was no man's puppet. He might even make a strong and able king, for he had his virtues, even though being a good husband was scarcely one of them!

If this frankness made Ramsay a little uncomfortable, it did not seem to disturb the others. Indeed it drew from Moray the comment that this was the one matter that he had against their father: that he had married off his elder daughter, as a mere girl, to a man more than twice her age, as a matter of policy, to endeavour to attach Dunbar more firmly to the national cause, unsuccessful as this had been. Although Mariot nodded, Agnes, shrugging, turned the matter by asking if this was not what earls' daughters were for? Wait until Johnnie had a daughter of his own! Of course, my lord Moray already had an unmarried sister . . . !

It was at this stage that there was an interruption, a quite noisy one as the Master of Dunbar put in a shouting appearance, three-year-old George, Agnes's son, his nurse in full cry behind him, a couple of deer-hounds also in attendance. For some time thereafter matters of defence, policy and filial duties were in abeyance.

Later, with the shutters closed against the night, the four of them sat within the ingoing of the great fireplace of the hall, on two cushioned benches on either side of the glowing, hissing log fire. It was delightfully snug and companionable there in the firelight, with the roar of the seas outside muted, all draughts excluded, sufficiently warm without being too hot; for the fireplace was no less than twelve feet wide, its lintel a massive slab of stone more than that in length, reputedly taken from a Pictish stone circle, so that the ingle was like a little open room of its own in the thickness of the walling. But although there was ample room lengthways for sitters to draw back from the blaze sufficiently for comfort, there was less space broadways-on, so that the pairs had to sit fairly close together – which suited Alexander Ramsay very well, for he shared a bench with Mariot. Inevitably this proximity involved a fair amount of touching and occasional pressures, which the man found very much to his taste, and which the young woman at least did not object to sufficiently to draw away to the limits of her corner. Separated from the other two by the fire, a pleasant intimacy was engendered, so that each couple tended to intersperse the general conversation with their own. Noting this, Black Agnes smilingly warned the pair opposite.

"Be careful what you murmur in each other's ears, you two," she advised. "If you look up behind you, Mariot, in the corner, you will perhaps discover a small hole in the stonework. That is the laird's lug! From it a pipe of sorts, a speaking tube, leads up to the room above, which is the Earl's private chamber. Where it opens in *his* fireplace. So sitting there he can hear all that is being said down here; a notable convenience on occasion, I am told! We do not have any such refinements at Doune, I fear!"

"Fear not," Mariot told her companion. "There is nobody up there tonight at least!"

Which was a comforting comment from her, he ventured to assess.

When, in time, Mariot announced that she would now seek her couch, and the men rose to stoop their way out of the ingle-neuk, Agnes remained sitting.

"Mariot will show you to your chamber, Sir Alexander,"

she said kindly. "I have something to discuss with Johnnie. Sleep well."

Mariot raised an eyebrow at her sister, but after good-nights, led the way out.

"Agnes, as Johnnie said, was always the masterful one," she murmured, as they climbed the two flights of the torchlit turnpike stair.

On the third floor, she led him to one of four doors, which opened on to a firelit bedroom, with a great canopied bed, steaming water-jugs and wash-basin, and a garderobe in the thickness of the walling with candle-shelf, stone seat and chute. The sigh of the waves sounding up that chute only emphasised the genial security of the chamber.

"I think that you will be comfortable here, Sir Alexander," Mariot said. "This is a well-run house, despite its position and its curious lord. Better than I run Doune, I am afraid."

"I was very well treated at Doune," he asserted. "But, as I recollect it, I – or rather we – escorted *you* to your room that night, not you to ours. The man's privilege, surely? And, and my friends call me Sandy. Will not you?"

"If you so wish, yes. Very well – but my room is this next door to yours, so you have no need to fare far. A good night to you, Sandy. May you sleep soundly, despite the sea noises."

"Yes. I thank you. And you, Mariot." He took the two or three steps with her to the other doorway. "I shall lie the more pleasantly for . . . for thinking of you . . . but through the wall!"

"Let not that thought keep you from your well-earned sleep," she advised.

He reached for her hand, to kiss it, as she opened her door.

It took him some time to sleep.

Next day, inevitably, the talk was again on the matter of strengthening defences, with Ramsay, experienced in soldiering, being asked for advice. After going out to inspect the works already projected, he could only suggest a still further-out ditch to be dug, in the rock, for the greater distancing of cannon and balista. Also he pointed out that the portions of the castle most liable to be hit by missiles, especially the parapets and roofs, could be thickened in the masonry, and reinforced to good effect. But it was the possibility of attack from ships which concerned him most;

and he proposed that he and Moray make a survey, by boat, to consider what, if anything, might be done protectively.

Early March was scarcely the time of year for pleasure-sailing, but the young women insisted on going along; and wrapping up warmly, they went down to the harbour and found fishermen to row them out in one of their high-prowed cobles.

The sea was choppy, and sitting still in the stern of the boat less than comfortable. But at least the conditions made clear the hazards for shipping approaching this coast, the innumerable rocks and reefs and skerries over which the rollers spouted and boiled, many just below the surface, and the greater danger therefore. The entrance to the harbour was by a clear channel for the last two hundred yards or so, unmarked but familiar to the fisherfolk, the rest a widespread menace.

This, of course, did simplify the problem of defence, since warships could approach only by that channel, with little room to manoeuvre. But the channel was wide enough and deep enough to allow quite large vessels to come very close to the castle-stacks, certainly well within range of their cannon and mangonels.

"Booms," Ramsay announced. "Booms of timber, held in place by chains. Slung across this channel, anchored to the rocks and stacks. A succession of booms. Cannon have a range of no more than two hundred yards, to be effective. So booms that will keep shipping beyond that. Mangonels throw their stones further, but not greatly."

"But, that would close the harbour to fishing boats also," Agnes objected. "Fishing is the people's living."

"Hang the booms so that their chains can be hitched and unhitched. Or, better, have them weighted down under the surface, so that even at low tide these shallow boats can pass over them, but deep-draught ships can not. Have your Dunbar smiths forge great chains. Your men cut heavy baulks of timber: oak, elm, beech. Have stones bound to these, to weigh them down. And . . . do not tell the Earl Patrick!"

The Countess clapped her gloved hands. "You are a wonder, Sir Alexander! Bless *you*, Johnnie, for bringing him!"

"Sandy is a knight who does not fail to rise to the occasion," Mariot observed.

"Sandy, is it! We progress! We poor women must be looking to *our* defences, I swear! How say you, Johnnie?"

Moray did his best. "I think that the boot may be on the other leg!"

After prospecting the places to put the booms across, dictated by the situations of suitable anchoring rocks, they returned to the castle. Ramsay was interested to note, in the passing, how as a couple of boats entered the harbour ahead of them from the fishing, under the bridge between the two outermost towers, they each provided a basket of new-caught fish to be hoisted up on ropes to men on the bridge, this seemingly how they paid their rents and harbour dues to their lord.

That evening, in the hall, Mariot entertained them with songs, accompanied by the harp, to their enjoyment; although Ramsay qualified his rapture by some regret that, there being insufficient room in their ingle-neuk for playing the harp, she had to perform outside it, and he was deprived of the nearness which he found so much to his taste. However, singing over, and Agnes bringing wine to sip, he got his companion back alongside for a little, before the bedward move was made. At that, again, Moray and his sister waited behind.

This time, at the bedroom doors, the man waxed a little more bold when Mariot wished him a good night's sleep.

"You are not the one apt for wishing me that, Mariot," he told her. "Last night, I remained awake for long, thinking of you. So near. Tonight, I am the more . . . engaged."

"Do I disturb you so?" she wondered. "You, a man of much experience, I am sure."

"Experience of some matters, perhaps – of fighting and warfare, of joustings and councils and the like. Not of women."

"No? Do not tell me that Sir Alexander Ramsay of Dalwolsey, renowned in the ranks of chivalry, has been deprived of all dealings with the female kind? That I cannot believe. You, who are not unattractive to women, I judge."

"To you, Mariot?"

She raised a cautionary hand. "Say that I recognise certain . . . felicities, sir!"

"Felicities? What mean you by that?"

"Why, but the opposite of failings, shall we say? You do

not strike me as ugly, nor mis-shapen, nor lacking manners. Given time, I might even think of more felicities, Sandy!"

"Time? How long a time?"

"Ah, now! Is impatience one of your infelicities, sirrah?"

"I think that it must be, Mariot Randolph. Where you are concerned."

"Then I must beware, must I not? I am warned. A good night to you." But she smiled.

That smile did it. Impulsively he reached out, to take her in his arms and draw her close. She did not resist, even when urgently he kissed her hair, her brow, her lips.

Then she stirred, sighing, and gently pushed him back. "As well . . . that *you* do not assault . . . this citadel!" she got out, a little breathlessly. "You storm to . . . some effect!"

Still holding her arms he searched her flushed features, wondering, wondering. He found no words.

"Again, goodnight," she said firmly, but still gently. Freeing herself, she entered her doorway. "Man of action!"

He spread his hands. "The motto of my house is *Ora et Labora* – Pray and Work!" he said.

"Then now try you prayer, Sandy Ramsay!" she returned, and quietly closed the door on him.

There are prayers and prayers, admittedly. That night the man did not altogether fail his fine motto. His orisons, however, tended to be interrupted by a recurring question. Had Mariot's lips moved under his when he kissed her? Or was that the wish fathering the thought? Again and again he tried to recreate that moment.

He slept even less that night than the previous one. Time, she had said, given time . . .

Unfortunately time was not what Ramsay was given, in that context. For the next forenoon a messenger arrived, sent by Seton at Berwick, with dire news. It was disaster in the West. The Regent's force had been all but annihilated. They had been caught up with at Dornock, east of Annan, on the shore of the Solway, by a fast-riding English host under Sir Anthony de Lucy of Cockermouth, who had crossed the shallow firth at lowest tide by the temporarily dried-out Knockeross sands, from Bowness in Cumberland. The Scots had been entirely unprepared for this, thus far into their own country, and were engaged in herding the great herd of Gilsland cattle across the Dornock Water's estuary, some one side of the river, some the other. It had been utter surprise and defeat, casualties grievous. The Regent himself had escaped but his nephew was captured, and the slain included Sir Humphrey Jardine, Sir William Carlisle, Sir Humphrey Bowes and innumerable others.

Appalled, Ramsay and Moray heard it all.

The courier had orders for them to repair at once to Edinburgh, where the Regent was to summon an urgent Council. So pleasant dalliance in the cause of defence strategy was to end. Unhappily the men were sent for from their temporary quarters in the town, and goodbyes were said at the castle. Ramsay certainly obtained a kiss and a hug from Mariot in farewell, but in front of the others it was not of the sort to analyse carefully; indeed he got a similar embrace from Black Agnes.

They rode off north-westwards without delay, worried men. Whither Scotland now? Will Douglas a prisoner. Who to lead, with only his amiable uncle as Regent?

6

The hurried Council in Edinburgh Castle did not, could not, solve many problems – and certainly did not produce any obvious new leadership. For one thing, there had not been time for the more remotely-seated lords to arrive, if indeed many of them heeded the summons; and the Balliol supporters, of course, remained absent. In the event, Ramsay himself made the most useful contributions to the debate, with the young Steward and Moray backing him, the Regent out of his depth and almost pathetically grateful for any guidance he could get. But there were earls present, Strathearn, Lennox and Ross, who were conditioned not to take over-kindly to too much prominence for a mere knight, even one of so illustrious a line as Dalwolsey. And it was the earls who could produce the great and so necessary man-power.

Ramsay's contention was that, despite the recent emphasis

on the South-West, Annandale, Carlisle and the rest, the key hereafter would be on the East March, particularly Berwick-on-Tweed. Edward Plantagenet was massing his forces at Bamborough, sixteen miles south of Berwick, not at Carlisle. Sir Alexander Seton believed that was where the main English assault would come – indeed Edward had said as much. He had ordered the strengthening of Dunbar Castle, thirty miles north of Berwick; why, if not because he intended to use it as his base against Lothian and this Edinburgh?

The Earl Patrick of Dunbar had now openly thrown in his lot with the English, and as Chief Warden of the Marches, was also in theory master of Berwick. Everything pointed to an eastern attack.

There was little disagreement with that. What to do about it was the problem.

There were the inevitable assertions that they must raise a great army to defeat the insufferable Edward should he dare set foot on Scottish soil, this earl promising his thousands and the next outdoing him. But specific strategies were sadly amissing, for few there were experienced soldiers, used enough to inter-clan battle and feud but not to full-scale national warfare against the English might, as their fathers had learned to be.

Sir Simon Fraser, one of the few veterans, made the first practical proposal. Dunbar should be replaced forthwith as Chief Warden, a suggestion which met with no opposition. It was left to Ramsay however to point out that Dunbar was not likely to tamely accept such demotion, and the attitude of his forces was uncertain, to say the least. His own men would support him, of course; the others, Border mosstroopers in the main, might or might not. But any new Warden might well have difficulty in taking over.

Fraser said that the new Warden then must be sent south well supplied with sufficient men to convince Dunbar's people.

Ramsay agreed, but suggested a refinement. If Dunbar could be lulled first into a false sense of security, it might all go more satisfactorily. The main issue was the defence of Berwick town and port, without which King Edward could not risk a major advance into Scotland by land. Transfer Sir Alexander Seton, whom they could trust, from being Keeper of the royal castle of Berwick to being Governor of Berwick town. So that Dunbar would be in no position to hand it over to the enemy. And appoint Dunbar himself in Seton's place, to the castle-keepership. Shut up therein, he would be detached from his Warden's forces and unable gravely to endanger the town, for the castle was outside the strong walls. Then appoint a deputy to take over the command of the Warden's duties and forces – possibly Sir Simon himself. Would not that help to solve some of the problems?

Even the earls present hailed this as an excellent plan, and Fraser was there and then appointed Deputy Warden of the Marches.

In the heady talk thereafter, Ramsay for one was very much aware of the lack of any particular tactics being put forward; all was generalities, and high-flown ones at that, almost as though the battle was already won. Presently he felt bound to pour some cold water on all this optimism.

"Suppose Edward does gain Berwick, my lords, and advances northwards – what then? or even decides to leave the town untaken behind him, but surrounded, as he might?"

That was met by stares, almost glares, as though he had voiced the unthinkable. What did he think the Scots army would be doing meantime? Standing by, idle? They would attack the attackers. Cross over into England and assail Edward from the rear. Blockade the port. Starve the English host.

He nodded. "But still, Edward may advance. He can field a much greater army than we can. I think that we shall not beat him in set battle; the Bruce taught us that, surely . . ."

"Bannockburn, man! Bannockburn," he was interrupted.

"King Robert, my lords, never wanted to fight at Bannockburn. Only his rash brother, the Lord Edward, forced him to it," and he glanced over at the Earl of Carrick, the said Lord Edward Bruce's second son, who had now deemed it judicious to desert the Balliol cause. "Bruce ever used the land to fight for him. I say that we should do the same, if need be."

"Yes, yes, Sir Alexander," the Regent said. "But how? At Berwick?"

"Not at Berwick, no. I see little choice there, other than stout walls and stouter hearts. But, if Edward moves north, there is hope. On the march. There is the close country just north of Coldinghame Muir, at Pease Dean and Bilsdean, between Berwick and Dunbar. There a host must string out. And there is no avoiding it. There a hidden few could hold up thousands. Then cut them up into gobbets, isolate the leaders . . . "

"Very well. We shall remember that, my friend. But hope that it may not be necessary, that Edward will never get so far. Now, my lords, as to numbers. You, my lord of Ross, how many can you raise? And how soon get them here from your northern lands . . . ?"

The remainder of the Council was concerned with such matters.

Ramsay went off to try to recruit more men in his part of Lothian.

He was soon recalled to Edinburgh. The Regent desired him, as proposer of the scheme, and as having already served with the Earl of Dunbar, to accompany Sir Simon Fraser down to the Earl's camp near Berwick, there to help that man inform Dunbar of the decisions made and to assist in convincing him to take over the keepership of Berwick Castle. Ramsay was less than delighted with the task, but consoled himself with the thought that at least the journey south would take them by Dunbar Castle again, and a call thereat would be possible.

Unfortunately Dunbar was nothing like a full day's ride from Dalwolsey, barely twenty miles, and by fair roads; and Fraser, a grizzled veteran, was scarcely the man to try to involve in an unnecessary overnight stop in the interests of romance, however chivalric. But at least a call could be justified, as advisable to inform the Countess of the situation vis-à-vis her husband.

So, much sooner than he could have hoped, Ramsay came seeking admission at the castle guardhouse once more, glad to see work already in progress on excavating the new outer ditch, and masons busy on reinforcing the parapets and towers, Agnes herself superintending. Their welcome was warm, even without the Earl Johnnie, Mariot's quieter than her sister's but no less kindly. In front of Fraser, Ramsay himself had to be more restrained than he would have wished, but at least Agnes's cheerful kisses allowed him to bestow a like greeting on her sister, Fraser looking on somewhat askance.

Over a hasty but adequate meal, the situation and plans

were discussed, Black Agnes approving heartily, almost gleefully, indeed going so far as to add an improvement of her own. Knowing her husband, if he could be led to believe that the royal castle of Berwick might be alienated from the crown and actually *given* to him for his services, he would be the more apt to accede to the arrangement, being a man of acquisitive mind. Mariot capped this by suggesting that, since the Earl Patrick would presumably intend to yield that castle should Berwick town fall to King Edward, he could expect a greater reward from that monarch if the castle was nominally his own, not just a crown possession. Ramsay asked Fraser if he thought that they could risk assuming the Regent's agreement to this, and grinning, that man averred that Sir Archie Douglas would agree to anything that spared him trouble.

When they presently rode away from Dunbar Castle, Fraser's attitude towards female participation in affairs had risen noticeably. A parting invitation from the Countess that, when he had finished his business at Berwick, Sandy Ramsay might come back and help supervise the sinking of the proposed booms in the sea, the timber for which was already being felled, was cordially supported by Mariot.

They had learned that the Earl Patrick had his base meantime at Holywell Haugh near Horndean, eight miles west of Berwick, a convenient location to encamp a standing force and to dominate the East March and the main ford of Tweed thereabouts, opposite Norham. It was here that, at the Competition for the Crown forty-two years before, Edward the First of England had met the Scots magnates and set in motion the actions which ultimately led to the Wars of Independence. Thither the emissaries now rode, through the Merse, another thirty or so miles.

It would not be true to say that they were well received at Holywell Haugh that evening. For not only was the Earl Patrick suspicious of anyone coming from the regency, but he happened at this juncture to be consoling himself with a local lady, in the absence of marital comforts. They did not in fact achieve an interview that night. They had time to assess the composition and probable loyalties of the force gathered there in the riverside haugh next morning, before the Earl Patrick would see them. It was very much a composite host, consisting of the Earl's own feudal manpower, the levies required by the crown, for the support of the Warden, from Border lairds, and bands of assorted mosstroopers belonging to various clans who found it profitable and expedient to ally themselves with the most powerful figure in South-East Scotland, the assembly at Holywell Haugh amounting to about three thousand. How many of these would actually and actively support an English attack on Scotland because Dunbar did, was the question. His own men would, of course; but the others were more doubtful. Some might well be Balliol supporters and go along with the Earl for that reason. Ramsay and Fraser reckoned that perhaps one-third might desert Dunbar when it came to the crunch. But if the Earl was detached from them, in Berwick Castle, and Fraser took over the Warden's duties here, then the proportion would probably increase.

When eventually they saw Dunbar, he was hardly forthcoming, being especially suspicious of Ramsay, whom he had heard had been visiting Dunbar Castle, and wanting to know why. Ramsay explained that his lordship's goodbrother, the Earl of Moray, had desired to see his sister the Countess whilst in the vicinity, as was but natural; and while there, they had learned that the defences of the castle were being strengthened, in view of possible attack by the English, and they had offered such small help as they could in this excellent work in the realm's interest. That was all.

Dunbar could scarcely take exception to that, and changed the subject. What did they want with him now?

Fraser and Ramsay had agreed that, since it was all the latter's idea and the former was a man of action rather than words, Ramsay should do most of the talking.

"My lord," he said, "the Regent, in this present coil, with English invasion threatening, has a task for you. An important task, in the realm's defence. None could do it better than you, and . . ."

"Task, sirrah!" the Earl interrupted. "What task may the Douglas ask of me, Dunbar and March? What task *dare* he ask?"

"Since he speaks in the name of the King's Grace, my lord, he can *command*. But you he *asks*. He desires that you take over the keepership of the royal castle of Berwick."

Dunbar stared.

"None can know better than your lordship the importance

of Berwick Castle," Ramsay went on. "Sir Alexander Seton is an excellent knight, but it is felt that a greater figure in the kingdom should hold this royal stronghold, in the King's name. Who better than one of the foremost earls of Scotland, at the very gateway to his own territories of the Merse and Lothian?"

"Perhaps so, Ramsay. But I have other responsibilities. I am Chief Warden of all the Marches."

"To be sure. But as such when you have to face King Edward's assault, it would be with an armed host, offering battle. Your potent force spurring you on." Ramsay picked his words with care, for he had rehearsed this more than once. "It would be clash and strife. Whereas, from Berwick Castle you could *speak* to Edward. Send an emissary, or yourself approach him under a flag of truce. Parley. Delay. Offer terms. Act the ambassador rather than the captain of cavalry. Which lesser men can do."

"So! Here we have it! Has the Douglas aught for me to offer Edward?"

"Yes." Ramsay was more careful still. "Edward, we are informed, tires of the man Balliol, who has failed him. Offer a treaty, if he will disclaim Balliol and his pretensions to the Scots throne. Offer peace and friendship, all outstanding issues to be discussed . . ."

"What is there in this for Edward Plantagenet?"

That was the nub of it, of course. "No great deal, perhaps, my lord, save to spare him a costly war. And to retain his own sister's position as Scotland's Queen, which Balliol dismisses. And he could gain much at a peace conference, without having to fight for it. For ourselves, it could do much also. Give us time. And get rid of the usurper." That was the essence of it, Dunbar's known contempt and resentment for Balliol.

"In Berwick Castle you would hold the key to much," Fraser put in. "And I would act your Deputy Warden here."

The Earl looked from one to the other, stroking his chin, weighing, assessing. They had baited their trap shrewdly. "When?" he demanded.

Ramsay could scarcely disguise his sigh of relief. "So soon as may be, my lord. Who knows when Edward may march?"

"And Seton?"

"He will move out. Down to Berwick town, where he will serve meantime as governor."

"And Berwick Castle could be yours, thereafter," Fraser added, for good measure, to clinch matters.

Ramsay had hoped not to have to bring this forward if it could be avoided. But now the thing was out and he had to make the best of it.

"Berwick is a royal castle," he said. "A crown possession. But, if this notable service is rendered by your lordship, it could be recommended that the Earls of Dunbar and March could be made hereditary Keepers. Or even that it could be transferred to your ownership." And heaven forgive him that invention!

The other licked his thin lips. "I will consider the matter," he said, and rose.

They retired, hopefully, but Ramsay slightly apprehensive over what they had done.

That evening at supper Dunbar came to them and abruptly, without preamble, announced that he would take over the keepership of Berwick Castle forthwith. Let them see that Seton was ejected. It was as simple as that.

Next morning, with no sign of the Earl, they rode on to Berwick.

Sir Alexander Seton was not in the least upset about being transferred down to the town. He had never asked to be Keeper of the castle in the first place, and being a man actively inclined, now that his wound from the Kinghorn affray was healed, found the confines of the castle irksome. The town and port would offer him much more scope, its preparation for defence, the training of its citizenry for siege conditions, its provisioning and the control of its shipping. He was confident that he, in the town, could resist any efforts of Dunbar in the castle to prevail against them – that is, providing the castle's cannon and mangonels were removed first and transferred to the town's walls and bastions, particularly to the port area. This was agreed, although Ramsay suggested that one or two of the smaller pieces should be left, to allay any suspicions of Dunbar. The Earl would no doubt be bringing his own personal troops with him, so Seton could take most of the present garrison down with him.

That man did not delay. The very next day the business was

commenced, the artillery being the first to be moved, Ramsay and Fraser helping to superintend. The townsfolk of Berwick were agog, and not a little apprehensive.

Three days later, on a fine April morning, Sir Simon Fraser rode off back to Holywell Haugh, to take over the Warden's duties, as Deputy.

Ramsay remained in Berwick, in the Governor's House, meantime, reluctant to leave until he saw Dunbar duly installed in the castle. He was much impressed by the strength, circumstance and indeed amenities of Scotland's foremost port. Edward the First had sacked the town in 1296, as an example to the rest of the country of what to expect if his take-over was opposed; but thereafter that megalomaniac prince had found it useful as a staging-point for his occupation of the northern kingdom. So he had not destroyed most of the buildings, along with their inhabitants, had even erected more and improved the walls and defences. Moreover, after Bannockburn, Bruce had actively encouraged the recovery of his war-shattered country by inviting Low Country merchants, wool-brokers, shippers and the like, Flemings in particular, to settle here; and they had brought much wealth and trade to the town, many having built fine houses as well as their mills, maltings, breweries and warehouses, John Crabb one of these. With a population of almost a score of thousands, the place was a notable monument to the values of industry and initiative.

Seton wasted no time in setting his men, and many of the citizens, to work of another kind, particularly digging new ditches to keep artillery at a distance. The port and town occupied an already strong position on the north side of the Tweed where it entered the sea, thus protected on two sides by water. Any land attack had to be from the west and north, entailing a prior crossing of Tweed, here quite wide. The area to be ditched therefore was comparatively limited, and part overlooked by the castle.

Three days after Fraser's departure a large new flag bearing the arms of Dunbar and March, a white lion on red, flew from the castle's topmost tower, indicative that the Earl had arrived. Indeed he further signalled his presence by sending down a messenger to order Seton to appear before him and inform what he was doing in Berwick town. This arrogant summons Seton ignored, for as acting Governor of Berwick he was in no way subordinate to the castle's Keeper, and held his appointment directly from the Regent. But Ramsay, concerned at this display of Dunbar's attitude, decided that he ought to stay on a little longer at Berwick, in Seton's support.

Very quickly, however, such preoccupations were swallowed up in vastly greater ones. Information arrived from deep in Northumberland that King Edward was already on the move northwards, earlier than anticipated, having left Newcastle the day before at the head of a great army estimated at sixty thousand, well equipped with cannon and siege-engines. This would inevitably be slow-moving, but it was only seventy miles from Berwick, so that they must expect him before the town within the week. He had left his young Queen at Bamborough apparently.

This news set Berwick in a stir of even greater activity, especially when, that same afternoon, a fleet of ships appeared off the mouth of Tweed, coming from the south, and turned in towards the port.

Seton and Ramsay hurried down to the outer walls and bastions above the harbour wharves and quays, where most of the castle cannon had been positioned, ordering the garrison troops to man the guns. It was all a very sudden call to action.

There were ten ships bearing down on Berwick. There were more than that number tied up in the harbour, although most of these were smaller, and all traders.

"Should these not get out, before the English bottle them up?" Ramsay asked. "The enemy will be stronger, but these could at least harry their flanks. Like light cavalry."

"I think not – even if we had time," Seton said. "The English will have larger cannon than these merchanters carry, and could sink them before they could get within range. But *we*, I think, have heavier pieces here than they can have on the enemy ships. These from the castle will be more powerful, with longer range than any that can be carried on shipboard. So, we let them come into the harbour approaches, the narrowing river-mouth, where they must bunch and slow to avoid running aground on the sand-bars, then pound them from here while still they cannot reach us effectively. Our shipping out there would but distract and scatter them."

"What difference in range? I know little of cannon."

"No great difference, but sufficient, I think. And pray! Ours, two hundred to two hundred and fifty yards; theirs, one fifty yards, no more. Or so I hope. Also, we shoot heavier balls, which is almost as important."

So they waited, cannon primed, crews eager, leaders anxious.

Seton's forecast proved accurate in the first part, at least. The approaching fleet, now seen to be wearing banners showing the Leopards of England, did slow down and bunch together as they approached the harbour entrance, to negotiate the fairly narrow channel. Their cannon were very evident, as they closed, crews lining the bulwarks.

Still Seton waited, calculating distance, gunners impatient at their dozen cannon, touch-ropes steeped in saltpetre smoking, fizzing, ready.

As it happened, it was the enemy who opened fire first, the leading ship suddenly letting off a ragged salvo from its starboard guns, in flame and smoke, as demonstration and warning presumably. Instinctively all on the walls and ramparts ducked, even Seton, who then cursed himself for a fool. However, although one or two balls did reach the land and even struck masonry, these were spent shot and did no real damage, the rest throwing up spouts of water harmlessly.

Nodding, Seton gave the awaited signal to fire.

Ramsay, even then, was scarcely ready for the deafening noise and percussion as the Scots artillery opened up, shaking the very walls, battering the senses and enveloping all in clouds of choking smoke. Ears ringing, he recovered himself and turned to peer through the reek.

When it cleared sufficiently to see, it was to reveal a dire sight. The gunners had been ordered to aim at the first two vessels, and at a bare two hundred yards' range they could scarcely miss. Some cannon-balls may have gone through between the masts, but clearly most had not. Masts, sails and cordage were down in tangled confusion, the proud ships suddenly mere lumbering hulks of wreckage emitting the screams of injured men. Some shots undoubtedly had hit the hulls also, but the effect of these was not so evident to the onlookers.

"Aim lower!" Seton shouted. "The same two ships. The water-line. And quickly! Fire on, fast as you can . . ."

Now the remainder of the English ships were opening fire; but these, behind, were still further out of range, and bunched as they were, some obstructed others. Their cannonade, although impressive, was quite ineffective.

Individually now and in no order, depending on how swiftly crews could reload, prime and fire, the Scots gunners worked their pieces, aiming lower, those two leading vessels taking terrible punishment. Utterly out of control now, these could not even fire back, for their port-side cannon could not be brought to bear. Sails and rigging trailing over the side, and bows noticeably down, the first ship swung broadside on to the current of the river, and into its flank the second crashed, both drifting towards the pole-marked shallows of the sand-banks.

"Now, the next two!" Seton commanded. "With God's help we shall block that channel!"

That was indeed what happened. In that narrow passage of navigable water, the clutter of ships had no room to manoeuvre. And with an east wind behind them they could not abruptly halt. Into the first two drifting hulks the next craft collided. And in the minutes which followed, this pattern was repeated. And all the while the Scots cannon thundered destruction.

It was the twin problems of overheating and running out of powder and ball which brought that one-sided battle to a close, to Seton's disgust. But by that time four of the enemy ships were wrecks, one was aground and two of the remainder sufficiently damaged to make it doubtful whether they would ever reach their home ports – which was most evidently the hope of the survivors, as they went through the difficult, desperate business of turning in the confined space and heading back out to sea.

Elated, the Scots leaders gave orders for boats and crews from the harbour to put out, to deal with the wrecked and stranded vessels and their people. There was no lack of volunteers for this duty.

This initial success heartened all at Berwick. So much so that a group of shipmasters and merchants came to Seton to suggest that a retaliatory gesture would be in order. Let them show the enemy that they were not the only ones who could attack by sea; and show also that the Scots could do it in less blundering fashion. A series of raids on northern English coasts and havens would be a salutary lesson, after this enemy defeat.

Seton and Ramsay were in favour, especially as this might well have a delaying effect on invasion moves.

So the next two days were spent in readying and arming a mixed squadron of available craft, merchanters all, but every one necessarily accustomed to using defensive artillery to protect themselves from the English pirates who infested the Norse Sea. John Crabb would have captained it all, had he not been captured; but other shipmen were eager to lead.

Just before they sailed, word reached Berwick from Sir Simon Fraser that Edward Balliol had crossed the Border in strength, in the Middle March, by the Note o' the Gate pass, and installed himself in his old base of Roxburgh Castle. Fraser would endeavour to contain him there.

Clearly this was a move in concert with the main English thrust. It would have the effect of largely preoccupying the Warden's forces, unfortunately.

That main thrust was not long in developing thereafter. Forward scouts came back to inform that the English might had reached Cheswick, a mere six miles to the south, and its vanguard would be before Berwick in a few hours.

Orders were issued for the cattle and geese to be driven in from the commons, the gates to be shut, the walls and bastions manned and all preparations for siege put into immediate operation. Ramsay was in two minds as to whether it was wise to allow himself to be bottled up in the town when his place arguably was with the Regent; but he decided that he might possibly play a more useful part here as Seton's assistant – and he ought to be able to escape by boat, at night, if necessary.

It was a strange experience to wait in that embattled and enclosed town, amongst the tense thousands.

In mid-afternoon the first glints of steel in the spring sunshine began to appear on the high ground of Scremerston Brae, and soon the long hill down to sea-level was covered in a vast tide of men and horses, armour gleaming, banners waving, under a faint haze of steam rising from thousands of beasts long ridden, muting the colours of plumed helmets, heraldic surcoats, painted shields and horse-trappings. On they came, ever more appearing over the crest of the ridge, the might of England on the move, the first major and full-scale invasion of Scotland since Bannockburn. Watching, even Seton was silent.

As the van drew nearer, the cluster of flags and pennons at the very front, under an enormous standard of the Leopards of Plantagenet, indicated the presence of King Edward the Third himself, although it was too far yet to identify individuals. The approaching host could not head directly for the town because of the suddenly-widening river-mouth, having to swing off somewhat to the left, westwards, to reach the Spittal or Town ford, the nearest crossing, whose natural shallows had been improved by an underwater causeway of stone slabs. But that causeway had had deep holes dug in it by the defenders these last days, and the intervening stretches strewn with caltrops, four-pronged iron spikes such as Bruce had used with such effect at Bannockburn, and which the many smiths of Berwick had been set to forging for the last weeks. That ford was going to make but a difficult crossing.

Quickly the English found it so, and considerable confusion developed there as the foremost horses stumbled and floundered and oncoming ranks piled up with the pressure of thousands behind. But this was a well-led and disciplined army, and blown trumpets and busy outriders soon restored order. The Spittal ford was abandoned and the van turned still further west. There were other fords.

The next one was the Castle ford, so named because it lay directly under the castle rock, although almost two hundred feet below. As they watched the enemy approach this, Seton and Ramsay nodded grimly. It was entirely within range of even the smaller cannon left in the castle, although depressing the muzzles sufficiently downwards would mean that only the far side of the ford would be bombardable. When the enemy front ranks reached there, and the first horsemen rode warily in to try this ford, no cannon-fire developed from above.

"As we thought!" Seton commented. "Dunbar shows his true colours!" The Castle ford was out of range of the town's artillery. The English host was able to cross unhindered, although it would take a long time to do so in its entirety.

Berwick was a slantwise town, sloping up northwards from the harbour area, its outer walls halfway up to the castle. But there was a quite large terraced space between, and it was up to this that the enemy van, with the Leopard standard, wound its way. It could never have reached there, and settled, of course, had the castle guns opened fire. Ditches old and new kept the new arrivals from too close an approach to the massive town walls, but, to be sure, this also applied in reverse; the enemy were just out of range of Berwick's cannon.

Nevertheless, Seton and his lieutenants, watching from the parapet of the main North Gate, decided that a warning salvo would do no harm, and show Edward that they were not all like the Earl of Dunbar. They had brought most of the pieces up from the harbour defences, not anticipating another seaborne assault meantime. These now crashed out a defiant discharge. Hostilities had commenced.

Although the balls fell harmlessly short, the enemy pressed back. The English artillery was not yet forward, being oxen-drawn and therefore the slowest-moving section of the army. So there was no response, save yells. That is, until a large white flag was hoisted and a party of resplendent heralds beneath it, these proceeding to pick their way heedfully in and out of the ditches, towards the North Gate.

The embassage had a trumpeter, and he blew a resounding flourish. When he had finished, a voice hailed.

"I am Montague, Earl of Salisbury, and speak in the name of the most illustrious Edward, by God's grace King of England, France, Ireland and Wales, and Lord Paramount of Scotland. His Majesty demands to know why this cannonade is fired against his royal person and by whose orders?"

"I know of no Lord Paramount of Scotland save His Grace David the Second, King of Scots." Seton shouted back. "I am Sir Alexander Seton of that Ilk, Governor of this town and port, and the cannon are fired on my command and with the authority of King David's Regent."

"You are insolent, sir, as well as misinformed!" came back. "The child David Bruce is no longer King. Therefore can have no Regent and you no authority. King Edward is now overlord of this northern kingdom."

"Not yet, he is not!" Seton declared strongly. "So back and tell your Edward so, my lord."

"You are foolish as well as insolent, sirrah." Salisbury returned. "But His Majesty is patient and merciful. Open these gates to him, and your folly will be overlooked and peace will prevail. Remain obdurate and you will hang for your presumption, and many others with you. And this town will be spoiled."

"Only when Edward Plantagenet has taken it! He will need more than your loud voice, Englishman!"

"Then you are warned, fool . . ."

Seton halted further profitless talk and sent the emissaries hurrying back with a single cannon-shot above their heads.

Thereafter it was something of anticlimax. Nothing happened meantime, at least that was evident from the town. The English columns kept arriving, but of course only a small proportion of the great host could move up to occupy that terrace position. Even the area down at the riverside would not hold them all, so that the legions had to make various other encampments, scattered wherever there was suitable ground.

Next day, still awaiting the arrival of the artillery, the English were not idle. They set to work cutting down trees and brushwood, far and near, to drag up to the terrace, to fill in the ditches – or at least, the two outer ones, for when they came to the inner ones it was promptly demonstrated that they were within range of the defending cannon. After this infilling, the enemy demolished cottages, barns and the like to provide stone and rubble to top the rest firmly, all done in businesslike fashion. The defenders could only watch.

The artillery began to arrive the following day, large and small, but none, so far as the Scots could see, more powerful than their own. These were dragged laboriously up to the terrace, and there ranged along the line of the filled-in ditches. They did not proceed to open fire however – no doubt because the heavy cannon-balls were yet to come.

It took two more days for these to appear, in a lengthy convoy of ox-drawn sledges which could only move painfully slowly. But once the first of these did arrive, Edward Plantagenet lost no time in testing their quality. From just beyond the outermost ditch, he opened up with his largest pieces.

It was much the same situation as with the ship attack. Despite all the sound and fury, the balls either fell short or were so feeble at long range as to strike only dust from the town walling.

The next step, of course, was to push the cannon nearer, over the first filled-in trench. This brought them fully forty yards closer. This time balls did strike the walls, some going over the top, but no real damage was done.

145

Seton deliberately waited, anticipating that they would come nearer still. They did. Then he ordered his gunners to fire, before the enemy could do so. And now these were well within range. He urged his men to aim at the cannon themselves; but this was difficult to do with such clumsy pieces, with considerable trial and error involved. But certain hits were registered, casualties created amongst the English gunners, and what was almost as important, great holes and craters made in the infilled ditches.

The enemy cannoneers withdrew; but not all their pieces were able to do so.

Later, with the gaps in the outer ditches filled up again, a second and similar attempt was made, with the same results.

It appeared to be stalemate.

Edward tried something different. That night he set his people to work in the darkness, filling holes in the trenches and moving the cannon forwards again. But this could not be done without noise, especially the last, and hearing it the defenders lit first torches and then large beacons along the walls and opened up with their guns. Aim was doubtful but sufficient to send the attackers hurrying back. Orders were given for the fires to be kept alight each night.

So it became a siege of attrition, as the days and nights went by. The English did try rushing tactics, sending dismounted men to reach the walls by sheer weight of numbers. But this was unsuccessful also, for the casualties were unacceptable, and though some did reach the masonry, over all the ditches, few burdened with ladders and scaling-ropes managed to do so, and these were easily repulsed by the defenders on the wall-tops. Arrows, crossbow-bolts and throwing-spears flew, but the enemy were much the more vulnerable, and the attempt failed.

Berwick was well placed to withstand siege for a time; but two score thousand people take a deal of feeding, and provisions began to grow short despite severe rationing. They might have been supplied by sea, but the English had more ships than that first fleet driven off, and presently many vessels appeared at the mouth of Tweed, not to attempt attack this time but to patrol up and down, blockading the harbour. What had happened to the Berwick raiding squadron was not to be known; but the chance of any of its craft being able to penetrate the blockade, even by night, was minimal.

There was another and more immediate danger than slow starvation: supplies of ball and powder running out. As the daily cannonading went on, this shortage grew ever more dire. It was only a question of time – unless help arrived.

King Edward must have guessed this, or possibly some English sympathiser had slipped out of the town by night in a small boat undetected, which was quite possible, and informed him of the situation. For on the tenth day he sent forward another deputation under the flag of truce to declare that he knew well of the shortages in the beleaguered town and that they would soon be in desperate straits. The besieged could not win. They had put up a sufficiently worthy defence and could yield with honour. He was a merciful prince and desired no unnecessary bloodshed. He was willing, if they gave him a suitable hostage to ensure their good faith, to allow Berwick ten more days of siege, whereafter, if they were not relieved by the so-called Regent, they must surrender. He would allow them half a day to consider this generous offer, otherwise the fullest attacks would continue.

Seton, Ramsay and the other Scots leaders did their considering. They had not a great deal of choice. Powder and shot would not last another ten days of cannon-fire exchange, nor anything like it; and by then food would be exhausted however drastic the rationing. Was the Regent Douglas never coming?

Ramsay decided and declared that he had been mistaken in staying on in Berwick thus long. He should have gone days ago and alerted the Regent to the situation, to come and relieve the town. He must know of the siege, but presumably did not realise the urgency of their need. He was no soldier and lacked experienced military advisers. He, Ramsay, should leave that night, by boat. If he could get up to Dunbar Castle, he could borrow a good horse there and be in Edinburgh five hours later.

This was accepted as advisable – even though, if the Regent and his army were still at Edinburgh, it would demand every effort to get them down here in time. But Ramsay might meet them on the way.

Before darkness fell, and the attempt could be made, Edward's heralds came back for their answer. And proof that an informant had indeed reached Edward from the town was provided by the fact that the emissaries now demanded that the required hostage should be none other than Seton's own son, a young man whom he had brought with him to Berwick on his first military venture, unfortunate a start as this had turned out to be.

When Ramsay took his leave that night, Seton had not decided whether or not to comply. His son admittedly would almost certainly be in less danger as a hostage than if he remained in the town. And the father had the well-being of thousands to consider.

It was proved that night that it was not difficult to escape out of Berwick, however hard it might be to enter it. Beacons were kept ablaze along the walls protecting the harbour and adjacent coastline in case of any infiltration attempt by boat, from the English ships out there for instance; but so far nothing such appeared to have been attempted. But by failing to light two of the beacons that night, a four-oared fishing coble was able to slip out, unseen save by the immediate guards. Ramsay's parting with Seton was reluctant. He felt, somehow, as though he was deserting; and he had grown much to admire the older man. But he would be befriending him, and all others here, better by going than by staying.

Clinging as close inshore as the rocks and reefs of that dangerous coast would allow, the four fishermen rowed him northwards. Strangely, it seemed less dark out on the water than on land. The sea was not rough, but there was quite a heavy swell, and the noise of this breaking on the reefs and skerries to their left was daunting to the uninitiated. But the oarsmen, chanting a low, endless rowing-song to their slow rhythmic strokes, seemed unconcerned, used to infinitely worse conditions than this.

It was slightly over thirty sea miles from Berwick to Dunbar, a very long row, much too far for any one night, whatever the conditions. They could keep up between four and five miles in each hour only for so long, for even strong and accustomed muscles tired. Fifteen miles north, they put into St Abbs haven, under the mighty headland of that name, just before dawn, and went ashore for a few hours' rest in a hay barn.

The fishermen knew some of their fellows at St Abbs and felt in no danger here. Indeed they were given a meal, more substantial than any they had been able to enjoy at Berwick for a while, before they set off again.

The next fifteen or so miles were easier, not so much because it was daylight but because, once past that towering headland, they were rowing west by north and the wind and tide were now behind them. By mid-forenoon they could see Dunbar's towers ahead; and by noontide they were under the outer castle-bridge, with Ramsay shouting up his name to the watch and asking for the Countess Agnes.

His reception by the sisters was heart-warming, and there was regret all round that he could not stay any time, that haste was vital. The young women had heard that Berwick was besieged and that the English army was none so far off, but they did not know the details, nor of course that Ramsay had been involved. They were concerned to learn of conditions in the town and well pleased to hear that the Earl Patrick was now Keeper of the royal castle of Berwick. They said that no English forward scouts had been reported anywhere in this vicinity; nor had the Earl made any direct contact with them.

It took much will-power for the man to drag himself away, presently, on one of Dunbar's best horses, but consoled and heartened by receiving the best kiss, on parting, that had yet come from Mariot Randolph.

Thereafter it was just a case of hard riding the thirty miles through green Lothian, by Hailes and Haddington and Musselburgh, for Edinburgh, which he reached before night-fall. He went, knowing that the fishermen were being sent back to Berwick with a boatload of provisions, and even some powder and ball, from Dunbar, with offers of more.

Ramsay found the Regent Douglas installed in Edinburgh Castle, with a host of lords and chiefs, including no fewer than six earls, a most illustrious company, waiting there while their forces massed and were added to on the adjacent Burgh Muir. Ramsay was perhaps less respectful towards this lofty assemblage than a young knight ought to have been, in his concern for the Berwick situation. Not that the Regent himself was in any way offended by the new arrival's immediacy and frank speaking. Indeed he was next to apologetic, declaring that levies from the furthest corners of the land were still on their way, and that the greater the army the better. He had had little idea of the dire straits prevailing at Berwick nor that time had all but run out.

With young Moray's and the Steward's help, Ramsay

persuaded him not to wait any longer for the arrival of the Earl of Sutherland's and the Ross levies, but to march for the Border forthwith.

Even so, it was a couple of days more before the great host, now estimated at between fifty and sixty thousand men, set off southwards from the Burgh Muir of Edinburgh for Lauderdale and the Tweed.

7

The army moved down Tweed steadily, scouts well ahead, aware that King Edward would be informed of its presence by now. Or at least its mounted divisions did for, as usual, it had left its slow foot, the majority inevitably, far behind, speed being so important for Berwick. There were only two days left until the expiry of the English ultimatum – be relieved or surrender.

Even so, they amounted to some ten thousand men, a gallant and glittering array of knightly chivalry and armoured strength. They reached the great river at Old Melrose, at the foot of Lauderdale, and followed it down to Kelso, where they had made contact with Sir Simon Fraser, who was not exactly besieging Balliol in Roxburgh Castle but containing him there, with the Warden's force, to prevent him joining Edward Plantagenet at Berwick. Fraser, impatient at so inactive a role, persuaded the Regent to relieve him and appoint a replacement Deputy Warden, and now rode on with the main cavalry host. They reached Gainslaw, not much more than three miles from Berwick, and Ramsay for one was becoming agitated. Strategy and tactics ought to be preoccupying the leadership rather than this simple advance. In all the galaxy of great lords his comparatively junior status restricted him from proffering advice and suggestions. He missed the vehement assurance of Will Douglas.

But, a little further, where Whiteadder joined Tweed, and with the nearest of the English encampments liable to come into view within the next mile or so, he could no longer restrain himself. He spurred forward to Moray's side, urging him to bring him to the Regent, earls or none.

"My lord," he exclaimed, "the English forces are divided into a number of camps around Berwick, for the land offers no single place sufficiently large. The nearest is not far ahead – or was, when I left the town."

"So you told us last night, Ramsay," the Earl of Strathearn observed dismissively. "And so much the better. We shall roll them up the more readily, one by one."

"My lords, it will not be so easy as that, I swear. The English King is no fool He must know that we are approaching. He has more men than have we, even if not all mounted. We can only approach them on a narrow front, because of this river valley's construction. He could chop us up into flitters."

"Tough flitters!" the Earl of Ross interjected.

"Perhaps, my lord. But broken up, nevertheless."

"What do you suggest, Ramsay?" the Regent asked. "You know the position here."

"First, that we cross Tweed. Most of the English are on this side of the river, naturally, since they besiege Berwick. Therefore put the Tweed between Edward's main array and ourselves . . ."

"But then, man, how can we attack them?" Strathearn interrupted. "The river between."

"Is that what we should be aiming to do, here?" Ramsay put to them. "To attack them? What have we come for, in haste? To relieve Berwick town, within the time set by Edward. The English will be expecting us. They have a greater host waiting. Much cannon. Let *them* do the attacking. Across Tweed. Which gives us the advantage, and keeps us out of range of their artillery."

"Ramsay is right," Sir Simon Fraser, who had come up, agreed. "Edward cannot sit there, besieging the town, with us here. He will have to turn on us. So have him do it from across the river. We have no cannon. And no foot here."

Fraser's friend, Sir William Keith, Knight Marischal of Scotland, supported that.

"Very well," Douglas acceded. "Where shall we cross?"

"There is a ford around the next great bend of the river, at the Yair or Yarrow, where the Berwickers net the salmon. A spit of sand and gravel, brought down by this Whiteadder, makes shallows there. Cross that, my lord. It is not like to be guarded, with English on both sides of it. Then on down the far bank, to assail the English camp at the Spittal. Leaving our own guard on that side . . ."

No better plan being put forward, this was decided upon, the prospect of assailing this Spittal encampment appealing. Forward scouts reported that the enemy were massing at two points ahead, at their large camp below the castle hill and also nearer the town, but that the Yair ford itself was not guarded. It might be something of a race, then, once the Scots were in sight and it was perceived that they were going to cross, with ten thousand horsemen to get over. Word was passed down the long column to close up, and to be ready to make a dash for the ford.

In the event, it went well enough, and the period when they were especially vulnerable passed without assault. Fortunately the Yair ford was a wide one, so many horsemen could take it abreast. Rounding the great bend opposite East Ord, they suddenly came into view of the English forces massing over a mile ahead. But these did not move forward at this stage, although they were as close to the Yair as were the Scots. Still they waited, as the Scots came on at a canter. Even when the foremost ranks reached the ford-end and without pause turned in, to splash across the two hundred yards or so of shallows, there was no immediate change, the enemy obviously taken by surprise. Half the Scots were over before the English decided to come on, but by then it was too late to effect a halt to the crossing. Some crossbow-bolts were shot, but at extreme range these proved harmless.

On the south side of Tweed, the Regent left Fraser with some five hundred men, to prevent an enemy crossing behind them. Then, with only a few hundred yards separating them now from their foes, they set off seawards.

Now there was another hazard to counter, the final Town or Spittal ford. Since this was under the cannon of the town, at least on the Scots side of the river, it was unlikely to be guarded. But the English encampment at the Spittal could close it, on the south side. Ramsay himself took a detachment and raced ahead therefore, knowing the position.

The Spittal camp was round another major bend of the river, the last one, and not actually in sight. So the possibility was that the leadership there, if any, would not be fully aware of what had just developed. At any rate, Ramsay reached the Town ford relieved to find no one there. At the riverside, he turned and waved from the saddle towards the town walls and bastions, urging his men to cheer. An answering cheer came over to them, thin but prolonged.

But now there was a competing outcry sounding from around the bend of the river. Presumably the English at the Spittal realised that something was amiss and were coming to see what. Before anyone appeared, however, the Regent arrived in force.

At Ramsay's shouted message, the Scots chivalry formed up from column into as wide a line abreast as the terrain would allow, and wasting no time, advanced at the trot.

Once round the bend, they were confronted with the sight of a mass of men hurrying towards them, a few hundred yards off, some mounted but most afoot, in no sort of order, spread and strung out over perhaps quarter of a mile of gently-rising ground, with the monkish buildings and its township behind, as well as the tented encampment. It was all, to be sure, a gift from the gods of war. Trumpets blared the Scots order to charge.

What developed was a massacre rather than any battle, as disciplined and prepared thousands bore down upon a scattered, unready and largely leaderless crowd, which could have had no idea that any enemy were on this side of the river. The English had no time to take any defensive measures, to form up into squares or hedgehogs, or even to present any unified front, before they were ridden down, trampled on, sworded, speared and completely overwhelmed. Many towards the rear bolted, but they had to bolt fast indeed to remain ahead of that thundering charge; and the river hemmed them in on their right. It was all over in bloody, yelling minutes, and the Scots swept on into the encampment itself.

No resistance developed there, nor could. Reining up, the Regent found himself master of the southern approaches to Berwick, and cutting off Edward of England from his own territories and sources of supply. Satisfaction, even glee at this initial success was, however, soon succeeded by doubts about what to do next. Taking over the monastic premises, there and then a hurried council of war was called. What would Edward's reaction be? He still outnumbered them perhaps five to one. Most certainly he would not take this initial set-back passively.

The first priority, it was agreed, was to hold the fords strongly, not only the two nearby but others some way up Tweed, to prevent their flank being turned. The next was to effect the relief of Berwick town, their immediate objective. But then, what? If Edward could not get at them here without the hazards of the river-crossing, neither could they get at him. No satisfactory answer to this problem was forthcoming meantime, but at least the situation gave them time for the main Scots foot army to come up. Messengers were despatched to inform its leaders, and to instruct them to cross Tweed early on, even at Kelso, and to advance up the south side.

On the subject of Berwick's relief there was some debate. What in fact was meant by relief? Could the arrival of this Scots army outside the walls be so considered? Some held that it could. Others, including Ramsay, declared otherwise. They would have to *enter* the town, and make their entry apparent to the besiegers, make it clear that the siege could be withstood for long yet, a new spirit of defiance engendered in the defenders. This was accepted; but Ramsay argued against a further proposal, namely that a new and more senior Governor be appointed to supersede Seton, with added authority. He claimed that this was not necessary, that Seton was an excellent commander and had put up a splendid defence. But some argued that a new and more resounding voice to address Edward would be more effective; also, sadly, that Seton's will to resist could well be weakened by having his son the hostage. Suppose the English refused to release that youth under some pretext, the father would be much constrained. This argument carried the day, despite Ramsay's protests, and it was decided to send Keith, the Knight Marischal, as one of the major officers of state, to head the relieving party and to take over the governorship meantime. They would cross at the Town ford, under cover of the defending cannon, and be admitted at the South Gate. Ramsay would accompany Keith.

There was no point in delay, nor any in waiting until darkness; the relief should be seen by the English to be effected and effective. So the encampment and the monastic township was scoured for foodstuffs and provisioning for the besieged – unfortunately no powder and ball was found – and

154

this loaded on to horses. Leading a long convoy of these, Keith and Ramsay rode to the ford and over, under the Knight Marischal's great banner, with a mounted escort, trumpets blowing, to draw maximum attention. Before they left, they heard the Regent declaring that if Edward Plantagenet sat tight and did not attempt any attack across Tweed, then he might lead the Scots force raiding deep into Northumberland, even as far as Bamborough where Edward's young Queen was known to be installed. That ought to fetch him.

To rousing cheers from the town walls, the relieving contingent came to the South Gate, which was ceremoniously thrown open to receive them, Seton himself there to welcome Ramsay with open arms. Burdens unloaded, the escort was sent back, horses and extra mouths to feed being undesired.

The gates clanged shut again, Berwick succoured, after a fashion, with a day to go.

Seton did not appear to resent being replaced in the governorship; indeed he might even have been somewhat relieved, for it was a grievous responsibility in present circumstances and he had borne it sufficiently long. He knew and was on good terms with Keith, and that man emphasised that it was only a temporary arrangement. The point about his vulnerability over his son was not mentioned specifically; but they learned that in fact that youth was not the only hostage, for Edward had subsequently demanded that a selection of the citizenry be yielded up also, including some mere children.

Next morning, the trumpets were blown at the North Gate and the Knight Marischal's banner hoisted, with shouted demands for King Edward to appear. That monarch was undoubtedly comfortably ensconced up in Berwick Castle, but after some delay the Earl of Salisbury did arrive, with heralds, and was informed that he could advance safely to near the walling.

"I am Sir William Keith, Knight Marischal of Scotland," Keith called. "Now Governor of this town, in the name of His Grace David, King of Scots, and his Regent. I have relieved this town, with men and provisions, within the time agreed between your King and Sir Alexander Seton, former Governor. I now require the return of the hostages and the retiral of all English forces from Scottish soil. See you to it."

There was no response to that stirring announcement. Salisbury listened, turned to the heralds in discussion, and then without further remark went back over the ditches. It was all something of an anticlimax.

Thereafter the Scots waited for an answer. None came. No unusual activity was evident in the English lines. Hours passed, and nothing happened, no reply, no deputation, no attack.

The same inactivity seemed to apply on the wider front, with the two armies static, no assault on the fords, where opposing guardians stared at each other across two hundred yards of water.

By nightfall there was nothing to report, as the beacons were lit.

The next day, there was some development but only on the Scots side. The first companies of the infantry began to appear along the south side of the river, making a brave show, however weary with forced marching. By mid-day they had arrived by their thousands. Was this what Edward had been waiting for? To learn the extent of the threat?

Then there was another development. After substituting strong infantry guards at the fords, in place of the cavalrymen, almost the entire Scots mounted force formed up and rode off, in companies, southwards, up the long hill of Scremerston Brae, to disappear eventually over the ridge into deeper Northumberland. Advisedly or otherwise, the Regent Douglas was doing as he had part-proposed.

What Edward Plantagenet thought of that the folk in Berwick could only guess. But they got an inkling presently.

In mid-afternoon, Salisbury was back under his white flag. He announced that the so-called Scots Regent and his main force had clearly abandoned Berwick to its fate, and had insolently chosen to invade England. The fact that Sir William Keith and a handful of others had surreptitiously managed to enter the town could by no means be claimed to be a relief and succour for the besieged. Therefore, the agreed time of respite now being overpast, King Edward demanded immediate surrender, as by that agreement.

This peculiar interpretation of events shook the defenders. But Keith replied stoutly that this was folly, and worse, shame. Berwick *had* been relieved in time. Succour and provisions had been brought in. Much of the Scots army

156

remained nearby. The town would nowise surrender. Tell King Edward so.

Salisbury retired, but was back again within the hour. The King's Majesty was wrath, he declared. The Scots, as ever, were guilty of major duplicity. Berwick was still besieged and would fall. Surrender now, or the hostages would be hanged.

This dire threat, of course, gave them pause. But surely it was *only* a threat? No Christian prince would do such a thing to innocent hostages? Keith looked at Seton, who stood nearby.

After a moment or two, that man nodded grimly. "No surrender," he said.

The Knight Marischal shouted back that since it was unthinkable that any such deed would be carried out, and a disgrace to the knightly code that it was so much as suggested, there would be no yielding up of the town. That was final.

That night Berwick seethed with the dread question – was it indeed only a threat?

In the morning there came an ominous indication, although it still could be but threat. Men advanced with beams of timber to the edge of the outermost ditch and there proceeded to erect a gibbet. When the hammering stopped and they withdrew, it was noted that a rope hung from the cross-beam. But only one.

Then a resplendent party came forward, some mounted, under the Leopard standard of England. On one of the horses was a slight figure, bound and blindfolded. This horse was led to the gibbet by two other riders, and the dangling noose put round the youth, Thomas Seton's neck. Thereafter, as the rest stood by, Salisbury advanced nearer.

"This is your last chance, obdurate Scots!" he called. "Yield not, and the hostage hangs. And thereafter Berwick will be sacked."

It was a desperate moment. Everywhere men held their breaths. Above the North Gate, all eyes turned on Sir Alexander Seton, Keith's and Ramsay's included. Seton stood as though carved in stone. He said no word.

"Well, man – well?" Keith got out hoarsely.

Seton moistened his lips. "So be it. And God have mercy on my soul! *His*, my son's, is safe. No . . . no surrender!"

Something like a moan came from the crowd of watchers.

Turning away, Keith raised his voice. "If you do this,

the Englishman, Edward Plantagenet's name will stink in the nostrils of all Christendom. As his grandsire's stank! Berwick does not surrender to threats."

Salisbury shrugged and went back.

They had not long to wait to discover whether Edward was in earnest or not. Hardly had Salisbury reached the others when the two men who sat their mounts on either side of the bound youth reined forward, taking the victim's beast with them. Jerked out of the saddle by the rope, Thomas Seton was left dangling in the air, swinging and twitching grotesquely.

A great cry compounded of rage, sorrow, hatred and vituperation went up from the town walls as the colourful company under the Plantagenet Leopards turned and rode back towards the castle, leaving the slight jerking figure to its dance of death.

Sir Alexander Seton stumbled away, a stricken man. None dared approach him closely, although Alexander Ramsay did follow him heedfully some way behind.

Edward gave them only until the following morning. Then his heralds appeared again. Did Berwick now surrender? Or were the remaining hostages to be hanged? They were given one day to decide. The body of Thomas Seton still hung from the gibbet.

Now the town was in turmoil indeed. No longer could the hanging be seen as a threat; it was now a promise. If the English would execute the son of Sir Alexander Seton, a noted Scots knight, would they hesitate over ordinary towns-folk? The citizens of Berwick were not prepared to wait and see. They had withstood siege, hunger and deprivation. This was too much. The merchants and better sort sent deputations to the Governor, and the common folk mobbed him and his lieutenants in the streets. He must yield.

Keith conferred with his colleagues, Ramsay included. He had a certain number of men-at-arms in the town, who could, probably, contain a revolt of the townsfolk, at least for a little while. But would that be justified? Or effective for long? If determined, the thousands must prevail and let in the enemy.

None could disagree. Ramsay it was who suggested temporising. After all, they still had certain cards to play. The Scots infantry army still sat there just across Tweed. And the Regent at his raiding could not be far away. Edward might be seeming to ignore these, but in fact he must be concerned. If the Regent and the cavalry could be brought back, and urged to make some sort of attack, or at least the threat of attack, Edward would have other things to think about than hanging hostages. Time therefore was needed. Edward had agreed to a time-limit before. He would not give them as long, probably, but he might allow a day or two.

Sir Alexander Gray, who had come with Keith, said that a promise to yield within a definite period, say four days, unless relieved by the Regent, might well be accepted, and save the hostages. Keep the townsfolk quiet meantime. This was agreed.

So next day when the heralds returned, Keith made such offer, adding that he must be allowed to inform the Regent of this for it to be effective.

Perhaps Edward indeed was reluctant to embark on that wholesale hanging; or may merely have assessed that this way he would force the Scots army into a rash and costly attack which he could repulse, and then get Berwick's surrender. At any rate, Salisbury came back to announce that his magnanimous prince had made this, his final decision. The town had the period asked for. By then it must be relieved effectively and beyond doubt, or his English army defeated in the field; otherwise full and unqualified surrender. By relief it was stipulated that at least two hundred armed men must be seen to have entered the town, with due provisioning. An emissary would be permitted to leave Berwick to apprise the so-called Regent of this arrangement.

So the thing was settled. Keith himself decided to go and try to find Douglas, and to explain it all. He hoped that he could do so quickly.

The news was relayed to the restive citizens that they had a few days' respite.

Keith left, with a small escort, by the South Gate and the Town ford.

In the event, the Berwiekers were given hope and encouragement sooner than they could have anticipated. Presumably Keith had found the Regent not far away, for only the day following the great cavalry host appeared over the lip of Scremerston Brae once more, to descend to the Spittal. New heart became evident in the town.

This was further enhanced later in the day, when, towards

dusk, the entire Scots army, horse and foot, was seen to be on the move westwards, back along Tweedside. At the Yair ford, in mass, they turned to cross, the English guards there prudently withdrawing to a discreet distance, while trumpets sounded in all the enemy encampments. Presumably the Regent had waited until almost darkness, so as to hide the Scots movements once across the river. The watchers from Berwick's walls presently could see them no more, in an overcast early summer night. But there was a sufficiency of stir and flaming torches amongst the nearby English positions.

The morning revealed a different scene. For the first time in weeks there was no mass of English soldiery on the terrace area, nor in the other visible encampments, although the tentage was still there, only a few enemy troops remaining between castle and town. Nor was there now any sign of the Scots. The centre of gravity had at last moved away from Berwick. No relief attempt was in evidence. So the Regent had apparently decided upon Edward's second alternative – challenge in the field. Although most there cheered, Ramsay was more apprehensive, knowing his Regent and those young earls.

They waited there, in Berwick, in a strange state of enforced inaction and suspense. No sounds of battle came to them, no indication that destiny was being decided not far off. It might not be, of course. The Regent might have decided on a strategic retiral, for instance, to lure Edward northwards or westwards into a position favourable to the Scots, perhaps even as far up Tweed as the Kelso area, where the Warden's force could be used to help defeat him.

By early evening, however, the first intimations of developments began to appear, in the shape of English units returning. And, ominously, these displayed no hint of defeat nor dejection; on the contrary. And when, towards the July gloaming, the royal-standard party arrived back and proceeded up to Berwick Castle with, even at a distance, an air of triumph unmistakable, the watchers' hearts sank. Whatever had happened, English spirits were high, and Berwick was still besieged. No heralds, however, came down to inform the town.

Information came otherwise. After dark, a small fishing boat from Burnmouth slipped into the harbour, with two

160

passengers aboard, one none other than Sir William Keith, the Marischal, wounded, the other his own esquire. Carried up to the Governor's House, in much physical pain, his mental pain proved to be more dire. In fits and starts he told Seton, Ramsay, Gray and others the sorry tale.

It was disaster again, entire, appalling. The Regent had led his army round to the north of Berwick, to the vicinity of Halidon Hill, about three miles north-west of the town, and between that hill and Mordington had halted, in quite a strong position, with marshy ground in front. In the early morning the English host had appeared. They did not attack but took up their stance on Halidon itself, covering that hill. And there, a mile apart, the two armies sat and looked at each other.

Ramsay all but groaned, guessing the rest.

Those proud young Scottish earls could not sit there for long. Against the urgent advice of Keith, Fraser and other veterans, they decided that the English were afraid to put it to the test; but *they* were not. They persuaded the Regent to advance to the attack. So they left their strong position, and in four great divisions under Douglas himself, Ross, Moray and the Steward, rode down to cross that marsh and to assault the hill. Halidon was no great mount, a mere five hundred feet high, but it was sufficiently steep on that west side, after the slow plodding through the bog, to greatly slow down and disperse the advance. Had the infantry been thrown in first, it might have succeeded, giving the cavalry time to regroup and adopt some outflanking tactics. But no, the knightly chivalry had to lead, and lead they did to utter and complete defeat. The enemy bowmen showered them with arrows, to break up any semblance of order; and the English horsed might, charging downhill, everywhere overwhelmed the Scots leadership by sheer weight and impetus. The Regent himself was one of the first to fall. All around, the other Scots lords went down like bowled skittles. The cavalry were toppled back on their own infantry, most of whom were never engaged. Groups did manage to stand fast, and to fight bravely, but not for long, with the English foot descending upon them in their thousands. Keith saw most of the leadership slain. Four earls, no five – Ross, Lennox, Strathearn, Sutherland and Carrick – fell. But still greater losses were Sir Simon Fraser, Sir Alexander Lindsay, Sir John the Graham and the two uncles of the Steward, Sir James and Sir John Stewart. He himself, wounded, had been led off that bloody hill by his own esquire.

"Dupplin Muir again!" Ramsay exclaimed, beating fist on table. "Oh, the folly of it! The purblind folly of men who would never learn! Bruce and Wallace taught their fathers how to fight the English might. And the sons throw all away in prideful stupidity!"

"The Regent is dead, then?" Gray said. "We have no Regent again?"

"Aye. The first to fall. He was not the man for the task, once Will Douglas was lost to him."

"And Moray? And the Steward?" Ramsay demanded.

"I know not. I did not see them. Nor heard of them. Their divisions were some way apart. But – Fraser was with Moray, and fell."

Grim-faced, Keith's hearers eyed each other.

Later that sorry night, Ramsay came to Keith's room, where he lay awake in pain. "What now, at Berwick?" he asked.

The Governor shook his head. "I have no choice, now. The agreement was to yield if not relieved, or the English beaten in the field. As Governor here, I can only surrender the town."

Ramsay nodded. "So I judged. A sore duty. But . . . you will not require *me*, for that? Nor Seton? Nor Gray?"

"No-o-o. You would leave? If you could?"

"Aye. Surely that is *my* duty. To continue the fight, not to become a prisoner of the English. I can do nothing here now. I have left this town once already, and can seek to do so again. By boat, as you came in. By night. *This* night, or it will be too late."

"As you will," Keith said wearily. "Would that I could go with you. But my place is here, to gain the best terms I can for this unhappy town. I fear, I fear . . ."

A couple of hours later the same Burnmouth boat which had brought the Marischal in picked its secret way out of Berwick harbour, with the three knights as passengers. Nor was it alone. Other small craft were leaving the stricken town, the news having got round, and its consequences all too clearly perceived. Many were seeking to get out while they could, so many indeed that Ramsay feared that they must be

162

seen by the blockading English ships lying off, for the July night was less dark than he could have wished. But if any were intercepted, the Burnmouth coble was not, hugging the shoreline, however hazardous its reefs and skerries, under the loom of the land.

They were off Burnmouth by sunrise, where the rowers rested awhile, for Ramsay had bargained with the fishermen to take them onward to Dunbar, in a repetition of the previous escape.

The passengers made a dispirited trio as they approached Dunbar Castle. Seton had hardly spoken to any since his son's death; Gray was never loquacious; and Ramsay not only again felt something like guilt at deserting Berwick in its hour of need, but did not relish having to tell the Randolph sisters the terrible news and the possibility that their brother might be one of the casualties.

However, when presently the knights were admitted to the castle, it was to find Moray and the High Steward themselves therein. They had, apparently, ridden in around dawn, after a hectic escape from the battlefield's carnage, the Steward's right arm in a sling. Great was the friends' relief at seeing each other, free men still, and warm Ramsay's reception from the two young women.

But it was not the time for lingering or relaxation. It would not be long before the English were at Dunbar, now that Southern Scotland lay wide open to their advance. Earl Patrick might well bring Edward himself here – who had paid for the improved defences. Dunbar, all agreed, would be a good place to get out of, since it was impossible, despite these improved defences, that it could be held against its own lord and the whole might of England's king. Black Agnes would leave along with her brother and sister, having no wish to co-operate in the treachery of her peculiar husband nor to act hostess to Edward Plantagenet. They had in fact been preparing to leave when Ramsay and the others arrived.

Moray and Robert Stewart had similar tales to tell of the poor leadership and rash foolishness at Halidon Hill, although being themselves young and inexperienced they did not see it in quite the same terms as had the veteran Keith. They could add some illustrious names to the toll of the slain; the list seemed to leave few of the great names of Scotland surviving. But at least they were more hopeful about casualties amongst the rank and file, especially the foot. The majority of these had probably escaped back across the marsh, they thought; indeed many had never been engaged. Where they all were now, who could tell, their own levies included? Making for home as swiftly and inconspicuously as possible, no doubt. It was the cavalry and the knightly host which had taken the beating.

Incidentally they revealed that the Northumberland raiding, as well as failing to draw Edward from Berwick's walls, had not achieved very much. A few villages burned and manors sacked, that was all. They had not got as far as Bamburgh, being warned by scouts of an English reinforcement army from Newcastle on the march northwards, which could have caused complications.

In mid-afternoon they left Dunbar Castle, well mounted and quite a sizeable company – for Moray and the Steward had managed to extract a group of their horsed men from the débâcle and ridden directly here. It was unlikely that any English advance-parties would in fact have got thus far as yet, but they went prepared.

They followed the River Tyne westward, by Hailes and Haddington. At this last, Seton left them, to make for his own castle near Cockenzie, with his terrible news. And at Musselburgh it was Ramsay's turn to say farewell, much as he was tempted to agree to the Randolphs' urgings and proceed with them over Forth to Doune of Menteith, so much more secure in present circumstances than would be Dalwolsey; for nothing was surer than that the English would be up to Lothian and Edinburgh before long, and Dalwolsey not far off their path. But he owed it to his brother and his own people to go warn and prepare them; also he hoped that some of his retainers and tenants, from whom he had been detached since Berwick, might have survived Halidon and would win home.

So, much as he would have liked to ride for Perthshire with his friends, in especial Mariot, he left them, to turn up Eskside, but promising to come to Doune before long. There would have to be some sort of Council meeting, anyway, held somewhere out of Edward's reach, to try to cope with the situation. It might well be near Doune.

Gray went on with the others meantime; his lands lay in Angus, north of Tay.

8

As Alexander Ramsay rode northwards some weeks later, alone and inconspicuously clad, not even on a very good horse, and hoping to be seen as some small laird or merchant of no interest to the present rulers of Southern Scotland and their minions, he mused on the ups and downs of fortune, in nations equally with individuals, how unpredictable these could be, for all the decisions, intentions and attempts of men, great and small. After Halidon Hill and the surrender of Berwick, surely none could have foreseen the sequence of events. Edward Plantagenet, instead of advancing victoriously into Scotland, had in fact hastened off southwards almost at once, to deal with urgent developments on a vastly different front which gravely affected his wider ambitions. In 1316 when Louis X of France died, he left no surviving son, only a sister and two daughters – and the sister was Isabella queen of Edward II of England. Louis had been succeeded eventually by the son of his uncle, Philip de Valois now Philip VI of France; but this had been challenged at the time by Edward III who claimed a possibly closer link through his mother Isabella. He held the French title of Duke of Guienne. Nothing had come of this then, but recently King Philip had had trouble with Flanders and therefore with the Emperor, and an anti-Philip party had arisen, which now was holding that the son of the late King's sister was more entitled to the throne than the son of his uncle. Suddenly this party had reached the stage of action, and were calling on Edward to come and demand the French crown, backed by suitable force. And that was a call the Plantagenet could not resist.

He had left behind all sorts of imperious and dire instructions, of course, anent Scotland; but lacking his personal presence the situation inevitably had changed notably. For one thing, Balliol again came to the fore, Edward in his haste changing his attitude and reinstating him, at least meantime,

165

as puppet-king, to carry out his orders as Lord Paramount. And Edward Balliol was not Edward Plantagenet, by any means, for which the Scots undoubtedly had reason to be thankful. For not only was he less than efficient and able, but because of his family preoccupation with Galloway and Dumfries-shire, and the South-West generally, he proceeded thereafter to consolidate his position there first, mainly to raise a new army for the conquest of the kingdom, since Edward Plantagenet was taking most of the force at Berwick south again to aid in the French adventure. Not only that, but because of Balliol's reinstatement as alleged King of Scots, Patrick, Earl of Dunbar and March was furious, gravely disappointed in King Edward, and reconsidering his allegiance again, his dynastic hopes dashed despite his aid at Berwick. And since Dunbar was the greatest lord in South-East Scotland, that important area which had been cowering in anticipation of full-scale sack and occupation, Lothian in especial had had something of a respite, as the Earl sulked. Ramsay, for instance, sitting in Dalwolsey and ready for instant flight – since he could by no means hold that castle against any major assault – had been left in approximate peace, as had Seton at Seton, and other Lothian barons. So, although Scotland was leaderless and stricken, it had not so far suffered the devastation expected.

Now the Chancellor, Bishop Bernard de Linton of Man, had called a Council meeting at Dunblane, for such of the loyal magnates as had survived, along with senior clerics. In the circumstances these churchmen were now important indeed, for they at least were not decimated in battle and represented a continuing authority, and, what is more, a comparatively wealthy one, Holy Church's coffers being seldom empty. Admittedly not a few of the bishops, abbots and priors were of questionable allegiance, too many following Bishop St Clair of Dunkeld's line, but by and large the Church was sound and the ordinary clergy basically loyal.

Dunblane was a bare six miles north of Stirling, across Forth, and therefore some forty miles from Edinburgh, a reasonable day's ride. But Ramsay elected to go by little-used roads and byways, to avoid possible interception and recognition, and it was late before he reached the cathedral-close and Bishop Maurice's palace, just to the south-west, where the Council was to be held. He found no large numbers assembled, and with a preponderance of clergy, but this was only to be expected. He was glad to see Moray and the Steward already there, and to learn that the Randolph sisters were safe in Doune Castle, only four miles away. So far there had been no trouble there, nor here.

The Council, when it met next forenoon under the Chancellor's chairmanship, consisted of only fifteen members, although there were some others, of less importance, in attendance for consultation, mainly churchmen. Of the bishops there were only two, apart from Bernard of Man and their host: Aberdeen and Brechin. Other than Moray, there was no earl present, although the High Steward ranked as equivalent. Hay, the High Constable, was the sole other great officer of state. Of lords and noble knights, apart from Ramsay there were Gray, Wemyss, Leslie, young Douglas of Douglasdale and old Sir Malcolm Drummond of this Strathallan. There were also the mitred abbots of Holyrood and Cambuskenneth and the Archdeacon of St Andrews and Dean of Glasgow, representing those two important bishoprics whose incumbents were not available.

Bishop Bernard opened the proceedings with a very heartfelt prayer for help and guidance, the amens to which were sufficiently fervent. Then, saying that he need not dwell on the present national situation in general, since all knew it only too well, he could not but pay tribute to the memories of so many who ought to have been with them but were instead attending a higher court. He besought God's blessing upon their souls. In especial, of course, they must remember the late acting Regent, whose loss left the realm without a resident governor and His Grace King David without representative and guardian.

All nodded, none choosing to mention that the late Lord of Galloway had scarcely been the most effective of regents, however amiable.

"Which brings me to our first duty and priority," the Chancellor went on. "Which is to our liege-lord David, his well-being and safety. He is at present, with the Queen, in Dumbarton Castle, under the care of Sir Malcolm Fleming. I cannot think that he may remain there secure. The man Balliol is now reported to be at Ayr, which is why there are no representatives from those parts here today. He, Balliol, could be outside Dumbarton in a couple of days, if he chose.

I advise that we send His Grace and the Queen to France forthwith, for safety. King Philip is our friend, and would guard them well."

"Is France the safest place, my lord Bishop?" Drummond asked. "Now that English Edward is planning to invade there."

"That, I think, will make Philip still the more our friend, Sir Malcolm. He may need Scotland's help, hereafter. And France is large enough to hide King David meantime."

It was agreed. The young King and Queen should be sent in the first available ship, in care of a suitable emissary.

"The next problem is that of the regency. We have lost four in the space of two years, to our grievous cost. How say you, my lords and friends?"

There was silence around the table, men eyeing each other. The choice was limited indeed, and the task unenviable.

"We need a leader experienced in war," the High Constable said. "Mar and Douglas were not that, and we have paid the price. Sir Andrew Murray was, but . . ."

"Sir William Douglas, Knight of Liddesdale, would have served, but he too is prisoner. And kept in chains, I am told," Wemyss said.

"Who else have we, sufficiently versed in war? For war it will have to be," Bishop Alexander of Aberdeen asked.

None there could give him an answer.

"I fear that we cannot hope for an experienced warrior," the Chancellor said. "But acting Regent we must have, to give authority and edict in the King's royal name"

"I propose the High Steward, then," Adam, Bishop of Brechin put in. "He is King David's kinsman, a grandson of the Bruce. The Steward for Regent."

"Acting Regent, my lord."

"Acting . . . ?"

"Aye – as was my lord of Galloway. Do not forget that we *have* a Regent still, even though he is not with us. Sir Andrew Murray is a prisoner in Carlisle Castle. But he is still Regent of the kingdom, appointed by Council and parliament, and sworn-in before the King."

That had not occurred to most there. It set Alexander Ramsay thinking, that and the mention of Carlisle.

Robert Stewart spoke up. "I am but eighteen years," he said. "It is too much. The responsibility. I am not well versed in the arts of war. The weight of it is too much for *my* shoulders, my lords."

There was a silence.

"Suppose that the burden was shared?" Ramsay suggested. "Since it is an *acting* Regent. Four shoulders instead of but two? Is that possible, my lord Chancellor?"

"I see no reason why not. Indeed, in the circumstances, it might be best."

"Then I propose my lord Earl of Moray. He and the High Steward are friends and work well together. So together they could act as Regent." ·

Moray began to protest and then changed his mind, glancing at Robert Stewart.

"Is it agreed? Good. Then, my lords, that can be arranged. A swearing-in before His Grace swiftly, at Dumbarton. Then, a ship for France." The Chancellor paused. "In the matter of France, here is a consideration. Scotland needs aid, direly. The French are our ancient allies. In these straits they could send us help. Experienced soldiers, which we greatly require. Arms. Moneys. This is of prime importance in our present state. An ambassador we should have, who can put our cause to King Philip with authority. And who can talk with that monarch face to face. It must be a man of rank. Who better than my lord of Moray? Joint acting Regent. Young King David must have an escort, also of rank. You, my lord, could fulfil both duties. If you would?"

Moray hesitated and looked again at the Steward.

"If my lord of Moray is in France, he cannot share the burdens of regency with me," that young man objected.

"He need not remain in France for long, my lord."

Two non-enthusiastic nominees for regency could think of no valid excuses meantime. Bishop Bernard gave them little opportunity.

"Now, the part Holy Church can play," he went on. "It must do its utmost, despite divisions amongst the clergy. Fortunately we have the highest authority on our side, as represented here by our good friends the Archdeacon of St Andrews and the Dean of Glasgow, the two foremost sees." He looked round them. "It may not be known to you all, but the Primate, my lord Bishop of St Andrews, has died. In France. He was a sick man when he went there. So we have no Primate meantime. This is a sore loss, but it could be used to our advantage also. For not a few will aspire to that high office. Some amongst those who might otherwise support Balliol, perhaps! So these may not wish to harm their chances at this present, either with the College of Bishops – on which some here present may have a certain influence – or with His Holiness the Pope, at Avignon, whom the Scots Church acknowledges and the English does not."

The other churchmen exchanged smiles.

"There is also the probability, to be sure, that Edward Plantagenet and his Archbishop of York will use the vacancy to advance their insolent claim to spiritual hegemony over Scotland by petitioning the Bishop of Rome, who also calls himself Pope, to appoint *their* nominee to St Andrews, and have Edward Balliol to accept it. That could create much trouble in the Church at large, as well as in Scotland, and we must be prepared for it."

The non-churchmen present were not greatly interested in this emphasis on ecclesiastical affairs, and were tending to show it. Sensing it, the Chancellor pointed out that Church and state were closely linked in this. Drily, he observed that the *people* were apt to be concerned over Holy Church, even if some of their lords were not! And in this present pass, with so many of their lords gone, the people's support for King David was the more vital. For the defence against Balliol and the other English would have to be different, from now on; more like Wallace's and the early Bruce's campaigns, no great armies and set battles but small strikes, ambushes, harassments, the constant hostility of the whole nation. Edward had a heavy hand, and would care little for that. But Balliol would have to deal with it. Already Edward had provoked the ill-feeling in Church matters which would cost Balliol dear. He had ordered all Scots monks and priests, suspected of what he called rebellious notions, to be transported to English monasteries and charges, and to be replaced by suitable English clergy capable of teaching the Scots salutary doctrines. The blind arrogance of it! So far this had only been carried out in the Border counties, but it had provoked great anger and resentment. Even the Earl of Dunbar was furious. So here was opportunity to rouse the people to ever more active opposition to Balliol. Add to that the fact that Balliol had ceded, by charter, the counties of

170

Berwick, Roxburgh, Dumfries, Peebles and even Lothian to Edward Plantagenet personally, to be from henceforth part of England, not Scotland, and they would perceive something of the witches' brew which was being boiled up – and of which they must seek to take advantage.

Most there had not heard of these outrageous enactments and reacted in vociferous fury.

Ramsay waited until the noise had died down. "My lord Chancellor, all must agree on the need to show these invaders that they have over-reached themselves. But if we are to use the people's resentment to good effect, we must have a plan and policy, a strategy. How is this to be achieved, in our present state of weakness?"

"You are right, Sir Alexander. But I am no soldier. How say you, and the other lords here?"

Gone was the confidence of previous Councils. None there was brimming over with suggestions. There were mutterings about the impossibility of raising another large national army after the successive defeats of Dupplin, Dornock and Halidon. An army there would have to be, raised somehow, and under the Regents' command; but clearly it would have to avoid any large confrontation with the enemy for some considerable time to come, perhaps only when French aid might arrive. Meantime it would have to be small-scale war, and attrition.

"But how shall this be done?" Ramsay persisted. "There must be some control, some unity in it, some overall plan. We must all do what we can, yes, striking as we are able. But that will achieve little against the usurper and an occupying army unless there is some unity of purpose, some direction in it all."

"This Council must serve, under the Regents, for that," Bishop Maurice said.

"But, my lord, if we are all scattered over the land, attacking as we can, harassing, rousing the people to resist, we cannot keep running to this Council for guidance and authority."

"Wallace and Bruce achieved much without that," the Constable observed.

"Have we a Wallace or a Bruce now?"

That silenced all.

"It seems to me," the Chancellor said, "that we must use

the Council members, as well as others whom we may bring in, not only as such but as individuals in authority. Each in their own area. To act as leaders, in the Regents' names. All but independent commanders, most of the time. Meeting when possible at some centre but operating each to best effect in his own given area. I can see no other course, at this present."

Doubtfully they considered that, but none offered a better suggestion.

"We are sadly uneven in our territories," Bernard de Linton admitted. "Great areas not represented here. But leaders must be found for these. That at least is something we churchmen can do – seek out the necessary leaders. I think, in especial, of the South-West, Lanarkshire, Ayrshire, Dumfries-shire, Galloway, where Balliol is so strong. Sir William Douglas of Liddesdale would have been the man, but he is a chained captive. For Renfrewshire, Dumbarton and Glasgow, there is the High Steward himself, here. For Menteith and Strathearn, my lord of Moray. For Perthshire and north of it, the High Constable. For Gowrie and Angus, Sir Andrew Leslie. For Fife, Sir Michael Wemyss. For Lothian, Sir Alexander Ramsay. For Lanarkshire, my lord of Douglasdale." Almost apologetically he looked at that youth, a cousin of the Knight of Liddesdale, and another William, son of the Good Sir James's brother. That this sixteen-year-old should be sent to be the leader of Clydesdale seemed absurd, but beggars could not be choosers. The Chancellor went on, "You, Lord William, bear the Douglas name, which means so much in the South-West. Many will, I believe, rally to that name, despite your lack of years. Will you do what you can, there, in the name of your uncle, the late Regent, and your cousin, the Flower of Chivalry?"

The youth blinked, gulped and nodded.

Almost hurriedly the Bishop went on, to Ramsay now. "And you, my friend, on you will fall a heavy burden. For Edinburgh will assuredly be Balliol's important target, and all Lothian with it. Not only so, but the Border Marches, in especial the East March, where my lord of Dunbar is supreme, remains unrepresented in all this, and can most readily be reached from your Lothian. So you could perhaps assume authority for that also, meantime. Until we can find others. And you best know Patrick of Dunbar."

"He is my lord of Moray's goodbrother," was all the excuse Ramsay could conjure up there and then.

"But my lord of Moray will be in France. At first, at least. When he returns . . ."

This so very sketchy planning could please none there; but no better scheme was forthcoming, and out of much discussion and many expressed doubts, the thing was agreed.

They went on to discuss the raising of manpower and moneys.

It was at the end of that long meeting that Ramsay put forward the suggestion which had been simmering at the back of his mind almost from the beginning.

"You said, my lord Chancellor, that Sir Andrew Murray was held captive in Carlisle Castle. I had not known of this. He is our most able soldier, and still Regent in name, you say. Could he be rescued?"

They all stared at him.

"Carlisle is but a few miles from our border. The folk on either side of the borderline, in that West March, are but little hostile to each other, unlike the East and Middle marches. There is much coming and going. A rescue might be contrived."

"How, man – how?" Leslie demanded. "Carlisle is a strong castle."

"I know it. But it might not be beyond our wits to devise a plan. The Borderers, on both sides of the line, are scarcely concerned with being Scots or English, but rather as a special folk, a law unto themselves. We learned of that when we raided Dacre at Gilsland, with their help. If sufficiently rewarded, we might conceivably gain their aid in freeing Sir Andrew Murray."

Only Moray evinced any belief in the possibility of that.

"It was the Grahams of Netherby and Kirkandrews who gave me the notion. They are English, despite their name, but they aided us gladly enough at the crossings of Esk. For a consideration. They might do so again."

"If you think it is possible . . ." the Chancellor said, shrugging.

"With this Council's permission, I could try. It might not be for some time . . ."

They left it at that, and soon thereafter the meeting broke up.

Moray invited Ramsay and Robert Stewart to spend the night with him at Doune Castle.

The autumn evening was chilly and they were glad to sit round the well-doing fire in the lesser hall at Doune, companionably. But it was not quite the same as at Dunbar nevertheless, just a little less satisfactory, for Alexander Ramsay at least, in that there was no ingle-neuk here to enforce an enjoyable proximity; also it was five, not four, with Robert Stewart there, and that young man was obviously as much attracted to Mariot Randolph as heretofore; which made two of them. And since he was heir presumptive to King David and now acting Regent of Scotland, as well as a close friend of the lady's brother, Ramsay could not underestimate the competition. They sat on a settle on either side of the young woman, who sought to distribute her attentions all too fairly, while her sister grinned at them from across the hearth.

"It will take a deal of getting used to," Black Agnes observed, "to be sister to one of the new rulers of the realm, admirer of the other, and at the same time wife of one of their foremost problems! Heigho – will I survive it? You, at least, Mariot, have not got *that* problem!"

"Your problems are as nothing to mine," her brother asserted. "I know nothing of being a regent. And this of taking young David to France – some other should have that task. One who could talk of our need of arms and men to King Philip. I know little of such matters. Some experienced soldier should be sent . . ."

"You have served now in two great battles. And some lesser affrays," Ramsay said.

"But only as a captain of my own men. Never as a commander of an army. So I have little knowledge of what is required. What to ask from the French. You, Sandy, would have been the better choice."

"But I, a mere knight, am not the man to chaffer with kings and the like, to represent Scotland. Nor suitable to be King David's guardian . . ."

"Any more than I am to act Regent," Robert Stewart put in. "Who am I, at eighteen years, to seek to rule a kingdom? Even with the help of Bishops Bernard and Maurice. We are none of us suited to our new roles. Too young . . ."

"Since our elders have got themselves killed or captured,

we have little choice!" Ramsay said. "This realm is like a ship without a rudder, and its crew landsmen!"

"And what is *your* role, Sir Sandy – for which you are so unsuited?" Black Agnes asked.

"The good Lord only knows! *I* do not. Save that I am, it seems, to take responsibility, in the name of the Acting Regents, for Lothian's stand against the enemy, Balliol and the English. Somehow to rouse the folk to resist, to find other leaders, to organise and lead attacks. And not only in Lothian. In the East and Middle Marches also – where I will come up against your husband, Countess, I fear. Something that I do not relish."

"Patrick may not be so great a problem as he was," she said, slowly for that young woman. "He will be much aggrieved. Sore against Edward Plantagenet, over his putting Balliol back on his stolen throne. Hotter than ever against Balliol himself. Patrick is a man of moods. And his present mood will be one of much resentment."

"How far will that take him, think you?"

"Sufficiently not to work with Balliol, that I am sure."

"But still not to work with ourselves?"

"That I do not know. But . . . he might be persuaded."

"I think not by me! But *you* might try?"

"You say so? He does not often heed me in the greater matters, I fear."

"You – and the two Edwards, perhaps! It could be of much importance for this kingdom."

"We shall see, Sir Sandy . . ."

"And what do you plan to do?" Mariot asked him. "All those sore tasks. To effect them where shall you start? At Dalwolsey?"

"Scarcely there, I think. Dalwolsey is all too readily reached, and no great strength. If Balliol is not a fool, he will take it early. For I fear that I shall be a marked man. No, I shall go to a lesser place, not far off. A small castle on the North Esk – Dalwolsey is on the South. Hawthornden. It is not mine, an Abernethy house. But the Abernethys were Comyn and against Bruce and suffered the consequences, losing their lands. The castle is now little better than a ruin, but it may serve. It is very strongly placed on a cliff-top above the river's gorge. But, more important, it has below it, in the cliff, caves, hidden and reached only from its well-shaft.

Many caves, linked together and cut in the soft rock, it is said by the ancient Picts. There would be a safe refuge. From this Hawthornden, I think, I might sally out and be a thorn in the flesh to Edward Balliol."

"So! You have considered it all, Sandy. Already. I knew that you would fight on. But to have planned all, so soon . . ."

"Not all. Only a beginning, it may be . . ."

"Would that Scotland had more like Sir Sandy Ramsay!" Moray said. "We would not be where we are now. He even thinks to rescue Sir Andrew Murray from the English!"

"That is only a small hope, very small. But, who knows, it might be possible."

Mariot looked at him, with something of anxiety clouding her accustomed serenity. "You will be careful?" she said. "I know that you are scarcely a careful man. But have a little care, Sandy. For the sake of . . . others."

He reached out to give a quick squeeze to her arm. "I *will* take care, yes. That I may stay alive and effect the more. Also, I hope, I hope that I may have much to live for!" That was as much a question as an assertion.

She nodded gravely.

The Steward clearly felt that it was time that he made some of the running. "I am going to require help, much help, to act the Regent," he declared. "Not just from bishops and old men, but from such as yourself, Ramsay. Your caves may be very well, but you will have to be with me, at times."

Ramsay shrugged. "I am at your command, my lord Regent."

"Not command," the younger man said, leaning around Mariot's person, almost urgently. "To seek your aid, your advice, your goodwill, Sir Alexander."

Touched, Ramsay nodded. "The last you have already. The first, whenever you ask it. The advice, such as I can offer, at any time. But – I am no paladin, no wise councillor. I pray that you may have better counsel than mine."

The young woman between smiled kindly on them both. She patted the Steward's hand and pressed Ramsay's.

Mariot presently sang for them, accompanying herself on her harp, of love and sorrow, joy and laughter and tears. Agnes was no singer, but where the melodies lilted suitably, she rose and danced lightly or gracefully or spiritedly, her brother joining in once or twice, the two visitors less accomplished in this respect. Clearly the Randolph family had grown up a happy and talented one, despite the stresses and strains of the time.

When it was time for bed, as before in this house, Robert Stewart was first on his feet to offer, bowing, to take Mariot to her chamber. Ramsay half rose, and then reconsidered, and sat back. As the girl looked down at him, brows raised, he inclined his head, and then glanced over to the Countess.

"The Lady Agnes also deserves an escort," he said. "Not always her brother, surely?"

That sister skirled a laugh.

"Then a good night, Sandy. Sleep well," Mariot said.

"The better for your . . . kind consideration," he said.

Agnes pointed at him when the other two were gone. "You play your own games, Sir Sandy?" she suggested.

"At times, perhaps. But . . . not here," he told her.

"No? Then, are you foolish? Or very clever?"

"More the first than the last, I would think, Countess. In most matters."

"I wonder! How say you, Johnnie?"

"I say nothing," her brother answered. "Not knowing what you are at."

"Then *you* are the foolish one, Regent or none!"

The men exchanged doubtful glances.

"Have it as you will, Sir Sandy. Come, conduct me to my room, then."

Agnes explained, as they climbed the narrow twisting stairway, that her chamber, from childhood, had always been on the topmost floor of the highest tower, where she had felt safest from interference, by parents and other spoil-sports. But alas, that would not interest Sir Alexander Ramsay of Dalwolsey, she feared?

Coughing, he murmured something indeterminate.

When they came to her door and she opened it, she sighed, dramatically. "Should I invite you within? Or am I to be a better sister this night than I am a wife?"

What was a man to say to that? "I think that you are better in both than you pretend, Countess," was the best that he could do.

"I wonder! Ah, well, it looks like a lonely, virtuous couch for both of us, does it not?" She reached up, threw an arm around his neck and gave him a vigorous hard kiss on the lips.

177

"A good night, nevertheless, Sandy. I will remember what you said anent seeking to prevail on Patrick."

"I thank you. Sleep well . . ."

In the doorway she turned. "See you – I cannot think that young Robert Stewart is still at Mariot's door, down there. Nor within it! A tap thereon might repay your trouble!"

"You . . . you think so?"

"*I* would, were it me."

"I would not wish . . . would not seek . . ."

"Nor I think you a faint-heart! Is not the motto of your house Pray and Work? Off with you – and good fortune!"

On the floor below he remembered Mariot's door from the last time. At it, he hesitated for a little, then knocked, but softly.

A voice answered, but Doune's doors were massive, even within, and he could not distinguish words. He did not want to shout and inform the whole establishment as to what he was at. He knocked again, no more loudly.

Another murmur and then movement. The door opened, if only a little, and Mariot peered out.

"Sandy!" she exclaimed. That only.

"Forgive me! I, I but seek a word with you, Mariot. I did not see you alone." He racked his brains desperately for some excuse, and could conjure none adequate, for his wits were scarcely functioning at their best. This on account of what he saw before him. The young woman had presumably been either in bed or about to go there, and had hastily thrown on some sort of loose bed-robe, under which she was fairly evidently naked. This robe was less than effectively tied up, with the result that, above, it gaped somewhat to reveal not a little of a very lovely bosom, and below parted to show considerable length of white leg. She admittedly made some attempt to draw the ends closer, but not in any agitated or prim fashion, for she was not that sort of person. The man was understandably preoccupied with this vision. "I . . . ah . . . am sorry!" he got out a shade breathlessly.

"Sorry? For what, Sandy?" she asked. And perhaps she was just a little breathless herself; certainly that bosom heaved a little more obviously than might be normal – although of course hitherto, aware of it as he had not failed to be, he had not observed it thus.

"For . . . intruding. On you. When, when . . ." He swallowed. "It was your sister said . . ." Hastily he amended that; it would be grievously unfair to involve Agnes. "I just had to see you."

"Yes? Then you need not apologise," she nodded. "What did you wish to say to me, Sandy?"

Still he had not thought of any suitable pretext. Suddenly it came to him that this was ridiculous. He was not some callow youth, but a grown man, who had lived and fought and killed, aye and had women – although not such a woman as this – easy women. Why cast about for excuse?

"It was important," he jerked, almost roughly, although that was unintended. "I had not kissed you goodnight."

She blinked a little, a pink tongue appearing to moisten her lips, then smiled. "Important, to be sure," she agreed. "A grave omission!" Without actually moving nearer to him, she somehow gave the impression of closer proximity, perhaps a slight leaning forward.

That was all that he required. In a single stride he had his arms around her, and holding her tightly he kissed her hair, her brows, her upturned face and then her lips. And, glory be, those warm, moist lips moved under his own, and opened just a little. Strongly, vehemently, he possessed them, while time stood still.

If time did, it may be that they themselves did not, or not entirely, for there was distinct movement in their persons, of one sort or another, more than that bosom heaving, with deepened breathing and stirring of limbs. At any rate, positions changed a little, and in the process that bed-robe opened somewhat further, and, without any deliberate contrivance, the man's hand slipped most naturally inside, to cup one of those delicious cool breasts, and so to remain while the rest of his body pressed the closer.

Not for long, however. That so intimate contact presumably spelt its own message to Mariot Randolph, for after a few blissful moments she withdrew her lips from his and then brought up a hand gently to remove his from what it held. Almost imperceptibly she moved back.

"It is good night, then," she said, her voice now frankly uneven. "Good for *this* night." The emphasis was palpable. "Your duty done, Sandy, my dear. So, go and sleep soundly."

"Yes." He nodded. "Yes." He found nothing else to say.

Smiling again, she drew her robe more tightly, touched his arm, and turning, moved within and slowly shut the door.

Ramsay looked at the stout timbers for some time before he too moved off, his mind in a turmoil. But it was a turmoil of joy, delight, gratitude, nowise disappointment. Perhaps his body was less than content, but not his mind, his real self, his honest emotions. As he walked along that stone-lined, torchlit corridor to his own chamber, his step was light and his whole being sang, albeit soundlessly. It was all so good, so excellent, so right. Now he could face Edward Balliol, Edward Plantagenet, Patrick Dunbar, the Devil himself, and care naught. That Ramsay motto was effective, after all: Pray and Work. He had been praying for this, after a fashion, for long. And now the work had worked. Or so he esteemed it. Bless Mariot Randolph! Aye, and bless Black Agnes of Dunbar!

Part Two

9

The men, some forty of them, unloaded the horses, the captive ones and their own, of their booty of armour and weapons, carrying these through the thin, chill drizzle of the February night into the castle courtyard to the lip of the circular well-shaft, there piling it up. Back and forth they went, cursing as they stumbled in the dark, for the approach to Hawthornden Castle was anything but level, perched on its cliff-top above the deep, steep ravine of the North Esk. All these horses could not be got into the small courtyard, and anyway none were wanted there. Ramsay and his fellow-leaders carried their share, for this band did not behave as masters and servants but rather as companions in effort, trial and danger.

With the last of their useful haul of gear unloaded, about a dozen men went off with horses, taking them by a carefully chosen route over stony ground to a sizeable burn-channel which wound its way downhill to the river far below in the wooded valley, and down which the horses were led, splashing and often slithering in the water. This was by no means the first time that they had taken this strange route. It was a nuisance, but necessary unfortunately. The tracks of many horses leading to that ruined castle would have been revealing and highly dangerous, so after each foray the beasts had to be taken away in such fashion that their hoof-marks would not show, to be bestowed thereafter in sundry farmeries and crofts on the other, west, side of the river. In the morning, two or three more men would sally out, clad as the humblest of peasants, to look for and clear away any horse-droppings which daylight might show. Nothing must indicate that the derelict Hawthornden Castle was in fact no longer abandoned.

Actually, the castle, part demolished by Robert the Bruce for good reason, *was* abandoned, save by the bats, rooks and owls. It was deep below it that Ramsay and his band had their so secret refuge. That well-shaft in the centre of the little courtyard was the answer. Down it a rusty iron step-ladder was rivetted to the lining masonry, this descending deep into the bowels of the soft sandstone cliff. Down this narrow circular shaft the present trophies of victory on a small scale, swords, maces, lances, helmets, chain-mail shirts and the like, were awkwardly carried or lowered by tired mud-spattered men, none wounded on this occasion happily, into a candlelit corridor, and there stowed in one of the many chambers which opened off, hewn out of the solid rock. For down here was a honeycomb of such chambers, some part-natural caves but most cut painstakingly by human hands in the sandstone, long before, Pictish hands presumably, to turn this into a hidden underground fortress and refuge. Bruce himself had used it as such, and Wallace also, during the Wars of Independence. There was one 'back-door' exit at the end of a long narrow passage, opening eventually into a clump of thick bushes on the hillside; but this was deliberately seldom used, lest it might be revealed to the keen-eyed or men with dogs. Two entirely visible openings did let in daylight to part of the labyrinth, but these were natural cave-mouths in the sheer cliff below the castle, and care was taken never to appear obviously therein, for these could be seen plainly from the opposite side of the ravine. Cunningly, one of these natural caves had been utilised as a dovecote, with hundreds of nesting-boxes cut in the soft stone, and duly occupied by scores of the birds – which could provide a source of food. Their flying in and out of the cave was ages-old and aroused no comment locally.

The booty stowed away and their own armour and weapons doffed, the men gathered in the largest of the chambers, quite a sizeable apartment, where a cheerful fire burned, the smoke finding its way up through apertures in the roof which led out to various escape-holes sufficiently dispersed to ensure that no tell-take wisps of smoke were evident. Here Will Ramsay and a couple of servitors from Dalwolsey, who had not been on the foray, had prepared a meal for the returning warriors, simple but adequate – for they had no lack of food, well supplied from the surrounding Ramsay lands – soup, a great stew of beef, porridge and honey, washed down with milk or ale. The lairdly ones drank no wine in these circumstances.

Over the meal, Alexander Ramsay reported on the day's

doings to his brother. "We rode in small groups, to the valley of the upper Tyne, above Crichton. This English convoy which Brother Cuthbert at the Soutra Hospice informed us would be coming up Lauderdale and through the Lammermuirs, would almost certainly be making for Crichton Castle to spend the night, there being a Balliol garrison there, before riding on to Edinburgh next day. Where the man Balliol is at present. So we lay in ambush in the narrow valley, a mile or so above Crichton. They did come, just as it was darkening. At the end of their day's long riding they were careless. The scouts who rode ahead kept in a bunch on the road. We let these past, and fell upon the main convoy, chopping it up into three parts. They had no chance, in that narrow place."

Will sighed, but said nothing.

"When those scouts came hastening back, we had them also. It was almost too easy. But profitable. We gained much of arms and gear. Even some gold and silver."

"Who would have thought that Sir Alexander Ramsay of Dalwolsey would turn robber! You took no prisoners?"

"No prisoners." That was flat. "We cannot afford the luxury, man. In mercy, or for ransom. To bring prisoners here would be to betray our hiding-place, sooner or later. You must see that."

"Many . . . dead?"

"Many. Some few escaped into the woodland . . ."

He was interrupted. Wattie Kerr, who had been in charge of the horse-disposal party, arrived, to announce that they had a would-be visitor, seeking Sir Alexander, none other than my lord Bishop of Dunblane. They had found him, with two servitors, enquiring at one of the farms. Wattie knew that his master was friendly with the Bishop, but did he want him brought here to their secret hidey-hole? And if so, how to get him in? That heavy prelate would never get down the ladder.

Wondering how Bishop Maurice had known approximately where to come, but happy to welcome him, Ramsay told Wattie to fetch him in, and by the little-used escape-tunnel which ended in the bushes.

Presently the Bishop, panting, wet and dishevelled, with his two apprehensive-looking attendants, was ushered in, to warm greetings. Exhausted, the older man took some little time to recover from his wanderings. In fits and starts he

185

informed them as to how he had learned of their where-abouts. He had gone from Edinburgh to Dalwolsey, but had learned little there from the cautious castleton villagers; the castle itself was now occupied by Balliol's minions. But he had recollected that Sir Alexander's esquire was young Pate Ramsay of Cockpen. So he had made his way to that smaller laird's house, convinced Pate's mother as to his identity and trustworthiness, and learned from her about Hawthornden – but not how to find his way into it. It had been fortunate that Wattie Kerr had stumbled upon him enquiring at one of the farms . . .

"You went to much trouble, my lord, to see us," Ramsay commented. "I am glad that you did. But, why? It must be important?"

"It is," the other nodded. "Have you heard of this so-called parliament? No? Well, Edward Balliol called a parliament at Edinburgh these last days, summoning all to attend. As a bishop, I received a summons. My first thought was to scorn it. Then, on second thoughts, and in consultation with the High Steward, I decided to attend, that we might learn more of Balliol's plans and affairs – aye, and of those who now support him. So I went, and it proved a sorry business. Scarcely to be believed. Balliol indeed is but a puppet. All is controlled by the English. They tell him what to do, and see that he does it. All positions of any power are held by the Plantagenet's men, partly the former dispossessed lords that we know of, but mainly newcomers from England. In charge of all, acting as Chancellor, was the Lord Scrope, Lord High Justiciar of England, as representing King Edward. Master of Ceremonies was Sir Ralph Neville, Seneschal of England. Others deciding matters were the Lord Montague, the Lord Henry Percy, the Lord Mowbray, Lord Richard Talbot, Sir Edward Bohun and more – I cannot mind them all. These confirmed that most of Scotland south of Forth, the city of Edinburgh itself, this Lothian, the counties of Roxburgh, Peebles, Dumfries, the constabularies of Haddington and Linlithgow, and the forests of Jedburgh, Selkirk and Ettrick, were from now on and for ever to be part of the kingdom of England and . . ."

The clamour of fury, indignation, disbelief drowned the prelate's words. But he held up his hand.

"That is not all, my friends. The lands of all who fought at

186

Halidon Hill are forfeited and given to Englishmen – and that includes your Dalwolsey, Sir Alexander! Richard Talbot is now Earl of Mar. Henry Beaumont, one of the dispossessed lords, is now Earl of Moray as well as Earl of Buchan. David of Strathbogie, that turncoat Earl of Atholl, is now High Steward of Scotland! Percy is given Annandale, Moffatdale and the castle of Lochmaben, the Bruce's own lands. The Earl of Surrey is given much of Galloway . . ."

Again he had to pause on account of the din. When he could make himself heard, he went on.

"I will spare you more of this. But . . . it is beyond all crediting, I agree. Still, see you, there could be some possible benefit in some of it, for us. For despite their fine new titles, the dispossessed lords are becoming restive. Much of the land which they believed should come to them is being given to these other Englishmen. They, the dispossessed, do have some stake in this kingdom, being either married to Scots heiresses or the sons of such by English fathers. But they see these arrogant lords, sent up by Edward Plantagenet, being given all the key positions in the realm, and granted the best lands, controlling all. And they do not like it. That much I learned, at least. Patrick, Earl of Dunbar, likewise!"

"He was there? Taking part?" Ramsay demanded.

"Aye. But growing the more unhappy as time went on."

"And you believe that there may be trouble? That these former dispossessed ones may make trouble for Balliol?"

"I will be surprised if they do not. Some of the Comyn lands have been grasped by these incomers; and many of the dispossessed had Comyn links, as you know, married Comyn women. There is naught so apt to cause hatred and strife as losing lands. But that is the least of it. This alleged parliament carved up Scotland into gobbets . . ."

"And it was agreed? The Scots present agreed this dastardly shame and treason? Even Dunbar?"

"They did – Balliol's creatures. See you, there were no great numbers of Scots present. Most entitled to be there had stayed away. And not a few of those there took little or no part, did not speak, hung their heads, as well they might! Dunbar himself, an unhappy man. But they dared not to vote against, with the English watching all like hawks."

His hearers gazed at each other, exclaiming, muttering.

"All this you should know," Bishop Maurice went on. "But

that is not what brought me here this night. It is . . . other. You said, Sir Alexander, at that Council meeting, that it might just be possible to rescue Sir Andrew Murray from Carlisle. I come to beseech you to try to. Desperately we need him back. Robert the Steward is a fine young man, but he is not yet twenty years and with no experience of managing so much as a sheriffdom, not to say a kingdom. Bishop Bernard and I do what we can to advise and encourage him, but we are old men, clerks not soldiers, well enough for councils and statecraft perhaps but not for winning back a kingdom from an occupying power. Robert Stewart, with my lord of Moray away in France, is at his wits' end as acting Regent. He roosts in Rothesay Castle, comes to Dumbarton to meet us now and again, but can achieve little in the realm at large. You here do more for Scotland, we hear, much more. He, the Steward, urged me to come to you."

"I was perhaps unwise to suggest this of trying to free the Regent Murray, my lord," Ramsay confessed. "It may not be possible; indeed the more I ponder it the more I doubt! But . . ."

"But you will try, my friend?"

"If you think it worth the attempt . . ."

"I do. In this pass. Forby, it is the acting Regent's command that you do! We need Murray, a leader and warrior, with a name all men respect."

"It may take time, patience, money for bribes, much secret talk and persuasion . . ."

"The revenues of my bishopric of Dunblane are yours, for this, Sir Alexander."

"I have some moneys here, captured moneys . . ."

"Then go you and try. So soon as may be. You do excellent work here, yes, by all reports, harassing, waylaying, unsettling the enemy, encouraging our friends and the common folk. But this of Murray could be greatly the more important for Scotland."

"Very well. I will attempt it . . ."

All were weary, for it was well past midnight of a very full day. But before seeing Bishop Maurice bedded down in one of the lesser caves, Ramsay asked him if he had news of the Randolph sisters.

"I saw the Lady Mariot a few days past, yes. She is well, but much missing her brother and sister. The Countess Agnes has returned to Dunbar and her husband. When he is there!"

"Ah. Yes, she said that she would go and . . . seek to change his attitudes."

"It is important, to be sure, that he be detached, if possible, from the English interest. After this of Sir Andrew, *you* might go see the Earl? Try to persuade him to change sides. That the Scottish cause would serve him better than the English. Or Balliol's. He hates Balliol. He was a very unhappy man at this parliament . . ."

"The pity that we should have to seek the goodwill and aid of such traitors and self-seekers! We could never trust him."

"True. But he is very powerful, and influences many in the Borderland. If at least he was not fighting *against* us."

"Perhaps. And the Lady Mariot? She is now alone at Doune?"

"Yes. I see her when I can. A fine young woman. Very different from her sister, to be sure. But a true daughter of her father, God rest his soul. She speaks of you."

"She does? I, I admire her greatly."

"As well you might. Goodnight, my son."

With that Ramsay had to be content – although contentment was scarcely a word that applied to him these days. He sought his own hard-lying couch.

Two days later, with Pate Ramsay and Wattie Kerr and a dozen of his men, he was riding down the Ewes Water valley towards mid-Eskdale, having traversed the Ettrick Forest diagonally from Peebles to Hawick, and crossed the watershed thereafter by the high pass of Mosspaul, by little-used routes. They had met with no trouble, seen no sign of enemies, carefully avoiding the vicinity of the towns and castles where such might be looked for. Now, in Armstrong country, they felt comparatively safe. The Armstrongs, although far from the loyalest subjects of the Scots crown, were even less impressed by that of England, a law unto themselves, like some other of the Border March clans, and well-placed in their Eskdale and Liddesdale fastnesses to maintain that independent stance.

They reached Langholm in late afternoon, well aware that for the last couple of hours they had been discreetly shadowed by various horsemen, glimpsed only occasionally, no doubt Armstrongs, who would in all probability have sent word ahead as to their progress. Ramsay had carefully decided on the numbers of his party, not sufficient to pose a threat to any, but enough not to be attacked without due consideration.

He was looking for the Armstrong chief, Mangerton, but scarcely expecting to find him at Langholm, for Mangerton was some distance up the almost parallel dale of the Liddell Water. But Langholm was the Armstrong 'capital' and things must be done in due order if this most delicate venture was to have any chance of success.

In the event they were met, almost a mile north of the township, by a swaggering company of some fifty superbly-mounted, heavily-armed mosstroopers, as ruffianly a crew as could well be imagined, but as fleeringly sure of themselves as they were most evidently critical of anyone daring to ride through Armstrong country without express permission. Fortunately, Ramsay recognised one of their leaders from the Gilsland expedition, Armstrong of Whithaugh, and could hail him by name, a hatchet-faced, lean individual with a pronounced cast in one eye – it was this cast which jogged Ramsay's memory – and who appeared to appreciate being treated as an equal by so eminent a knight as Sir Alexander Ramsay. So the first hurdle was surmounted. They were fortunate in more than that, for on being informed that they were there seeking Armstrong of Mangerton, Whithaugh admitted that Mangerton had in fact been in Langholm that day and had gone to spend the night at Gilnockie, only six miles further south down Eskdale. He, Whithaugh, would escort Sir Alexander there in person.

So, under the wing of the most effective authority in all the Debatable Land, however infamous, they continued on down Eskside, Ramsay making himself consistently pleasant to Whithaugh and his companions.

At Gilnockie Tower, which he remembered from the previous occasion, he did indeed find Mangerton, a quiet and reserved man to be the head of so turbulent a clan, but with his own strengths. Gilnockie, some sort of cousin, was a very different type, younger, brash and arrogant. But he entertained the visitors adequately, indeed feeding them royally, informing them, as before, that the beef was prime English and the wine likewise, in that it was straight from the excellent cellars of Lanercost Abbey, the good churchmen being selective in such matters!

This indication of a cross-border traffic offered Ramsay an opening. He had thought much on his preliminary approach to Mangerton, so important.

"You, or your people, still make sallies into Cumberland, then?" he put to the older man. "I am interested in making such a sally."

His hearers eyed him unspeaking.

"It is no ordinary raid or reiving," he went on. "It will be difficult. I think that only the Armstrongs might achieve it. With Graham help, perhaps." That was carefully said. Mangerton's sister was wed to a Graham on the English side, he recollected, and he it was who had aided Douglas on the Gilsland raid, with the Grahams of Netherby and Kirkandrews.

He had their interest, at least. "No raid is too difficult for us!" Gilnockie jerked.

"Even into Carlisle Castle?"

That had them staring.

"Sir Andrew Murray, Regent of Scotland, is a captive in Carlisle Castle," Ramsay went on. "If he could be got out, there would be rich reward for those who contrived it."

The Armstrongs eyed each other.

"If it is too much for you to consider, tell me. And I shall try elsewhere."

"Where else?" Gilnockie demanded.

"I would try the Grahams. They must know Carlisle Castle passing well."

"Tell us what you purpose?" Mangerton said quietly.

"Sir Andrew Murray has been prisoner in the castle for many months now. With no rescue attempt. They will not be looking for anything of the sort. It is too strong a place to assault. But we might extract one man therefrom, using our wits, and a deep purse. Scotland needs Sir Andrew Murray."

"How much?" Kilnockie asked baldly.

"Enough for even Armstrongs! You have my word on that."

"This would take some prior contrivance," Mangerton said.

"Admittedly. Hence, I thought, the Grahams. If they were sufficiently . . . persuaded."

There was another silence, minds undoubtedly busy.

"It would be a deed to sing of, hereafter," Ramsay observed, shrugging. "How the Armstrongs lifted a regent, not a parcel of cattle, from the English!"

Perhaps it was that last that did it, or at least tipped the scales. Mangerton nodded.

"We will ride to Netherby tomorrow," he said.

Kirkandrews Tower was no more than six miles south of Gilnockie, on the Scots side of Esk, with Netherby just across the river on the English bank. Andrew Graham, at the former, listened to Mangerton's, rather than Ramsay's, brief account of what was envisaged as though it was the most normal of projects, making little or no comment other than that they must go and see his kinsmen at Netherby. He would accompany them.

Over the same almost private ford which they had used on the Gilsland occasion, they crossed Esk into England, with no more ado than fording any other stream, to find Netherby awaiting them, well aware of who was coming, so efficient was the Border intelligence system. Whether or not he knew *why* they had come was another matter, but he listened interestedly, an elderly greybeard with a shrewd eye and a strong, stocky figure. He too appeared to find nothing particularly odd about their actual proposal, although he scratched his beard over the details. It might be a little difficult to arrange, he suggested. And costly.

Ramsay had come prepared for that last, but was suitably tactful about how the matter should be put, in case their present host was touchy on the subject of finance, unlike for instance Armstrong of Gilnockie.

"I recognise that some quite substantial moneys may be required," he said. "Bribes for guards and gaolers, hiring of men and horses, and the like. I have authority to offer £300 Scots, to cover all . . . expenses."

There was a silence at that. £300 was a large sum, even in Scots currency, with cattle, the normal form of exchange in these parts, fetching less than £1 per head. But, of course, it would not do for the others to sound impressed. Netherby was at his beard again.

"Aye. Umm," he said. "There could be not a few to pay. Carlisle Castle is well guarded. There would require to be . . . negotiations. Certain folk would have to be paid to look the

192

other way, of a night. I fear, aye, I fear a little more might be required."

Ramsay glanced at Mangerton. "I will put a further £100 in the hands of Mangerton here, to cover all possible extra charges. That is as far as I can possibly go."

Mangerton nodded gravely. "A wise provision," he commended. "I think, Will, that should serve."

Kirkandrews agreed. "We might pick up some beasts on the way home, to help eke out," he suggested.

"I had thought of that, yes," Netherby admitted. "But not on the way home, Dand. Earlier. See you, if a large raid on lands near to Carlisle was made just before dusk, it would draw away many guards belike, cause much upset. Take attention away from the castle. Say, to Houghton or Drawdykes, north of the town . . ."

"Better still, two days hence is market-day in Carlisle," Mangerton put in. "There will be many droves coming in, to the town-muir. A raid on these would arouse more outcry than just on some lord's or squire's land and cattle. Bring out the town guard, even some of the castle people, it may be . . ."

Kirkandrews slapped his leather-clad thigh. "Good! We could do both, by the Mass! I have been looking for just such a ploy, for long . . ."

"And I am with you!" Gilnockie asserted. "We will attack in force. Make it just after darkening. Descend on the town-muir. Then back over Eden, defending the crossing, to let the beasts get well on their way. We should do royally!"

"All wearing Armstrong colours, mind you," Kirkandrews added. "So that it is seen to be a Scots ploy. No Grahams seen . . ."

"Yes, yes . . ."

Ramsay was interested that this cattle-raiding project seemed to be of more concern to some present than was the release of Scotland's Regent. And even more so when Netherby added his own refinements as to timing and getting back with the herd implying evident acceptance of the original proposal. It seemed that the attempt would be made.

The discussion eventually got down to dealing with the major issue. Various names were mentioned, none meaning anything to Ramsay. Questions of how much, in money, kept arising, to that man's private amusement, so tiny were the sums debated compared with the £300, despite all the previous emphasis on the expense of bribes. Since time was so short, with the market in two days, it was decided that Netherby's two sons, known apparently as Will's Will and Will's Dod Graham, should go to Carlisle that very day, to sound out the necessary individuals and make arrangements. Considering how delicate was the entire operation, and how secret it all must be kept, Ramsay was distinctly doubtful about committing all to the discretion of these young men, neither of whom looked notably responsible. But everybody else seemed to judge them reliable, and he was in their hands now.

These emissaries, of course, required the moneys to effect their bribery. There was considerable discussion as to how much they should have – not so much on Ramsay's part as on that of their seniors, who obviously were concerned that their own shares were not unduly whittled away. Listening, it did not fail to occur to Ramsay that, with their evident fondness for gold and siller, and their reputation as rogues, it was something of a wonder that they did not just grab all that he had, there and then, and forget the Carlisle project, since they were very much in a position to do so. Presumably it was true that there could be honour among thieves, perhaps Border thieves in especial, with their own codes of conduct.

In the end, it was decided that the Graham brothers should take £30. At the same time, Ramsay handed over the £100, plus half of the remainder, to Mangerton, as earnest of mutual trust, if that was the word.

They returned to Kirkandrews Tower for the night, as the brothers rode off.

Next day, while Grahams and Armstrongs were assembling in large numbers for the cattle-raid, Ramsay and his little party had to wait, with what patience and calm they could muster, for more effective developments. It was mid-afternoon before word was brought across Esk that the Netherby sons had been reasonably successful at Carlisle and that all should go ahead as planned. It was less than a dozen miles to Carlisle, ninety minutes' riding. The cattle-reivers were about to leave, taking a roundabout route so as to give no warning of their descent upon the town-muir at darkening, there to cause major alarm and distraction. The castle-party would not leave until well after dark, to allow maximum numbers of guards and men-at-arms to be drawn off.

They watched some one hundred and fifty horsemen ride away, almost due eastwards, with mixed feelings. These could create a distraction, certainly; but they could also alert the entire Carlisle area for trouble that night.

It had been decided that the best time to arrive at Carlisle Castle would be around midnight, when the town guard and others, it was hoped, would not yet be returned from trying to rescue the cattle, and the castle garrison itself should be bedded down for the night. So the long-awaited move was made, from Netherby, about ten o'clock, on a chill night of fitful moonlight and rain-showers. The group, as well as Ramsay's own people, included Gilnockie and Kirkandrews and Will's Dod, with some of their men; Will's Will had stayed on in Carlisle in the interim, to keep the situation there under review. Mangerton and Netherby elected to remain behind, leaving it all to the younger men.

It was a relief, at least, to be on the move, and making the attempt.

They rode by the direct route, about thirty strong, since there was nothing to be gained by hiding, at this stage. Because of the crescent moon, it was only half dark, but the locals knew every yard of the way. So, going by Longtownmoor and Hopesyke, they crossed Lyne by the ford at Westlinton, and thence by Harker and Lowryhill to the Eden. There was a bridge over Eden into Carlisle, of course, but this was to be avoided in present circumstances. However, the Grahams – and the Armstrongs too – knew all the fords of all the rivers, and there was one at Etterby, about a mile downstream. From there Carlisle Castle was a bare mile ahead.

Will's Will Graham was waiting for them at the far side of the ford, a cheerful character who, by his confidence and general attitude, had probably passed the waiting time in an alehouse, imbibing. But, according to him, all was in order, or as good order as they might contrive. Moneys had been accepted, assurances given – and threats of dire reprisals made on any backsliders. There had indeed been a great to-do in the town and castle at dusk when the raid on the town-muir had commenced, and satisfactory numbers had flooded northwards over the Eden bridge to try to deal with it. Few if any had come back as yet, he believed.

They rode on through the scattered outlying skirts of

Carlisle, outside the walls, past the leper-town, until the massive black outline of the great fortress loomed up before them. They were fortunate in that the castle was an integral part of the walled city, its bastions forming a section of the northern walling of the town, so that no city gate here had to be negotiated. The North Gate, leading to the Eden bridge, would presumably be open, because of the cattle-raid, but the other gates would be shut for the night.

The Graham brothers led them, dismounted now and going quietly, to a sector of the outer castle walling where, a little west of north, a postern gate was situated, small and little-used. This would be securely locked and barred, to be sure, and the Grahams had been unable, indeed wisely had not tried, to entice the sergeant of the guard responsible for this sector from his duty. But they had managed to bribe a couple of that night's sentinels, who would be patrolling the walls in that sector, to move away elsewhere when they heard an approach being made. These assured that the gate-porter, an elderly man, slept all night in his little lodge in the walling, and would be easily dealt with.

The perimeter wall was high, perhaps twenty-five feet, topped by a parapet and wall-walk. But they had come prepared for this, with a couple of scaling ropes tied to spiked grapnels, the hooks of which could catch on projections and grip, the ropes themselves being knotted at intervals, to aid the climbers.

There was no sign of sentinels up on the wall-walk, no sign of life about the place at all indeed, effective bribery or otherwise. The ropes were thrown up, and after a number of attempts did catch and hold secure – although the noise made by the grapnels clattering on stonework sounded enough to wake the entire castle, to Ramsay's sensitive ears. No reaction was evident however, and Will's Dod and an Armstrong promptly set about clambering up the ropes, feet against the walling, hand over hand. Hoisting themselves over the parapet itself was apparently less easy, but no sooner were they up than another pair followed on.

There was a pause, the party waiting in mixed anticipation and apprehension. Then a creaking noise signalled the opening of the postern door. Dod Graham came out, waving.

They surged inside, none troubling to ask after the gate-porter. Will's Will had made a point of learning where the Regent Murray was immured, in a range of semi-subterranean vaulted cellars below the great north-west bastion of the inner bailey. This, although not far from the postern, meant that they must get inside that same inner bailey, itself protected by another lofty wall. So, although the bastion they sought was to their right here, they had to hurry round to their left in order to find the gateway. This was unlikely to be shut or barred at night, except in siege conditions, despite having its own gatehouse; if it was, they would just have to do some more rope-climbing.

The gateway-pend proved to be open. There might be men asleep in the gatehouse, so they entered the arched entrance quietly and left half a dozen of their people there to guard it and block the gatehouse door.

Hurrying on now, still without seeing or hearing anything of the garrison, the leaders in the venture had no difficulty in locating the north-west bastion, a squat but massive square tower at the angle of this inner bailey. It had only the one entrance, and the door was shut, but proved not to be locked. This groaned loudly as they opened it, but snores from the vaulted guard-room on the right seemed to indicate no disturbance of the guard. Four more men were left to watch this, and the remainder of the party moved on, and down a steep, straight flight of steps into evil-smelling pitch darkness.

They had brought flints and steel and tinder and candles, and these they now lit. A narrow vaulted corridor, dripping damp, was revealed in the flickering glow, with four doors off, all on one side. Two of the doors stood open. The other two had great keys in their locks, on the outside. Which?

Unlocking the first, Ramsay peered into a filthy, stinking cell. A man lying on dirty straw stared up. Shaggy-bearded, with greying matted hair, thin and gaunt and in ragged clothing, he appeared to be some wretched beggar, imprisoned for heaven knew what offence in this hell-hole. Muttering a sort of apology, Ramsay withdrew and closed the door.

The next cell proved to contain two inmates, both youngish men, haggard and bearded, but obviously neither Sir Andrew Murray. What, then? Had they been misinformed? The Regent not here after all? Tricked? Or – could it be . . . ?

Ramsay went back to the other cell again. The man was sitting up on his straw.

"You! Your name?" he demanded, peering.

"My name? I, I have near forgotten it. But it is my own. Who are you to ask it?" The voice, although hoarse and cracked, was Scots, and proud.

"Lord! Can it be, can it be Murray? Sir Andrew? The Regent? Can it be you, truly?"

"Andrew Murray, yes. As to Regent, God knows! Who are you?"

"Ramsay, my lord – Alexander Ramsay of Dalwolsey. Come to win you out of this evil place."

"Ramsay! Young Dalwolsey! Of a mercy . . ." The sitting man started up, voice breaking, but lost balance and fell back.

Ramsay stooped, reached out to aid the obviously weak and unsteady man. Others crowded into the cell, with the candles.

"Is this your man?" Gilnockie demanded. "*This* your Regent?"

"Yours also!" That was harsh. "Ill-treated, curse them! Help me with him, man." And to Murray, "Fear nothing, my lord. We will have you out of here. Up with you . . ."

The older man muttered something, but concentrated his efforts on rising and keeping his feet.

Supporting him on either side, they got him, tottering, out of that grim dungeon. Closing the cell door behind him, they all but carried him along the corridor. Murray was a big man, but this was but a shadow of his former self, thin, wasted and stinking. Getting him up those steep steps was difficult and far from soundless, their charge gasping and groaning.

They found a new situation at the guard-room, the door open and one of their men standing therein, the other three inside. The snoring having suddenly ceased, the two guards had apparently come to the door, and been dealt with. Details as to this dealing were omitted.

They all moved out into the inner bailey, Murray saying nothing, concentrating on putting one foot before the other, breathing uneven. At the gatehouse there were no complications and they picked up their half-dozen watchers. Ramsay was worried about the postern situation, for he doubted if it would be possible to get Murray over that high wall. However, all was well there, and they passed through the gateway without problems, and bore their charge along outside the walls to where the horses waited.

Now there was a new anxiety. Could Murray sit a horse and

ride, once they had hoisted him up into the saddle? Or would he have to be carried in front of someone else, like a child? Ramsay put it to him.

The Regent made his first coherent statement since leaving that cell. "I . . . will . . . ride," he said.

They had brought two extra horses, and somehow they got him up on to one of them, where he slumped forward in the saddle. Concerned for him, Ramsay mounted and moved close, offering to take the reins and lead the beast. But the other waved him away.

"There is the ford to cross," he warned.

"Ride . . . slowly."

They rode, strung out, down to the Etterby ford, to splash across, Ramsay remaining close to Murray in case he needed help. But in the saddle that man seemed in better control than on his feet; or perhaps it was just the fresh night air after the stench of that underground cell. He rode reasonably well.

It was not until they were over Eden and trotting past the Etterby cot-houses and cabins that it really came to Ramsay that they had done it, that the great project was actually achieved, the all but unthinkable accomplished, and with the minimum of trouble. Indeed it had been almost too easy, seeming to diminish the importance of it all. But that was folly. They still had to get the Regent back to his own land.

So, despite the impatience of the mosstrooping fraternity, they rode slowly the dozen miles back whence they had come, with frequent glances behind, fearing pursuit. But nothing of the sort materialised, and the country folk, if awakened by the sound of many hooves, had the good sense to shut ears and eyes again. Nothing was to be seen nor heard of the cattle-raiders.

Sir Andrew was reeling in his saddle long before they reached Netherby, Ramsay afraid that he would topple to the ground. They dared only go at a walking pace now, at least Ramsay's group did, with some of the Borderers hurrying on ahead. Nevertheless it was agreed that they must get Murray across Esk and into Scotland before they let him rest. Somehow this seemed important.

That last fording was done at a snail's pace, with Ramsay's horse reined close enough to Murray's for his arm to be intermittently around the other's sagging person, although the unevenness of the going made it difficult. At length, at the door of Kirkandrews Tower they more or less lifted the Regent down and carried him inside, where the women of the house took over, to cherish and wash and put him to bed.

Relaxing in relief, Ramsay drank a celebratory cup of ale with the others and made a gesture at eating some of the fare provided, before he sought his own couch, thankfully.

Scotland had its leader again – although it looked as though it would be some time before its Regent would do any actual leading.

Even though Murray was in no state for further riding so soon, it was decided that he must move on the very next morning, deeper into the Border fastnesses. Once the English authorities discovered that their important prisoner was gone, it was inconceivable that they would not come looking for him, sending out companies to scour the land; and they would surely assume that it would be into Scotland that he would be spirited. The Grahams were all too well aware of this, and eager to see the backs of the visitors. The cattle-lifters had returned, with the dawn, well pleased with themselves, their bellowing beasts making the neighbour-hood loud with alarm. This four-footed booty had to be dispersed quickly and driven off in small parcels into all the valleys and hidden pastures of the Debatable Land, 'beef-tubs' as they were known, so that Netherby, and Kirkandrews too, could deny all knowledge of the night's doings if challenged. After all, there were many other Border reiving clans on the West March, on both sides, Robsons, Elliots, Salkelds, Maxwells, Johnstones, Musgraves and the like. So it was agreed that Ramsay should take Sir Andrew the fifteen miles or so to Mangerton in Upper Liddesdale, along with a due proportion of the cattle, there to rest up for a day or two. It would be a bold Englishman indeed who led anything less than an army that deep into the Armstrong sanctuary.

Paying over the remainder of the money to those who had so effectively earned it, they set out northwards amidst mutual expressions of esteem, it occurring to Ramsay that perhaps he had made useful friends here for the future. At least, travelling with the cattle, they did not have to hold back their pace to accommodate Sir Andrew.

10

Alexander Ramsay sat his horse waiting, not exactly impatiently but very conscious of the waiting. These last months had seemed to be largely a matter of waiting, trying for a man of his temperament. Not that he regretted it or felt that he had in any way wasted his time, but that time had seemed to pass very slowly. Moreover, although his wits told him otherwise, a different part of his mental make-up could not escape some sense of guilt. This spot where he had waited was so fair, so peaceful and so remote, that it seemed no place for one concerned with Scotland's cause and freedom to be lingering through a fine spring and summer. Not that he had been at Avoch all the while; he had made sundry brief journeys away, on the realm's and the Regent's business, but none sufficiently far south to bring him into the area where Balliol and the English ruled, or into any real danger, where such as he ought to be involved, struggling, fighting, instead of waiting upon the needs and commands of an ageing man, even if that man *was* the true ruler of Scotland.

And yet, and yet – those wits of his told him that what he had done was right, for the best, in the land's best interests. Small-scale fighting, raiding, ambushing, was all very well, and personally satisfying if successful; but such would never gain Scotland's freedom, however much it might help in the process. Only large-scale war would, or could, in the end, drive out the invaders, and only such as Sir Andrew Murray had the authority and the experience and the reputation to rally the nation and bring about victory, if even he could do it. So, since March – and it was now September – Ramsay had brought the Regent back to his northern lordship on the Inverness Firth, stayed with him in his weakness and recuperation, all but nursed him back to such health and fitness as was possible, acted his attendant, assistant, lieutenant and delegate.

Now, at last, there was to be action of a sort, a start.

He gazed due eastwards, over the heads of the great assemblage of men gathered on the level ground between the castle and the shore, across the sparkling waters of the firth, to the coasts and blue mountains of Moray. Thither they were bound, when the Regent saw fit to send them on their way. It would be a long march, for although that opposite shoreline was not much more than five miles away, they would have to make the long detour round this Inverness Firth and then round the head of the Beauly Firth, by Inverness itself, and then east again, to Petty, some forty-five miles. To save the still frail Murray this tiring progress, he was to take a boat across, and they would rejoin him at Ardersier, to march on the further seventy-odd miles to Dundarg Castle, in northern Buchan, their objective – their *first* objective, that is.

At length the rest of the leadership group emerged from the castle gateway, the Regent in close converse with Sir Alexander de Mowbray. Ramsay was not very happy about this association with Mowbray, for he did not like nor trust turncoats, of which the Scots nobility seemed to be all too full these days. Yet without Mowbray this present venture would not have been attempted. He was one of the former disinherited lords, with their strong Comyn connections, no Englishman but who had taken Balliol's side in the present troubles, his father having fought against Bruce. Now, like some of the others, he had fallen out with Balliol over the usurper's appointment of Englishmen to the important offices in the realm, and left his court. But while these others were content to retire to their lands and castles, Mowbray had gone further. His brother Geoffrey had recently died, leaving only two daughters, and he, Alexander, had claimed the family's wide lands; but Balliol had decided against him and given them to the daughters and their husbands, who happened to be also amongst the former disinherited, for all these Comyn descendants tended to cling together and intermarry, for the sake of the vast lands involved. In fury, Mowbray had taken the major step of changing sides, and come north to join the Regent at Avoch, with a large body of men. Not only so, but advocating an attack on Sir Henry de Beaumont, now styling himself Earl of Buchan and sulking at his strong castle of Dundarg, husband of one of the sisters. Dundarg should be his, Mowbray asserted. Murray was not interested in the man's ambitions but recognised the opportunity to drive a wedge between these English-inclined lords, strike a blow at Balliol and try to wrest the great province of Buchan from the usurper's sway. Ramsay saw it as a first blow in a new campaign, and disciplined himself to be civil to Mowbray, since they were to be in joint command of the present force until the Regent rejoined it.

Murray, although only in his fifties, looked an old man, and although vastly better in health than when he had come back here, was still thin and stooping. Ramsay, who had grown very fond of him in these months, recognised that even this comparatively modest expedition would tax the other's strength and stamina.

"All ready, Sandy?" the Regent asked. "I wish you well on your march. I cannot think that you should meet with any trouble, other than the miles themselves, till we meet at Petty. It will take you three days, I reckon. I will sail for Ardersier tomorrow, and hope that I will have some hundreds more of my Petty people to join our host. My lord of Barnbougle and yourself will do very well." There was just a hint of warning in that, for them both. Murray knew very well Ramsay's feelings in the matter.

Barnbougle was Mowbray's ancient barony in Lothian, almost the same distance west of Edinburgh as Dalwolsey was south. That man, a few years older than Ramsay, sallow-skinned but handsome in a saturnine way, made no comment, but mounted his horse to ride off down to the waiting assembly.

Ramsay wrung Murray's hand. "So starts a notable enterprise, my lord. The beginning of great things, I hope."

"Pray God so, lad . . ."

Mowbray was no more enamoured of the other's company than was Ramsay. Since the latter by this time knew this countryside the better, he rode at the front of the company of about twelve hundred men, while Mowbray remained with his own people towards the rear. But this was no mounted array, such as the Lowlands and Borders could produce, but in the main a foot host. Up here, on the outskirts of the Northern Highlands, good riding horses were in short supply. Nevertheless, progress was faster than might have been expected, for these clansmen, lightly clad and armed, were used to moving at a trot, which they could keep up for great distances, seemingly tireless. They could not go as far and as fast as cavalry, of course, but they made a very mobile force for all that – and they could go where horses could not, through marshland, over rock and up steep craggy heights.

They went now due westwards and round the head of the long firth-like Munlochy Bay, and on by Kilcoy to Tarradale, at the neck of this great peninsula between the Inverness, Beauly and Cromarty Firths, known as the Black Isle, although in fact it was no island, nearly all of which was part of Murray's lordship of Avoch. After Tarradale, they reached what might be called the mainland, and could turn due south to Beauly, the town and priory at the head of its firth. Here, because of their delayed start, they camped for the night, a mere fifteen miles covered. Mowbray put up in the priory but Ramsay stayed with the men.

The next day they proceeded on, eastwards now, by Lintran and Bunchrew to Inverness, to cross the River Ness there. Its castle had been destroyed by Bruce and never rebuilt, and the town was now an appanage of the Earls of Ross. But Earl Hugh, who had married Bruce's youngest sister, had fallen at Halidon Hill and left only a child heir, and Balliol had sent up emissaries to retake the former Comyn castle of Urquhart nearby. These were now isolated and not sufficiently powerful to impose their sway on Inverness itself, which was in consequence a sort of no-man's-land in the present power-struggle. The Avoch force encountered no opposition there, but did not linger, moving on a few miles north-eastwards along the Moray Firth shore now, to camp at Allanfearn. This was already in the barony of Petty or Petyn, Murray's second great lordship.

They were at Petyn Castle, near the head of its hook-shaped bay, by the mid-day following, to find the Regént already there and assembling men from his far-flung domains, the lordship stretching for many miles along the coast and well up into the hills of Strathnairn, where it marched with the earldom of Moray. Sir Andrew said that if they waited another day they would have an extra thousand men, mainly Highlanders.

So it was quite a major force which set out, two days later, on the long eastwards march to Buchan, seventy miles at least, through the sheriffdoms of Nairn, Forres, Elgin, North Moray and Banff; country where Balliol's rule did not run, but over which occasional forays from the great Comyn lands of Buchan traversed to keep them quiet. Ramsay heedfully suggested a horse-litter for the Regent's journey, but the proposal was brusquely dismissed and Murray rode with the rest.

Fortunately the weather remained good, and even allowing for Murray's frailty they could average almost twenty miles a day. They met with no hostility, and the Regent's name, announced by scouts ahead, ensured consistently warm local reception. On the evening of the fourth day they approached their destination.

Dundarg was a strange place for Henry de Beaumont, kinsman of the great English Earl of Warwick, to hole up in, quite the most northerly and remote of the Buchan strong-holds, which he had inherited through his wife, a daughter of the last Comyn Earl of Buchan. But it was one of the strongest and least accessible, and had not been demolished by the Bruce regime. If he wanted to dissociate himself meantime from his far-out kinsman Edward Balliol, here was as good a place as any, perhaps.

The castle, on the site of a former Pictish fort, hence the name, the Red Dun, occupied a rather extraordinary position on a narrow and thrusting promontory, high above the waves. It would be no easy place to take, and there was no cover from view in the approach from any angle. Undoubtedly the arrival on the scene of a host of over two thousand would not have gone unreported, so there was no point in seeking to make any attack by night. They approached openly therefore, along the cliff-ridge from Aberdour and down the grassy slope to the precipitous shoreline, with the westering sun at their backs. Needless to say they found the castle all shut and barred against them, the drawbridge up and the nearby cot-town empty of its inhabitants.

They wasted no time in preliminaries. The leadership group advanced on horseback, carefully, having to cross two deep dry ditches cut in the rocky ground to prevent artillery being brought close to the walls, but halted well before the final water-filled ditch which the drawbridge could span, just out of bowshot of the gatehouse. They flew the Lion Rampant flag of Scotland's monarch and the banners of Murray, Ramsay and Mowbray. A trumpet was blown, and shouting being unsuitable for Murray, Ramsay raised voice for him.

"I speak in the name of Sir Andrew Murray, Lord of

Avoch, Petty and Bothwell, Regent of this realm for David, the King's Grace. He is here present. As is also Sir Alexander de Mowbray, Lord of Barnbougle, your kinsman, who claims that this castle is his. I am Sir Alexander Ramsay of Dalwolsey, and would speak with Sir Henry de Beaumont, calling himself Earl of Buchan." That took hard shouting, over the distance and against the noise of the waves breaking on that iron-bound shore.

That produced an immediate response from the gatehouse. "I am Buchan," a voice came thinly, but clearly. "I recognise no Regent and no King David Bruce. I deny that this house is Alexander Mowbray's. It is mine, in the right of my wife. I require you all to leave my lands forthwith."

That was predictable.

"What you recognise or do not is of no import, Englishman," Ramsay returned. "The Lord Regent, in the name of the King, demands the immediate surrender of this hold."

"Then he is fool as well as impostor! Let him try to take it!"

So that was that, the necessary routine gone through – or not quite all, for a shower of arrows came winging over from the castle walls, to a chorus of derisive shouts, none finding a target at that range. The Regent's group retired to the cot-town, having anticipated nothing other.

It had to be siege, therefore, and siege without cannon to assist. Some sort of mangonels and slings for throwing rocks they might construct, but in effect it would be a matter of starving the defenders out. Which meant time. Their unheralded arrival would almost certainly mean that the castle would not have been stocked up with food to stand a long siege, especially with presumably extra mouths to feed from the abandoned cot-town. And no large-scale provisioning by sea would be possible, on account of the rocky and reef-bound shore below, although on a calm night a small boat might just be able to land something, to be hoisted up the cliff. How long, therefore, Beaumont could hold out was a matter for guesswork. But that was not supremely important; not to the Regent anyway. His main objective was to let Scotland know that its leadership was on the offensive again, assailing one of the usurping earls, threatening the province of Buchan and more, and conceivably drawing a relief force northwards to Beaumont's aid, which might itself be ambushed and destroyed in this comparatively empty country. David de Strathbogie, Earl of Atholl, another of the Comyn brood, was known to have retired to his Atholl fastnesses, on the other side of the Mounth, and might be enticed to venture this far. Others, also.

They took over the cot-town of about thirty cabins, to provide what comfort was possible, and in the next days the men would be set to constructing hutments for themselves, felling timber for firewood and collecting food from the countryside; this all to be duly paid for, on Murray's strict instructions, for retaining the goodwill of the local folk was important.

They settled in, to wait for hunger to work for them.

After the first few busy days, of course, time began to hang heavily for those of an active disposition – which certainly included Alexander Ramsay. Also he was having to see all too much of Mowbray, who did not improve with enforced proximity. The castle might have been empty as far as developments went. The rest suited Murray well enough in his present state, but the men inevitably tended to grow restive, and undisciplined in consequence. Therefore, since two thousand were by no means necessary to watch Dundarg, unless there was a serious attempt at relief, Ramsay proposed that he should take a mounted company, say two hundred, which was as much as they could produce horses for, and, as it were, show the King's flag round Buchan and adjoining parts, making it clear to the population that the royal forces were now in command again here. They might also be able to drive out any Comyn sympathisers, and possibly gain earlier warning of any would-be relieving force's approach. Murray found no objection to that, but said that they must keep in fairly constant touch, by means of mounted couriers, in case of emergency.

So a move was made, there being great competition amongst the men to be included, although many were no accomplished horsemen and therefore not suitable. It was good indeed to be riding free again, with no hard-and-fast remit, a whole province before them, Pate of Cockpen, Ramsay of Redheuch and Wattie Kerr enjoying it equally with their lord. It was possibly of no great consequence in Scotland's cause, but at least it was activity.

With all of a wide land before them, Ramsay chose to head first along the coast eastwards, for this was where the main population was based, in fishing villages and havens. Inland, there were fewer people, the province never having fully recovered from the terrible harrying meted out by Edward Bruce after his brother's victory at Inverurie, the notorious Hership of Buchan. Besides, the land was hilly without being mountainous, and not very fertile, with great areas undrained and barren moor. They went by Rosehearty and Pitsligo, where there was a castle, but a Forbes place not Comyn, and its elderly laird wished them well. There was another castle at Pittulie nearby, but this had been all but demolished and never rebuilt. On past Sandhaven and Phingask, they followed that attractive coastline of intermittent cliffs and sandy bays to the great thrusting Kinnaird's Head.

There was another small castle here, little more than a tower, which provided a beacon-light for shipping and alleged protection, and in return took a proportion of the fishermen's catch, as at Dunbar. It was a Comyn place, but left in the hands of a local keeper, a frightened man when he saw the two hundred riding up to his door. He made no attempt to confront them. With no hostility towards the people there, Ramsay considered it to be his duty to destroy this little stronghold, as an example. He informed the keeper so, told him that he and his could remove anything they wished from the tower. He could, and should, erect his beacon anywhere on the headland itself, but the castle was to be burned.

Ramsay did not enjoy this sort of thing, although some of his men seemed to get satisfaction out of the destruction. He saw the people here as fellow-countrymen who could not help their lords' treasons.

They spent the night at the fishertown, the castle now only a smouldering shell, and rode on still eastwards next morning, after sending a courier to Dundarg.

This was approximately the pattern for the days which followed, although they did not always find convenient strongholds for them to burn. Some were too strong for them to take, but more had been destroyed already, Edward Bruce's work of twenty years before evident everywhere. But they did make their mark on that part of Buchan, proceeding as far east as Rattray Head, and ravishing the Cheyne castle of Inverallochy, linked with Comyn, before turning to cut back inland by the Loch of Strathban, Lonmay and Rathen. They had been gone for a week.

There was no change in the situation at Dundarg. But there was news. Messengers had reached the Regent from the South. The Steward, who had been holed up secure but restricted in his island castle of Rothesay on Bute, encouraged by the tidings of Murray's return, had slipped out, taken boat to Dumbarton Castle on the Clyde estuary, and had been welcomed there by Sir Malcolm Fleming, the loyal Keeper. From Dumbarton he had sent word to the tenants of his great Stewartry lands of Renfrew and Paisley to muster. These had risen, to much good effect, and Balliol's occupying forces, not strong thereabouts, had fled. Encouraged by this, Sir Thomas Bruce, a son of Edward, had raised the men of Carrick and Kyle, with some success. Hearing of this, Sir William Carruthers had assembled a host in Dumfries-shire and Galloway. This of course was Balliol's own country, and he could not achieve much there; but he had moved north to join Carrick and Kyle, and these again had linked up with Renfrew. So that now there was a fairly solid belt of the South-West in loyal hands, separating the Balliol lands of Galloway from that usurper's headquarters in central Scotland.

As well as this there were other reports, less good but interesting. Earl David de Strathbogie had moved north from his Atholl lands up into Badenoch. He had inherited much territory, with the island castle of Lochindorb there, from his Comyn mother. Why was he doing this? As crows flew, Lochindorb was only some forty-five miles from Dundarg, although across mountainous country. Could he have had information about this siege of Beaumont – he was married to Beaumont's daughter – and intend to come to the rescue?

This thought worried Murray, for a besieging force, down in this hollow of the seaboard, could be very vulnerable to attack by any major company on the higher ground behind. It might not be that, but the possibility was there. The Regent suggested that Ramsay might use his restless energy to go and make a quiet investigation. No challenging of Atholl, at this stage, just a discreet scouting.

Ramsay was not averse. He took a mere dozen of his Dalwolsey men, and with Pate and Wattie Kerr, set off next day. Riding fast and free, they went west by south across upland Buchan, with a local man as guide. Twenty rough miles over the hills of Troup and Overbrae and Tillymould, they came to Turriff, where they rested their mounts. Then on almost as far again, in the same general direction, through the north of Strathbogie, whence Atholl took his name but no longer owned. They were getting into lofty country now, moving out of the green Buchan hills into the skirts of the great mountainous spine of the land. They halted for the night at Croughy in Glen Livet, part way up the narrow valley of the Conglass, this developing into a sort of pass leading to the strange and remote upland township of Tomintoul.

They did not head upstream next morning however, but swung northwards for the mighty strath of Spey. They were coming into Badenoch now and it behoved them to go warily. Seeking to avoid townships and villages – for the Spey valley was wide, fertile and populous – they had difficulty in finding a ford of the great river which was not near the haunts of men. A well-armed and horsed party of a dozen, they were not likely to be attacked, but their presence could be noted and word sent to Lochindorb.

Eventually they chanced on a wandering Benedictine friar, who informed them of a ford at Dellachapple, near Cromdale, where there was only a small monastery. By and large the churchmen were loyal to King David, for the Bruce had been a good friend to Holy Church, which had in the main supported him. And the Bishop of Moray, who ruled here, was sound. So they felt that they could trust their friar, and revealed their identity. He added, then, that the Earl of Atholl was indeed at Lochindorb, and reported to be assembling men from far and near; it was the talk of the countryside. Why was not known, but it was assumed that it was for an attack on the Regent, who was known to be in Buchan.

Ramsay, of course, needed more than this, and must somehow try to obtain it. But he was beholden to the friar for more than that. For he had tidings about another of the former disinherited lords, the Lord Richard Talbot, calling himself Earl of Mar, an Englishman married to the daughter of the Red Comyn, slain by Bruce at Dumfries. He, having raised many men in the Comyn lands in Galloway, had marched them eastwards along the Border, for purposes unknown. But he had been careless, and Sir William Keith of Galston, kinsman of the Marischal, had ambushed his force and defeated it with great slaughter, killing Talbot himself.

So now, with the successes of the Steward, Thomas Bruce and Carruthers, the South-West was almost entirely in loyal hands.

This was excellent and encouraging news, indicating that the blight on the land after the disaster of Halidon Hill was lifting, and the Scots spirit arising from the ashes.

They crossed this ford at Dellachapple and rode directly northwards into the high heather moors of Dellafure and Auchnahannet and Dava, desolate country and womb of waters, where the Rivers Divie and Dorback were born, the land known as Braemoray. With the peak of Knock of Braemoray soaring ahead of them out of the brown moors, they swung left, westwards, and presently came in sight of Lochindorb itself, lying in a vast amphitheatre of green land amongst the desolation. What to do now, Ramsay was not sure. How to find out Atholl's intentions? If they could perhaps capture one of his people, who knew something . . .?

In the event they did rather better than that. For where the heather changed to rolling, grassy slopes, cattle-dotted, more like Buchan again, and they began cautiously to ride down in the direction of the loch, they perceived a commotion ahead, at a cot-town surrounding an old and decayed hall-house. Prudently they drew aside into the scattered scrub woodland which patched these lower slopes.

They had quite some time to wait before they saw three mounted men ride away from the cot-town shepherding a group of perhaps ten obviously reluctant young men, these last in ragged kilts and plaids. They led them off downhill in the direction of Lochindorb. Women and children and older men stared after them sullenly.

"Unwilling recruits for Atholl's host," Ramsay said. "We might learn something here. These folk do not like it."

Waiting a little longer, they moved down to the hamlet. Their arrival was watched with ill-concealed hostility. Smiling reassuringly, Ramsay called out that they were friends, not Atholl's men. They would buy food, meats. He emphasised the word *buy*.

That gained them some slight acceptance, producing money a little more. He asked whose hall-house this was, to be told Mackintosh's of Corrycharcle. He recollected that this was Clan Chattan country before ever the Norman

211

Comyns grasped it. Leaving Pate to purchase provisions, he made his way on foot to the hall-house.

There he found the elderly tacksman in considerable resentment over the forcible taking of his young men for the Southerner's wars. What right had this Atholl to come demanding levies? The Mackintosh was his chief, not this Frenchman!

Ramsay smiled to himself. David de Strathbogie would not relish being called a Frenchman, although he was of course of Norman extraction a few generations back. But at least this attitude gave him the opportunity to declare that he was King David's man, Ramsay by name, sent by the good Regent Murray, and against this Atholl – which met with approval. And more, with questioning. Was the Regent nearer than they had heard, then? The word was that he was on the Buchan coast, near Aberdour. That was where this Frenchman was going, with a great host, to surprise Murray. But, if Murray was nearer, was *he* about to surprise Atholl?

Ramsay had to admit that this was hardly the situation, not yet at any rate. Later, perhaps. How many men did Atholl have assembled down there at Lochindorb?

A great many, he was told, three thousand at least, and more being brought in daily, like his own laggard people.

How reluctant? Ramsay demanded. Was this unwillingness general, here in Badenoch? For, if so, these Highland levies would fight the less stoutly.

Mackintosh agreed. He did not see the local clansmen, Macphersons, Shaws, MacGillivrays and Davidsons, as well as Mackintoshes, fighting with any fervour for the Frenchmen.

So Ramsay had got what he had come for. He thanked the tacksman, urgent that he and his people said nothing about their brief visit, declared that he would commend him to the Regent, and took his leave.

Well provisioned, they set out on their return journey.

In two days they were back at Dundarg with their news, which much interested Murray. He decided that something must be done about it. There was no knowing when Atholl might reckon that he was strong enough to come to the rescue of his father-in-law; but it would take an unmounted host, as his must be, perhaps five days to reach the Buchan coast.

They could not rely on having more than another week, then. And if Atholl already had over three thousand, then numbers were in his favour even though enthusiasm might not be. And Beaumont might be able to sally out and aid him, in an attack.

The Regent, therefore, proposed a diversion. If Atholl could be led to believe that an assault on his own base down in Atholl itself was envisaged, then he might well return there to beat it off, instead of coming to Dundarg.

Ramsay agreed. But how was such an impression to be given? Where could they raise the men for it?

In two ways, the older man suggested. One, whilst Ramsay had been away, they had had information from the South, from Bishop Maurice of Dunblane, that young Moray was returned from France. If he could be persuaded to raise as many men as he could from his Doune of Menteith lands and march them north into Atholl, that would help. And if he himself were to leave Mowbray in charge of the siege here, and take say seven hundred of their men south-westwards out of Buchan and into Mar, then this could be seen as a threat to Atholl also, just across the Mounth from Mar. Murray's own wife was at Kildrummy Castle, the seat of the Mar earldom, which Talbot had never been able to take, and she, Christian Bruce, could produce more men. So there could be the threat of a thrust into Atholl from two sides. When David de Strathbogie heard that – as he would be sure to hear, given time – he would surely move to counter it. Time was the problem. How quickly could he, Ramsay, get down to Doune and convince Moray to act?

Ramsay calculated. Forty miles to Aberdeen? Another fifty to Perth, although he would have to avoid Perth itself, where Balliol was making his headquarters. Then twenty more. Some hundred and ten miles to Doune. If he was unhampered by a following of men, he could do it in two days' hard riding.

Murray nodded. Do that, then, without delay. He himself would start out next day, for Kildrummy. It ought to work.

So Ramsay was to horse again, this time with only Pate and Wattie Kerr, leaving Redheuch to command the Dalwolsey contingent at Dundarg. Now it was merely horsemanship, on and on, keeping going. They had fine beasts, and would need them. One thought above all others beat in Ramsay's head, as they ate up the miles. The probability was that he would be seeing Mariot Randolph shortly, as well as her brother.

Weary and travel-stained they arrived at Doune Castle just after the October darkening of the second night, hard riding behind them, their horses all but foundered. The drawbridge was up and the great gates barred – no doubt because of Balliol's presence not so far away – so that they had to do a deal of shouting and identifying before they could gain access. Which resulted in a notable reception once over the lowered bridge, with both Moray and his sister come down to welcome them. Mariot's greeting was the most frankly warm with which she had yet favoured Alexander Ramsay, she actually throwing her arms around him, more as her sister Agnes might have done, crying how good it was to see him, where had he come from, was he well, she had thought of him so often, and the like. He was duly if rather dazedly appreciative.

Moray was almost as glad to see him, if in a different way. Apart from their friendship, he was eager for news, being very largely ignorant of the current situation in Scotland, save what Bishop Maurice could tell him. Since he had got back from France he had been more or less cooped up in this strong castle. Rumours and conjectures there were aplenty but little hard news. It was said that Sir Andrew Murray had been ransomed, which sounded very unlikely, for the English would surely never allow Scotland's foremost leader to go free. There were more circumstantial tales of Robert Stewart's doings in Renfrew and Kyle, and he was proposing to go there and join him, if he could have it confirmed. But no details and no more general information as to the overall state of affairs.

So over a much-needed meal Ramsay was able to tell them the situation as he knew it – if disjointedly, for he was very tired. Pate indeed fell asleep at the table. He informed Moray as to the Regent's wishes in the matter of Atholl and urged him to move quickly, stressing the time factor. The other was agreeable enough to do as suggested, indeed was so relieved at not being called upon to be acting joint Regent any more that he would have agreed to almost anything.

Later, by the hall fire, while Moray was telling him of his adventures in taking the young King and Queen to France,

Ramsay nodded off. And seeing it, Mariot took charge. It was bed for him, forthwith, she ordained. No man should ride over one hundred and ten miles in two days and then do anything more than eat and sleep, certainly not discuss the nation's ills. He was to follow her.

So it was that young man's turn to be escorted up to his bedchamber by Mariot, instead of the other way round, and once there no nonsense about parting at the door. She led him in, took him over to the great canopied bed, turned back the covers, pushed the warming-pan into a new position, found some more fuel for the well-doing fire and poured out a cup of wine for the bedside table. When, sitting on the edge of the bed, he reached up arms to draw her to him, she yielded only momentarily, stooped to kiss the top of his head and then moved back, quite determinedly.

"Not tonight, Sandy," she said. "There is a time for all things. Tonight, for you, it is sleep. Only sleep. To bed with you, my dear. A good night!"

He tried to protest but the words did not come. In fact, as the door closed behind her, he could barely summon the energy to take off his clothes. Toppling into bed, he was asleep before he had time even to commiserate with himself over her departure.

Next morning, recovered although still stiff, Ramsay went with Moray on a tour round the Menteith area, for Doune was really the dun or fort of Menteith, or more properly Monteith, the hilly lands between the Rivers Forth and Teith. Mariot rode with them, saying that she had had enough of being confined within the castle precincts. Moray sought out his lairds and vassal land-holders, ordering them to assemble the maximum numbers of men available at very short notice, and to have them at the castle by the very next morning, armed and mounted. Yes, it was very little time, but that was the situation's requirements. Tomorrow, before noon.

This barony of Doune of Menteith, separate from the greater earldom of Menteith, a Stewart fief with a child as earl – his father, Earl Murdoch, having been one of the slain at Dupplin Muir – was only a modest part of the large earldom of Moray, although its castle the favourite seat of the late Regent. The main lands were in the North, in the great province of that name, with others down in the West March of the Borderland. These lands would have to be raised for men, in due course; but for the present venture, Doune must serve. It could muster five hundred perhaps – but scarcely in so brief a time. Three hundred or so tomorrow, the rest to follow on. Moray would now go and see the mother of the child Earl of Menteith, to try to get her to send a contingent. They were Stewarts, after all. If Ramsay would go and see Bishop Maurice at Dunblane? He could produce forty or fifty more, surely . . .

In mid-afternoon, when Moray headed westwards for the Countess's castle of Inch Talla in the Loch of Menteith, Ramsay turned eastwards for Dunblane, with Mariot declaring that she preferred the Bishop's company to that of the young Earl's mother. Unfortunately, perhaps, he still had Pate and Wattie accompanying him as well, even though these did follow a discreet distance behind. But it was good to be riding together. It was becoming something of an obsession with Ramsay to be alone with this young woman.

The few miles to Dunblane through the green, cattle-dotted slopes, were all too short. The man learned that Agnes was still at Dunbar, where her peculiar husband was more or less sulking, hating Balliol and all his works, angry with Edward Plantagenet whom he considered had grievously failed him, but not yet prepared to throw in his lot with the Regent. Agnes was trying to persuade him, but . . .

Bishop Maurice received them kindly, indeed in almost fatherly fashion towards Mariot, of whom he was obviously very fond, and genially towards Ramsay, of whose exploits from Hawthornden he had heard some garbled tales. Churchmen were apt to hear more than most, through their travelling friars, although accuracy could not always be vouched for. As to the Regent, he had heard only that he had somehow been ransomed and had returned to Scotland and was in Buchan. He was delighted to hear of the true situation now prevailing and agreed that he must do all in his power to help. He could promise sixty men from his Church lands, perhaps forty horsed and ready tomorrow. For his part, the Bishop told of stirrings and small uprisings reported from many parts of the land, all heartening news.

Despite his admiration for the good prelate, Ramsay was not for lingering. He calculated that Moray's visit to the Countess of Menteith would take some time, with further to go and persuasion to be applied, and probably lesser lairds to

216

approach also. So that back at Doune they should have the private quarters of the castle to themselves for a while – and that was something to be desired and made to last as long as possible. He could not actually urge Mariot to leave her friend, of course, but he probably made his wishes apparent.

Presently they were riding back to Doune.

Cousin Pate was the next problem. He could not just be dismissed, nor of course sent to the servants' quarters with Wattie, but his pleasant company was not required meantime. However, Pate Ramsay had sufficient perception to see that his services to his lord were not urgently required at the moment, and found convenient business elsewhere.

So Alexander Ramsay was in something of a hurry when at last they were in the private hall, laying a hand on his companion's arm. "Mariot, I so seldom can see you alone. I, I long to, always."

"Do you, Sandy?" she asked gravely.

"Yes. You see, I have grown very fond of you. I think . . . you must know it?"

"You are kind."

"No! It is not kindness that I feel for you, Mariot. It is a deal more than that."

She smiled. "I am the more . . . flattered."

He shook his head, frowning. "This is difficult to say. I fear to say too much. I fear to offend. To say anything which might spoil, injure our friendship. For you have been most kind, friendly. I fear to risk damage to that . . ."

"So fearful? The bold Sir Alexander Ramsay of Dalwolsey, who all say fears no man, no odds! This fear I cannot believe."

"Yet it is true. You see, so much is at stake. For me. I want to retain your friendship, so fear to hazard it by, by saying too much."

Gently she did the arm-pressing. "Yet now, I think you *are* saying too much! Too many words. Like fear and spoil and hazard. Perhaps you should just say what is on your mind, Sandy. Am I so great an ogress, so harsh a female?"

"You are the most lovely, kind, fair and dear woman in all this land! And, and . . ."

"That is better, Sir Alexander! Much better. Say on! You do very well, now that you have reached the point."

"But that is *not* the point, Mariot! To my sorrow. The point is that you are a great earl's daughter and sister, and of kin to

217

the royal house of Bruce, daughter of the beloved Regent Moray. You could wed any in this kingdom. Worse still, the High Steward much favours you, I know well. He would wed you, I think, if he might. Your brother's friend. And *he* is heir presumptive to the throne! King David is a mere boy, and may well not survive. Edward of England would slay him if he could, nothing more sure. Balliol would also. Then the Steward would be King of Scots, Bruce's grandson. And his wife would be Queen!"

"Ah! So you would have me Queen of Scotland?"

"*I* would not, God knows! But you could be, if, if . . ."

"If I would? I do not love Robert Stewart. I like him, yes. But . . ." She shook her attractive head. "And this troubles you, Sandy? That I could, one day, be the Queen, if Robert Stewart asked me to marry him."

"To be sure. It is ever on my mind. What could *I* offer you? So little, by comparison."

"And, you think me, as it were, in the market? Seeking the highest bidder? The highest price!"

"Ah, no. But I cannot shut my eyes to that price. And John, your brother. He will have some say in the matter . . ."

"Johnnie would never have me do what I did not want to do. And although he likes Robert Stewart well, he greatly admires you. He has said so, often. We all do. So, do not be so fearful, in Doune Castle, when you are unafraid elsewhere!"

"You, you tell me to be bold, then, Mariot?"

She laughed, the first laugh of that somewhat awkward conversation. "Now what have I done! Not too bold, Sir Knight . . .!"

He put an arm around her, and drew her to him. He kissed her brow, her eyes and her lips – and hers opened and moved slightly under his.

"I love you, Mariot," he said, against those lips. "How I love you!"

"I guessed . . . as much!" she got out.

"My Sweet! My Precious! My heart's desire . . ."

She pulled away a little. "You have . . . recovered your . . . courage, I see!"

He drew a deep breath and released her. "I am sorry. Forgive me. I, I forgot myself."

She waved a now free hand. "For a moment, so did I! But . . . there is a time for all things, perhaps. Not now! Not here."

And she pointed, "Old Andrew has been waiting to give us our meal, this while."

"Sakes!" In his preoccupation with his personal problems, he had not noticed the elderly castle chamberlain waiting over near the service door from the kitchen stairway, and now staring fixedly in the other direction. "I am sorry," he repeated. "I did not know, did not see."

"No matter . . ." Mariot moved over, and said a word to the old major-domo.

So, in minutes, the servitors were bringing up food and wine for the table, and intimacies were perforce suspended. And during the meal Moray arrived back, pleased with himself. He had got more men out of the Countess than he had expected, two hundred no less. It would mean waiting until at least noon tomorrow for them, but worth it. So they should be almost six hundred, to deal with Atholl.

What was left of the evening Moray spent in readying his people for their departure, provisioning, and ensuring that the necessary horses were brought in from outlying farms; and in all this Ramsay felt it to be his duty to offer assistance. There was no further opportunity for private converse with Mariot.

It was late before they were finished, and Ramsay was afraid that the young woman might have retired to bed. But she was waiting for them, to say goodnight when they got back. He was, of course, urgent to escort her to her room, almost forgetting to take suitable leave of his host.

He held her arm climbing the twisting turnpike stair. At her room door he halted.

"Tomorrow I will be gone," he said.

"I know it," she answered, low-voiced. "To my . . . sorrow."

"Then that, at least, I can take with me – your sorrow. But, sakes, I want more than that, woman!"

"What do you want, Sandy?"

"Lord? I want *you*!" Hastily he went on, lest he had gone too far. "But since I can scarce have you now, perhaps ever, I want something, something which I can take with me. To have. To hold on to." He was holding on to her person now, in fact, more strongly than he realised.

"If I can give you aught, Sandy – what would you?"

"But a word or two. I have told you that I love you, Mariot.

219

If I could believe, dream that one day you could think possibly to say something of the same to me, some word of hope . . ."

"But, my dear, I said so! I told you, did I not, that I was fond of you? Can you not tell it? Would I be here, your arms around me, if I was not?"

"Fond, lass, and I am grateful. But I seek more than fondness, see you. Love, that is what I seek, long for, need!"

"Then love, yes. For I do love you, Sandy."

"You do? You do? Dear God, you *love* me? Mariot! Mariot!" He all but shook her in his joyous extremity.

"To be sure. Is it so strange? Have we not been . . . close? For long now?"

"Close!" He embraced her comprehensively, to demonstrate his notion of closeness.

"Not here, Sandy!" she got out, a little breathlessly. "Johnnie could come . . ."

"Then inside." And he pushed open her door.

She hesitated, but yielded to pressure. "For a moment or two, only . . ."

"Yes, yes . . ."

With the door closed behind them, he took hold of himself, as well as of her. "Forgive me, my dear, my heart's darling. I am so much overjoyed. I forget myself. It is so good, so much what I have longed for."

"I know, I know. But . . ."

His lips closed on hers, his hands enclosed her breasts. Somehow they found themselves sitting on her bed.

"I do not think . . . that this is wise, Sandy," she said, after a minute or two.

"But if we love each other . . .?"

"Yes. But we can go . . . too far. Too fast! And I am weak, I fear. A very frail woman!"

She knew her man, undoubtedly. That of frailty, implying her being at the mercy of his strength, was sufficient to arouse his masculine protective care, his sense of chivalry. He took himself firmly in hand.

"Yes. You are right. Fear nothing. As matters are, we must be careful, discreet. I know it. But one day, my dear, God aiding me, I will come for your hand. In marriage. If you will have me. And then, ah then . . .!"

220

"Then, Sandy, I will be waiting. And, and . . . all yours. I am yours now, I promise. But then, ah then . . .!"

"Surely. Hasten the day! But now – you would have me go?"

She eyed his face searchingly in the half light, biting her lip as though uncertain. Then she nodded. "If you will, my dear. I, I think that it would be best. Tonight."

"Tomorrow I leave you."

"I know it, I know it. But, I know myself, also, you see. And – oh, Sandy, go, go quickly!"

"So be it." One last passionate kiss and he was on his feet. "I will not sleep, but still I will dream!"

"Goodnight, my love . . ."

The next day, at noon, Moray's force moved northwards.

To avoid the dangerous Stirling–Perth approaches, they wound their way up through the hills of the Ardoch Water area to Glen Artney, and then over to Comrie in upper Strathearn, some fifteen miles. On through the ever heightening mountains of Breadalbane, by Glen Lednoch and over to Ardtalnaig on Loch Tay, a similar distance. They camped by that lochside. Next day, riding north-east to the foot of that great sheet of water, they turned up the Strath of Appin to reach the head of Loch Tummel. Now they were into Atholl, with Blair-in-Atholl itself, the Earl's seat, no great distance off. They went slowly, in roundabout fashion now, to Kinlochrannoch and up Glen Errochty; for their objective was not to seek to assail the powerful castle of Blair but to let all Atholl know that a strong force was advancing northwards through the earldom, so that word would be sent to the Earl himself up in Badenoch, it was hoped at approximately the same time as he would be learning of the Regent's move south-westwards through Mar. This ought to ensure the Earl's immediate and hurried march south for Atholl, and the hoped-for encounter, with the loyal forces trapping the enemy between them. So they did not hurry now, burning sundry clachans and townships on their way, as much to send up great smoke-clouds as anything else to indicate their presence and make the message clear.

They met with little real opposition, the entire Atholl area obviously having been more or less drained of men to make up the host taken to Badenoch. They were well aware of being watched, of course, all the time; but six hundred was too strong a company to be assailed by any but a comparable force.

Avoiding Blair Castle itself, they joined the main strath of the Garry at Struan, and turned up-river, still delaying in order to give good time for reports to reach Lochindorb, almost seventy miles to the north – if the Earl was still there.

He was not, as it proved. For at Dalnacardoch, just south of the great high pass of Drumochter, a courier reached them from Murray. Their strategy had worked. The Regent's progress through Mar, with much of his strength from Dundarg, had duly drawn Atholl back towards his threatened home territory. He had headed south by Glen Livet, Tomintoul and the Mounth passes. Murray, reckoning that the enemy would continue on that line, cross Dee near Ballater and head over the watershed to Atholl, had hurried ahead to Deeside, to a position on the long rounded hill of Culblean, north of Ballater. The Atholl force could pass on either the east or west side of this hill, and Murray planned possible ambushments on each side. In the event, the enemy came on the east, and where that drove-road narrowed between the head of Loch Kinnord and the steep gorge of the Burn o' Vat, the Regent's people had taken them utterly by surprise, cutting up the long column of between three and four thousand men into gobbets, most of which were then left leaderless, and many far from eager to fight. It had hardly been a battle, so total was the surprise, even though the vanquished much outnumbered their attackers. David de Strathbogie himself had fought bravely, seeking to rally his fleeing men by basing himself against a rock and shouting that it would flee as soon as he. And he had died beside that rock.

So now, the courier reported, the Regent was returning to Dundarg, and called on Sir Alexander Ramsay to rejoin him there. Moray was to take over the province of Atholl meantime and from there pose a threat to Balliol himself at Perth. Once Dundarg fell, which it was believed would be soon now, he, the Regent, would join Moray in Atholl and march on Perth.

So it was parting, north and south, for Ramsay and Moray.

By the time that he arrived back at Dundarg, that castle had in fact capitulated. Whether it was the shouted news of Atholl's defeat and death that did it, or merely that supplies had at last run out for the defenders, Beaumont surrendered. Murray chivalrously did not maltreat nor even imprison him but sent him south to England, on parole, to collect and bring back a substantial ransom – which would be very useful.

There was nothing now, after demolishing Dundarg Castle, to keep the Regent's force in Buchan. They set out on the long march back to Atholl.

They duly found Moray at Blair. But there proved to be no need for a joint approach to Perth, for all Atholl and Gowrie rang with the news that Balliol had taken fright over all these reverses, and the uprising of the loyalists' spirits, and had departed for Berwick-on-Tweed, . calling again for King Edward's help.

Scotland was not free yet, of course, for its greatest fortresses and castles, other than Dumbarton, were still in English or pro-Balliol hands: Roxburgh, Home, Caerlaverock, Lochmaben, Murray's own Bothwell, Edinburgh, Stirling, Dunnottar and the rest. But for the moment the tide had turned. They must keep it that way.

Murray would start trying to reduce those castles, beginning with his own Bothwell, in Lanarkshire, near enough to the Borderland to be available at short notice if required. For it was the Borderland which was now the vital area again, with Balliol at Berwick and anticipating Edward Plantagenet's help. And the key man on the Border was Patrick, Earl of Dunbar and March. Ramsay must go to Dunbar.

11

It was good to be making for Dunbar Castle again, even though Ramsay scarcely relished the prospect of trying to persuade its owner to start behaving as a Scots earl should. But Black Agnes was excellent company, if of course less so than her sister; and Mariot would somehow seem the closer in her company, he anticipated.

It was good, also, to be riding openly through Lothian, without fear of attack by Balliol's supporters or the English.

His own castle of Dalwolsey was in enemy hands still, as were many other strong places in these parts; but in present circumstances the garrisons tended to keep their heads down, not looking for trouble as hitherto.

He rode down the River Tyne, from Haddington, avoiding Hailes Castle, and on by Bielhaven to the coast. With the red stone town of Dunbar in sight ahead against the sparkling sea, he saw that the great flag of the earldom was not flying from the castle's topmost tower, as it would be apt to do were its lord in residence. Was his errand, therefore, doomed to be abortive?

The drawbridge, however, was down, and he had no difficulty in gaining access to the first of the rock-top towers. No, the Earl was not there, he was told, but the Countess was. Indeed, presently, Black Agnes came running over the bridges to greet him, arms wide, not caring who observed her smacking kisses. He could not but rejoice to be so well received, even if the object of his visit was not to be attained.

The Earl was at Ersildoune in Lauderdale, she told him, the seat of his second earldom, of March. He did not spend more time with her than he must, she added frankly; nor was she cast down therefor! She had not managed to persuade Patrick to throw his considerable weight on to King David's side, no. He was very disgruntled, however, at odds with everyone, including herself, believing himself to be ill-used by all. If the Regent had something to offer him, something substantial, it was conceivable that he might be induced to commit himself to the loyalist cause.

Ramsay admitted that Sir Andrew Murray had more or less given him a free hand in this matter. He would go on to the Earlstoun of Ersildoune next day.

That evening, by the fire, the man rather gained the impression that if Agnes Randolph had not been so devoted to her sister, and his own preoccupation with Mariot recognised, he might well have been the object of even more friendly attentions than already prevailed. He was a little cautious, in consequence.

Perhaps she perceived his wariness. For presently she went straight to the point, in typical fashion.

"You and Mariot, Sandy?" she demanded. "How is it with you? I know that you are fond of her. How far has it gone?"

He blinked a little at this forthright enquiry. "I . . . we . . . ah, we are friends. Good friends. I greatly esteem her."

"I know that, man. Anyone can see it. You have been at Doune recently. Have you come together? Do you progress?"

"We enjoy each other, I think."

"Think! Enjoy! A mercy – if you enjoyed her fully you would not say *think!* Out with it, Sandy, where are you at?"

"I have told her . . . she knows that I find her . . . desirable. And, and more than that."

"Save us – is that all? Desirable!"

"Damnation – I love her! And she loves me, she says."

"That is better! Why could you not say so, at the first? So, you love each other. As I guessed. What now, then?"

"What mean you, now?"

"I mean that you are, I swear, a lusty man. And Mariot is no shrinking flower. Love does not stand still, for such as you."

He frowned. "I would marry her, to be sure, if I might. But, as you must know, it is difficult. This war and battle – no time to start a marriage. And, why should she marry *me*? She could wed anyone, the highest in the land. The Steward, who one day may be King. He thinks much of her, I know. She could be Queen . . ."

"And you think that matters, if she loves you?"

"It must matter. It is her life. And I could be slain at any time."

"As could Robert Stewart."

"Perhaps. But – if she had a child by Robert Stewart, a son, he could be King one day."

"You believe that would weigh greatly with Mariot? Having husband or son King? A sure promise of a troubled life! Instead of wedding the man she wanted."

When he shook his head, she went on.

"See you, Sandy, few women of our sort obtain the privilege of wedding the men they want. Most of us are married off to men our fathers deem as desirable goodsons! For their wealth or lands or position. As was I. Wed to Patrick, a man old enough to have been my sire, when I was fourteen years. A man I could not love nor even greatly respect. Tied to him, because he was Earl of Dunbar and March and controlled much of the Border. The like should not happen to Mariot. She *could* wed for love. As could you. And why wait? You say that you might be slain. Any of us could die tomorrow. We must grasp what happiness we can while we can. Do not delay, man."

"How often have I told myself all this, Agnes. But . . ."

"But nothing! You are Sir Alexander Ramsay of Dalwolsey, a paladin in Scotland's struggle. Do not shrink from *this* challenge! Ask her to wed, and soon. I swear that she will say yes. If she does not, she is scarcely sister of mine! I could wish, could wish . . .!" she left the rest unsaid.

"I may take your advice," he told her carefully.

Next morning he set out south-westwards, through the Lammermuir foothills and diagonally across the wide, green and fertile plain of the Merse; Home country although under the overall authority of Dunbar, much of it devastated by repeated English raiding. He rode by Duns and Greenlaw and Gordon, some forty miles, to the valley of the Fans Water, which led down into Lower Lauderdale. And down at its foot, where the Fans met the River Leader, was Ersildoune, a famous name in Scotland's story.

This, of course, was the home of the renowned seer, poet and ballad-maker, Thomas the Rhymer, Sir Thomas Learmonth of Ersildoune, who had cut such a wide swathe some fifty to sixty years previously, in the reign of Alexander the Third. He, to be sure, was but a small laird, whatever his qualities of mind and heart, a vassal of the then Earl of Dunbar and March, his modest tower-house down in the riverside haugh. But up from this, on the higher ground rising to the White Hill, was the great castle of his lord, surrounded by its large castleton, known as the Earlstoun of Ersildoune, the seat of the March or Merse earldom.

Here Ramsay met with a very different reception to that at Dunbar, cool, suspicious, verging on the hostile. The Earl was away, visiting vassals' properties up Lauderdale, he was told; but enquiries elicited that he would be back with sundown.

The visitor waited, rather noticeably shunned.

He heard Dunbar and his party ride up, but it was some time before the Earl deigned to send for him. He found him at meat in the lesser hall, and obtained his first refreshment since arriving at Ersildoune, since it could hardly be denied him in the circumstances.

"I am told that you come from Murray, Ramsay?" Dunbar said, without enthusiasm. "Where is he now?"

"At Perth, my lord. Which he has taken over from the man Balliol, fled. He sends you his greetings."

"No doubt. But not only greetings, I warrant. What does he want from me?"

Thus bluntly demanded his business, Ramsay was left with little scope or opportunity for finesse or preliminary soundings, such as he had envisaged.

"He seeks the goodwill and co-operation of one of the great earls of Scotland. And one of the most powerful. As is surely his right, as Regent of the kingdom."

"Right, man? Who made him Regent? *I* certainly did not!"

"A parliament did, my lord. Confirmed by His Grace. And he is married to the late King Robert's sister, the aunt of King David."

"*I* am married to the daughter of King Robert's nephew! So what of that?"

Ramsay tried a different tack. "Under Sir Andrew Murray's leadership the realm is being freed of the usurper. Everywhere the land is rising to arms. But Balliol is only at Berwick, and seeking English Edward's aid again. So this East March is vulnerable. And you, my lord, control the East March."

"I do." That was curt.

"Edward Balliol is no friend of yours. And King Edward has spurned you, has he not? The Regent believes that it is in your interests to join him and free Scotland from its enemies. And from yours."

"I conceive *myself* to be the surest judge of my interests, Ramsay."

"No doubt, my lord Earl. But would you not require to know all the . . . advantages before making your judgment?" He rather emphasised that word advantages.

Dunbar did not fail to notice it. "There are advantages? For me? As well as the privilege of fighting Murray's battles for him!"

A hot retort rose to the younger man's lips, but he swallowed it. "There are, yes. You would be appointed Chief Warden of the Marches . . ."

"I am already Chief Warden. Always have been."

"Shall we say, appointed so by parliament and the Privy Council?"

The Earl snapped his fingers, eloquently enough.

"The office of Lord Chamberlain is vacant. It was Sir Alexander Fraser's, slain at Dupplin Moor. It is one . . of profit."

The other sat silent.

"The Balliol family own vast lands, some in Lothian – Penston, Hoprig, Adniston, Elvingston and others. These will fall to be forfeited, like the Comyns' lands. You, my lord, could receive some of them."

He had Dunbar's attention now. "Which?" he demanded.

Ramsay swallowed, wondering how far he dared go. "That is not for me to say. A matter for . . . negotiation, my lord. With the Regent. But substantial lands, I am assured . . ."

"I have long sought for lands in Galloway and the West March. I have properties in the Middle March. And the barony of Morton, in Dumfries-shire, is my wife's. But Galloway . . .?"

"I have no doubt that could be arranged, my lord."

"Aye. Well, we shall see. Tell me, Ramsay, was it in truth Murray who sent you here? Or your friend Douglas?"

"Douglas? Sir William, of Liddesdale? He is a prisoner in England."

The other raised his eyebrows. "He *was*. You have not heard? You did not know? I thought . . ." He shrugged. "Douglas has escaped. He is back in Scotland, at his house of Hermitage, in Liddesdale. Or was . . ."

"Lord, is this fact? True? Here is news! We have heard nothing of it. When was this?"

"I learned of it some days past. From Armstrongs."

With the distinct impression that this was a more important development than any grudging support bought from Dunbar, Ramsay saw no point in seeking to prolong the interview. Nor did the Earl show any inclination so to do. Clearly they had got as far as they were going to at this stage. With no offer of hospitality forthcoming, and too proud to ask for it, the visitor decided that anyway he would prefer to spend the night in the castleton than in this unwelcoming hold. He had noted a small monkish hospice attached to the nearby church. That would probably serve. Declaring that he would inform the Regent that his lordship was considering a change in his attitudes, in return for due advantages, he took his stiff leave.

The hospice accommodation was spartan but sufficient, its custodians more friendly than those of the castle. He left at sunrise.

Now he rode not north-eastwards, whence he had come, but in the opposite direction, down Lauderdale to Tweed, then over the eastern shoulder of the Eildon Hills, the Romans' *Trimontium* and Thomas the Rhymer's alleged meeting-place with the Queen of Elfland. Then on by St Boswells to the Teviot valley at Ancrum. Up Teviot he turned, in the Middle March now. Avoiding the Cavers—Hawick vicinity, which was Balliol land, he stayed to the north of the riverside, by Minto and Wilton. There he worked round the town of Hawick to the Slitrig Water, up which he turned. Now he started to climb, and would go on climbing, up and up through the high watershed hills which divided Southern Scotland, the spine of the land. As well that he was an excellent horseman and finely mounted, for this was major riding, a fifty-mile journey over taxing country, with no convenient hospices nor inns for travellers in these empty uplands. Fortunately the weather was kind.

He reached the lofty narrow pass of Shankend with the sinking sun and all Liddesdale, Eskdale and Lynedale ahead of him, a vast panorama of green slopes, far-flung ridges and shadow-filled valleys and cleuchs, the country of the Armstrongs and the Elliots and the Johnstones, where Douglas was in theory overlord but in fact was a merely tolerated incomer who might be useful.

It was all downhill now, by the Whittope Burn to its junction with the Hermitage Water. And there, rearing tall and dark and menacing on its terrace above the rushing river, was the powerful castle of Hermitage, bearing surely an odd name for a stern, frowning stronghold in wild country.

Admission to that place was no easier than at Ersildoune. And when eventually he was inside, no Will Douglas came hastening to welcome him. When he ran his friend to earth it was to find him, crouched over a fire in a small tower-chamber, staring into the flames.

Starting forward with a cry of greeting, Ramsay actually faltered in his stride as the other looked up. He was in fact barely recognisable, a changed man from the big, vigorous, confident, even brash individual of heretofore. Thin, bent, haggard, he looked withdrawn, almost furtive. He made no attempt to rise.

"Lord, Will, what is this? Save us – what . . . how . . . man, what have they done to you?"

The other took his time to answer that. "Well may you ask!" he said, at length, his voice dull, toneless.

"But, this is beyond all! You look . . ." He stopped himself. "Will, you are sick? Ill?" He went to grip those stooping shoulders. The other shrank from his touch.

"You could say so."

Ramsay stared, nonplussed. "I heard that you had escaped. Heard it from Dunbar, of all men! I came, at once. Tell me, Will."

Douglas shook his head. "You could have spared yourself the haste."

"But . . ." Ramsay sat down, although unbidden, the other apparently no more pleased to see him than eager to communicate. "There is a deal wrong here," he said, picking his words now. "Can you not tell me? I am your friend. We have shared much together, Will."

"What is there to tell? Save folly and malice and spleen. None of that new, or news!" Having said that, with evident effort, he appeared disposed to say no more.

"But – you cannot leave it there, man!"

When that produced no reaction, Ramsay spread his hands. "At least, you can offer me some refreshment! I have ridden from Lauderdale."

That seemed to get through to the man. Straightening up, he reached for a bell, which he rang. When a servitor appeared almost immediately, indicating that he had been waiting just outside the door, he curtly ordered meats and wine for Sir Alexander Ramsay.

This delayed gesture appeared to produce some slight relaxation in Douglas's attitude for as they waited uncomfortably, he volunteered a remark. "You are dealing with that snake, Dunbar?" he all but snarled.

"Sent by the Regent, by Murray. To try to win him to our side, in this present coil. We need his power, to my sorrow. Murray escaped also, you will have heard?"

The other did not comment on that.

"How did *you* effect your escape, Will?"

Douglas stared away from him. "By . . . devious means," he said shortly.

"No doubt. But . . ." Most clearly the man did not wish to speak about it. But Ramsay could scarcely leave the matter there. "Where were you held?"

"In many places. I was moved."

This unprofitable exchange left Ramsay as perplexed as ever. Food and drink arrived, providing a diversion of sorts.

Thereafter Ramsay launched into some account of what had happened in Scotland since Douglas's capture, talking almost for the sake of talking. Not that his hearer appeared to be particularly interested; perhaps he had heard most of it already.

One item did seem to concern him however, and that on the face of it a late and comparatively unimportant one.

"This of the Balliol lands," he interrupted. "For Dunbar. Not Cavers, in Teviotdale. *I* want Cavers."

Surprised at this, the first display of any animation and on an unlikely subject, Ramsay sought for some reason. Why this sudden concern for lands? Or was it just Cavers? Douglas had never seemed greedy for property; it was power he was interested in, challenge, war. The Flower of Chivalry, he was the hero, not the land-grabber. An illegitimate son of the Good Sir James, he had inherited no great estates. This of Liddesdale was large enough, but unproductive, largely barren hillsides, its wealth in cattle and stock mainly Armstrong and Elliot-owned. Could that be it? Wealth required? Cavers was a rich barony, and the superiority of the town of Hawick valuable. Had Douglas committed himself to a heavy ransom payment to gain release, and now be concerned as to raising it?

And yet, would the English have let this man go, at any price? Any more than they would Murray? He was the foremost of Scotland's warriors and a born leader. They would have been fools to let him return, to rejoin the fight. For mere money. Yet he *had* returned, and now seemed to be in a strange state of agitation, as well as in sorry physical condition.

"I think that Dunbar was most eager for the Galloway lands," Ramsay said. "No doubt, if you desire Cavers, the Regent will see that you get it. Are you short of siller, Will? After your long absence from your properties?"

231

The look he got at that was sharp. "No!"

"I thought . . . ransom, perhaps?"

"I made . . . escape."

"Yes . . .?"

But no more was forthcoming. Ramsay realised that he was going to get no details of that escape, for some reason.

So he told Douglas of the rescue of Sir Andrew Murray from Carlisle Castle, to little comment.

When he sought his couch that night, early enough, he was as perturbed as he was mystified.

In the morning there was little change in the situation, with Douglas reserved and uncommunicative still. Whatever was wrong, it was evidently not for discussion. The nearest they came to any explanation was when Ramsay, by wondering about the other's actual capture at the Lochmaben affray, did unleash a brief flood of vituperation over the indignities inflicted upon him on and after that occasion, the vileness of making him, Douglas, walk on foot, in chains, right down through the centre of England, an object for jeering, hissing and the throwing of filth. And thereafter imprisonment in iron fetters, at Edward Plantagenet's express command. The bitterness thereat was clearly deep and festering, perhaps the only clarity in the entire situation.

Another clarity, however, was that Douglas was by no means eager for his visitor to prolong his stay. So apparent did this become that Ramsay could not ignore it. Besides, his duty was to report to Murray without delay. He decided to leave that same day.

Before he went, he did broach the subject of future operations. Douglas was obviously a sick man. But his experience and abilities were much needed. How soon did he think he would be able to play his part again? *Some* part? The Regent would want to know.

The answer to that was no more informative than the rest. It would depend on much that went unspecified apparently.

Only at the actual parting did Will Douglas let his guard drop a little. Gripping the other's arm, he said, "Sandy, it is hard, hard! Do not . . . think too ill of me. It is not, not . . ."

"Not what, Will?"

The other frowned, biting his lip. Then the frown

hardened, and he shook his head. "Nothing!" he jerked. "Nothing. Off with you, man – and forget Will Douglas!"

"That I shall never do."

"Then more fool you!" And he turned his back dismissively.

12

Ramsay's reports to Murray, at Perth, regarding Dunbar and Douglas, important as they might be, were overshadowed by the tidings from England. Edward Plantagenet had answered Balliol's appeal for help all too fully and promptly, despite his involvements elsewhere; although whether it was in fact aid for his puppet or the furthering of his own ends, was a matter for debate. He had come north in person, arriving at Berwick by sea, and was now in process of assembling a great army from the North of England counties. And Berwick's great harbour was reported to be filling with his ships of war.

This, of course, was dire news, for however successful the Scots had been recently they were in no state to take on the full might of England. It had been hoped that his French ambitions would inhibit Edward from northern adventures meantime, but apparently not. There was much alarm in the Regent's camp.

Whether the Earl Patrick had had any knowledge of this when Ramsay saw him was anybody's guess; for of course it could greatly affect his attitude. But the fact that he had at least seemed to consider throwing in his lot with the Regent's cause, even at a price, gave the impression that he had been unaware of Edward's move. The Plantagenet coming north by sea, to be sure, could account for any lack of information reaching Dunbar or Ersildoune. Black Agnes, certainly, had known nothing of it.

Since Douglas's escape had not been looked for, his present strange state did not arouse so much concern in Murray and others as it did in Ramsay. But the Regent said that he would send a courier at once to Hermitage urging the full and immediate mustering of the Douglas manpower, not only Sir William's own, which was not so very great, but all of the name, largely leaderless since his uncle's death at Halidon Hill and his own capture, Sir Archibald's heir and present chief of the family, William, being a juvenile. Ramsay did not volunteer for this errand.

It was back to the grim familiar business of large-scale assembling of forces, therefore, and this time with precious little enthusiasm evident throughout the land, as the word of Edward's personal presence spread, with all that implied. One slight consolation developed, however, as accounts came in of a comparable reluctance to provide men on the part of the North of England barons and squires, in turn wearying of endless fighting and warfare. The extent of this disillusionment was emphasised when a reliable report was received that no fewer than fifty-seven Northumbrian and Cumbrian land-holders had risked their liege-lord's wrath and refused to man the army of invasion. This must be deeply worrying for Edward, who was said now to be importing mercenaries, by sea.

Murray's options as to manoeuvre were inevitably severely curtailed. Outright confrontation, set battle, was out of the question. Ambuscade was impracticable against a major army. Outflanking tactics demanded very large numbers of men. Counter-raids into England might achieve something but were unlikely to halt a full-scale invasion. The Regent had little choice but to adopt the age-old strategy of retiring before the outnumbering enemy, deeper and deeper into the heart of Scotland, drawing him on and on, extending his lines of communication and seeking to deprive his men and horses of sustenance by destroying all food and forage stocks as they retreated, driving off cattle and sheep, even poisoning wells. It made a sore strategy, devastating for the territories thus harried by friend and foe alike. But it could be effective, gradually weakening the invaders' will and ability to fight, causing them to range far and wide for provisioning, and so offering opportunities for ambush, cuttings-off, harassments. And the centre and northern parts of Scotland were hilly, mountainous, full of rushing rivers, narrow glens, steep gorges, lochs and bogs, ideal country for the few to confound the many.

This decided upon, they could only await Edward's moves. But an extra worrying factor was that English fleet at

Berwick. That could change so much, outflank, land enemy troops behind them, bombard with cannon. Those ships were apt to come between the Scots leaders and their sleep.

No word came from the Earl of Dunbar, nor yet from Sir William Douglas.

Murray gave Ramsay an unexpected and not particularly welcome assignment. He was to go back to Hawthornden, stock up its caves with provisioning and arms, arrange secret places where the horses could be kept secure, and then seek to organise groups of men all over those parts of Lothian, these to remain in their homes meantime, in hamlets, cot-towns, farms, mills and the like, but ready to act, on Ramsay's orders. If Edward advanced through the Merse, as was likely, and up into Lothian, nothing was more certain than that they could not halt him before Edinburgh. So when the Scots army retired beyond Forth, it would be valuable to have such groupings in existence behind the enemy, ready, where they could cause major disruption and alarm. When Ramsay observed that this was not a very martial and notable role for him in the forthcoming great struggle, Murray declared that, on the contrary, it was a most important and vital charge which he knew no other capable of fulfilling. Ramsay would be far more use to their cause thus employed than being just one more knightly captain of cavalry, leading endless rearguard actions.

So, taking his own people with him, to serve as nucleus for his undercover force, he set out for his home country.

Hawthornden Castle remained as they had left it, an abandoned ruin above the steep, deep gorge of the North Esk, occupied only by its pigeons and bats. They came to it, advisedly, by dark, leaving their horses hidden, as previously. This matter of the horses was likely to be the greatest single problem, but vital for success. Ramsay anticipated much more difficulty in finding secret accommodation for their mounts than in finding men.

The underground cave system was dank and cold, but they had left ample stocks of wood, and they soon had a cheering fire going. They would start making the place as comfortable as possible on the morrow.

Thereafter they spent busy days and nights, for there was much to be done, and it had to be done discreetly, with the minimum of indication that 'Hawthornden was in any way involved. So they moved about the country only in twos and threes, not to draw attention to themselves, on foot and dressed in old clothing. The finding of suitable places to keep their horses, where they would not be obvious, took up a deal of time, for riding mounts would stand out amongst farm animals; and such refuges had to be within reasonable walking distance of their castle. This part of Lothian was fairly populous, being fertile farmland, and, below the Pentland and Morthwaite Hills, well provided with streams and rivers for the driving of mills. These mills, in especial, were useful, for they tended to have considerable storage accommodation for grain, only seasonally required, and such could be converted into temporary stabling. Within a two-mile radius of Hawthornden there were over a dozen mills, as well as innumerable small farmeries, and amongst these the horses were bestowed. Much of the land, of course, was Ramsay's own, Dalwolsey itself being only two miles to the east; but since his castle was occupied by an enemy garrison, however modest in size, care had to be taken in that direction.

Food and forage was less difficult to find and store away, especially when the farmers and cottagers were told that it would be paid for, and that when the English army arrived it would all be requisitioned by them anyway and certainly *not* paid for. So hidden storage for provisioning was a priority. Also plans were made for driving cattle and sheep up into secret valleys and hollows in the nearby hills, after the fashion of the Borderland beef-tubs, before the enemy arrived. Indeed, many of the country folk themselves proposed to go off with the beasts, when the time came, preferring the hardships of camping in the uplands rather than awaiting the attentions of an invading army.

The actual recruiting of the men proved to be the easiest of their tasks, for there was no lack of fighting spirit once a lead was given. Some elementary training was necessary, of course, and Ramsay and his lieutenants spent the evenings coaching the volunteers in the use of weapons, unorthodox methods of quiet killing, ambushing, the use of cover, and the like.

That valley of the North Esk and its surrounding area was probably better prepared for invasion than anywhere else in the land, that early autumn of 1335. Still Edward Plantagenet delayed, probably in order that the Northern English harvest might be got in and more men freed for military service by their masters. It allowed the Scots harvest also to be reaped and gathered and then hidden away as much as possible.

It was hardly a time for considering proposals of marriage, but that did not prevent Alexander Ramsay from much contemplation of the subject.

Then, at last, at the beginning of November, a messenger arrived from the Regent to say that Edward had crossed Tweed in strength and was marching into the Merse, burning and harrying, while Balliol had been sent to do the same on the West March, and was advancing through Dumfries-shire. The Scots forces would seek to delay only, at this stage, falling back before the enemy to and beyond Forth and Clyde.

So, it was last-minute preparations and warnings, the herding of cattle and taking to the hills. November was scarcely the ideal season for it. Edward would not take long to reach Lothian.

Ramsay's people required no announcement as to when the invaders arrived, for although the main English army did not come thus near the foothill country, keeping to the coastal plain where, if necessary, they could be aided and supplied by their shipping, flanking cavalry detachments did advance into and through their area. There were reports of another enemy force coming up Lauderdale and into Lothian by Soutra Hill. Soon the smokes of burning townships and villages were darkening the already grey November skies, and by night the ruddy glow of flames lit up all. Penicuik, the nearest town, provided a major conflagration.

In the caves deep below Hawthornden Castle Ramsay's people waited, feeling much frustrated at having to lie thus low, hidden, whilst savagery reigned around them, but hoping that their hour was coming.

They were kept well informed, with men making their secret way to Hawthornden from all around. As well as Penicuik and the village of Roslin – which they could actually see from the cave-mouth in the cliff – being burned, so also were Dryden, Bilston, Bonnyrigg, Polton and Lasswade. But so far most of the farms and mills had escaped, the enemy concentrating on the centres of population. Oddly enough, one of the lesser places which *had* been destroyed represented something of an advantage to themselves, for the castle of Roslin was almost directly across the valley from Hawthornden and had all along been something of a danger to them. It belonged to the St Clairs, but its lord had been slain along with the Good Sir James Douglas taking the Bruce's heart on crusade, and his young heir lived with his mother in Caithness, this castle being left in the care of a keeper of doubtful allegiance. Now, at any rate, it was sacked and part demolished, so no longer any sort of threat.

Now the wave of invasion had passed this area meantime, with Edward's army concentrated before Edinburgh, which walled city would almost inevitably fall to the attackers, although its great fortress-citadel on the rock would probably withstand siege. Ramsay had anticipated this, and sought to plan his moves accordingly. It was important that their first attempt should be successful and if possible fairly dramatic, in the interests of morale, something which would have a real impact on the local population as well as on the enemy. So it had to be carefully planned, its location as well as its execution. And the actual attack, in whatever form, should not take place too close to Hawthornden, since afterwards there would almost certainly be attempted reprisals and a scouring of the neighbourhood by the angry English, and it was essential that their sanctuary in the caves remained undiscovered.

The solution occurred to Ramsay one day when they were faced with the inevitable problem of having to change the hiding-places of their horses, where the millers required the granary accommodation for the storage of grain and flour after the harvest. He was at the Mill of Kirkettle, about two miles upstream from Hawthornden as the crows flew but three times that as the river wound in its glen, perhaps the furthest out of their horse-refuges, but one of the most hidden and out-of-the-way of the mills. The miller, a tough, youngish man, was incoherently apologetic for having to eject the beasts from his barn, but pointed out that there was plenty of secret pasturage for horses, even in winter, nearby, not under cover but sheltered enough from wind and weather. On doubtful enquiry about this, the man indicated that upstream from this Kirkettle, the Esk had cut a most peculiar and contorted course for itself through the foothills, something to do with the rock formation no doubt. All the upper valley of this river was through deep and steep wooded gorges, admittedly, as at Hawthornden itself; but this, for some winding miles above Kirkettle, was especially tortuous, twisting and turning in tight loops, crooks and bends, between high naked shoulders of bare red sandstone. But in between these bends were hidden and unexpected crescents, dells and dens of excellent grass, deep, sheltered and unseen from above, because of the prevailing hanging woodlands of the upper slopes. Pasture there for many horses. Cattle also, the miller himself keeping beasts in one of them. All this explained less than eloquently, but cogently.

Ramsay went exploring, with Pate, the miller leading, and was much impressed. It all made very difficult going, getting round the thrusting sheer headlands of rock, soaring for hundreds of feet above. But the series of hidden combes and bottoms were extraordinary in their rich pasture, although narrow and usually crescent-shaped. The problem, of course, was access. Here was ideal secret grazing for the horses; but they would have to be led carefully, in single file, along narrow rocky paths around those bluffs and headlands.

It was when they came to a larger dell with a number of cattle in it, that Ramsay suddenly saw the possibilities. How did those cattle get there, he demanded? These could not be herded along those constricted and difficult paths. The miller agreed. They were his own beasts. He said that they had to be herded for some distance and then led down from directly above, from the more level ground through which the river was cutting its way. There were one or two zigzag routes down into these further-away dells, through the steep woodland. But these tracks could be very slippery and dangerous for the stock in wet weather, so the dens were little used.

That was it, then, Ramsay declared, suddenly excited. Fill one of these hidden hollows with cattle. Then have someone to act the informant. Tell the English foragers, who were bound to be desperate to find meat for the invading army. Lead them there, down into the ravine. And then – ambush, slaughter!

None could see any flaw in it. And so long as there were no enemy survivors, the thing could be repeated. All this would be taking place a fair distance away from Hawthornden, with little likelihood of any connection being guessed at.

They had not long to wait before they heard that the invaders were indeed sending out foraging parties throughout the countryside, an inevitable development, with thousands to feed. Edinburgh had not yet fallen, thanks to its stout walls and the citadel's artillery and bombards. But the word was that English ships were now unloading cannon at Leith, so it was feared that it would not be long before the city was battered into capitulation, even though the castle itself might hold out.

The Roslin area was only some nine miles from Edinburgh and bound to have its quota of foragers. Ramsay arranged that one of their volunteers, whose family had gone off into the Pentlands with their stock, should act the informer, find a foraging party and tell them of the cattle hidden in the Woodhouselee den, asking for due reward for so doing, and then leading the enemy thereto, his brother coming hot-foot to warn them at Hawthornden. The timing of it all would be important, so that the ambushers could be there first.

It was two days, during which the ominous booming of cannon from the Edinburgh direction was fairly constant, before young Drew Hogg came in haste to tell them that he and his brother Jockie had come across a mounted patrol of about a score of the enemy in the Dryden area, not a couple of miles nearer Edinburgh. They all seemed to be mercenaries from the Low Countries, only the officer being English. Him Jockie had told about the cattle, after soliciting reward. Since clearly the foragers had been unsuccessful until then, the officer had not been difficult to persuade, promising payment by results. Jockie was going to lead them to the Woodhouselee part of the Esk Valley by roundabout ways, to give time for the Hawthornden party to reach the den first. So the utmost haste was required.

Ramsay, well aware that they would be apt to get little notice in this sort of attempt, had planned routes and procedure beforehand. About two dozen of them set off almost immediately, on foot necessarily since their horses could not be readily available. At the run, they crossed the open country, south of the Esk's valley, cultivated land, pasture and moor, by Gorton and Gourlaw, but avoiding those now more or less abandoned hamlets and keeping to the scrub woodland and whins, for cover. It was a fully two-mile run, and they were carrying swords and dirks; but they were all fit, and though panting and breathless they reached the lip of the gorge in little over some twenty minutes, sufficient time, they hoped, for what had to be done. Down into the den they fought their way through the dense, steep woodland and undergrowth, scratched by hawthorn and brambles.

There they found the decoy cattle grazing undisturbed – so they were not too late. They hurried across the crescent of grass and splashed over the river beyond, almost waist-deep, for the enemy would be brought along the other, north side of the valley, from which the zigzag cattle track descended. Up this they went, careful not to leave footprints in muddy patches.

Almost anywhere on this track an ambush would be possible. But near one of the uppermost bends there was a stretch where there was a little cliff of naked sandstone rising above one side, and the normal thick wood and scrub on the other. Ramsay could use that cliff-like rock.

Sending a man up to the top of the track to keep watch, he disposed his little force. Two-thirds of them he had climb to the top of the stretch of rock, an uneven twenty feet or so above the track, to space themselves along, not all bunched together, and to then cover themselves with brushwood and faded bracken. The rest were to hide in the trees and undergrowth at the other side. All had their instructions, and none were to act before a given signal.

In the event, they had quite some time to wait, uncomfortable for some of the men on the cliff, indeed Ramsay himself, for some of their perches were cramped and awkward. They need not have been in such a hurry.

Then the watch came running down the track. The enemy were approaching. He was directed to join the people in the bushes, at the trackside.

They heard the newcomers well before they saw them, the clop of hooves, jingle of harness and chatter in a foreign tongue. Then the leaders appeared around the sharp bend, the officer and another man, who had Jockie Hogg mounted behind him, to show the way, followed two by two by the file of men-at-arms. The officer wore a shirt of chain-mail, but the others had leather-scaled jerkins. They all had helmets, but most were carrying these at their saddle-bows. For this foraging duty they had left their lances behind and were armed only with swords, maces and daggers. Twenty-two of them, they rode on unhurriedly past the hidden watchers. As well that they had no dogs with them.

The waiting now was tense. Presently they could hear shouts and halloos as the cattle were rounded up. The yells continued and soon came closer, as evidently the herd's ascent of the track commenced.

When eventually the enemy appeared around the nearest bend, however, there was a complication. Ramsay had assumed that the foragers would just drive the beasts before them up the slope, the men in a column behind. This was indeed what they did, only they had sent two horsemen ahead to lead the way, for some reason. And here was a problem. These two would have to be let past. There were perhaps two dozen cattle, and these would occupy fully thirty or forty yards of the path, at certainly no more than three-abreast. And the following riders must not be warned. But it was essential that none of the enemy should escape. The probability was that those two men in front, when they heard uproar behind, would turn and come back, to see what was to do. But they might not; they might just flee. In which case this project could not be repeated, for this would become a marked site.

Ramsay had only moments to make up his mind. He could not shout instructions to the others, for that would warn the two horsemen; anyway, there was no time to relay any instructions. He had to act on his own. Pate crouched next to him, and he gripped his shoulder and whispered urgently to wait, wait until at least half of the enemy main body were past before jumping. Then punching the next man on the back, to follow him, he flung himself backwards into the bushes behind – and prayed that the oncoming riders would not be looking up that height to see any disturbance.

It was a difficult, indeed crazy business, but he had no time to think of anything better. The undergrowth was thick and prickly and the slope steep. But somehow he and his follower had to fight their way through its entanglement, along parallel with the track and behind the line of their crouching colleagues. Bent, much of the time on their hands and knees, and over broken, rocky ground, scratched, whipped by branches, they clambered on, hoping that the disturbance would not be evident from below.

Fortunately the horsemen were riding only slowly, at a walking pace, for a herd of cattle could not be hurried up a steep, winding track. Moreover, blessedly, only about twenty-five yards further up was another sharp bend. Once round that, they themselves ought to be able to clamber down on to the path and be out of sight for a few seconds.

Struggling on in breathless, but cursing haste, Ramsay sought to think out ultimate action.

At last they were round the next bend and, thankfully, he half plunged, half rolled down and on to the track, his colleague not far behind. On up the path they ran, stumblingly. How far to go? It was vital not to be too far ahead; anyway, they had not time, before the horsemen would be round the bend and see them. But not too soon, or the commotion would halt the herd early, and give some sort of warning to the main party behind.

Damn those two outriders!

About thirty yards up Ramsay decided must serve. Jerking one panting word to his companion, he pointed to the bushes on the left side, while he flung himself into cover on the right, drawing his dirk as he did so. The other seemed to understand, and disappeared into the opposite shrubbery.

They were only just in time. Hardly were they in position when the horsemen appeared. At least these two were chattering together, obviously quite unconcerned. Only a few yards behind came the first of the cattle.

Ramsay drew deeply, to steady his uneven breathing, hating what he was about to attempt. Then, as the men-at-arms came level, he leapt out of the leafage, dirk raised. Only a second or so later his companion followed suit.

The riders could not fail to see them, of course, one on each side of the track. Almost automatically they reined up, reaching for swords. They would have been better to have spurred on.

It takes only moments for even startled men to draw swords from scabbards, and to be able to wield them to effect. But fewer moments still were required for what the attackers were going to do, for this was the most simple of slashing striking, given all but stationary targets. Stooping low, the two Scots struck, and struck again, with their daggers, not at those riders but at their horses, at their vulnerable rear legs. It took less time than it takes to tell, as they slashed through the great tendons behind the knee or hock. Hamstring had been the single word Ramsay had barked at his colleague.

With high whinnying screams those two animals staggered, their hind-quarters collapsing, throwing the riders backwards

243

inevitably. Down men and horses crashed, one drawn sword clattering far, the other still clutched, but limply. And Ramsay and his companion used their dirks the second time. The mercenaries had no least chance. Helplessly sprawled on the ground, they were stabbed, in the unprotected throat above the leather jerkins. A couple of thrusts and each lay jerking in death throes. The only danger for their assailants was the wild kicking of the fallen beasts.

There was no time for assessment of the situation. The foremost cattle, only a few yards behind, had halted in terror at sight of the disarray and carnage in front, and were now trying to turn away, back, but of course were being pressed on by the others behind. There was bellowing, uprearing pandemonium on that track to add to the horses' screaming. Ramsay prayed, if that is the word, that it had not all taken place too soon.

He and his partner could not see what went on further down the track. And they could not win through the struggling confusion of cattle. There was nothing for it but to climb up the hillside some way, although not on the steeper side Ramsay had used, and struggle through the bushes, above the herd.

Round the bend was a scene of further and even more dire turmoil, at first seemingly entirely chaotic, men and horses in milling, rearing, yelling disorder behind the last of the cattle. But the prepared and trained eye soon established that the confusion was one-sided, that purpose and method of a sort prevailed in part, the attackers' part. All along the line of riders the men up on the little cliff-top had leapt down on top of the horsemen, dirks out, at the same time as their friends at the other side had burst out from the shrubbery; these last primarily concerned with the horses, restraining them, pulling them back and round, even hamstringing one or two, but also seeking to drag down any riders who were not being adequately grappled with by the others, or already down on the ground. The surprise had evidently been complete, and the horsemen wholly at a disadvantage, being either knocked out of their saddles, thrown by suddenly rearing mounts, winded by the impact of bodies from above, arms pinioned by their attackers, or simply stabbed there and then. Scots crashed to the ground too, of course, but these were ready for that, expecting it indeed, and apt to be on top. On prior instructions, the people on the far side were to seal off any possible attempts at retiral down the track, and the tight-packed frightened cattle prevented any escape upwards.

By the time that Ramsay had worked his way back to the main killing-ground, it was all but over. The enemy were either dead or dying, without exception, for there were to be no survivors and the merely wounded were being finished off without mercy. Even Jockie Hogg had strangled the man he was riding behind. It was grim savage work, but war, and necessary; and the atrocities committed by Edward's mercenaries on the Scots population left little scope for pity.

In only a few minutes they had achieved complete victory, and at little cost, some bruising and one man with an ankle sprained when falling with his victim from a rearing horse. And they were richer by much gear, arms and seventeen mounts, after putting the hamstrung beasts out of their misery.

They were not finished yet, however. Twenty-two dead men and five horses had to be disposed of, an off-putting and difficult task for the elated warriors. These bodies had to be securely hidden and no traces left of the massacre. Just dragging them into the thick woodland was not sufficient for Ramsay, since dogs could smell them out, by chance or in search. So some hollow or pit had to be found, where they could be covered over. But dragging these dead horses through that shrubbery would leave an obvious trail. The men would be less of a problem.

It was Pate who came up with a suggestion. These soft sandstone cliffs in this valley? If there were caves underneath Hawthornden Castle, admittedly part man-made by the ancient Picts, there could well be others which might serve their purpose, as hidden sepulchres, much better than any attempt at pit-digging. All agreed with that, and parties were despatched up and down the twisting valley to search for possible suitable caves, whilst others herded the cattle back down into the riverside pasture.

Ramsay's group were unsuccessful in finding anything adequate in the way of holes or caverns downstream, but presently Wattie Kerr sent a man to inform them that he had discovered an area of possible cavities upstream, not far away, crevices rather than caves, in the sandstone right down at the river's bank, large enough he thought to take the dead horses. Ramsay went to see. The crevices, deep splits in the redstone rock, had presumably been cut by floods. With fallen stone to fill up and effective man-handling, these should be sufficient to hide much more than five horses and many men's bodies. Also, being down at the river's edge, would not demand dragging through woodland.

The men themselves had to haul those bodies, equine at least, down the track to the haughland and then along over the grass and riverside shingle, at great labour; for no amount of coaxing would make the live horses drag the dead ones. They would carry men's bodies slung over their saddles, but shied and refused at their own kind. So the business took a long time, and effectively dissipated any atmosphere of triumph over their victory. Rolling and heaving great stones and boulders on top of the corpses, and then going back and cleaning up the track to show no signs of the slaughter, as far as possible, completed that inglorious but necessary part of the proceedings. It was dusk before, wearily, they led their captured mounts back to the Kirkettle Mill pastures, and then headed for Hawthornden, reaction to their so merciless killing setting in.

Reaction or none, Ramsay was well satisfied, in the military as distinct from the private and emotional parts of his mind. The enemy patrol would just have disappeared without trace. None in the English camp could know where, nor how. It might conceivably be inferred that disaster had happened somewhere in the Esk valley area of Lothian; but that could cover scores of square miles, with nothing to indicate where. Being mercenaries, they might even be thought to have slain their English officer and deserted. So the thing could be done again, for the need for meat for Edward's army would be insistent. Admittedly, once a second lot disappeared there would surely be investigation, but where would that start? What clues could offer the enemy a lead?

Two days later, with the Hogg brothers sent off to try a repeat of their decoy act, a similar sally was staged, this time with a forage patrol found at Lasswade. And it all proved still more easy, not only because the ambushers were more practised and confident but because the patrol was smaller, and all Englishmen, and when herding up the cattle did not choose to send any outriders ahead. So there were no complications and, thankfully, no need to hamstring horses, which in turn meant that the corpse disposal afterwards was much simplified. Again there were no survivors.

How long could they continue with this curious campaign? Ramsay, although gratified at his success, was scarcely proud of it. Brought up in the knightly, chivalric tradition, such killing was far from admirable, he felt, however effective. And just how effective it might be, in the wider sphere, he could not be sure. In a great army of thousands, would the loss of such small patrols, however unexplained, be considered significant? And even if it was, what lasting effect could it have? It was, to be sure, giving his group of volunteers experience and expertise, and raising spirits perhaps in this part of Lothian – for however much he insisted on secrecy as to details and locations, he could by no means prevent his people boasting somewhat and spreading the word around; indeed this of morale-lifting was part of the objective. Nevertheless this was not Alexander Ramsay's notion of warfare nor knightly conduct. He could only hope that it might lead to better things.

At Hawthornden they remained isolated, largely uninformed as to the situation elsewhere in Scotland. The boom of cannon-fire had ceased from the Edinburgh direction and local gossip was that the city had fallen but that its castle had not. It was said that most of King Edward's army was now marching westwards along the south shore of Forth, making for Stirling, the Scots still retreating before it and ravaging the land as they went. Surely, at the barrier which Stirling and its bridge represented, the Regent would make a stand? And, if the enemy had now largely left the Edinburgh area, presumably there would be no more foraging parties hereabouts for them to attack? Was their role at Hawthornden over?

Then, with Ramsay beginning to wonder whether it was worth remaining there in the circumstances, a messenger arrived from Murray. He told that the Regent had been unable to halt the enemy at Stirling, on account of the English fleet ferrying troops across Forth from Leith, and these getting behind the Scots army, from Fife. So they had had to retire further. Since Edward was reported to be making for Perth, and the same manoeuvre could be repeated there with ships in the Tay estuary, the Regent was regretfully withdrawing, all the way into Atholl, behind the Highland Line. With winter weather now prevailing, Edward was unlikely to risk campaigning north of Perth and facing the snow-filled passes. So there should be a breathing-space. Balliol was reported to have reached Renfrew and seemingly going to pass Yule there.

Sadly, however, Edinburgh Castle had fallen, powder and ball for the artillery exhausted. So that city was wholly in English hands. There was work for Ramsay to do in Lothian, yet. The English there would have problems of supply, with their shipping involved elsewhere. Reinforcements as well as provisioning were said to be coming up from England. Any interception and disruption of such convoys would be a major help in this situation, keeping the English looking over their shoulders, and encouraging the Scots folk. Already there were stories abroad of Sir Alexander Ramsay's doings in the enemy rear. Let him seek to build on that useful foundation.

So now there was a new challenge, and more after the fashion of what had been originally planned.

The first requirement was information. Supply-trains would be apt to be slow-moving, and reinforcements would probably be used to protect them, and therefore have to go at the same pace. Next day, Ramsay sent Pate and two others south-eastwards by the coastal road towards Berwick-on-Tweed, and Redheuch and two more southwards by Soutra and Lauderdale for central Tweeddale, the two obvious routes for English-based convoys to approach Edinburgh, to try to obtain prior warning of any such, so that they had time to plan interception.

In the event, time was what they were not given. For Pate had not been gone four hours when one of his men arrived back at Hawthornden with the news that a large cavalcade of men-at-arms and laden pack-horses was on its way north, presumably from Berwick, and had in fact got as far as Dunbar already, but was still coming on. Pate was shadowing it, but it was probably too late to do anything about this one.

Ramsay, eager for action, decided that at least an attempt should be made. It was all haste, therefore, haste to collect horses, haste to ride eastwards; and not in such numbers as he would have wished. Planning, such as it could be, would have to be done in the saddle.

As they rode, fast, by Redheuch itself and then by the ford of Tyne at Pathhead, and on down that east-flowing river, he calculated urgently the factors of time and land. The first was probably the most vital. It was now afternoon of a late December day, dark in a couple of hours. A large convoy would not want to proceed in darkness, even though well guarded. Nor would it, or at least the leaders, wish to camp out in any exposed position in these circumstances. But they would be far too many to put up at any monkish hospice. So they probably would be halting within two hours. But where? They had passed Dunbar when this messenger started back. Fast as *he* might have ridden, the enemy would have had time to get perhaps another eight miles, maybe more. Where would that get them? Haddington, in the Vale of Tyne, the county town, was about twelve miles west of Dunbar. Would they make for Haddington's shelter, behind its walls? A slow convoy, that would mean riding for an hour or more in darkness. Preston-on-Tyne was the village before that. Would they elect to settle there for the night? It was a small place, although there was a monastery of the Trinitarian Friars at Houston nearby. But between the Haugh of Preston and Haddington lay Hailes Castle, a strong place in the gut of the valley, now with an English garrison. Was that not the obvious answer? Hailes. It was set where it was for the most practical of reasons. For some two miles, the river, and the road which perforce followed it, here ran through a narrow defile, not so deep nor wooded as their own Esk but equally constricted. And Hailes Castle was placed in the midst, dominating river and road, so that no travellers could pass in either direction without paying toll to the castle – a quite normal piece of feudal planning. In hostile territory, would not that convoy almost certainly make for the cover of Hailes Castle, with night falling, where its leaders could expect hospitality and their pack-train protection?

Ramsay, to be sure, could not do anything about the castle itself; but the trough-like valley below Traprain Law . . .?

Time? Always time! Riding their hardest he and his score or so of men avoided Haddington, to the south by Morham Glen, and back to the Tyne beyond at Stevenston. The light was already fading, but the mighty mass of Traprain reared looming ahead a couple of miles. This had once been the capital-hill of the Southern Picts, under King Loth, who indeed had given name to Lothian. Deep below that whaleback hill lay Hailes. Would they be in time to achieve anything?

Between hillfoot and river-gorge was a sort of long grassy terrace, whin-dotted, where Hailes cattle grazed, once Pictish farmland, perhaps one hundred feet above castle and river-bank – which admittedly was a grievous weakness for the fortalice where cannon could be sited to fire down upon it if barrels could be sufficiently depressed. But the place had not been designed to withstand artillery siege but purely as a wealth-making armed toll-house, dominating the road. That the English thought it worth garrisoning now would be precisely because of that domination of the main road north from Berwick.

Up on this terrace and well out of sight of the castle, Ramsay led his people. Dismounting, he ran to the lip of the decline and peered down and along. It was hardly wooded here, for that would have been a further and unnecessary weakness of defensive capabilities, there being only broom and whins and a few hawthorns, hiding little of the road below. And that road was empty at the moment.

So – the convoy had not yet come. Or was not coming.

Ramsay sent a scout eastwards along the terrace, to where a view of the road's approaches to the ravine could be obtained, near to Preston Haugh. He then went hurriedly prospecting.

There was fully half a mile of road eastwards, the castle being set a similar distance westwards. Between, road and river snaked along in coils and bends, the former narrow, the latter whitely rushing. No cavalcade could thread that valley floor in more than double-file, if even that. Led pack-horses would be apt to go in single-file. Therefore a very long, strung-out procession. And he had only this score of men.

If there was little wood above that ravine there were at least stones, rocks, boulders; no doubt most of these had been originally cleared from the cultivation-rigs by the Picts and later farmers. These must be their ammunition – if the enemy came.

He set his men to gathering and rolling the stones, the larger the better, to spaced heaps on the lips of the gorge. The light was almost gone, and he feared that it was all to no purpose, the enemy having camped elsewhere.

Then his scout came racing back. A large mounted company was entering the valley from near Preston. How many he could not tell in the half-dark.

The likelihood of this being other than their quarry was remote. Hurriedly Ramsay divided up his little force. Ten he kept with himself, to occupy the end of the line nearest to the castle. The remaining dozen he formed into three little groups, to station themselves each about one hundred yards apart, beside those heaps of stones. Then he turned his busy attention to the shrubbery, the broom rather than the prickly whins. Telling his ten to pull up as many bushes as they could in the short time available, he plunged down the hillside to survey the road itself. He selected a tight bend reasonably near their main heap of boulders. It was perhaps six hundred yards from the castle, but of course out of sight.

He could not risk shouting, but had to clamber up again, to have his people drag down their broom bushes and place them in the road beyond that bend. They would make no very effective barrier, but in the dusk it would not be clear what they represented, and once identified as only bushes, would force the leading horsemen to dismount and pull them aside. And those horsemen would almost certainly be the men in charge of the convoy, heading for the castle's shelter.

He hurried back up the hillside.

He was only just in time. Barely up, panting, he saw the first riders appearing round one of the bends below, as anticipated, two by two. It was some seventy yards further to the bend with the bushes. In the gloom it was impossible to distinguish details as to the horsemen.

At least there was no question about timing now, nor how many files to let past. The enemy themselves would decide that for them. All but holding their breaths, the watchers waited.

Then the inevitable happened. The leading files of horsemen were brought up short as they came upon that barrier. This naturally caused confusion down the line, as horses over-rode each other and nobody could perceive the cause. Ramsay raised his hand, and the first boulders were pushed over and went trundling down. With their crashing descent there was no need for further silence. Ramsay's horn blared out its signal for action down the line.

Bounding and crashing, the rocks hurtled down upon the lengthy convoy. Loud the yells of the attackers resounded – and it is extraordinary how much noise twenty-odd men can make when they try. After the boulders, their hurlers came leaping.

In mere moments there was widespread disarray; so few against so many admittedly, but the many not knowing that, not knowing what went on indeed, in the half-dark of that deep valley, strung out for the best part of a mile, most men leading laden pack-horses and therefore isolated save for those immediately in front or behind, their leaders out of sight, themselves weary and less than alert after a long day's march. Small wonder if most of them fell into panic.

At the front, Ramsay's ten flung themselves down upon the leaders who, as anticipated, were having to clear those bushes blocking the road. And here at least the odds were in the assailants' favour, for they outnumbered the four pairs who had rounded that bend, half of whom were now dismounted and dragging at the bushes. Eight bewildered and disorganised men had no chance against eleven determined attackers with daggers drawn – and no notion as to how many more there might be behind. The enemy went down like ninepins, most not even having time to draw their weapons.

Ramsay wasted no time. Whenever he saw this group overwhelmed, he shouted to his people to help drive the frightened horses back round the bend on top of the next advancing files, some of the beasts already bolting back of their own accord. So there was further confusion there, with yelling attackers before and behind. Horsemen desperately sought to be elsewhere, some turning back, more throwing themselves down from their saddles and running down to the river, a few even trying to climb the hillside, anything to get away from that surprise assault.

Leaving his busy group, Ramsay grabbed a riderless horse and vaulted up, to beat it into a canter and dashed down the line shouting, "A Ramsay! A Ramsay!"

He found the same situation prevailing all along, or at least as far along as his four little parties extended, hopeless disorder on the part of the enemy, vehement purpose in his own men. His own shouting presence added to the English derangement.

His concern now was over the tail of the convoy. He had no idea how far this might stretch eastwards, and what might be happening there. Reining up amidst the last of his groups he

252

called for two of these to mount abandoned horses and come with him. Accompanied thus he hurried on.

Three horsemen waving swords and dirks might not seem a grievous threat to a long column. But when that column is in more or less single-file and consisting largely of led pack-horses, with nobody in command and no effective view forward because of bends and darkness both, three menacing riders can represent real threat, especially when they might be only the first of many.

Forward riders turned and bolted back, in fact, and that of course spread havoc and alarm in those behind. Quickly the remainder of that narrow, twisting road became as much a shambles as the rest.

Hoarse and all but exhausted, presently, not far from the first houses of Preston Haugh, Ramsay pulled up, satisfied. How many had escaped, he had no idea, but in this instance that did not greatly matter. How many were slain or wounded would be equally uncertain, possibly no great number in the end. But the convoy was destroyed and a quite major blow dealt to the occupying forces. Enough was enough.

This time there was no need for butchering of wounded; these could be left for the castle garrison to deal with. Ramsay was worried about that garrison now. Could they have remained totally ignorant of what was taking place less than half a mile away? Had the shouting and clash not penetrated that far? The rushing noise of the river might have drowned it. But might not an investigating company sally out? Or a fugitive reach there with the news? His people were in no state now to meet any concerted counter-attack. He hurried back, past all the litter of the ambush, bodies dead and wounded, riderless horses, discarded weapons, to the front of the line again.

No resistance continued, indeed there had been little of it from the first. His men were elated, congratulating each other, whilst rounding up prisoners and examining booty. He stopped all that. They wanted no prisoners. All to mount. Leave the dead and the wounded. Collect such pack-horses as had not bolted. Then away from here. The Hailes garrison might be on them at any moment.

Sobered, the victors did as commanded. Presently, with a string of some thirty led animals and pack-horses they climbed out of that dark valley on to the terrace and headed westwards into the night. No signs of the garrison, no pursuit, materialised.

Back at Hawthornden, they assessed their gains. As well as having delivered a resounding blow to the occupying forces and their morale, they had done it under the very walls of an enemy-held castle, which must have its own significance. And they had captured a great stock of miscellaneous gear, arms and armour, gunpowder, clothing, provisions including wines, even money, coin. Not to mention the horses. Storing it all away was a problem in itself.

But there was to be no resting on their laurels. The very next day Redheuch arrived back from Lauderdale with the news that another English pack-train, presumably also from Berwick, was heading north-westwards up Tweed, and when last seen was nearing Caddonfoot. Going in that direction the probability was that it was making for Balliol's camp at Renfrew. If so, it would almost certainly cross the watershed from the upper Tweed at Broughton, over to the Clyde valley by Biggar and Lanark. And there were numerous possible ambush-places in the upper Tweed valley.

Too good an opportunity to let pass, Ramsay organised an almost immediate start, his men nothing loth.

The most direct route to the upper Tweed from Hawthornden was by Leadburn Muir and down the Eddleston Water to Peebles, some sixteen miles. But Ramsay was concerned that this new convoy might have got beyond Peebles by the time that they could reach there, and he wanted to be in front, not behind it. Caddonfoot was only fifteen miles from Peebles. In the time Redheuch had taken to come back to tell them, and their own journey there, the enemy could have covered that. So at Leadburn, instead of turning south for the Eddleston Water, he carried on over the open moorland between the Morthwaite and Pentland Hills, by Cowdenburn and Halmyre to Romanno, where there was a ford of the Lyne Water. The Lyne was a tributary of the Tweed. Down its narrow valley, between quite high hills, they turned, due southwards now.

They had come some sixteen miles, and over fairly rough country, almost as far as to Hailes in the opposite direction, and dusk was already falling. At Drochil, the Lyne was joined by another sizeable stream, the Tarth Water, and swung away eastwards. Four miles more and they would reach Tweed at

Kirk of Lyne. The convoy would probably be halted for the night by now. But where? Would they themselves be better to halt and camp, waiting for the morning light, and the enemy on the march again? They could stop at the site of the Roman fort of Hallyne, a couple of miles ahead, which he knew well. They would have that secluded place to themselves, amongst these sheep-strewn hills.

Which was where Alexander Ramsay was wrong. For rounding the base of the shoulder of Hamildean Hill, he abruptly pulled up. Ahead of them the valley was ablaze with small fires, camp-fires, obviously, in the vicinity of the Roman fort.

Hurriedly he halted his column, to consult with Redheuch. Who could this be? Could it be the English convoy? Could it, in fact, be anything else? All these fires must represent a sizable force. Who would be camping up in this empty valley?

Ramsay of Redheuch was nonplussed.

"Wait you," Ramsay said. "Suppose that they have someone with them who knows this country well. Well enough to tell them that the northern tip of the Ettrick Forest around Drumelzier and Broughton is namely as a haunt of broken men; not leal subjects of the King of Scots, but rogues, outlaws and the like. The sort who would think nothing of pilfering a pack-train encamped. Coming towards night, might not such guide tell them that, if they came up this quiet Lyne valley, they could camp secure. And on the morrow go on north-westwards, by Drochil and Castlecraig and Elsrickle, to Lanark and the Clyde, almost as quickly, avoiding the Forest." Without waiting for comment on that hypothesis, he ordered Wattie Kerr, always just at his back, to slip down to the encampment and to spy it out, numbers, positions, guards. Then he turned his people back round that bend in the valley, to wait.

Wattie was back inside half an hour, with good news. It was the English convoy, sure enough. And if there were any set guards or sentries, he had seen no sign of them. Although the fires were dying down, there had been glow enough to reveal that most of the men were already lying down to sleep. Better still, they had tethered their horses upstream of the camp, in this direction. He grinned as he announced that.

If Ramsay did not actually grin, he at least nodded

significantly. He had his men dismount, at once, told them briefly what he intended, which indeed was simplicity itself, left two to watch over the horses, and led the rest quietly downstream.

The sinking fires gave sufficient light to show up, presently, the dark mass of the enemy horse-lines, where the animals were tethered loosely to graze on the waterside meadow, perhaps one hundred beasts. Telling his men to spread out, not to bunch and to approach casually, so that the creatures would not be alarmed, he led the move in.

In methodical fashion they mingled with those horses, causing no great stir, and began to untie the tether-ropes, and where the knots were difficult, to slash them through with their dirks. When he judged that all were loosed, Ramsay gave the first signal, a life-like curlew's wheepling cry, for his people to move back to the upper edge of the lines, furthest from the camp, and mount beasts there, still unhurriedly.

With all up, he gave the second signal – a very different one. For now there was no need for silence, quite the reverse. "A Ramsay! A Ramsay!" he shouted, and brought down the flat of his sword on his own beast's rump.

All did the same, taking up the cry, and in moments the scene was transformed from quiet peace to pandemonium, as the Scots drove their mounts into the midst of the untethered animals, yelling and beating about them with the flats of their blades. Thus abruptly alarmed, the mass of horses bolted, and in the only direction open to them, with the assault behind, the river on the right and the steep hillside on the left. Down upon the sleeping camp they stampeded, in a thunder of hooves and shrill neighings.

Nothing, of course, could withstand nor deflect that charge of frightened horseflesh, certainly not recumbent men rousing themselves to sit up, blinking, around those dying fires. The fires themselves added to the chaos, for the horses could nowise all avoid them, and pounding through them, scattering blazing wood and embers, they further maddened themselves as well as the more confounding the enemy.

In the circumstances there was little for the attackers to do, the horses doing it all for them. Such Englishmen as were not trampled down rolled clear and fled, either downstream, into the river itself, or up the hillside.

Through the camp area, with the crazed horses streaming

on, Ramsay sought to turn his men around, to ride back and
deal with survivors. But that was less than simple to achieve,
these mounts also being in a state bordering on panic, and,
without harness, hard to control. It was a very ragged return
they made, seeking for men. But in fact nothing of the sort
was necessary. Those Englishmen who remained were either
dead, injured or standing about in dazed bewilderment, none
in a state to put up any resistance.

So the thing was done, almost too easily to be credited.
Ramsay was content. He wanted no prisoners. The enemy
survivors could be left to look after their injured. He sent for
their own horses to be brought down, and set his men to
loading the convoy's gear and baggage on to the captured
horses, somewhat overloading them admittedly. They calculated that it had been a smaller train than the Hailes one,
perhaps fifty men and fifty led pack-horses, and they had
collected only about a score of animals. But these must serve.

Presently they started back northwards, up Lyne, through
the nightbound hills, with their booty, almost bemused by the
ease and scope of their success. Could they hope that this sort
of attack could be maintained for any length of time? And
what effect was it having on the enemy high command?

13

Ramsay, now engaged in the so far neglected part of his
programme, that of organising groups of potential fighters on
a wider scale throughout Lothian – risky, since there was
always the danger of enrolling a traitor or loud-mouth who
could endanger all – was provided with some answer to his
questions on the strategic situation. Another messenger
arrived at Hawthornden from Sir Andrew Murray, calling
Ramsay to a parliament to be held at Dairsie, in Fife. That the
Regent assessed such a thing as possible and desirable was in
itself a good sign; but the courier brought other good news.
Edward Plantagenet had returned to London – not unexpected in the circumstances, since the monarch of a great

realm could hardly spend the unproductive months of winter kicking his heels in such as Perth; but his going heartened the Scots. Also Balliol was still at Renfrew, less than active. Scots sallies up and down the land were taking place, small-scale, but their effect cumulative; and Ramsay's exploits in Lothian were being talked about throughout the length of the land, probably exaggerated and inaccurate but boosting morale. And there had been one larger-scale success. One of the few important castles still held by the loyalists, Lochleven on its island, had been assailed by Sir John de Strivelin, one of Balliol's supporters. But Sir Alan Vipont, the Keeper thereof, had managed to turn the tables on the enemy, loading the castle's armament, light cannon, mangonels and arbalests on boats, by night, and bombarding the besiegers' camp on the mainland, to such effect that he had won a sizable victory, capturing much material and many prisoners, including de Strivelin himself.

So spirits were rising, and the Regent had decided that a parliament, much overdue, would accelerate recovery, and was prepared to risk coming south to Fife to hold it, from his Atholl security.

So leaving Pate and Redheuch in charge, Ramsay set out with only Wattie as companion, and one man to return with the horses, for north-east Fife – and cheerfully. Although Dairsie was almost exactly the same distance from Doune Castle as was Hawthornden, it somehow seemed to be nearer, in the right direction; and surely could provide opportunity and excuse for a visit?

Rather than risk the long and dangerous journey through occupied territory, by Linlithgow and Stirling and Fothriff, he chose to ride secretly by night down to the Forthside fishing port of Cockenzie, a few miles east of the Esk's mouth at Musselburgh, and there bargained with a fisher crew to take them in their coble across the estuary. It meant leaving the horses there, and having to buy new ones on the Fife side, but at least he was not short of money, with all the captured loot.

After a distinctly choppy voyage they were landed at the harbour of Earlsferry next mid-day. There they found difficulty in obtaining suitable mounts – which seemed ridiculous considering all the horse-flesh they had left behind them. But eventually, on very indifferent nags, they set off due northwards through Fife, for Dairsie, another fifteen miles.

Ramsay asked himself why the Regent had chosen such a place as Dairsie for a parliament? It was a small, out-of-the-way parish in Stratheden, between Cupar and St Andrews, and although there was a castle there, belonging, if he recollected aright, to the Learmonths, it was only a small hold. It seemed an odd venue. Possibly the proximity of St Andrews, the ecclesiastical capital of Scotland, was the answer, where Bishop de Linton, the Chancellor, was apt to base himself, and other important clerics were to be found? Was the Church, then, expected to play some special part in this parliament? In which case, why not at St Andrews itself?

He learned the answers to some of his questions when he arrived at Dairsie Castle, on its mound above the Eden, six miles from St Andrews. It was no larger than he had anticipated. But roomy premises would not be required, apparently, for no large numbers were expected; indeed it must have been one of the smallest parliamentary attendances on record, with many Council meetings even being more numerous. And it could not be held at St Andrews itself, for it seemed that Edward had appointed a warlike cleric, an Englishman named William Bullock, as Chamberlain of Scotland, and he had chosen to make his headquarters at St Andrews Castle, the episcopal seat, dispossessing Bishop de Linton. The Bishop-Chancellor, now ageing and frail, was still sharp in his wits, and his advice much needed. But he could not travel long distances, hence this venue, near St Andrews but hopefully secret and far from obvious.

Ramsay found a mere dozen or so commissioners assembled, in addition to Murray himself and the Chancellor, including the High Steward, Moray, Sir Alexander Mowbray, Sir Malcolm Fleming from Dumbarton, Sir Michael Wemyss, Sir Alexander Leslie, Sir Alan Vipont, Sir William Carruthers, Bishop Maurice of Dunblane and one or two other clerics. More were hoped for. But nothing would make this a representative gathering, and Ramsay learned that the only reason for calling it a parliament was that certain important decisions to be made would have the full force of law and authority, greater than any mere Council meeting could command.

He was surprised to find himself treated by most of the

others as the hero of the hour. It seemed that his exploits from Hawthornden had been noised abroad all over the land, and exaggerated in the process. Vast were the alleged numbers of the enemy slain, huge the booty captured, great the consternation of the occupying forces. Much as Ramsay sought to play down all this and to emphasise reality, even he could not but recognise that the main object of his efforts, the worrying of the enemy leadership and the improvement of morale in Scotland, had been largely achieved.

The reunion with John Randolph and Robert Stewart was, of course, of especial satisfaction, and the trio had great things to tell each other of their various activities. It did not take long for Ramsay to be asking after Mariot Randolph, to be assured that she was well, still at Doune and frequently seeking news of himself.

With the so-called parliament due to take place the next day, they had an accession of strength that evening, and a distinctly embarrassing one. For who should arrive but Patrick, Earl of Dunbar and March, and with a train of followers fit for a king. For the sake of the essential secrecy, nobody else had come with any large escort; this great entourage of Border lairds and mosstroopers could not but have drawn widespread attention, especially as they obviously could not have travelled, horsed, by sea, and therefore must have come all the way round by Stirling, held by Balliol's people as that strategic place was. Yet here they were, to the doubts and surprise of all.

The Regent could not even be sure whether Dunbar had indeed at last decided to change sides, for he certainly did not say so, indeed made no declaration of any sort, but acting in his haughtiest and most overbearing manner, seemed to assume not only that he had every right to be present but that all should be suitably impressed. There was no room for all his company, of course, at Dairsie Castle, and they had to more or less take over the nearby village, to much local offence. But then, that man had never sought popularity in any quarter.

The session due to start at noon next day, and all assembling, they were treated to another surprise, the arrival of Sir William Douglas, the Knight of Liddesdale – and eyed almost as askance as was Dunbar. Nor was he much more forthcoming than the Earl, stiff, wary. He was looking better, physically, than when Ramsay had seen him at Hermitage, but his attitude towards all was as reserved, defensive, almost sour. He brought with him a younger half-brother, Sir James Douglas, whom he seemed to use as a sort of buffer, a shield and mouthpiece, between himself and the enquiries of former colleagues. Approaches and questions were very noticeably unwelcome. Ramsay was treated with a little less caution than the others, but still far from frankly.

What the English had done to the renowned Flower of Chivalry was debated on every hand.

With these two important but extremely doubtful acquisitions, the Regent called his parliament to sit in the hall of the castle, the Chancellor to conduct the business.

Bernard de Linton opened the meeting suitably with prayer, indicating the realm's great need of divine aid. Then he explained why this of a parliament was necessary. Philip de Valois, King of France, had sent an envoy to inform the Regent that he had reason to believe that Edward of England was about to invade France in fullest force, and even have the effrontery to declare himself *King* of France, on the grounds that his mother, Queen Isabella, was the daughter of the late Philip the Fourth of France. This situation would demand the fullest co-operation of the partners in the Auld Alliance against the arrogant Plantagenet. To help give King Philip time to assemble his fullest strength to resist invasion, he requested the Scots to mount a series of raids over the Border, in order to keep the greatest possible number of English troops in the North of England and to cause Edward maximum apprehension about the security of his rear. This request came with the backing, indeed the royal command, of the King of Scots.

Most there stared at each other with a mixture of astonishment and exasperation. What did Philip de Valois think they were at? Did he not realise that they were an occupied realm, struggling desperately to keep some vestige of independence and defiance against the invader? How in God's good name could they invade England? The French King must be mad. They should tell him so.

The Chancellor, glancing at the Regent on what served for a throne, held up his hand. "Think on this," he said. "For there is more to it than you may at first perceive. Indeed, this may be the best news that Scotland has had for long. If it is true that Edward is to proclaim himself King of France and invade there, then that means that he will be busy for years to come, involved in a great war which will drain his resources to the utmost – and which he is unlikely to win. He will have little time, then, nor strength, to spare for Scotland. The man Balliol will be left to fight his own battles, and Balliol, I think, we can deal with."

"I agree," Dunbar jerked, to the surprise of all.

Ramsay looked at that Earl thoughtfully. Was this why Patrick Dunbar was here? Had he somehow heard of this vaunting ambition of the Plantagenet and recognised that Edward would have more than enough to do without coming to rescue Balliol, and so decided that his own best interests and hopes of power lay on the Scots side?

"But this of invasion of England," the Steward said. "How can we contemplate anything such? Weak as we are."

"Raids, not full-scale invasion," the Regent put in. "We might try to mount some raids over the Border. I say that we *must* try."

"Why?" Sir Alexander de Mowbray demanded. "Do we love France more than our own realm? This may help Philip de Valois, but to *our* grievous cost. It may delay Edward's invasion of France, if that is the truth, but will it not bring him back, meantime, to punish us?"

"It may," Murray admitted. "But that may not prove so ill, perhaps. For the French envoy brought more than the request. He brought promises of arms, ships, money. And he says that King Philip, to gain time, is also going to propose a truce to Edward, a truce meantime between England, France and Scotland. He believes that Edward will accept such truce, hoping thereby to lull France into unpreparedness. Then to strike. But he, Edward, would wish to settle with Scotland first. So he would come to us, offering this truce, if he deemed that we were sufficiently a danger to be worth it. These raids would serve that purpose."

This involved and subtle scheming was quite beyond most there, and there were shrugs and head-shakings. But Murray went on.

"Whether or not we agree with all this, there remains the fact that it appears to be a royal command to us from our liege-lord. King David is now fourteen years, and to be sure he is in the care and keeping of King Philip. So no doubt he will do as Philip tells him. But he is still our monarch and his command constrains us. That is why I called this parliament, not any Council. I, as Regent, must pass on any express royal command. I cannot change nor controvert it. Only a parliament can question a royal command."

There was silence at that.

"Need any controvert it?" Moray asked. "To me, it seems to make sense. Surely we can make some such raids into England. If Sir Alexander Ramsay, with only a few men, can do what he has done, causing the enemy to look behind him all the time, could we not all do something of the sort? I, for one, will lead a raid over the Border."

"And I," Robert Stewart added.

Thus encouraged, others said the same, and the thing was decided in principle, details to be thrashed out later. Will Douglas, noticeably, was not amongst the volunteers.

There were sundry other matters to debate but these were minor and soon dealt with. It was agreed that attacks should be made on the lesser castles held by Balliol garrisons, although the great strongholds would be beyond them. A series of such assaults, widespread, would surely force the usurper to stretch his resources and thus make it less likely for the projected raids into England to be hampered or intercepted. Dunbar, in his abrupt way, was strong on this, asserting that Balliol must not be allowed to retain a single hold in the Merse or in the Borderland generally – which, coming from that man, raised some eyebrows.

Many there were anxious to get away as quickly as possible, before word of this meeting could reach the occupying enemy, in especial this churchman Bullock, at St Andrews Castle, whom the Chancellor declared to be efficient and determined, probably the most useful man Balliol had; and he was, after all, only some six or seven miles away. The fear was that, secret as they sought to keep the assembly, Dunbar's arrival with his great company might well arouse attention and bring repercussions. So prompt dispersal appealed to most, the Douglases not the least anxious to be off.

Ramsay had found it difficult to have a private word with Will Douglas, for that man kept his half-brother close at his side all the time. But when James Douglas went to get their horses, Ramsay took his chance.

"Will," he said, "it is good to see you looking better, more yourself. I was much concerned for you, at Hermitage. Perhaps you and I might together lead one of these raids into England? Like old times . . ."

"I think not," the other returned, curtly. "I have seen enough of England!"

"To be sure. But – you will not sit idly by, Will? At Hermitage. Less than a dozen miles from the borderline! You will do *something*, in this coil?"

"Anything I do will be against *Balliol*, man. The usurper. Not playing the reiver across the Border. I leave that to my Armstrong neighbours!"

"But this of bringing Edward Plantagenet to a truce . . . ?"

"Fools' talk! Think you Edward is a bairn, to play games with?"

Ramsay shook his head. "What has come over you, Will? You are a changed man, indeed." And when he got no reply to that, he added, "See you, if it is indeed this of ransom moneys, I have captured much booty of late, English gear. And not a little money with it. I shall pass this on to Murray. But some could be well spent, perhaps, coming to you. English siller to pay English ransomers!"

"No! I told you. I do not need your charity. Nor want it." And Douglas strode off.

Sighing, Ramsay went to find John Randolph.

He found him with the Regent, Robert Stewart with them. He liked the Steward, but could have done without him on this occasion. He did not mention his conversation with Douglas, promised Murray that he would make a raid into England at the earliest opportunity, suggested that he might co-operate with Moray in the matter – and then, as casually as he could, added that he might return with Moray to Doune forthwith, when they could decide on arrangements.

His hearers seemed to think that an excellent plan, and unfortunately that included Robert Stewart, who declared that he would join them in the raid and, of course, come with them to Doune.

Ramsay did his best to look pleased at this.

Murray asserted that this was very good, and wished them well. Meantime, they could all escort Bishop Maurice back to Dunblane, by suitably hidden routes.

And once again Ramsay was less than enthusiastic, much as

he admired Bishop Maurice. That prelate was an old man and would ride but slowly, whereas he, as usual these days, was in a hurry. It would be fully forty-five miles from Dairsie to Doune. Young and hard riders could cover it in five or six hours, hilly as some of the way was; but it would take the Bishop almost a couple of days. Fortunately Moray evidently thought along similar lines, and announced that, time being important, they would be better hastening ahead; besides, the Bishop would probably be safer without them, as a cleric travelling about Church affairs.

The three young men, with their personal attendants, set off westwards with the minimum of further delay.

It was dark as a late May evening ever is, in these parts, and touching midnight, before they rode up to the massive ramparts of Doune Castle on weary spume- and mud-spattered mounts, having covered the long Howe of Fife, crossed the Ochil Hills by Glen Devon and Sheriffmuir and forded the Allan Water, without incident other than one horse going lame at Fossoway and having to be left behind, with its rider.

With horn-blowing and shouts for the castle to be opened for its lord, the drawbridge presently clanked down and the portcullis creaked up, and they clattered through the gatehouse-pend into the inner courtyard.

They were dismounting, Moray calling for sleep-bemused servitors, when Mariot herself appeared in the keep doorway. In the half-dark it could be seen that she was wrapped in some sort of loose fur robe, and peering out. Ramsay had to restrain himself from running to her.

In fact, Robert Stewart, who was nearer the doorway, strode to her first, and reaching for her hand, kissed it eagerly. She laughed, and told him to have a care or he would be ruining her reputation as a modest woman – and clutched her covering closer with the other hand and arm. Her brother called that she should have stayed abed.

It took a moment or two for her to realise, in the gloom, who the third arrival was. Then she gasped. "Sandy!" she cried, and forgetting about her modesty, hurried forward, both hands out to him. Ramsay was aware of gleaming white amongst the dark moleskin, and then she was in his arms. The Steward, standing by, could not but have drawn depressing conclusions.

Moray chuckled and went to clap his friend on the shoulder, before leading the way inside.

When incoherences finally gave way to more reasoned greetings and explanations, Ramsay, after the first feelings of bliss in her mere company, found himself all impatience to get Mariot alone, her undivided attention. He had waited for this, anticipated it, for so long. But that was not so easy. She had to play the good hostess, having lamps and candles lit, summoning up food and drink, ordering bedchambers to be prepared, asking how the parliament had gone, and the like. And eating, his companions seemed to take an interminable time about their food, and prepared to sit at their wine thereafter indefinitely, discussing where they should strike over the Border, and how.

It was Mariot who eventually got some movement, by announcing that if *they* were not tired after their long day and riding, she was, a mere weak female whose bed called. She suggested that they might plan their mighty future activities with clearer heads in the morning.

She had not finished before Ramsay was on his feet, to escort her. Brother John grinned, but the Steward did not.

They held hands as they mounted the twisting turnpike stair.

"I have been so anxious for you," she told him. "All this of war and battle. Your attacks and victories. Your name on everybody's lips, yes; but myself dreading every word of it, fearing what the next news might be. Need you be quite so much the hero, Sandy?"

"I am no hero, lass. Indeed, what I have been doing is far from heroic – ambush, surprising, slaying by night, acting the robber and cut-throat rather than the knight! Were it not on the Regent's orders and for the realm's sake . . ."

"Yet you are risking your life on every occasion. And I must wait here and dread each caller's tidings."

"You, you care so much, Mariot?"

"Of course I care. Need you ask? But that, I fear, will not stop you riding off tomorrow and doing it all again!"

They had come to her bedchamber door, on the floor above the hall. Ramsay's had always been on the storey higher. He drew a deep breath.

"It is possible . . . I thought . . . I might have other plans for tomorrow! If, if . . ." He left the rest unsaid.

266

"Yes? If what, Sandy?"

He reached for the door-handle. "May I come into your chamber, Mariot? For a little while. Not long. While I tell you." He looked down that corridor. "I fear that we may be disturbed. Your brother . . ."

She made no bones about entry this time, and led the way in.

With the door closed, he reached out to embrace her, and she made no attempt to hold him off. Urgently his lips sought hers. Standing there between door and bed, in the light of a single flickering candle, they heard Moray and Robert Stewart pass along the corridor, talking.

"Alone! With you. At last," Ramsay whispered, between kisses. "Mariot, oh Mariot, my dear! I have longed for this. Ached for it. Dreamed of it."

"I have . . . thought of it . . . also!" she admitted, a little breathlessly.

They stood there for long moments, content to hold each other, although content began quite quickly to be superseded in the man by a more pressing emotion, for he could not but be aware, much aware, of the feeling of her person through the moleskin robe, now less than tightly covering her. Indeed, loosest inevitably at top and foot, the neck gaped open somewhat and one white shoulder was bared. Clearly she wore nothing beneath the robe. When he bent his head lower to kiss that also, he could by no means ignore the rich swelling of flesh which began to project just below. He had to hold back his busy lips.

Presently she reminded him, gently. "You were going to tell me something. Of your plans, Sandy?"

"Yes." He drew up, taking a grip of himself and clearing his throat.

"It is important. To me, at least. Yes, to you too. Or . . . could be. You see, I . . . I . . ." He stopped. This was not how it should be done, standing there, whispering. He reached for her hand and led her over to the bed, and sat her down on it. Himself, he remained on his feet.

"So serious, Sandy?" she put to him.

"Yes. I have thought much on this. I have considered it. And not only for myself. And I think – now. No longer waiting. Will you marry me, Mariot?" There, it was out.

He heard her quick intake of breath, actually heard

her swallow. But when no words followed, he went on swiftly.

"I would have waited. I *have* waited. But – to what end? This warfare could go on for years. As already it has done. I see no real end to it. I could wait and wait. And, I have to . . . put it to the test. To know my fate. To know if I have any hope. Your sister Agnes told me to ask you. Not to delay. She said, she said . . ."

"Aye, what did Agnes say, Sandy?"

"She said that she thought . . ." No, that would not do. He could not have Black Agnes doing it for him, the craven's way. "She said to take my courage in both hands," he improvised. "And not to wait overlong."

"Good for Agnes!" Mariot observed, if a little thickly.

He stared. "You . . . say . . . that!" he got out.

"Why, yes. If Agnes it is who has brought you to it!"

"But – you, you *wanted* me to ask you?"

"To be sure. For long."

He wagged his head. "You did? Does this mean . . . ? Or is it . . . ?" Urgently he bent and gripped her by both shoulders, one bare. Almost shook her. "Mariot Randolph – answer me! Are you saying that you *will* marry me? Or, or but torturing me!"

"You can ask that, Sandy Ramsay, of the woman you would have to wife? Yes, I will marry you." Then her voice, which she had somehow kept so calm, so assured, broke. "Oh, Sandy, Sandy my love! At last! How I have waited for this. It has been so long . . ." And she reached up to draw him down to her.

They dispensed with words for a while.

Not unnaturally in the circumstances, that bed-robe fell still a little more open, both above and below. Not did its wearer make any unsuitably prudish attempts to draw it together again. The man's hand went wandering, as men's hands are so apt to do. Soon they were cupping her full, rounded breasts, oddly and deliciously cool. She did not deny him.

When his lips went prospecting in the same general direction, freeing hers, she found her voice. "You still have not told me what you plan for tomorrow?" she got out, panting a little.

That arrested him in some degree. "Why – it was . . . if

you said yes . . . if you did not think it . . . if you would be so good . . ." He bit his lip. "Save us – I thought to go to Dunblane and have Bishop Maurice marry us!" That came out in a rush.

"Tomorrow . . . ? Today, indeed?"

"Yes. Today. There is so little time, Mariot. I know that it is overmuch to ask. So quickly. For a woman. But, I must be gone, after. So soon. We all must be. Your brother and Stewart also. It is damnable! But this is war. If not now, this day, then it may be long before we can wed."

"Yes. You are right. It will be a strange wedding. But – yes, that will be best."

"Bless you, lass! I know well what I am asking of you."

She stroked his hair. "I count my blessings. And am happy!"

They accepted that happiness thereafter without further debate. That is until the man's hand, leaving those delectable breasts, slipped down to caress an almost equally delectable thigh, cool also. And in due course slid upwards, with the cool giving place to warmth. Then, still gently, she reached to still that hand.

"My love, think you we ought to, to go so far, tonight? I know how it will be, for you. For myself also, for I am not strong tonight. But since we will be wed tomorrow, in but a few hours, would it not be best to wait? Having waited so long. One night. We, we might feel the better before the Bishop's altar tomorrow! No?"

He moistened his lips. "If you wish . . . ." That was less than enthusiastic.

"I cannot deny you anything this night, my dear. But – I think that it would be . . . suitable." She mustered a little laugh. "Besides, it is already late, and I at least need some sleep before my wedding-day! I say that it should be bed, for us. Our lone beds, this last night!"

"Aye, you are right, as ever." Almost abruptly he rose, releasing her. "I will go – while I still have the strength to go! And that only just! But I doubt if I shall sleep!"

"I am loth as you," she admitted. But she too rose, to escort him to her door, and in the process all but defeated their joint resolution. For the motion, after all the previous disturbance, caused her robe to fall completely open, and even in the pale candlelight the impact on the man was considerable. Perceiving it she covered herself quickly.

"Forgive me!" she whispered. "But . . . tomorrow night!"

He got out of that room more swiftly than he had entered it, almost forgetting to say goodnight; and then had to be called back to be given the candle to light his way upstairs.

Ramsay must have slept after all, for he was roused by Moray beating on his door, in the morning light, to come in and shout his congratulations. Mariot had just told him the news. He was delighted, happy to have so puissant a goodbrother. Gathering his wits, it occurred to the bridegroom that perhaps he ought to have asked the Earl's permission, as head of the family; but it all seemed to be accepted – and this was scarcely the occasion. Downstairs he found Robert Stewart less enthusiastic, although he did manage to wish them well. Mariot herself was brisk, bright and businesslike, giving him only a single smacking kiss. It was as though last night had never been. But that he had not dreamt it all was evidenced by her announcements as to wedding arrangements, apparently all thought out. A messenger had already been despatched to Dunblane, to inform Bishop Maurice, whom John declared would probably not arrive there from Dairsie before mid-day. So they had the forenoon to undertake such preparations as were essential: duties, guests, clothing, the subsequent marriage-feast and the like. It would necessarily be a very simple bridal, of course. She would have to dispense with a wedding-dress, even a bridesmaid. John would give her away. Whom would Sandy wish to act groomsman?

Ramsay had to confess that he had not thought of that. There did not seem to be much choice. Doubtfully he looked at Robert Stewart.

There was only so much that young man could take. Hastily he declared that unfortunately he would not be at the ceremony. If he was going to play his part in the forthcoming raid into England, he would have to be on his way back to Renfrew and the Stewartry lands thereabouts, to gather men. He must leave forthwith.

Due regret expressed all round, this announcement meant that an alternative subject to weddings fell to be discussed before the Steward left – hostilities. And here the younger men, of course, looked for guidance to the now veteran bridegroom. Having asserted that her brother must just double the roles of giver-away and groomsman, Mariot, with something like exasperation, went off to make all the nuptial arrangements herself.

Ramsay, perforce focussing his mind on military strategy, suggested that since speed and secrecy in their projected raid was of the essence, the swiftest descent on English territory was indicated, avoiding enemy-held strongpoints and occupied areas so that there would be no warning for the victims. Berwick-on-Tweed and vicinity, although near, was out of the question because of the strong English armed presence there. The Roxburgh Castle area was similar. Jedburgh, Carter Bar and the Redeswyre would probably serve, but once over the Border there they would be into the long valley of Redesdale which had to be threaded before they could reach the peopled Vale of Tyne; and taking a largeish force down that twisting, narrow route could allow warning to be signalled ahead by beacon-smokes or fast riders. So he proposed an approach in between – for further west they would be into endless empty hills – by Morebattle and Yetholm and so into the quite populous and fertile valleys of the river College and Glen and Till. That would be only some forty-five miles from Lothian's limits, so that, well mounted, they ought to be able to do the excursion in three days.

This commended itself to the other two, who certainly had no better suggestions, and it was agreed that the three parties should meet at a secluded rendezvous below Soutra Hill, in five days' time, to ride down Lauderdale. They could scarcely manage it before that.

As well that Mariot was not sitting in on this conference, reflecting on her honeymoon period.

The Steward rode off in mid-forenoon, Mariot bidding him a warmer farewell than usual for a bride.

Soon after noon they set out for Dunblane, Mariot looking very lovely in a silken cream gown under her riding-cloak, Ramsay merely in the clothing he had come in, Moray at his most splendid.

They reached Dunblane's fairly modest cathedral to find Bishop Maurice only just arrived. But well aware of the urgency of the military situation, and out of his affection for Mariot, he made no fuss about playing his part in these strangely hurried nuptials, indeed expressing his satisfaction in her choice of husband and commending their decision to wed at such short notice.

In the circumstances, he agreed that the ceremony should be pared down to the bare essentials. They would use only the side-chapel of St Cathan, uncle of the Celtic missionary St Blane after whom the cathedral, town and see were named. They would dispense with processionals, choirs, incense and suchlike. Perhaps one day there would be opportunity for a formal confirmatory ceremony.

So, with only minimum delay they went in through the fine west doorway, with its notable blind arches and bay-leaf carvings, and into the narrow vaulted chapel of St Cathan under the especially wide clerestory. One or two of the diocesan clergy, the abbot and prebends, with a few monks, attended, to make the chapel look less empty. One sweet-voiced young vocalist sang them in.

Ramsay, mind in a whirl, found himself before the little stone-carved altar with its candles and Celtic cross, Moray next to him and Mariot on her brother's right. It suddenly occurred to him, just as the singing stopped and the Bishop began, that he had forgotten all about a ring. In something like panic he nudged Moray and whispered. The young Earl grinned and jerked his head towards his sister. Leaning a little forward she smiled sweetly and held out her hand, cupping a handsome gold circle. Moray handed it over.

This relief, it is to be feared, did not wholly free the bridegroom's wits for due and proper attention to what Bishop Maurice was saying to and about them – but then, does the privileged male participant ever really follow the service word by word on these occasions? All unbidden, pictures of the previous night's activities tended to rise before his mind's eye, and when he dismissed these, contemplation of *this* night's programme came along instead. He was firmly rejecting this also when he remembered Mariot's suggestion that their restraint in her bedchamber might well make them feel the better before this altar today, which, although it brought a warm glow of righteousness momentarily, also produced a vivid mental reconstruction of that situation, to further complicate matters.

He was clutching the ring in his hand, hoping that the slight pain of it might help concentrate his thoughts, when his eye lit upon a handsome sculptured standing-stone against the chapel walling, obviously Pictish, carved with another Celtic cross, intricate scroll-work, a man on horseback and a creature which might have been a dog but looked more like a pig. Could it be a pig? Would the ancient Picts find reason to link pigs with sacred crosses? He had, come to think of it, seen the sculpture of a pig playing the bagpipes at the Abbey of Melrose, where Bruce's heart was buried. Was there some odd connection in their religious attitudes between pigs and piety?

This interesting train of thought was interrupted by the Bishop moving down to them, and Moray announcing that he gave this woman, and then coming round to Ramsay's other side, allowing Mariot to edge up next to her groom. Matters were evidently reaching a climax.

The business of the ring went without any hitch, thankfully, and as in a dream he heard himself and Mariot being declared man and wife; heard, although the reality did not really sink in. As they knelt for benediction her hand reached for his, and squeezed it, and that undoubtedly helped.

Instead of full nuptial mass, they received thereafter the reserved sacrament from the altar sanctuary; and then it was over, with the Bishop coming to kiss Mariot and press Ramsay's shoulder, Moray making hearty congratulatory noises, Ramsay himself still distinctly bemused. Perhaps he had had an insufficiency of sleep that night, after all?

"Husband!" Mariot whispered to him, starry-eyed.

He looked at her searchingly, as though to see if she was any different, this beloved woman whom he had ached for so long. His, now. He held her close, wordless.

The Bishop offered them refreshment at his little palace, but Mariot said that they should get back to Doune, where a feast of sorts awaited them and where she hoped that he, the Bishop, would join them, although she realised that he would be tired after his so recent journeying. He agreed that he would come, presently.

They rode westwards again, Ramsay in a state of burgeoning euphoria.

The repast which followed, considering that it had been unplanned prior to that morning, was a notable tribute to the new wife's housekeeping ability, the size of her larder and the efficiency of the castle's underground ice-houses, with a variety of soups, trout, salmon, duck, grouse and venison, as well as beef, sweetmeats in abundance and choice wines with it all. It seemed just a pity that there were only the four of them to appreciate it all; although, of course, the castle household was celebrating also, in the greater hall, and nothing would be wasted. The Bishop fell asleep over his wine.

At least the sparsity of company ensured that there would be no folly about a traditional bedding ceremony, so beloved of many guests after a wedding-feast, with a general move to the bridal chamber, the males undressing the bride, the females the groom, and putting them together on to the connubial bed, with encouraging instructions as to subsequent procedure; not that Ramsay would have permitted anything of the sort on this occasion, however clamant the demands.

When Moray began to look soporific – after all, he had not slept for long the night before either – Ramsay raised an eyebrow at his wife, and she nodded.

They rose together, and Mariot announced to her heavy-eyed brother that they would now go down to the other hall and visit the assembled company there, as would be expected. No doubt he, Johnnie, would see the Bishop to his chamber presently?

Moray summoned sufficient initiative to offer the required well-wishes as to sound sleep and pleasant dreams, much lacking in originality.

Downstairs the atmosphere was very different, anything but soporific, uninhibited high spirits prevailing. The noise did abate somewhat at the newly-weds' appearance, but the jollity did not, ale and whisky seeing to that. Nor would they have wished it to. The seneschal or chamberlain, senior there, sought to gain silence by banging on a table with his tankard, but without much success. He then made some announcement, presumably well-wishing, but it went largely unheard; even he, probably, was not at his best and most lucid. Whatever he said, the company cheered him to the echo, and he collapsed back on to his seat well pleased.

Mariot and Ramsay went round, smiling, chatting here and there, appreciating all the goodwill, the man rejoicing in the obvious affection in which Mariot was held, respect to be sure but a deal more than that, real fondness, not always given opportunity of expression.

They worked their way back to the door and left the company to its merriment, waving.

And now, at last, they were on their own, constraints gone – save for such as they might produce for themselves. They held hands, but were strangely silent as they mounted the stairs.

In her own room, Mariot clung to him, head against his chest. "I am all yours now, Sandy," she murmured, all but mumbled. "What we have waited for – man and wife. At last. But . . . am I a fool? For now I am . . . afraid. A little."

"Afraid, lass? Why? Of what? Why should you be afraid? Of *me*?"

"No, no – not of you. *For* you, perhaps. Afraid that I may . . . disappoint. Always, before, I have known . . . what I am at. My way. Known myself. Even when I have felt weak. But now, I do not know. This is all new, to me. All new. So, I fear that I might . . . fail you."

"That you could never do, my dear," he assured, much moved. Always this young woman had been notable, at least to him, for her calm serenity, a sort of quiet assurance. He had never seen her like this, uncertain, apprehensive. Yet her fears were for him, not herself. "Care nothing – save that we are together, belong to each other, now."

"Yes. I tell myself that. But . . ."

"Last night you were not afraid. Even when, when we . . ."

"No. I am a fool. Forgive me."

"We shall do only what we did last night, lass. If that is your wish."

"No, no . . ."

But he led her over to the bed, and sat her down, as before, to lean over and kiss her, her brow, her eyes, her lips, gently at first, then more vehemently; and she responded, but deliberately rather than eagerly. His hands slid over her person, and she pressed those hands firmly to her with her own, but he could feel her body tense, unyielding. It was different, all different.

"Why, Sandy? Oh, why?" she asked, and that was almost a wail.

"Perhaps, perhaps a moleskin bed-robe has its advantages? Over a wedding gown? However fine!" he suggested thickly.

"Ah, yes. Perhaps." She sat up, even mustered a little laugh. "Wait you."

She rose and went across the rug-strewn floor to a great wardrobe which took up much of one wall, almost a small room in itself, and opening one of its doors, slipped inside. Waiting, as instructed, the man took the opportunity to loosen some of his own clothing.

Presently she came back, in that bed-robe, and stood before him, wordless.

He drew her to him and rested his head against her, whispering endearments. Then he drew aside those furry folds, finding them unfastened. In that position her breasts, uncovered, seemed very prominent, almost to thrust at him. He buried his face between the delights of them. He kissed each nipple in turn, fondling them with his tongue. They rose in response, with their own thrusting.

He could hear her breathing deepen, with consequent stirring of that delectable bosom. And suddenly more than her breasts responded for, uttering a little cry, she clasped his head to her, rocking him back and forth in her arms, crooning something breathless. Then shrugging that robe off her bare shoulders so that it fell to the floor, she was down on the bed beside him, in all her naked loveliness, warm, all but urgent, inhibitions past.

They accepted nature's guidance thereafter joyfully, with all the night ahead of them.

It was only that one night of bliss, unfortunately. For to meet the Steward at the Soutra rendezvous in time, with a suitable company of his own men, entailed a start the very next day. But they had known that all along, part of the compact. Their parting, the following noon-day, was bitter-sweet indeed. But man and wife now, they could look forward to the future with a glowing satisfaction, doubts and fears behind them. Only be careful, she whispered, as she stood at his horse's side, be careful. For he was no longer only his own man.

14

The three young men rode down Lauderdale, southwards, at the head of nearly five hundred horsemen, Moray and Robert Stewart in high spirits, the latter apparently having decided to make the best of his emotional situation, and bearing Ramsay no evident grudge. That man was rather more serious, since clearly the raid's responsibility was his, and his mind was active with planning and visualising.

There were two main problems: the reaching of the Border with England undiscovered by the occupying forces; and the finding of a suitable fairly populous area thereafter to ransack, while still leaving themselves time and an escape-route, to get back without interception by a stronger enemy. So he had to consider in advance every mile of their chosen route, to avoid strongpoints and Balliol-aligned and possibly hostile areas. He still aimed to cross the Border in the Yetholm vicinity.

Whilst he rode, cogitating, his companions were discussing Will Douglas, trying to fathom the extraordinary change in the man. Ramsay had told them of his ransom theory, so large as to be beyond his ability to pay; but this did not altogether convince them, nor himself. Surely that would not have depressed that forceful character so greatly, even allowing for the terrible conditions he had been kept in and consequent ill-health? And would, in fact, the English have let so renowned a leader and warrior come home, at any price? There must be more to it than ransom-moneys. Moray thought that Douglas must be sickening for something; and the Steward, perhaps out of his own recent experiences, suggested that he might have fallen in love with some high-born Englishwoman, possibly the wife of his captor, who had contrived his release and now he was in thrall to her.

They avoided Lauder town with its nearby Thirlestane Castle by swinging off right-handed to cross the high ground of Threepwood and so reach the upper Allan Water, which led them down its quiet, all but empty, valley to its junction with Tweed at Langlee, thus also avoiding the Earlstoun of Ersildoune, since none of them trusted its owner's conversion to their side. They forded Tweed near Darnick and rode on due southwards, to the west of Melrose, to climb over the high shoulder of the South Eildon Hill and so down across Bowden Muir to the valley of the Ale Water. Following this down, they came to the Teviot at Ancrum, and turning eastwards along that great river, by Nisbet, they forded it at Crailing, having thus kept well away from Jedburgh where

Balliol held the castle and abbey. The Cheviots were now rising before them, glowing in the evening light, as they reached Kale Water, up which they turned, to Morebattle. Yetholm, Ramsay reckoned, was only four or five miles ahead, and the Border itself another mile. They had come about thirty-five miles.

With men and horses tiring, they decided to halt after Morebattle village, in safe Kerr country. Better to enter England rested, with the dawn.

None of them were very sure about the location of Northumbrian townships and villages ahead, in the valley of the Bowmont Water. So they halted at Mill of Tofts, where they paid generously for provisioning from the distinctly apprehensive miller, and sought to pick his brains as to the lie of the land beyond the borderline, Wattie Kerr seeking to reassure his fellow-clansmen as to their honesty. Actually Wattie succeeded so well with the miller's family that he got a son, a shepherd, to volunteer to accompany them as guide, he apparently knowing the cross-border area intimately.

In the small hours of the morning they were on their way again, soon leaving Kale Water, which swung away in a great bend southwards, whilst they continued eastwards over higher ground to the next valley, of the Bowmont Water, their spirits at this hour noticeably lowered. Yetholm, on the Bowmont, was a small place, and they clattered through it without pause. If any of its people were wakened in alarm, they did not show themselves; sensible folk, they had been keeping their heads down for generations, to survive the situation.

There was nothing to reveal the march when they crossed it below Shatton Hill, in the half-dark, although their guide informed them of it.

Now they had a choice of routes. They could continue on down Bowmont Water, for Kirknewton and Wooler; or they could cross the hilly ground, due northwards, for Branxton and Flodden and the valley of the Till. They decided on the latter. Wooler would be over ten miles away and might present more dangers in getting back unassailed. And the Till was the greater, richer vale and therefore more populous, also nearer to the borderline.

After crossing Bowmont and marshalling again beyond the ford, Ramsay took the opportunity to address the men. They were here of a set purpose, he emphasised. They were not seeking battle, nor were they out to slay nor take prisoners. Nor to steal cattle, for herding cattle homewards would grievously hold up their progress and endanger their return. This was, to be sure, no ploy for heroes! They were here to show the King of England that the Scots were not cowed, that they could raid into England at will, that he should have a care. This was to be the first of many such raids, showing too that the man Balliol could not prevent them. What they had come to do was to destroy, damage, spread fear and alarm. They would pay especial attention to mills, barns and grain-stores, each man to take home with him such meal as his beast could carry without delaying its pace – for as they all knew, there was near-famine in many parts of their country, on account of English laying waste of the land, and the fields not having been tilled. So the good Regent had ordered that as much English grain as possible be brought back from these raids. So, all would be done in order and by due command, no raping and murder, slaying only when opposed in arms. Was it understood?

The response to that was unenthusiastic, almost sullen, but backed by Moray and the Steward, Ramsay was heeded, his reputation helping.

As they proceeded over the quite high shoulder of Mony- laws Hill, in the half-dark, country identical with that on their own side of the Border, Ramsay questioned their Morebattle guide as to the places ahead which might be worth devastat- ing, how they should be approached and in what order, always remembering the priority of a safe retiral. The young shepherd told him that there were only hill-farmsteads just ahead – Monylaws itself, Tithehill, Branxtonmoor and Branxtonhill. Then the quite large village of Branxton itself. They reached the Till there, and could turn either west along it, or east. West would bring them to Pallinsburn and Learmouth and Cornhill-on-Tweed; east to Crookham and Etal and Ford villages. Ramsay said that they would see how they fared when they got to Branxton. He rather grimly told himself that this cautious, inglorious attitude would make him sound to all anything but a paladin; but that was probably good for his soul, lest he become the swollen-headed hero. And Mariot would approve, at least!

Dawn found them moving down from Monylaws Hill's east

shoulder upon the property of that name, no great establishment, a small stone tower-house with attached farmery and half a dozen cottage hovels. It seemed somehow a poor first target for five hundred armed men, especially descending on it by surprise, and Ramsay had to remind himself of his own recent instructions to the company about lack of heroics.

In fact, it proved to be almost a non-event. Surrounding the place, the attackers aroused no sign of life, save for the barking of a couple of dogs; and riding in, the leaders had actually to hammer on the barred door of the little tower to inform the owner that he was being raided, while the rank and file, or some few of them, less courteously, merely burst into the cot-houses and drove the sleeping inmates out, men, women, children and poultry.

In only a few minutes the bewildered and unhappy inhabitants of Monylaws were herded into the convenient sheep-pens, and the place entirely in the invaders' hands. The problem now was what to do with it all. The obvious thing was to burn all that would burn; but that would be unwise at this early stage in the raid, for clouds of smoke rising into the morning air would certainly attract attention over a wide area and might well give warning of trouble. So, with no least relish, orders were given to tear the thatches off the hovels, drag out and smash plenishings, slaughter stock and purloin meat, smoked meats and the like, and load these on to such horses as were available.

Scarcely proud of themselves, they left the sad folk to bewail their lot – although they may just have recognised how much worse it could have been. The punitive force rode on.

Tithehill was the next farm, about a mile away, of similar size but lacking any tower-house. Instead it boasted a bastel, a towerlike refuge for its folk in time of trouble. Unfortunately for them they did not recognise this trouble as it came, for although people were stirring here, with sun-up, they either did not see the company coming through these foothills, or else assumed them to be their own English, for no refuge was sought. Astonished, indignant and then in hand-wringing agitation, thereafter they watched their homes being ransacked and their farmstead destroyed and pillaged. Then, without delay, they too were left to their grief and outrage.

According to their guide, the next two places, Branxtonmoor and Branxtonhill, were fairly close together, some two miles on. This would demand more or less simultaneous assault, so Ramsay divided his force, asking Moray and the Steward to attack the one whilst he led against the other, both parties to use the upheaved nature of the land as far as possible to hide their approach. All now perceived the wisdom of not having set fire to the earlier places.

Branxtonmoor was a larger property, with its inhabitants now going about their daily work. This proved no disadvantage for the raiders, for it meant that the menfolk were dispersed, although it could have allowed one or more to escape to nearby Branxtonhill with warning had that not been foreseen and taken care of. As it was, this establishment proved no more difficult than the others, although productive of more booty. And when the attackers moved on to Branxtonhill, they found the other party equally successful, and pleased with themselves.

Ramsay perceived the danger now of complacency. It had all been too easy, to pick off these undefended places one by one. The real test would lie ahead, when they assailed Branxton village, even though they were told that it was no very large community.

It was almost mid-forenoon now. They were able to scan the land-lie ahead. The village was not to be seen. Indeed there were no major prospects from here, with small hills all around. Their guide named them: Flodden Edge to their right, Barley Hill to their rear, Monylaws Hill to their left and Hill of Branxton in front, the village they sought hidden behind its quite lofty ridge, which sloped up moderately on this side but seemingly dropped sharply beyond.

This location meant that their approach would be hidden for much of the way – save from anyone up on the hilltop. But was it likely that anyone would be up there? They could see cattle grazing on its slopes, admittedly, and there might be herd-boys. But for such, if any, to decide that it was enemy approaching, and then to run back over the hill to warn the village, would take as long as it would for the mounted force to ride there.

Ramsay asked their shepherd as to the lay-out of the village. Was it a cluster of houses or a long street? Both, he was told, houses close together where two roads joined, and more strung out eastwards. This last concerned Ramsay, for eastwards less than two miles lay Crookham, another village

281

and larger, in a bend of the Till, which he had thought to make their next objective. And folk escaping from the east end of Branxton could flee to warn Crookham. So he decided on another two-pronged approach, round either end of this Hill of Branxton. It would have to be carefully timed so that they attacked in unison. Difficult, when they would not be able to see each other and did not know the exact lie of the land on either side.

Their guide had a suggestion. He had been up on this hill more than once. From up there one could see down to the low ground on each side. If he, and one or two others, rode up there and then spread out along the ridge, they could signal down when both forces were in a position to ride on the village at the same time. Commending him, Ramsay agreed.

They split up as before, himself to lead the west-about group, Moray and the Steward the east-about, part of their task to see that no escapers got away in that direction. Two men to accompany the shepherd to the hilltop.

The plan worked adequately. Once round the base of the hill they found themselves facing the wide vale of the Till. Ramsay went cautiously ahead, alone, to spy it out. He could see the village now, about half a mile to his half-right, only cattle-dotted grazing slopes between. There ought to be no problem of approach. They would be seen, of course, but riding fast they ought to cover that distance in less than three minutes, too short a time for any real precautions to be taken against them.

Back with his men, Ramsay issued his instructions. They had to wait for a little for the trio to climb that hill. Then the signal came, a man waving both arms. With a shout, Ramsay dug in his spurs.

It was at least a heartening charge over the grassland, scattering the cattle, a thousand hooves thundering. Some men, working on the rigs near the houses, looked up, to stare in uncertainty before bolting for the village. The horsemen reached there almost as soon as they did.

There was a large bastel-house at this western end, then a double row of cottages, leading to a small church and what looked like a hospice for travellers at a junction of roads. Beyond, more cottages stretched eastwards with a larger house at the far end, with trees around. From behind these trees suddenly they could see the other company bearing down.

Ramsay, reaching the roadway, waved his men to a halt. It was narrow, and would not take more than four horsemen abreast, so that two hundred and fifty would be far too many for easy passage. Shouting for some to go round the backs of the cot-houses on both sides, to prevent escape, the rest to remain where they were meantime, he led about two score cantering down the village street, swords drawn, where folk were emerging from the houses to peer – most of them to dart fairly promptly back in again.

They gave no time nor opportunity for any sort of opposition. Near the road-meeting they came up with Moray, the Steward having taken a party along the side-road, southwards. Their men were now, in fact, blocking the streets in every direction, far too many for the task. Branxton clearly was theirs, without a blow exchanged; but what to do now? None of them had any experience of this sort of warfare, if such it could be called.

Ramsay came to a conclusion, swiftly. Instead of the five hundred proceeding onwards, they would divide up. Leave perhaps one hundred here, to round up these villagers and ransack the place. The rest to hurry on to Crookham. Being, they were told, larger, it might require more men to take it, but not four hundred. So another two parties could go on to Etal and Ford, which lay approximately one mile and two miles ahead. There, all being well, they could at last use the weapons of fire, for thereafter it would be a dash back over the Border, and the smoke-clouds rising would be too late to endanger them.

Imparting something of this to Moray, they left Robert Stewart in charge of Branxton, with five score men. When he saw smoke rising eastward, he could start burning here, but not before. And not to burn the church. The remainder rode on.

Crookham, down near the riverside, sheltered and tree-girt, was no more prepared for their arrival than the others had been, and although it was larger, a place of lanes and alleys, it was no more difficult to take over. Leaving Redheuch in command here, with one hundred and fifty, the twelve score pressed on down Till for Etal.

Ramsay knew that there was a castle there, which would

have to be avoided; he believed that it was not a large one. Fortunately, as they drew near, they found it was sited at the other side of the river, before the village was reached. He thought that it could safely be sealed off.

As they passed it, across Till, he left two score men to guard the foot between it and the village. There was no sign of reaction therefrom.

Etal was a scattered place, with a fine church and two mills. The visitors encountered no unified resistance here either, although there were protests, swiftly put down. Those mills would yield much meal. Leaving half their remaining men here, with Pate, charging him to keep a close line with the ford-guarders near the castle, Ramsay and Moray led onwards for their final target. Ford, according to their guide, lay less than two miles south-by-west. He took them by a road cutting across a great bend of the river.

There was danger in this scattering of their force, they were well aware, but the chances of major attack on them were not great, with the surprise and the fact that the English garrisons on this East March were, naturally, near the borderline itself and all some miles off – Wark, Twizel, Tillmouth, Norham and Berwick-on-Tweed itself. No escapers were likely to reach any of these in time to endanger them.

Ford, as its name implied, lay at a major crossing of Till, a small town rather than a village, and with quite a large castle overlooking it. Ramsay recognised the dangers here also, but saw it as something of a challenge and opportunity – and hitherto there had been no real challenges. They could not hope to destroy any large proportion of the place; but if they could cause panic and alarm and burn some part of it, and under the walls of its castle, that would probably have more impact on the English authorities than all that they had done so far. Ford Castle, then, a Heron place, was the key.

Nearing the little town, he divided the party again, he hoped for the last time. He and Moray took half, and rode boldly up on the approach to the castle itself, on its mound, the rest, under one of Moray's lairds, to go on and wreak as much damage as they could at this end of the town and to raise fire as quickly as possible.

As they neared the castle they could see that the drawbridge was down and the portcullis up, no trouble looked for. Ramsay was almost tempted to try to rush the gatehouse, although this had not been his intention; but he quickly decided against it, for if by any chance they were trapped inside the castle, as could happen, then this entire raid could end in disaster if Moray and himself were captured. Anyway, it would not have proved possible in fact, for when only about two hundred yards from the place, the portcullis suddenly clanked down, effectively barring entrance. Presumably the gatehouse guard, uncertain as to the visitors' identity – although they could not know that they were Scots, for they were displaying no flags nor banners – decided to play cautious.

Halting their men, Ramsay and Moray rode forward alone, to comfortable hailing distance. The former raised his voice.

"Is this the house of Sir William Heron?" he called. "If so, here is the Lord John, Earl of Moray, seeking Sir William."

There was no immediate reply. That would take a little digesting.

"Did you hear me? The Lord Earl of Moray requests Sir William Heron's attendance."

From a gatehouse window a voice answered, doubtfully. "Earl of where . . . ?"

"Moray. Son of the late Regent of Scotland. Do not keep him waiting, man!"

"Scotland? I, I will go tell Sir William . . ."

Moray grinned. "I fear our friend had never heard of me! Think you this ploy will work, Sandy? Suppose this Heron has more men than we have, in his castle?"

"He would need time to muster and equip them. And I doubt if he will keep over fifty horses within those walls. To sally out, on foot, against us, would be seeking trouble indeed. No, it is arrows that I fear. I scarce think that he will have cannon here."

They had to wait there for some time. But at this stage that was to their advantage, providing opportunity for the wrecking group to get busy.

Eventually another more authoritative voice spoke from the gatehouse. "I am Heron. Who are you that come shouting at my doors?" That was gruff and sounded as from an elderly man.

"I am Sir Alexander Ramsay of Dalwolsey, Sir William. You may not have heard of me. But even you, sir, will have heard of the Earl of Moray, here?"

285

There was a pause. "Is it truth, then? That you are from Scotland?"

"Aye. From Scotland. Seeking redress! *You* have ridden raiding into Scotland in your time, I swear! Now, it is your turn!"

"Are you crazy – mad . . . ?"

"If you think that, Heron, you will learn otherwise! My lord of Moray demands the surrender of this castle."

"You *are* mad! Begone, miscreants, while still you may!"

"Not so. We require that you yield this house . . ."

"Fools! Insolent fools! Try you to take it!"

"We might. But first we shall burn your town." A quick glance over his shoulder revealed no smoke arising as yet. "We have many more men there."

There was silence at that.

"Come, sirrah, let us waste no more time. Do you yield? Or does Ford town burn? And its folk suffer."

"You will pay for this dearly, you scoundrelly Scots . . .!"

"Scotland has already paid. In advance! Your turn now. We have taken and destroyed other places. Etal and Crookham and Branxton. Now it is this Ford . . ."

Moray spoke at his side. "Smoke, Sandy!"

Glancing over, Ramsay saw with relief the first black columns coiling up above houses down there, as thatches were set alight. Now he need not feel that he was talking against time. He pointed. "Your town, Heron!"

He got no answer to that.

"You yield, Heron?"

"No! Never!"

"Very well. Your people will pay." More smoke rising. "Unless, Sir William – since you are knight – you will *act* the knight? Come out here and fight me. In single combat. Or, if your years restrain you, send another to act your champion. Or more than one. We will settle our differences in fair fight. For your honour's sake!"

He got a positive answer at last. Two arrows came whistling past, close, whether aimed to hit them or merely as warning there was no knowing. But the message was clear. He and Moray reined round and rode back to their men, ordering the whole party to move back some way out of range, there to wait.

But not for long. For now that the smoke was rising high, it would be seen from afar and acted upon, first by their own folk and then, eventually, by the English garrisons, no doubt, miles away. The time factor was now against them. Ramsay sent a couple of horsemen to order Moray's laird to break off the ravaging, not to worry about booty, and to return here forthwith.

It seemed quite a long wait before the others arrived back, with Ramsay becoming concerned. Once reunited, they wasted no time in learning the details of the assault on Ford town, but reined round at once to ride back whence they had come. What Sir William Heron thought of this was not to be known.

Before they were halfway to Etal they could see two great columns of smoke towering ahead.

At Etal, they found Pate, with most of his men lining the riverside opposite its castle in case of attack from its people, who could be seen massing outside, across the ford; not that this seemed very likely, for there appeared to be considerably fewer of them than of the invaders. Pate was worried, however, that they might have sent warning messengers northwards to inform the nearest garrison. The village was aflame, and its unhappy folk huddled under watchful guards. No doubt everyone there, friend and foe alike, was relieved when Ramsay ordered prompt retiral.

Redheuch had all under control at Crookham, his men still firing roofs and heaps of plenishings. From there they could see the smoke from Branxton rising high. They did not linger here, either.

The company reunited at Branxton. Ramsay asked their guide whether there was any shorter route back to the borderline than by the way they had come which did not take them by Morebattle – for he did not wish any seeming link with that place, for fear of reprisals. Their shepherd, much agreeing with this last, said that the shortest way was by Learmouth and Pressen. But this would bring them over-close to Wark Castle, a major English stronghold. However, if at East Learmouth they swung south-westwards between Pressen Hill and Brown Rigg, they could reach the Border near Hoselaw and so avoid both the Wark and Morebattle areas. This was accepted. Incidentally their guide now announced that he wished to be enrolled in their company hereafter, finding this activity more to his taste than shepherding.

Their dash for the Border went without incident, as they avoided villages and the haunts of men, and left all the devastation behind them. The actual crossing back into Scotland represented a purely illusory security, of course, since any English pursuit would pay no attention to it; but it produced a good feeling nevertheless. In fact, all were in cheerful mood, although weary and many smoke-blackened and sore-eyed. They had achieved what they had set out to do, made quite a dramatic impact, suffered no casualties and gained almost one hundred captured horses, laden with grain, meal and various provisioning. Only the leaders, Ramsay in especial, tended to feel somewhat uncomfortable over the distinctly un-knightly nature of their activities, however effective and valid the cause. Tired as they all were, they rode on as far as the great woodlands of Haddenrig, not far from a Tweed ford at Sprouston, where they felt that they would be safely hidden, to spend the night.

Next morning, refreshed and with no sign of pursuit, they headed northwards, avoiding Kelso, and so across the Merse to Lauderdale and the way they had come. Over Soutra Hill, Ramsay and his own people left, to make for Hawthornden, while his friends and the larger company continued on northwards for their own areas, with the booty. They would stage another raid soon, they promised each other.

In fact, there were several raids thereafter, not all quite as successful and expeditious as the first one, in two of which Ramsay took part, others conducted by different leaders but all following approximately the same pattern of swift dashes by unfrequented routes to fairly isolated English communities, particularly in the Middle and West Marches, carefully avoiding the strongly-held and fortress areas of Berwick, Hexham and Carlisle. As well, Ramsay led two night attacks from Hawthornden on Balliol establishments, one on a supply-camp on Edinburgh's Burghmuir, the other on Cavers, near Hawick in Teviotdale, which was a Balliol family possession, as serving warning on the usurper that he too was the target for this renewal of the Scots' intransigence.

In it all, Ramsay came to discover himself to have become the renowned paladin, little as he assessed himself as deserving of anything such. He learned that his name and fame, ever magnified in the recounting, was being used as a rallying-cry, an encouragement to others, by the Regent and his lieutenants. Indeed he was told that many young men were actually seeking to be allowed to join his band, as a sort of apprenticeship in the splendid trade of arms. All of which was greatly embarrassing to an essentially modest man.

He heard nothing of any raids conducted by Will Douglas.

Then, in August, word came from Murray that the Franco-Scots strategy appeared to be working. Edward had agreed to a truce with Philip – who was insisting that Scotland should be included – and the Plantagenet was reported to be coming north himself again, presumably to negotiate the terms of the truce. There was also news, from other sources, that Balliol, feeling the mounting pressure, had moved south to Roxburgh Castle, only a few miles from the borderline.

Matters were clearly approaching some sort of climax.

But that climax, when it eventuated, was other than anticipated. Perhaps the Scots were naive in judging King Edward by normal standards, for the Plantagenets seldom acted normally. If he was coming north to establish a truce, he did it in his own peculiar way. For he brought with him an army of forty thousand, and sent a fleet of ships into the Forth estuary – and not merely to emphasise his power and majesty. Crossing into Scotland at Berwick, as usual, he marched on, burning and slaying, as though any truce was the last thing to cross his mind.

Not having anticipated this, the Regent had no great force assembled. He was still based on Atholl and, hearing that Balliol had left Edinburgh for Roxburgh, was preparing to come to Edinburgh to meet the Plantagenet in conference, when he heard the news of this new invasion. He sent out rallying-calls at once, but of course it would take time for any comparable host to assemble, especially in the Highlands. The courier who came to Hawthornden ordered Ramsay to remain where he was, and if possible to harass Edward's rear, as before.

So all seemed to be back to the sorry normal.

Edward did not waste time. In three bloody days he was at Edinburgh, captured the great fortress-castle, and leaving a keeper and garrison there, marched on to Stirling, which had remained securely in Balliol's keeping, the strongest fortress in the land. Then on to Perth, clearly seeking to confront the

Regent in person. Murray, still without a major army, retired ever northwards through the mountains, where the huge enemy force would be at a disadvantage. Edward, recognising this, left most of his foot in the Perth area and led his ten thousand cavalry on after the retreating Regent, ravaging the land as he went – although there was not a great deal to ravage in these Highland glens.

Meantime Ramsay did what he could, attacking supply-trains and ambushing foraging-parties and the like, and at this he was now expert indeed. He found himself receiving constant reinforcement, not really desired in the circumstances, springs of nobility, young men ambitious to be heroes, adventurers and the like. These he did not want at Hawthornden itself, nor could he put them up there, limited as the accommodation was and secret as it must remain if possible. So he established a camp for them in the hidden Esk-valley dens where they kept their horses. He also brought into use another series of cliffside caves at Gorton, not far from Hawthornden, of similar type and origin but provided with no castle above them. Many of these, reputed to have been a haunt of William Wallace, he was using to store arms, armour and other captured gear. He was active, busy, effective and successful in his ventures; but often he ached for Mariot, and cursed Edward and all things English for so making a mockery of his marriage.

One of his later recruits, who came from Fife, told him a strange story. Apparently the English lord, Henry de Beaumont, who called himself Earl of Buchan, he who had been captured at Dundarg by the Regent and allowed to go south, on parole, to gather his ransom, had so far abandoned knightly behaviour as not only to fail to send the ransom back, but actually had joined Edward's army against Scotland. His daughter, widow of the late Atholl, was still at the island-castle of Lochindorb in Braemoray, and the Regent had sent some of his northern vassals to besiege it. She had somehow sent a plea to the Plantagenet to come to her aid, and this he had indeed done, in person, playing the chivalrous prince for once, but sacking Aberdeen, with much slaughter, on the way. So now he was as far north as the Inverness area, with Sir Andrew Murray still retiring towards his own country of Avoch and the Black Isle of Cromarty. Whether Edward would continue the pursuit as far as that none knew; but surely his lines of communication were becoming mightily stretched, and the gathering strength of the Scots, mustering throughout the land, would make them even more vulnerable.

No doubt this consideration did not fail to occur to Edward himself, for the next they heard of him at Hawthornden was that he and his mounted host were returning to Perth.

Ramsay kept up his harassing tactics in Lothian and its vicinity. One more major gesture he made, down to Roxburgh itself, with Moray. They did not aspire to any assault on the great royal castle itself, this being far beyond their capabilities; but they did demonstrate a challenging presence in the neighbourhood, entering the large castleton, practically a small city in itself, and actually drove away many of the Balliol force's horses at pasture in the vicinity – this just to emphasise to the usurper that he would be safer in England, and fairly deep therein at that.

Then the news broke. Edward had departed for England, leaving his brother, the Earl of Cornwall, not Balliol, in charge of Scotland, at Perth, clear indication of his contempt for the usurper. But there was to be a truce offered, after all, although apparently it was below his dignity for Edward himself to haggle over terms, his brother to do that. This last savage invasion had been merely the Plantagenet way of preparing the ground. The Regent was to go to Perth, under safe-conduct, to discuss conditions and details. So King Francis had been right in his assessment of the situation; only, two could play at the game of preparing ground.

A few days later, a courier from Murray reached Hawthornden. The Regent had met Cornwall at Perth and thrashed out terms. There would be a parliament in ten days' time, at Dunfermline, to decide on acceptance or otherwise. Raiding activities were to be halted meantime.

Ramsay rode for Fife the next week, light of heart. The long-awaited truce was more than welcome, of course, if the terms were such as could be accepted. But it was not so much that which gladdened him. Mariot! He could surely now start acting the married man? And Dunfermline was not so very far from Doune.

The parliament in the great abbey was a deal better attended than that at Dairsie. From the first, the Regent made it clear that he personally advised homologation of the conditions he had managed to negotiate at Perth. They were not entirely satisfactory, needless to say; indeed the entire truce was something of a farce and fraud. But it was better than war against an enemy ten times as numerous, under an ambitious tyrant; would give them a breathing-space; and ought to militate gravely against Balliol's interests, for which Edward clearly cared little. The Plantagenet would break the truce whenever it suited him, all knew; but meantime they could strengthen and consolidate – and seek to wean Balliol's supporters in Scotland from him. The terms they had to swallow were none so grievous. The English garrisons in Stirling, Edinburgh, Renfrew, Roxburgh, Berwick and Caerlaverock Castle to remain, but lesser castles and houses to be vacated; all attacks on supply-trains and the like to cease; raids over the Border likewise. On the other hand, all Scots who had trespassed against the occupying power were to be pardoned; the liberties of the Scottish Church were to be maintained; and the laws pertaining at the death of Alexander the Third would be observed.

The parliament did not take long to agree these terms, however arrogantly put, and to ratify the truce. Will Douglas curtly moved acceptance, Dunbar seconding, and in doing so mentioning that he had it on good authority that the man Balliol had now removed himself from Roxburgh to Berwick, although leaving the former castle strongly garrisoned.

After the formal session, Ramsay suffered the less-than-welcome experience of being all but feted as something like the hero of the hour, the Regent himself leading the acclaim. According to him, none other had done so much and so consistently worried the English aggressors. Moray and the Stewart also won their measure of praise, but to nothing like the same extent. Ramsay was besieged by volunteers to join his company when the time came again for military activity – as come it would, all accepted.

To escape all this, he retired early, after gaining a promise from Moray that they would depart for Doune fairly promptly the next day.

It was only some thirty miles from Dunfermline to Doune, by the Cleish and Ochil hillfoots, Dollar and Causewayhead and Dunblane. On the way, Moray informed that Robert Steward was going to wed, when was not clear. It was no great love-match but a sensible arrangement with the daughter of one of his major vassals in the Renfrew lordship, Sir Adam Mure of Rowallan. Elizabeth Mure, whom the Steward had known since childhood, was a cheerfully amorous character who probably would do Robert very well; although whether, in the event of young King David producing no offspring, she would make a good Queen-consort for Scotland was another matter. Undoubtedly he had been on fairly intimate terms with this young woman for long, but only on Mariot's marriage had he decided that he might wed her.

Mariot received her husband with frankest joy. She had been expecting him, to be sure, and had a feast prepared. He decided there and then that not only was she the most delectable person he had ever known and the fairest sight he had ever feasted his eyes on but also was the most desirable creature ever to come his way – and he was tending to demonstrate the impact of all this forthwith and had to be laughingly restrained.

"Soon!" she whispered. "Soon! But, I rejoice to hear it, sir!"

Later she exhibited little more restraint than did he, all maidenly modesty and inhibitions gone. They knew utter fulfilment at last, that night, in each other's arms.

Surely there was now some future together for them, even though it might well be comparatively brief?

15

Two days later they were on their way, after a call on Bishop Maurice. It seemed strange indeed, for the man at least, after all the years, to be riding openly, no longer furtive nor prepared for battle, with only Wattie and four others as escort, down through Central Scotland. They led a trio of pack-horses, laden with Mariot's clothing and some personal possessions, and did not hurry. Moray had offered to provide a large company for their safety but Ramsay had declared a truce to be a truce, and great armed bands parading the country were contrary to the spirit of the thing. Nevertheless, when they reached the junction of Teith and Forth, in the area north of Stirling, they carefully avoided the Causewayhead vicinity and the narrow Stirling Bridge itself, under the frowning ramparts of the huge rock-top castle, and made a detour westwards to cross Forth by the Ford of Drip and so to reach the safe anonymity of the great Tor Wood, wilderness area second only to the Forest of Ettrick in size, in the southern half of Scotland. Just in case the English in Stirling were not yet fully truce-conscious.

Mariot was a good horsewoman and assured her husband that the fifty-odd miles from Doune to Hawthornden was by no means too much for her in the one day. He would have taken her direct to her new home-to-be at Dalwolsey, had he been certain that the enemy occupiers had vacated it yet, under the general terms of the truce, and had he known in what condition they might have left it. Besides, she was eager to see Hawthornden and the famous caves and refuges from which so much had been achieved, and determined to spend at least one night in the romantic underground. Ramsay had never thought of it as romantic, but acceded that her presence therein would make it so for him thereafter.

So again to avoid enemy-held Edinburgh, they turned south-eastwards in the Linlithgow area to make for the Calders and skirts of the Pentland Hills and so round to the Esk valley.

Mariot's reception at Hawthornden was all but riotous, not only as their leader's wife and the Earl of Moray's sister, but as the first woman to have graced the cave-system, in recent times at least; however many of the company had desired otherwise. That she was going to spend the night with them added to the appreciation. Details of the truce terms and parliament, in the circumstances, made only a moderate impact. For her part, Mariot found it all even more dramatic and exciting than she had visualised, especially the sing-song before turning in, held in the firelit and somewhat smoke-filled cavern which was the living-chamber, with all the strong male resonance rendering ancient ballads of love and war and longing, not all of them delicately worded but all rousing, particularly in that strange, secret, echoing setting. Her harp was still amongst her gear with the pack-horses, but she did not fail to contribute two or three songs of her own, in her clear, melodious voice so different from the others, rapturously received.

That night, in their private little cave, romance most assuredly blossomed in and blessed underground Hawthornden.

In the morning, Will Ramsay, who had throughout acted more or less caretaker and warden of the caves-refuge, as well as organising the quite difficult administration of provisioning, went off to discover the present situation at Dalwolsey. He presently came back to inform that, while the English garrison had already left the castle, they had also left everything in a deplorable mess, with quite a lot of plenishings missing. He had set some of the castleton women on to cleaning up, but it was to be feared that the place was in no suitable state for presentation to its new mistress. Mariot declared herself unconcerned about that, but since she was in no hurry to leave Hawthornden, it was decided that they should wait for a day or two before making the move. Meantime she wanted to see the other caves at Gorton and all the secret deans in the Esk valley and the spots where some of the actions she had heard about had taken place.

After two more days they rode the few miles to Dalwolsey, on the other, South Esk, at last. Mariot was delighted with the redstone castle's appearance and situation, so different from Doune; and the interior, after the ministrations of the local women, was better than they had feared. Some new furnishings, tapestries and hangings, floor-coverings and tableware would be necessary to replace items stolen by the occupying troops, but it all might have been much worse. Mariot promptly set about turning the place into more of a home than it had been for years. She was, after all, an experienced housekeeper. Ramsay wondered how Moray would get on without her at Doune. He also would have to find himself a wife.

Ramsay was exceedingly doubtful as to the efficacy of this odd truce, and for how long it would last, not trusting King Edward an inch. He believed that it would not be long before the English garrisons returned to their aggressive tactics, whether ordered to or not, and raids over the Border recommenced. Balliol, after all, was almost bound to try to recover his usurped throne. And once Edward Plantagenet was ready to invade France, Scotland would once again be fair game. So Ramsay did not disband his company entirely, but sent most of his people home meantime, prepared for swift recall. He kept a small nucleus at Hawthornden, however, and took his own personal following to Dalwolsey. But all could reassemble in a couple of days.

The Regent had now based himself at Linlithgow, which was a royal palace but insufficiently strongly-sited for the English to have considered worth taking over. This was less than twenty-five miles from Dalwolsey; and after a week or so, Murray sent for Ramsay to attend a Council meeting there. Since her brother would almost certainly be present, Ramsay took Mariot with him, for the two were very close.

The main object of this informal Council, about a dozen attending, including the Steward, was to discuss how they might best use this breathing-space, in Scotland's favour. For there was, of course, a danger in it – as Ramsay had recognised in his own arrangements – that, lulled by a probably false sense of security, men would immerse themselves in their own affairs, the lords disperse their armed forces and the nation revert to a peace mentality, so leaving the country open to sudden assault by the fortress garrisons or by Balliol's supporters. The Regent was open to suggestions to counter this tendency, but himself had a proposal, to keep the martial spirit to the fore and to serve a sort of warning on the enemy that they were ready for trouble at any time, without being so aggressive as to *provoke* that trouble. His idea was that certain of their lords and knights should issue challenges to English leaders to personal combat on the tourney-ground, in a series of tournaments, joustings, duels and knightly competitions. This would also give excuse for the Scots champions to retain parties of armed men with them, as suitable escorts, and indicate to Balliol and Edward's commanders that the Scots were very much alert. It might well also enhance their chivalric reputation.

It was at this stage of the debate that Murray looked at Ramsay. His name and reputation was now renowned, his exploits on all lips. If he was one of the foremost Scots champions at these tourneys, that would make a notable impact on the enemy, for sure. Sir William Douglas, who had been known as the Flower of Chivalry, had not come to this meeting, but Sir Alexander Ramsay was bidding fair to outdo his friend and possibly steal that title from him. If he would demonstrate to the English that he could perform as well on the tourney-ground as on the field of battle, Scotland would much benefit.

Ramsay, of course, was much disconcerted by all this praise, protesting that his activities were greatly exaggerated, and that anyway he had no especial prowess as a tournament-fighter. He could not refuse to play his part, but asserted that others were more likely to distinguish themselves in the lists than was he. He agreed, as did others, that the project was an admirable one and should be proceeded with quickly.

But how was it all to be initiated?

Ramsay himself it was who made the suggestion. Berwick-on-Tweed, where Balliol was now roosting, although occupied by the English and on the very borderline, was Scotland's principal seaport. Why not challenge the enemy to meet them there, thus emphasising the fact that it was Scottish soil, embarrassing Balliol they hoped, and making it difficult for the English notables to refuse to take part?

This was accepted with acclaim.

There followed a compiling of names of knightly challengers on the Scots side and particular English and Balliol supporters to dare on the other. A proposal was put forward that Edward Balliol himself should be named, but it was decided that this would be doing too much honour to the wretched usurper. By the same token the various challenges should not be sent through Balliol but through Edward's brother, the Earl of Cornwall. No lack of names were put forward, of Englishmen and renegade Scots who had distinguished themselves as deserving of being taught a lesson, including the Earls of Norfolk, Arundel, Salisbury, and Derby; the Lords Henry de Beaumont, parole-breaker, and Richard Talbot; and the knights Sir Roland de Vaux, Sir Anthony Lucy, Sir John de St Michael; and the renegade Scots, Sir John Stirling and Sir Laurence Abernethy, one-time owner of Hawthornden Castle. Some of those present at the meeting volunteered to take part, and other known experts with lance and sword and mace were suggested for approach. The challenges were to be sent to Berwick by the Regent as soon as possible.

Ramsay returned to Dalwolsey just a little apprehensive about his ability to distinguish himself in tournament-fighting, although he had done not a little of it in years past when Bruce's peace prevailed; but to take on English champions . . . ? Mariot was less than happy about it also, for jousting could be as dangerous as true warfare, often.

Much of the pride and quality of Lowland Scotland seemed to be *en route* for Berwick-on-Tweed a month later, partly out of policy but as much out of interest and a kind of defiance. The common folk from the Merse and Tweed valley were there too, for this was something unique, promising to be a spectacle such as none had ever witnessed, and one day would be for recounting to their children's children; an encounter between Scots and English, where all could watch without danger – or so it was claimed and hoped. Famous men would be there to display their prowess and represent their nations. It would all be a sight to see.

The English had readily agreed to the tournament idea, Cornwall actually to welcome it. Balliol's attitude was not known, but some of his supporters, Beaumont and Talbot amongst them, had accepted the challenges, as had many of the English leadership. After all, it was in accordance with the knightly code.

Murray himself had been going to attend, but had been persuaded not to. They dared not trust the English that far, truce or none. The easy capture of Scotland's Regent might have been just too much of a temptation. So he had nominated Moray and the Steward, as former joint Regents, to represent him. They had left him at Dunbar Castle, although his hostess had not remained there with him, for Black Agnes was not going to miss this entertainment. Her husband, as usual, was elsewhere, presumably at Ersildoune. Ramsay and Mariot were with Moray's party.

Reaching Berwick, along with so many others, they found that the tourney-ground in front of the castle there had been deemed too small for the present event and an alternative venue organised down on the links of the coast just north of the city walls, where there was room for thousands. Here many pavilions and tents had been erected, great and small, flying the banners of English nobility, lists marked off and enclosures railed. Some of the Scots had brought their own tentage but it made a poor showing beside the colourful striped and heraldic flourish of the others.

Moray's and the Steward's first problem was over Edward

Balliol. They must not do anything which could be construed as recognising the man's authority. They did not want even to meet him. Possibly guessing what their attitude would be, the usurper seemed equally anxious to avoid them, for he did not put in an appearance at all, although presumably he was in the castle. John Plantagenet, Earl of Cornwall, a somewhat weedy-looking young man, was in command; but in fact all was being directed by William de Montague, Earl of Salisbury, an older man, at least superficially jovial, who greeted the Scots in hearty, patronising fashion. They kept themselves, in consequence, the more warily remote.

This reaction grew the more pronounced as Salisbury and his colleagues proceeded to take charge of everything, as though very much the hosts and begetters of it all, directing the Scots this way and that, announcing fixtures and arrangements, and providing bounteous refreshments for all. Neither Moray nor Robert Stewart were aggressive personalities and found it difficult to assert the fact that this was all Scots initiative. They could have done with a personality such as Will Douglas.

Without consultation or warning other than a flourish of trumpets to gain him silence, Salisbury presently announced that the high and mighty Lord John of Cornwall decreed that the day's proceedings would commence with a twenty-a-side jousting, with lances only, this confined to those of knightly rank.

Moray was about to protest at this assumption of authority, when Ramsay pointed out that Englishmen around were laughing and declaring that the Scots did not *have* twenty knights to muster. It was a trick, to embarrass, to make them look weak, feeble. Let them accept this, then.

"But *have* we twenty knights, man?"

"Probably not. But we can . . . adopt some! No? In armour, these English will not know the difference! They will have no notion as to who are knights and who are not. Promote, for the occasion, some of our best fighters . . ."

Robert Stewart agreed. The trio then went hurrying round, seeking volunteers. Between them they raised fourteen knights and knighted lords, themselves included, and a round dozen veteran fighters, lairds and esquires, Pate and Redheuch amongst them. It was a deceit admittedly, but then this engagement sprung on them was almost certainly a crafty artifice, intended to produce humiliation.

The problem now was choosing the six to reject, without offence. Ramsay declared that Moray and the Steward should not take part in this mass encounter, since they were representing the Regent – that is, unless Cornwall himself also joined in, which did not seem likely. One or two of the older veterans agreed to drop out; and one of the knights also, actually a kinsman of Ramsay's own, Sir William Ramsay of Foulden, conceding that his eyesight was not of the best. So there were eleven knights and nine others.

William, the young Earl of Ross, whose father had been slain at Halidon only a mile or two away, was premier noble present, but he insisted that Ramsay should take the lead. So that man, in full armour now, went forward to arrange procedures with Salisbury who, it seemed, was not himself taking part, the Earl of Derby to lead the English side. Ramsay named sufficient of the Scots knights to sound impressive, and picked up a few of the English identities, including, interestingly, the Lord Dacre of Gilsland, Sir Anthony Lucy, the Lord Henry Percy, Sir Thomas de Musgrave and Sir Roland de Vaux. It was agreed that at the second blast of a trumpet the two sides should charge in line abreast. Those who succeeded in reaching the other's base-line would then turn and charge back, the side with most knights still upright in their saddles to be accepted as the winners.

It is feared that, drawn up in line, the Scots made a less impressive showing than did their opposite numbers. Their chain-mail was apt to be rusted, plate-armour dented, fewer helmets sported tossing plumes and the heraldic-painted shields were less ornate. Also, the English horses were better, or at least larger and heavier, the renowned Flanders destriers, which could greatly affect the issue in a headlong clash. Ramsay pointed out to his nineteen this danger. Try to avoid any actual contact with these destriers. Their own lighter beasts could be knocked aside and bowled over by sheer weight and impetus. On the other hand, their own horses would be more nimble on their feet and manoeuvrable. Use that, to dodge and wheel, where possible. It was lances only, but a sideways-swinging lance could unseat an enemy almost as effectively as a conventional head-on thrust. Use that other weapon allowed, then, surprise.

The Scots had one advantage denied to their opponents – the ladies. Few if any of the English notables had brought their women, so that Black Agnes, as Countess of Dunbar and March, found herself to be more or less Queen of the Tournament, with Mariot her deputy and other Scotswomen to cheer on their menfolk. Ramsay's lance bore two favours tied to it: Mariot's silken scarf and one of her sister's gloves, the other bestowed on Sir William Keith, the Knight Marischal.

At the first trumpet blast, both lines lowered lances to the couched position, helmet-visors snapped down. Ramsay and Derby each raised a steel-gauntleted hand to signify readiness. The second trumpet blew.

Inevitably the start was distinctly ragged, the horses scarcely trained for this, and bearing heavily-armoured riders. But at least the Scots start was the better, for their lighter beasts were quicker to move. Derby, in the English centre, sought to keep his knights more or less in line, which meant holding back for the slowest; but Ramsay did not trouble with this; he was not concerned to present a solid, massive, thundering front.

The course was three hundred yards in length, so that not a great deal of time was available for the horses to gather speed before the clash. From the first the Scots sought to surprise and confuse, by spreading as far apart as possible in the confines of the enclosure, whereas normal tactics were for a close-packed solid front. This forced the English to try to open out likewise, or they would have been able to assail only a few in the centre of the oncoming line. This in turn reduced their pace further, as Derby waved them left and right, so that the Scots on their faster mounts had opportunity to cover fully two-thirds of the available length and gain maximum speed before the impact.

That shock in itself was very uneven owing to the Scots strategy of not keeping in any very straight line, so that the charging horsemen met each other raggedly, the English losing the advantage of mutual weight and impetus; more especially so as just before the moment of impact, with lances aimed at each other's persons, their opponents almost all jerked their horses aside, this way and that, and then, as they passed, swept their lances round sideways with all their force, a difficult manoeuvre not always achieving contact, but when

301

it did having a dire effect on the balance of the enemy, tensely poised for a forward not a sidelong clash. Some English knights toppled from their saddles and crashed to the ground.

For his own part, Ramsay, in the very centre, was probably the least able to perform his own advised tactics effectively. Recognising this, he hastily sought an alternative surprise. Expected to aim at his opposite number, Derby, he rode directly at him, lance levelled, until, only a yard or two off, he violently pulled his mount's head to the left, so that they drove past each other, the Earl's spear-tip missing him by feet. Then, in almost the same motion, he brought his own lance round across his front, to strike the back of the English knight on his left, close by, who was aiming at Keith the Marischal, the next Scot. The unfortunate victim of two assaults toppled sideways to the earth with a heavy crash.

Then the two lines were past each other and plunging on towards the opposite starting base. The Scots had lost two lances, one man was reeling as though drunken in his saddle, and five English were unhorsed, one risen to his feet, one seeking to rise but three lying still.

A single glance showed Ramsay all this, but he wasted no time on the survey. Now was their opportunity. They had much the shorter distance to go to the turning base than had their opposition. Reaching it, he yelled to his people to wheel round and dash back, with maximum speed. They were cantering over the course again before ever the slowing English had reached their turning-place, although the injured Scot, Sir David Annand, dropped behind.

As a result, there was confusion on the enemy line. They had to cross the marked base before they might turn, and they must do this now as though they were being pursued, a humiliating situation. The reining round of the heavy destriers thereafter was a slower process again, amidst Derby's shouts for haste. Some English knights started back before others, and it became every man for himself.

The terms of this engagement being that the side with most riders still in the saddle, back at their own base, was the winner, meant that in fact the Scots had already won – if they could avoid further casualties. But Ramsay was well aware how unheroic it would look if his people all now sought to dodge and jink combat. They must do better than that, for honour's sake. They were seventeen effectives against fifteen, but head-on clashes could still favour the English weight, even though this was now much dispersed. He had to leave it now to his folk to use their own judgment.

For himself, spurring ahead now, he was three-quarters of the way back to his own base when he found an Englishman bearing directly down on him. Waiting until the last moment, he deliberately jerked his beast aside, without contact, although the other's lance-point scraped his shield. He hated doing this, but *Derby* was his target, not this unknown knight. The Earl's great white charger and blue and white helmet-plumes were readily distinguishable. Pulling over to the right sharply, Ramsay headed therefor.

Derby, in fact, was making for the Scot immediately in his path, Sir Patrick Graham, so to some extent Ramsay was thus advantaged, for the eye-slits in the helmet-visor did not give the best sideways vision. But the Earl did see the attack coming in time to pull round his destrier with a few yards to spare, and for a moment it looked like full-scale collision. But pulling back his mount's head violently so that the beast reared up, forefeet pawing the air, Ramsay pivoted it round in avoiding action. The other's lance did strike his shoulder-armour a glancing blow, but only that. Round and still further round he dragged his teetering horse's head, until it came down on all fours again directly behind the Englishman, Ramsay cursing his long, unwieldy lance when what he needed now was a sword. But seeking to foreshorten the thing for a jabbing motion, he thrust at the Earl's person as Derby tried to wheel back. Caught sidelong by the blow, that man slewed in his saddle, sought desperately to retain his seat, but the destrier's clumsy turning defeated him. Lance spinning away, he toppled over with a resounding crash, Ramsay's own lance splintering with the impact.

Graham's horse, seeking to avoid Derby's beast, cannoned into Ramsay's own, and the latter all but fell, likewise. Somehow, both managed to remain up, distinctly shaken.

Urgently Ramsay pulled himself together, to gaze round, with his own limited vision. It was at first hard to tell friend from foe, individual duelling being in process. But the heavier horses indicated identity – and Ramsay heaved a sigh of relief. There were many more riderless destriers than Scots horses. With a waving motion of his broken lance, he called all to break off and return to their starting base.

303

As the others came in, some obviously injured, some without lances, the final result could now be established. Eleven Scots remained in their saddles and only seven Englishmen were still mounted. Of the fallen men, six remained sprawled motionless – for falling in heavy armour could be stunning if not worse – the others on their feet, some staggering, these last including the Earl of Derby.

The cheering from the Scots spectators was loud and long, as esquires and attendants hurried out to assist the fallen.

Dismounting stiffly, his shoulder hurting, Ramsay himself walked out to inspect the prostrate half-dozen. Only one proved to be a Scot, none other than Redheuch, and he was stirring and seeking to rise, as were three of the others. But two English knights lay inanimate. His satisfaction impaired by this fact, Ramsay led his people over to the stand where the ladies sat, to receive their praise and congratulations, which included hugs and kisses from the Randolph sisters, Agnes' hearty, Mariot's tense. Appreciative as he was of these, Ramsay's attention was distracted nevertheless. Standing a little way behind the women's party was Sir William Douglas of Liddesdale, the Flower of Chivalry himself.

Much surprised to see him there, Ramsay raised a gauntleted hand. The other nodded briefly, and turned away.

Salisbury came up. "How does your victory smell to you, Sir Alexander?" he asked. "Achieved in such fashion!"

"Do you find fault with our Scots methods, my lord?"

"They were . . . unusual, shall we say?"

"Is not surprise always worth half a battle?"

"This is chivalric diversion, not war, sir."

"I call it mock war. And offered you mock surprise! As did you to us with your twenty-a-side challenge. There are more challenges than one! My lord, two of your knights seemed sore stricken?"

"They are dead. Necks broken, both." That was curt.

"I am sorry . . ."

"The next bout is individual combat. With lance and sword or mace."

"I think, my lord, that it is for us, the Scots, to say what the next shall be," Ramsay told him quietly. "But, I dare say that we can agree to individual combat. I shall consult my lord of Moray and the High Steward."

"Do that, Ramsay . . ."

Making for his friends, he saw Douglas standing with some of his people. He went to him, hand out. "Will, how good to see you here. You came to watch the sport?"

"Not to *watch*, no."

"Ah! You come to take part? That is good," Douglas was indeed looking more like himself – and he was, of course, the best-known tournament-fighter in Scotland. "Moray and the Steward will rejoice that you are come. I go to them now. Come, you . . ."

Moray's and Robert Stewart's rejoicing at sight of the Douglas was somewhat muted, unsure as to how to take him, the more so as the latter's attitude to them was distant. They were quite agreeable to the next affair being single combat, with lance, sword or mace, but hesitated when Douglas abruptly announced that *he* would be the first challenger, and took it for granted that this would be so. Ramsay, glancing at his friends, nodded slightly.

Douglas wasted no time. Although it was in theory the Knight Marischal's duty to make the announcements, he summoned one of his own lairds, went forward and had a horn blown loud and long. Then, in stentorian tones, the laird shouted that the puissant and renowned Sir William Douglas, Knight of Liddesdale, hereby sought the satisfaction of personal combat. His challenge was expressly to one man, Sir Edward Balliol, who wrongfully and insolently called himself King of Scots. Let the said Sir Edward come and prove himself.

The gasps which greeted that were not all on the English side, as men stared at each other. Ramsay, for once, was intrigued. Such a thing had never occurred to him and implied surely some reassessing of his thinking about Douglas's present attitudes.

There was a pause thereafter, until presently a herald on the English side had a trumpet blown and then declared that the high and mighty Lord Edward, King of Scotland, was not present on this occasion and therefore could not consider the Knight of Liddesdale's challenge.

The Douglas laird was commencing some reply to this when his master silenced him, and himself raised voice, and a powerful voice at that.

"I, William Douglas, understand that the miscreant Balliol

is lurking in this castle of Berwick. Let him come and answer this challenge, or forever bear the name of craven!"

Again there was an interval for deliberation across the lists, and then Salisbury himself came forward.

"The Lord Edward would, no doubt, meet you, Douglas," he called. "But he is not available. That is final. Choose you some other champion, or retire."

"Very well. All now know that the usurper Balliol is craven, and hides behind yonder castle's walls! So I must needs meet a braver man, as his deputy. But, see you, it must be one of *his* creatures, not some honest English knight!" Again there were gasps.

In a little, Salisbury was back. "The Lord Richard Talbot, Lord of Badenoch will meet you, Douglas," he said.

"The Lord of Badenoch has been safely dead these many years, God be thanked!" he was told. "But I will meet Richard Talbot."

Douglas came back, to prepare himself and his mount, and to don jousting armour. He made no comments as to Balliol.

When the trumpet blew for the start, Douglas surprised all by not couching his lance but leaving it upright, base in its socket, and drawing his sword. This was highly unusual, the normal procedure being to fight first with the lances, and if they failed to achieve results, to continue with the swords or maces. It would certainly confuse Talbot, who was charging ahead with lowered lance.

All watched eagerly. Would Douglas lower his lance at the last moment? Or would he seek to dodge and turn? Either way he was taking a major risk.

In the event, that man did neither. He drove straight at his opponent, as it looked to utter disaster, lance still high. Talbot must have expected him to pull aside, to divert, but instead, when only a few yards off, he swung his sword sideways across his chest, and then his shield, on his left arm, directly in front of him, so that it was based on the great sword. Then, almost in the same motion, bending low and crouching forward behind both, he drove on straight at the menacing lance-point.

What Talbot thought was anybody's guess. He might have wavered, a little.

Douglas did not waver. He used that sword-backed shield, their mutual impetus, and an explosion of his own muscular strength, to turn himself into a battering-ram. The impact of the lance-tip on a shrinking or unready man could have been devastating; but this man actually thrust out that shield to meet the lance, his bent arm serving to absorb part of the shock. The crash seemed to jar all there watching. Douglas's horse was thrown back on its haunches, although the heavier destrier plunged on. But the lance, deflected upwards by the force and Douglas's thrust, snapped its shaft. Talbot all but toppled forward at the sudden break in pressure. Then his destrier took him past.

Douglas, with a barked laugh loud enough to be heard by most, hollow as it sounded within his helmet, transferred sword to left hand and grasped his own lance at last, waved it in the air and then cast it mockingly from him.

The Scots cheering was ecstatic.

But Douglas, even whilst waving, was dragging his beast's head round hard. His right hand now free, he grabbed sword from the left and spurred after the Englishman.

Possibly Talbot realised his danger. But his destrier was a deal more slow than the other's mount, and not good at turning swiftly in its tracks whilst charging. He was half-round in his saddle and glancing back when Douglas bore down on him. With a furious sideways swipe of the sword that man struck the other at the neck-gorget. Talbot, still clutching his broken lance, reeled over, lost balance, and fell to the earth.

Douglas reined up, ignoring his fallen foe, and raised the visor of his helmet. He had to wait until the cheering died away.

"Send me another!" he shouted towards the English lines. "Another of Balliol's dupes. If any such dare!" And he rode back to his own base.

Talbot managed to pick himself up and limped back to his lines.

Ramsay, along with others, was congratulating the victor – who scorned the customary visit to the women's stand – when the English herald strode out again, to announce that the valiant and esteemed knight, Sir Edward Bohun, challenged Sir William Douglas to single combat.

Douglas shouted back. "I thank Sir Edward Bohun. But I did not come here to fight good Englishmen, only Balliol supporters. Find me one of them, if you can! If not, I leave here."

Ramsay was pondering this strange behaviour when the herald reappeared. He declared that with the King of Scotland absent, few of his people were present and none could be found meantime to take up the Knight of Liddesdale's challenge. If he would not fight Sir Edward Bohun, that knight challenged any other Scot soever to single combat.

Douglas snorted, turned away, shouted for his people to prepare to ride, and began to doff his jousting armour.

Ramsay protested that the day was not over yet and that much more could be achieved, but the other was adamant. He had done what he had come to do, shown up Balliol and his crew for what they were. He was for off. Ramsay and his friends were welcome to the rest.

As Douglas rode off, Ramsay's kinsman, Sir William of Foulden, came to announce that he wished to take up Bohun's challenge. This Bohun would no doubt be some kin to the Sir Henry whom Bruce slew in single combat before Bannockburn. He claimed the privilege of fighting him.

Ramsay was doubtful. Foulden was of middle years now, and although quite namely as a fighter when younger, was not the man he had been. And he had admitted that his eyesight was not of the best. But it was not for him to say who should fight and who should not. When the other added that this might well be his last jousting, and he wished it to be a notable one, he held his peace.

The Knight Marischal made the announcement that Sir William Ramsay of Foulden would fight Sir Edward Bohun. The answer came back; after all the lance-work, this bout would be on foot, with sword and spear. The English were still laying down the conditions. Foulden declared himself not averse to this gladiator-type contest.

Presently the two knights paced out, heavily in their armour, short stabbing-spears in one hand, swords in the other. They met and shook gauntleted hands, then stepped back. Immediately Bohun launched himself forward again, making a pass with his spear. Foulden jerked aside only just in time to avoid it, but not quite to avoid the vicious sword-thrust which followed swiftly, and which struck him on the left shoulder. He reeled back but recovered, lashing out wildly with his own sword. The other had to side-step, with a lumbering jump, and his long spurs caught in each other. He all but fell. Full armour was not an aid to agility on foot. Foulden was just too late with his spear-jab.

They each stepped back, panting already.

Bohun was again the first to attack. Sword weaving, he sought almost to dance in front of the other, footwork however less than nimble, but sufficient to keep the Scot guessing. Then, as Foulden dodged aside, Bohun bent low and thrust his spear out between the other's legs. His opponent fell with a crash.

Bohun stood aside, to see if the other would rise.

Foulden did, struggling somehow, obviously shaken by the concussion in his armour.

Seeing him back on his feet, Bohun resumed the assault, swinging his sword back and forward in a figure-of-eight motion. Foulden sought to intercept this with his spear – and the sword's sharp steel sheared the wooden shaft clean through. The Scot, lurching over with the force of the blow, sank on one knee. Bohun smashed down on his helmet with his sword, and once again stepped back, as Foulden fell forward on his face, clutching only a foot or so of wood.

Astonishingly the older man managed to pick himself up again, although he must have been all but stunned. He stood swaying, but held out his sword-tip to show that he was still in the fight.

There were mixed cheers from the onlookers.

Once more Bohun lunged, and as he came, Foulden hurled that piece of wood at the other's helmet. It struck him full-face, with sufficient force to shake him, and his sword-thrust went askew. Dizzy or not, Foulden swung his own sword down on the other's sword-arm, and the weapon went spinning to the ground. For moments the two antagonists stared at each other, panting. Then with both hands the Scot raised sword for the felling stroke. As it came, Bohun, with both hands available now also, jabbed his spear with all his strength in the other's face. And by an extraordinary chance, its steel point drove in between the slots of the visor, the metal bulging aside with the force. Deep in, the spear sank. The victim stumbled backwards, fell flat, and lay still, the short spear still sticking upright from his visor.

When it was seen that there would be no rising this time, Bohun raised a hand high, signalling victory. From both sides, after doubtful cheerings, men hurried out, Ramsay amongst the first.

Stooping over his fallen kinsman, he spoke urgently, and received a sort of gargled reply. But what to do? The spear had wedged the visor shut and it would not open. From the depth that the thing was in, Ramsay judged that it must have gone right through the left eye-socket and into the skull. That the man was still alive seemed a miracle. Desperately he sought advice.

He found the Earls of Salisbury and Derby there, gazing down.

"A brave man!" the former said. "I fear that he must be dead?"

"He is alive. I heard him speak. But, what can we do? I cannot open the visor. Unless I pull out this spear. And then . . . then . . !" He left the rest unsaid.

An English friar was amongst those who had come to peer down. He shook his tonsured head. "He cannot live," he declared. "I know something of hurts and healing. This knight – he goes to his Maker!"

"Can you do nothing, man?"

"I can shrive him," the other said simply.

"Aye, do that," Derby said. "He fought well. Do your best for him, clerk."

The friar knelt by Foulden's side, and intoned a brief office for the dying. He made the sign of the cross over him.

When he stood up, Ramsay exclaimed, "I thank you. But we cannot just leave him so. Like this." He bent an ear, to listen. "He speaks again, I think. This accursed visor . . . !" He tried again to withdraw the spear.

"If you pull it out now, it will be the end," the friar declared.

"You have said that he is as good as dead now! He tries to speak. Let him have that, at least! Before he goes."

"Ramsay is right," Salisbury nodded.

That man rose. "God forgive me!" he breathed. He took the spear-shaft in his two hands and tugged. It did not move. He put his foot on Foulden's helmet, and against the pressure heaved again. The spear came out, with the scrape of metal and bone, and a gout of blood with it. A strangled yell came from inside the helmet.

Ramsay knelt, to open the visor, blood and fluid seeping

out. Astonishingly, Foulden struggled to sit up. All around shouted to him to lie still. But, grasping Ramsay's arm, he managed to drag himself to his feet. Swaying there, he stiffly raised a hand.

"I . . . soon . . . shall ail . . . nothing!" he croaked, and choking on that last word, pitched forward headlong on his face, and lay still.

All gazed down at him.

"So help me, God – this brave knight shrived with his helmet on!" Derby exclaimed. "A happy man I'd be, with such an ending!"

"What stout hearts these . . ." Salisbury began, when Ramsay, who had sunk to Foulden's side again, looked up.

"He has gone," he said. "He no longer breathes."

For a little longer they all stood there, much moved.

"I think – no more jousting this day," Ramsay said.

Salisbury nodded. But Lord Richard Talbot, eager to redeem his name for prowess, objected that he had challenged Sir Patrick Graham, whom he had crossed swords with in France, to a joust, and had been accepted.

"Tomorrow will serve for that," Salisbury decided. "Enough for this day."

Later, Ramsay told Moray and the Steward that, for his part, he would not be at the morrow's tournament. The least that he could do for his late kinsman was to escort his body back to Foulden, in the Merse, and break the news as best he might to the bereaved widow. Mariot announced that she would go to aid him in that duty.

So ended that strange day of chivalry.

16

In the March of 1337 Edward Plantagenet announced himself to be King of France, and Philip de Valois to be but a usurper; and the English parliament authorised all necessary means for the obtaining of the French throne by force of arms. As a corollary, Thomas Beauchamp, Earl of Warwick, was appointed 'captain and leader of the army of Scotland, to represent the person of the lord King', and sent north to co-ordinate moves against the Scots rebels. Mention was not made of Edward Balliol, but this appointment of Warwick appeared to institute a new standing-army situation.

So the time for chivalrous games was past. It was back to normal in Anglo-Scottish relations.

There was no delay in the renewal of hostilities. Berwick-on-Tweed and Roxburgh were turned into huge English armed camps, preliminary probes began into Scotland, and all the garrisons of enemy-held castles, strongholds and towns recommenced aggression.

All was not wholly the same in Scotland, however. For although near-famine was rife in the war-devastated land, the truce period had achieved a growth in national spirit and a greater degree of unity, largely due to the fact that Balliol's cause was so obviously flagging, his support dwindling. Sadly however, Sir Andrew Murray was beginning to show his age, and failing in bodily strength, his authority having to be more and more delegated.

His orders were for Ramsay to return to Hawthornden and continue his campaign of secret assault, ambush and harassment, accepted now to be a major problem for the English. It meant leaving Dalwolsey, but then that house could well be taken over again by the enemy at any time; and the last thing its lord wanted was to be shut up and besieged within it. He was for sending Mariot either back to Doune or to her sister at Dunbar. But she declared that she had not married him to live apart from him; she would come to Hawthornden with him and seek to make its peculiar quarters more homelike for all concerned. She was sufficiently her father's daughter not to allow herself to be dissuaded. And it was extraordinary how, in only a few days, she managed to transform those caves to provide a fair degree of comfort and to introduce a much improved regime of meals, bringing two or three young women from Dalwolsey to aid her – in itself a highly popular innovation.

Ramsay recommenced his raids on the Edinburgh garrison's supply-trains.

News from the rest of Scotland tended to be sporadic and scrappy. But one item was sufficiently circumstantial and detailed to arouse much debate and to set Ramsay, in especial, pondering. This was that loyal forces had besieged St John's Town of Perth, under the Steward and Moray, but gained little headway until joined by two unexpected allies: these none other than Sir William Douglas, and, of all men, Master William Bullock, Balliol's Chamberlain of Scotland. It seemed that this curious but able individual had deserted the usurper, judging that cause in decline, had yielded up St Andrews and the castle of Cupar – in exchange for large personal grants of land – and, somehow linked with Douglas, had come to aid the siege of Perth. Cleric though he was, he appeared to have a genius for strategy. He persuaded miners to undermine the city walls, and not only to gain ingress but to drain at the same time the water from the surrounding moat and ditches back into the Tay. He, Douglas and the Earl of Ross were the first in under the walls, and although Douglas was wounded in the shoulder by a javelin, they kept the garrison engaged while the main army outside filled up the waterless moat with faggots and brushwood, and were able to scale the walls thereafter in great numbers. So Perth fell.

At first all this seemed scarcely credible, on more counts than one. Will Douglas had been so backward of late in tackling the enemy, save at that tournament, that it seemed unlikely, to say the least, that he should have taken this major initiative. And the warlike English priest, Bullock, was the last man to be expected to co-operate, and so effectively reputedly. But all accounts asserted that these two had transformed the situation outside Perth. Not only that, but they, with Moray, the Steward and Ross, were said to be now heading southwards to tackle Stirling itself, the strongest hold in the land.

Ramsay went over and over this strange circumstance in his mind, and in private discussion with Mariot, mainly concerned with Douglas's behaviour. It kept coming back to him that there was one feature which might possibly link the various aspects of the situation – Edward Balliol and his flagging fortunes. Douglas had come to that Berwick tournament for one purpose only: to challenge and show up Balliol and his supporters. He had refused to fight the English, as such. Now he was attacking Balliol's former base in Perth. Balliol's people still held Stirling, as they did Edinburgh. Bullock had been Balliol's very effective minion, but was now working against his late master, in league with Douglas. And

313

had been granted large lands. By whom? Was all this, then, some sort of personal Douglas campaign against Balliol but not against Edward Plantagenet? King Edward had apparently more or less abandoned Balliol, even as a puppet. Douglas had been failing to attack the *English* since his return from captivity, but was strongly attacking Balliol. Could he possibly have entered into some kind of arrangement with the Plantagenet whilst he was a prisoner in England – and thus account for his unexplained release? That he would help to bring down Balliol, who had become an embarrassment to King Edward, but not to damage Edward's own cause in Scotland? Was such an agreement too ridiculous to contemplate? It would answer sundry questions.

Mariot, who had never much liked Will Douglas, was prepared to consider it, although it seemed improbable.

The news came fairly soon thereafter that Stirling town had fallen and that Bullock had persuaded the Keeper of its all but impregnable castle to yield, on the grounds that Balliol was finished and that it behoved sensible men like themselves to make new arrangements, with either the King of England or the Regent of Scotland, or both.

When news came from Moray that he and the Steward were going to bring a force to join Douglas and this man Bullock in assailing Edinburgh, Ramsay decided to put in an appearance there.

When he came warily to the city's vicinity on a July morning, with Pate and only a small party, it was to find the joint loyalist force encamped to the north, its port of Leith already in their hands. Plans were being hatched for a double assault, as was necessary, for while the citadel, which dominated all from its towering rock, was the hard nut to crack, its garrison was comparatively small, the main enemy strength being stationed up on the Burgh Muir, to the south of the city, traditional mustering-place of Scots armies. This force, meantime, oddly enough, was largely composed of French and Flemish mercenaries, paid for by Balliol with Scots money to help fight his battles for him; he had of course been brought up in France, where his father King John of dire memory had been exiled, and had friends amongst the anti-Valois faction. In the present situation it was important that these mercenaries should not attack the attackers of Edinburgh Castle. So Moray and the Steward were to keep them occupied whilst Douglas and Bullock were making the attempt on the fortress.

Moray was glad to see Ramsay, not only for friendship's sake but because he knew the situation at the Burgh Muir better than they did; after all, he had been lurking about its fringes and approaches over many a night in his ambushes and assaults on the army's lines of supply. Ramsay reckoned that there were some two thousand men camped there, under the Flemish Count de Namur.

He was more than interested to meet the turncoat cleric Bullock, with Douglas. He proved to be a stocky, bullet-headed individual, of high colour and small pig-like eyes, less than attractive, abrupt of manner, far from a typical church-man. But whatever his failings in appearance and integrity, there appeared to be no doubting his military ability and shrewdness. The fact that this ambitious self-seeker had decided that Balliol's cause was no longer worth supporting was probably an excellent augury. Douglas, for his part, appeared to have close relations with him. He greeted Ramsay only coolly.

These two had concocted a scheme to win Edinburgh's fortress. A Dundee merchant shipper named Walter Currie, it was hoped, would provide the means of ingress. His ship was in Leith harbour, and would fly the English flag. He had apparently been used to supplying Bullock's castles at St Andrews and Cupar with food and wine. Now he was to seek to offer the same facilities to the Edinburgh garrison. He and his crew had shaved off their beards, to look like Englishmen, and he was to present himself at the gate of the citadel and announce that he had come from Newcastle-on-Tyne with a shipload of wines and provisions and powder-and-ball, sent by the English. If he could avoid the Scots army in the Leith area, he would bring up his cargo in wagons, for the castle's comfort, as instructed. If this was agreed by the Governor, when the wagons arrived and the portcullis was up and the drawbridge down, he would wedge the said wagons in the gatehouse-pend and the approach thereto, so that neither bridge nor portcullis could be worked, and men hidden under the bales and tarpaulins would leap out and deal with the gate-guard. Meantime, Douglas and his people, hiding nearby, would hurry forward and fling themselves into the castle, to overwhelm the garrison.

This was Bullock's scheme, and Ramsay had to admit that it sounded hopeful – if the man Currie could be taken for an English skipper. Douglas declared that he could speak like an Englishman; moreover, most of the garrison were Continental mercenaries under a French commander, de Limosin, who would be unlikely to notice differences.

That evening, Currie returned from his visit to the citadel to announce that the castle Governor, de Limosin, would welcome the arrival of supplies.

It was up to Moray, the Steward and Ramsay to arrange a distraction for the occupying force up on the Burgh Muir.

Ramsay, as usual now, was asked to lead; anyway, he knew best the lie of the land and the situation there, for the Burgh Muir, the city's common grazing, covered a large area. It was agreed that they were not looking for any major battle; the objective was to keep the Count de Namur and his men preoccupied while the attempt on Edinburgh Castle went ahead, timed for early the following morning. Wearing nondescript clothing, Ramsay went off alone on foot, that evening, to prospect.

The Burgh Muir of Edinburgh occupied the rising ground immediately south of the city walls, from the leper-colony area of St Lazarus or St Leonards on the north-east to Wryteshouse on the north-west, and from the Hospice of St Katherine of Sienna on the south-east to Merchiston Tower on the south-west, covering almost three square miles. The undulating and whin-dotted grassy slopes rose southwards towards the Braid Hills, crowned by the Bore Stane at its highest point, the traditional viewing-place for the monarch to review his armies about to march. The lowest ground, to the north, and nearest the city, was wet and boggy, containing the Burgh Loch, with its water-meadows. Normally the city's freeholders pastured their cattle, horses and geese on this common land, but in these days of war and invasion, all such stock had become early casualties. Now the only beasts there were the horses of the mercenary troops. These troops were apt to be camped on the higher, drier ground around the Bore Stane and Burghmuirhead itself, but patrols and sentinel-posts were established at various points around the perimeter, Ramsay discovered, and with the Scots force known to be only three miles away, at Leith, would be on the alert. So far there had been no move by the Count of Namur to march against the new arrivals.

Ramsay, pretending to be a townsman out for a summer evening walk, sauntered round most of the Muir's perimeter, observing. By the time that he won back to his friends near Leith, he had walked many miles, unchallenged, and was reasonably satisfied, planning an effective programme for the morrow. Moray and the Steward fell in with it, gladly enough.

So, well before sunrise, they were on the move up from the coast areas, a company of about fifteen hundred, mainly horsed. The enemy probably outnumbered them, but they hoped for the advantage of surprise. Well before they reached the city walls, now badly broken down by constant attack, they divided into three, and parted company. Moray took his five hundred east-about, down into the quite deep valley between the Muir and the steep slopes of Arthur's Craig, where they could ride unseen to the south-east extremity near the Sienna convent, or Sciennes as it was called locally; the Steward went west-about, with the city and its huge castle-rock hiding his party, using the lower ground beyond, on that side, to reach the Merchiston area; and Ramsay, with the foot, three hundred of them, and the remaining cavalry, waited, the closest to the enemy, but still out-of-sight.

Between the southern city wall and the edge of the Muir, flanking the Burgh Loch and water-meadows, a clutter of ramshackle hutments, hovels, stables, byres and the like had grown up over the decades, used by the citizens for dealing with their stock. All this was largely derelict now, but could still serve as cover for dismounted men. The problem was how to gain the shelter of it, without alarming the citizenry, even thus early in the morning? Not that it greatly mattered if the citizens were alarmed, so long as they did not communicate it to the soldiers up on the Muir. Most, undoubtedly, would not be disposed to do so, but there could be the odd individual who might, or mercenaries could be returning from a night out in the town with a woman-friend. And, unfortunately, there was bound to be some movement of folk out from the city, for this south side of Edinburgh was not adequately provided with drinking water, and many of the townsfolk went each morning out south-eastwards almost half a mile to a group of good wells at the western foot of Arthur's Craig, with pitchers, casks and water-skins for the day's supplies; these known as The Wells o' Wearie, on account of the weary trail there and back. Ramsay had decided that the way to deal with this difficulty was to bring his company west-about round the city wall, from the West Port area and up the climbing lane known as The Vennel just below the high, though broken, wall, to this vicinity, where a postern-gate was called the Well Port. There, still out of sight of the Burgh Muir, he used his two hundred horsemen, at this first stage, to form a barrier, a cordon, to prevent any access towards the enemy. His foot he led in amongst the huddle of shacks, sheds and pig-sties.

With Pate and Redheuch, he moved forward almost to the edge of the marshy loch to view the situation. At least there was no hurry, for they had to give time for Moray and the Steward to get into position, each fully a mile away. There appeared to be no signs of unrest on the Muir, indeed little movement visible of any sort, although blue columns of smoke from breakfast cooking-fires rose above the slight marshland mists. Immediately beyond the loch and the wet meadows, the enemy horse-lines were established, where the grazing was most lush. These lines were Ramsay's first objective. There were two or three sentinel-pickets watching over them, but not in any urgent fashion, indeed small fires were burning here also; after all, this large camp had been in being here for long months and had never suffered attack from the city direction.

It was a pity that there was no means of signalling between the three Scots groupings. Ramsay could only wait until he heard, or sensed, alarms and action away there to the south. Which of the groups would show themselves to the enemy first, Moray or the Steward, was not material, although a simultaneous appearance, east and west, would be best.

The waiting was trying, but it did give Ramsay and his lieutenants time to fully instruct their people. He kept in touch with the mounted cordon.

At last there were signs of alarm on the Muir, a distant stir recognisable, then actual sounds on the south-west breeze, shouting, clamour. The horse-pickets and sentinels nearby, roused, turned to stare, and presently two of them mounted and rode off southwards.

Ramsay sought to time his moves aright, for maximum

effect. When he saw some more of the guards at this northern perimeter begin to hurry back up through the horse-lines, he raised his horn and blew a succession of blasts.

Promptly his dismounted men surged forward out of the cover of their hutments, splitting into two groups, left and right, as they went. At the same time, the horsemen broke up their cordon and also divided into two parties, spurring east and west-about.

The reason for this two-pronged advance was, of course, the Burgh Loch. It was not large, only around quarter of a mile long and half that in width, but though shallow in summer it was still too deep in its central part for men to struggle through. At either end it was shallower, tailing off into marsh, and here men on foot could splash, wade and plowter across; but not horses, whose weight would sink them in the soft mud. So the mounted two hundred had to dash round the two flanks, where there was firm ground, while the three hundred on foot sought to cross more directly, but still having to avoid the central area.

It all made for an uneven, ragged and difficult advance, and no impressive charge, especially for those up to their waists in water with only soft basing for their feet, Ramsay himself amongst those nearest to the centre. But it did not have to be impressive or particularly fast at this stage, for it took the sentinels wholly by surprise, as well as outnumbering them ten to one. Turning to gape, for only moments, one and all they fled, not unnaturally. Some mounted nearby horses, but most did not waste time loosing tethered beasts but raced off up between the horse-lines.

This was as expected. The wet and muddy foot therefore found no one to fight, and were able to hurry on up to the lines of tethered animals, to slash the ropes with their dirks, and seeking to drive on the loosed beasts before them, with yells and wavings of arms. This was not entirely successful, and the cutting of many hundreds of tethers was not to be achieved very swiftly. However, their mounted colleagues soon appeared from either side, to aid in the work, and these had much more success in causing the enemy horses to panic and stampede off in a southerly direction, many indeed, in the general affright dragging out their own tethering-pegs and bolting with the rest.

Now it was the task of the horsemen to keep up the

momentum and direction of the stampede, leaving the foot behind. But many of these followed Ramsay's example and grabbed an enemy beast, to mount and follow on.

He, in the midst of the others now, was perhaps halfway up the grassy slopes, towards the Burghmuirhead, when he saw, away ahead, the anticipated development, large numbers of the mercenary troops, afoot, streaming down to collect their horses – and, of course, being confronted instead by a mass of panic-stricken horseflesh. The resultant chaos was all that Ramsay could have hoped for. Men and mounts were lost in indescribable confusion.

Now he had opportunity to look further afield. Beyond all the turmoil ahead he could not see far with any clarity. But he could distinguish enough to recognise that major hand-to-hand fighting was going on on two fronts, east and west, back there. And with Moray's and the Steward's people mounted, and the enemy almost all on foot, the battle should be much in the Scots' favour.

The impact of the charging riderless horses from the north completed the discomfiture and demoralisation of the mercenary force. By the time that Ramsay and his men arrived on the scene, it was all over. The mercenaries were either fleeing, or throwing down their arms, such as were not fallen; and of these last, probably no great number were dead or seriously wounded. It had not been intended to be a full-scale battle, defeat or victory, but had turned into one, largely thanks to Ramsay's favoured device of stampeding horses. The Scots leaders were able to congratulate each other, particularly in that Moray had captured the Count of Namur himself, quite a catch, for he was cousin to Edward Plantagenet's Queen. Other foreign knights were taken also.

The day's success, thus early, was further confirmed by the news brought from the city that Douglas and Bullock had achieved their objective, thanks to the man Currie from Dundee and his wagoners. De Limosin had yielded, and Edinburgh Castle was in Scots hands, for the first time in years. It was an occasion for national celebration.

Alexander Ramsay for one, however, did not remain to take part in any celebrating. He was concerned about all those escaped, fleeing mercenaries. Fully one thousand must have got away from the Burgh Muir, and could rally, given time. Even though they might not return in any organised way to Edinburgh, and might more likely seek to make their way to the Border and Berwick-on-Tweed, where was Balliol their paymaster, they could meantime represent a grievous threat and menace to the area between, which already had suffered sufficiently. Ramsay left his friends therefore and hurried back to Hawthornden, to pick up his company there and go scouring the vicinity for mercenaries, to keep them on the run until they were safely out of the country.

It was only after his return from this task some days later that he learned the sorry news that Moray, having agreed to ransom the Count of Namur for no less than £4,000, had courteously escorted his prominent prisoner to the Border, to go raise the ransom. And there, on turning back, he had been treacherously ambushed by English attackers and was now himself held captive.

17

There was more ill news for them all, in especial the Randolph family, soon afterwards. Edward Plantagenet, deciding that the Earl of Warwick was proving insufficiently aggressive as commander of the English army of Scotland, had replaced him by Richard Fitzalan, Earl of Arundel, with the veteran Earl of Salisbury as his deputy, with instructions to prosecute hostilities with a deal more vigour, in view of Balliol's continuing failure and the fact that almost all the great Scots fortresses save Roxburgh and Caerlaverock were now back in Scots hands. And Arundel, the new broom, had promptly sent Salisbury north over the Border to assail the nearest great castle to Berwick, Dunbar. Earl Patrick, as usual, was not there, but his wife was and, warned of the approach of a large English host, had raised the drawbridge, slammed down the portcullis and prepared for defence and defiance, in true Randolph spirit.

Mariot, still at Hawthornden, naturally was distressed and worried. But her husband sought to reassure her in some measure. Dunbar was a very special hold, built on its rock-stacks jutting out into the ocean. It would be very hard to capture, by its very position mainly out of range of most missiles from balista and all except the most powerful cannon. Admittedly cannon based on ships at sea could in theory get close enough to bombard it, but then any such would be in range of the castle's own artillery – which Edward himself had strengthened some time before – and wooden vessels made much more vulnerable targets than did massive stone walls and towers. So the probability was that Black Agnes could hold out for a considerable time, so long as she had provisions and ammunition, for there was an excellent well sunk within the gatehouse-tower's basement. And the Regent would, no doubt, seek to relieve the siege as soon as possible.

Mariot was not wholly convinced.

Her worries were by no means lessened by the arrival of further untoward tidings. Sir Andrew Murray, the Regent, had died. He had retired to his northern castle of Avoch, in Ross, a sick man, and there, after only a few weeks, had passed away. His loss, was, of course, incalculable, especially coming on top of John Randolph's capture. He had been the most respected and authoritative figure in the land. Scotland was again without a Regent and ruler.

Soon a call came for Ramsay to attend a hurriedly-convened Council in Edinburgh; it could not be a parliament since that required the Regent's royal authority. The principal business was, of course, to appoint a new Regent, and there could be little question as to who that must be. Robert Stewart and Moray had been reluctant joint Regents earlier, and now Moray was a captive in England. The High Steward and heir-presumptive to the throne was the obvious choice – although the Earl of Dunbar and March might have thought himself a more suitable candidate; but he did not appear at the Council, probably knowing that few would have voted for him, a man of such doubtful loyalties. Douglas came, but said very little.

Robert Stewart was far from eager to hold the position. Even to share it with Moray he had been loth. He only agreed now on condition that if and when Moray returned, it would be a joint regency again.

The Council had other matters to discuss then, notably the siege of Dunbar Castle. Few practical suggestions for its relief were forthcoming, since Salisbury was now known to have no fewer than twelve thousand men encamped at Dunbar, the main English host having moved up from Berwick; moreover an English fleet was patrolling offshore to ensure no succour by sea. Ramsay was urgent in his demands for some attempt to be made, but even he could not but recognise that the Scots were in no position to provoke a pitched battle against the English might mustered there. Black Agnes was acclaimed as Scotland's heroine – but that was all.

Ramsay then proposed some counter-stroke over into England, which might draw off part at least of Salisbury's force. Also he urged that they should try to capture some very prominent Englishman, whom they then might offer in exchange for Moray. In this he was rather surprised to be supported by Will Douglas who, in his obsession with Balliol, said that the usurper himself, still reputedly in Berwick Castle, should be their target. There were doubts about the possibility of this, and most believed anyway that the English now had so little respect for that man that they would be unlikely to consider him worth the exchange. Ramsay's proposal was agreed in principle, but details left to be decided.

Sundry other matters were dealt with, and the meeting broke up. Ramsay would have sought a private discussion with Douglas, but that man made off without waiting for any. All was not right with the Flower of Chivalry yet, undoubtedly.

Back at Hawthornden, Ramsay recognised that now he was in the distinctly odd position of being all but independent commander in the south-east of Scotland, with nobody to look to for orders or guidance – for it was fairly evident that Robert Stewart, who looked on him almost as *his* leader, was unlikely to send him instructions. Patrick of Dunbar and March was still, in name, Warden of the Marches, but that man was a law unto himself and no one knew what he might do, if anything. He might still be at Ersildoune, but he had other lands in the West and might have departed there. Certainly he was not showing himself around his Dunbar. As for Douglas, he had presumably gone back to Liddesdale, and would certainly take his own road. In these circumstances, Ramsay became the focus for attention and hope for the active and militant of a wide area who were anxious to strike a blow for their country. His reputation was now such that it was considered almost essential for any young blade with military ambitions to have served at least a little while with Ramsay's company. Volunteers began to flood to his standard in growing numbers.

Embarrassingly so, for that man did not look upon himself as any major commander but only as a guerrilla-fighter and captain of light cavalry tactics. Also, it made a nonsense of his hideout at Hawthornden, which could not cope with large numbers, and the secret location of which he did not wish to be generally known although, of course, all Scotland had heard of its fame by now. However, Balliol's garrison had departed from Dalwolsey meantime, so that he could now use that place, with ample room around it, as his headquarters, keeping only a small select unit at the caves.

In these circumstances he found himself in a position to lead quite a substantial mounted force, of some eight hundred, on his proposed challenge over the Border. This was to be no mere hit-and-run raid but a showing of the flag, one of its main objectives the capture of a prominent English lord. This last admittedly was not likely to be easy, and required not only planning but information. He could not hope to tackle Berwick itself, as Douglas had suggested; but some lesser place which was still important, perhaps the seat of one of the English Lords Marcher, as they were called – Norham, Heaton, Tillmouth, Twizel, Wark, Duddo and the like. He had to find out who might be holding these castles. He sent Pate and Wattie Kerr on a secret mission to find out.

They came back forty-eight hours later with at least some information. Most of the English lords and commanders were either at Berwick with Arundel or at Dunbar with Salisbury. The Marcher castles of Norham, Twizel, Tillmouth, Etal, Ford and Heaton were in the hands of keepers, in these circumstances, knights no doubt but insufficiently important to try to use in exchange for Moray. But Wark was presently being held by Lord Robert Manners, a member of the English parliament, for Northumberland, and a friend of King Edward's. Interestingly, he it was who owned Etal Castle, which they had shaken fist at on their previous raid into England and which had done nothing.

Wark, then, might well serve. And it was comparatively easy of access from the Scots side of Tweed, although a strong place in itself.

So a start was made for the Border, eight hundred strong.

By Soutra and upper Lauderdale they went, to swing off eastwards at the Mill of Carfrae, this to avoid the Ersildoune area, and then by Thirlestane and Gordon into the Merse, and slantwise across its wide expanse, to avoid Roxburgh and Kelso. They camped early, in the Birgham area, but well back from Tweed. Wark was only three miles away, as the crow flew, across the great river, and, as ever, surprise was of the essence.

Late in the evening, Ramsay himself went forward, with Pate and Wattie, to prospect. He also took their Morebattle shepherd, now an accepted member of their company, whose local knowledge might be useful. They decided on a crossing of Tweed by a ford near Carham, west of Wark a couple of miles. Then keeping well away from that strong place, on the morrow, they would circle round, to stage an attack on the small town of Cornhill-on-Tweed from the south. They would take their time about this last, time for the news to reach Wark, where surely no garrison-commander could just sit tight, ignoring the straits of the local community. Then, when the Wark force came to assail them, they would make a hurried retiral, southwards as they had come. On the previous, Branxton-Etal-Ford raid, Ramsay had observed a notable place for an ambush, on the Willow Burn near Pressen. There they would turn and fight. Lord Robert Manners, of course, might choose not to accompany his people on the Cornhill rescue, but that was a chance which had to be taken. If he did not come, they might thereafter try a sudden descent on Wark Castle itself – but it was unlikely that, surprise or none, they would be able to storm that major stronghold.

Prospecting the ford in the August half-dark, they cautiously crossed. It would be impassable in winter, but now the water came barely to the horses' bellies. They rode on southwards, actually here almost following the line of the Border itself, which at this point bent away from Tweed to cross Wark Common and on towards Yetholm. In about three miles they came to the Pressen Burn and turned down this, north-eastwards now. A mile further, carefully bypassing the farmstead of Pressen itself, they came to the projected ambush-place, where another two sizeable streams came down to join the Pressen, the three then forming the larger Willow Burn. This junction took place in a steep, restricted and wooded glen, between the shouldering green hills of Pressen and Brown Rigg. It had struck Ramsay as one of the best ambush-sites he had ever seen. Now, inspecting, peering about in the shadowy gloom, he decided that he had not been mistaken.

They moved on another two miles or so, avoiding the hamlet of East Learmouth, until they were on the southern edge of the Tweedside plain again, no great distance from Cornhill. Satisfied that they had it all reasonably clear in their minds, they turned back as they had come.

Ramsay had only an hour or two of sleep that night, for well before dawn he had his company on the move, taking exactly the route followed earlier. It was noticeable how much longer it took for eight hundred to cover the same ground as had four, the fording of Tweed in especial; however, all told, they had only some seven miles to go. It was only a little lighter than before when they passed the Pressen ambush-place, and Ramsay pointed out to his lieutenants their roles and where they were to go, on their hurried return, if all went as planned.

On past East Learmouth they came in sight of Cornhill, as the first of the breakfast fires were beginning to raise their blue columns in the morning air. Ramsay halted, and divided his force into three, with strict instructions, for once again timing and communication were vital. A small party, under Wattie, was to go off eastwards and round up the cattle grazing on Cornhill Common, and to bring them to this rendezvous; those beasts had their part to play. Pate was sent off westwards, in the Wark direction, to keep an eye on the castle, only two miles away although unseen from here. The two main groupings, under Redheuch and Ramsay of Carrington, were to go forward to deal with Cornhill itself, but to be on the watch all the time for signals from himself, ready to retire at once. The purpose was not the slaughter and ravishment of innocent townsfolk but the burning of the place, a demonstration. There was no great hurry at this stage – but there might be later on. Ramsay himself, with a few others, would take up a position on a grassy mound in front of them, about half a mile from the town, where he could be seen by all.

Everyone instructed, he gave the signal for action.

The two assault companies spurred forward, in horns left and right, down upon the unsuspecting Cornhill.

It was a strange sensation for Alexander Ramsay to stand back, inactive, while others did what had to be done. But today he was playing the general, the overall commander, not the captain, and his role was vital, however contrary to inclination.

It did not take long for the first murky smoke-clouds to billow up from the burning thatches of the doomed town. It gave Ramsay no satisfaction to see it, nor to hear the shouts and screams. He did not enjoy savaging communities; but this was war, and against an enemy who made a point of just such destruction, with added hangings, rapings and executions. Soon people could be seen running out from the streets and lanes, fleeing. Those to the east would see their cattle being driven off.

His attention was only partly on the town, his greater preoccupation being with Wark Castle. How long before its garrison learned of this assault? Would they see the smoke and send someone to investigate? Or come in force at once? Or wait until they received calls for help? They might send only a small company, at first. In any of these, Pate's information was all-important. And, of course, there could possibly be trouble from the other side, from eastwards. Berwick was only a dozen miles away in that direction, and the important castles of Tillmouth and Twizel only three miles, Norham seven; but there was considerable high ground in between.

In the event, it took what seemed to the watchers a very long time for any reaction to materialise. Which in one way was all to the good, for it allowed the Cornhill assault to proceed unchecked, the destruction of the town to be fairly complete. Soon the smoke arising was great, billowing black clouds mounting high, which must be visible far and wide. Surely this must fetch the Wark people?

Wattie and his group arrived, herding the cattle, scores of them. He was ordered to keep them available, nearby.

Then, at last, Pate himself came, in haste. A sizeable mounted company was coming from Wark, perhaps two hundred strong, with leaders in knightly armour, although no banners. It would be only minutes before they arrived.

This had been anticipated, of course, and Ramsay's

planned reaction was immediate. Horns blew and blew for the breaking off of the attack on the town, and prompt retiral. All would, indeed, have been waiting for the signal.

Men, many smoke-blackened, came streaming back in ones and twos and groups, to be sent straight on, back towards Pressen. Pate was sent with them, to organise their positioning at the ambush-area. Wattie had his cattle ready.

Anxiously Ramsay watched to westwards, at the same time seeking to count roughly the numbers of his men riding back from the town, a race against time indeed.

There was some woodland about half a mile west of the town, which would hide the enemy approach until then. Ramsay was congratulating himself that most of his men were safely out of the streets when he perceived movement, a mounted column emerging from the trees. Deliberately he waited just a little longer, to try to ensure that he and his remaining people were to be seen by the approaching force. Then he blew his own horn again, urgently, and wheeled his horse round.

Now it was to be the semblance of panic. The great majority of the Scots had already disappeared before the Wark contingent could have seen them. Only perhaps fifty remained in view, with Ramsay and Wattie and the cattle. These now went through the motions of hasty flight, some driving the cattle ahead but most seeking to force their way past or round the stampeding mass. Quickly the Wark company swung round in pursuit.

Cattle-beasts, however alarmed, do not run so fast as horses. The enemy, therefore, although they had started fully one-third of a mile away, quite quickly began to narrow the gap. This also had been foreseen, allowed for, but the timing was vital. This riverside plain on which all was taking place was about one mile wide; then the grassy hills began, southwards. So Ramsay and his people had almost half a mile to cover before they could reach the more broken ground into which the road penetrated on its way to East Learmouth and beyond. Once therein the cattle would tend to block the advance of the English, or at least slow it down. But until then, it was the Scots who were held up. They could, of course, abandon the cattle and get ahead, but this might have seemed out of character for what was intended to look like a typical Border cattle-reiving foray, which had only incidentally ravaged Cornhill; it was important that the Wark force should so esteem it, and not discover their mistake until too late. On the other hand, it would serve nothing for Ramsay and any of his people to be overtaken and captured. He and his present group, with the enemy only some three hundred yards behind, pushed on and around the edges of the stampede, leaving only Wattie and half a dozen others to keep herding it on, at the back, until the last moment.

They made the broken ground only just in time. Wattie had to gauge it exactly now too, for once the beasts were filling the narrowed confines of the valley road, it would be very difficult for horsemen to get through the crush and past. He dared not leave it too late or his little party would be casualties. They came spurring round the perimeter, only moments to spare.

There was now the danger that the cattle, with nobody driving them, would slow down, the stampede end and the enemy be held up little further. However, the thundering advance of the said enemy itself ensured that this did not happen, the alarmed herd merely exchanging one lot of drovers for another and larger contingent. So the English were held up considerably. Ramsay and his party had actually to slow down so that they remained generally in sight of the pursuit. This was important. They were the bait for the trap. They had almost two miles to go, into ever closer country.

Past the East Learmouth area, where another road branched off to West Learmouth, there was a widening of the valley, and here the Wark company managed to get past the cattle. Now there was no more holding back, both groups riding their hardest.

Only four or five minutes now till Pressen, with pursuers and pursued only three hundred yards apart. Ramsay's party pounded past the entrance to the first of the side-glens and its stream's confluence with the Pressen Burn, that on the west. This was only about one hundred yards from the one coming in from the east. All now depended on synchronised action on the Scots' part.

Ramsay rode on, and past the second opening. Glancing up it, he could see some of Redheuch's men, sitting their horses up there; there was no way that these could hide without going too far up. The other opening had been different, with a bend in it and trees, where Carrington's people should be lurking. However, even if the English noticed Redheuch's party and took alarm, no great harm would be done, for riding at the speed they were, their column of two hundred would not be able to pull up effectively, unready and at short notice, in less then fifty yards or so; and that would serve the Scots.

In the event, whether or not the Wark leadership saw the Redheuch men, they did not rein up, but came spurring on, chasing Ramsay's group up the main valley. It was that man who did the pulling up.

Shouting, and waving his arm in a circular motion to order a wheel round, he had his horse rearing high on its hind legs in a most difficult turn, his people all seeking as best they could to do likewise. For moments there was a shambles of stumbling, colliding horses and shouting men. Then, in no sort of order, they were round, facing back northwards to confront the oncoming enemy. And at the same moment, approximately, Redheuch led his four hundred out of their eastern side glen, lances lowered and swords drawn.

Because of the constriction of the valley, its road flanked by the river, the Wark company was inevitably strung out over quite a distance, and the Redheuch attack struck them more or less halfway. With the enemy files only three or four abreast, their column was cut in two straight away. Half of Redheuch's men swung left-handed to assail the rear of the front section of the English, while the other half swung right to deal with the rear section. Seeming utter chaos prevailed in that main valley by the riverside.

But the seeming chaos was one-sided, for Ramsay and his people knew exactly what they were at. He and his fifty now charged the head of the English column which was being attacked from the rear. And out from his western hiding-place rode Carrington and his three hundred and fifty, to splash across the river and attack the enemy tail.

Actually there was not a great deal of fighting. The Wark force, taken entirely by surprise and outnumbered four to one, had no least chance, and quickly perceived it. The leadership was all at the front, so that the detached rear was left without direction. Turning to flee, they found themselves facing Carrington's men, and recognised realities. Some sought to spur up the quite steep hillside, some to ford the river, but most just threw down their arms in surrender. The front half put up rather more resistance, but assailed before and behind, and tight-pressed in on themselves, they could do little that was effective.

It was all over in brief minutes, as everywhere men yielded.

Ramsay, panting a little, sidled his horse up to that of the only man there wearing a plumed helmet.

"I am . . . Alexander Ramsay," he got out. "Whom . . . have I the honour . . . to address?"

The other shrugged half-armoured shoulders. "I am Robert Manners," he said. "This is a sorry affair, sir. All craft and ingine, trickery. No honest battle."

"You have my sympathy, Lord Robert! We Scots cannot always afford honest battle! To my regret. May I have your sword?"

The Englishman shrugged again, and handed over his handsome weapon with a grimace.

Everywhere the Scots were disarming their prisoners. But what to do with them? Two or three of the better sort they could take back to Scotland, for ransom. But the great mass were just men-at-arms, with nothing of value to their captors save for their weapons, armour and, of course, horses.

Ramsay ordered that they were all to be dismounted, stripped of anything considered worth while, and left to find their way back to Wark or Cornhill as best they could. They themselves would ride back and collect those cattle, before they made for home. And they would look in on Wark Castle in the by-going. He put Pate in charge of the Lord Robert Manners.

So they left the scene of the perfect ambush, all craft and ingine as it may have been. They found the cattle milling about approximately where they had been left, and rounding them up, proceeded on their way at a comfortable pace – to scurrilous comments from Lord Robert anent reivers and cattle-thieves. They did not return to Cornhill but went by West Learmouth towards Wark.

They found that strong place all shut and barred against them, however, and even a shower of arrows greeting them, to ensure that they kept their distance. Evidently some of the mounted escapers from Pressen had got there first and given warning. Manners was conducted past his fortalice in silence.

Thereafter it was a straightforward ride back to the Carham ford, and over, a rearguard under Redheuch ensuring that they were not being pursued by any possible force from

Norham, Twizel or elsewhere. It was still only forenoon and they should be back to Dalwolsey by nightfall.

Ramsay sent the Lord Robert to Doune Castle, for safe keeping, and at the same time sent a messenger to the Earl of Arundel at Berwick announcing that he held Manners captive and was prepared to exchange him for the Earl of Moray. No other ransom would be considered.

They waited and waited thereafter, but no reply was forthcoming. Admittedly Arundel might well have to get King Edward's agreement for this, and that could take time, with that aggressive monarch campaigning against France. But week after week passed and there was not so much as a word from Berwick.

Mariot in especial was equally anxious about her brother and her sister. The siege of Dunbar continued with no let-up. None could remember so long a siege. It was making Black Agnes a heroine to be sung about, but it must be grievously affecting her, cooped up for months in that sea-girt stronghold. How much longer she could keep it up, none knew. Her husband did not appear to be making any efforts to relieve her. Indeed, how could he, how could any, with allegedly forty thousand English encamped against it?

Then a messenger did arrive at Dalwolsey, but from Dunbar itself, not Berwick. This was a fisherman who had contrived to slip out of Dunbar harbour by night in a small boat, eluding the blockade of the English fleet. He brought sad tidings. Agnes informed that she could not hold out much longer. Food supplies were almost gone and they were down to the last casks of powder, the last store of cannon-balls. Once these were gone, they would no longer be able to keep the English cannon at a sufficient distance to prevent them battering down the gatehouse-tower and so gaining access. If help was to come, it would have to come quickly.

This was an appeal which Alexander Ramsay could nowise ignore. He there and then went into an extended session of questioning with that fisherman.

18

It took a full week to mount the attempted rescue operation.
Provisions, powder and ball had to be collected, the last two
not so easy to come by in the prevailing state of Scotland.
Fortunately, Edinburgh Castle, when taken by Douglas and
the turncoat Bullock, had been found to be endowed with
large stocks of ammunition, and Ramsay was able to call on
this. Douglas had been rewarded for the citadel's capture by
being made Constable thereof, by the new Regent, partly to
try to involve him further in the national cause. He did not
lodge therein himself but left it to a deputy keeper, preferring
his own fastnesses in Liddesdale; but Ramsay's name was
sufficient to impress this deputy, and he allowed a fair
quantity of powder and shot to be taken.

Provisioning, wines and the like were little difficulty. But
all had to be transported down to the coast, the cannon-balls
in especial proving a problem. Ramsay had chosen Aberlady
Bay as starting base. Aberlady itself, admittedly, was the port
of Haddington and therefore less than secret; but its great bay
was tidal, its mouth almost three miles wide. At half-tide and
more, shallow-draught craft could sail or row out at the
eastern end, well away from the port area at the western end.
There was a small fishing haven at Luffness, at the head of the
bay, which would serve Ramsay's requirements, unlikely to
be spied upon by the English or their sympathisers. It
supported only six boats, and this was insufficient for his
purposes. So Pate was sent to hire another six, and their
crews, from the larger fishertown of Cockenzie, some miles
up Forth, and bring them to Luffness. There was no other
haven between this and North Berwick – which itself was too
near Dunbar for safety. Those English thousands were apt to
be spread out far and wide along this coast.

By night, Ramsay led his pack-horse trains of food and
ammunition to Luffness. The castle there, a Lindsay place
and strong, had been in Balliol occupation, like Dalwolsey;

333

but its garrison was now gone, although the Lindsays had not yet returned, having safer houses in Fife and Angus, leaving only a keeper and a few men in charge. Ramsay was distantly related to the Lindsays, and had no difficulty in persuading this keeper to allow him to store and hide his cargoes meantime in the castle outbuildings.

As well as hiring fishing boats at Cockenzie, Pate had been commissioned to collect fishermen's jerseys and canvas gear, for disguise. After the days and nights of preparation, all was ready. Timing, once more, was all-important. From the mouth of Aberlady Bay to the great Craig of Bass, off North Berwick, was eleven sea miles, partway to Dunbar. They did not want to be seen leaving the little haven of Luffness, twelve boats at once and heavily laden, which would be highly unusual. So they must go by night. And they wanted to be off the Bass before dawn, if possible, hidden behind its mighty bulk from the south-east and Dunbar area.

Ramsay had brought some forty of his own veteran fighters to add to the crews required to man the boats, these last cut down to a minimum, despite a flood of volunteers. All were dressed as fishermen, himself included. It worked out at about seven men to every boat, more than the normal fishing crew, but it was to be hoped that this would not be too evident to the enemy.

It was October now, with twelve hours between sunset and sunrise, which was a help. They had to wait until most folk would be abed before setting out, anyway, because of the tide. The night was dark enough, overcast, with a steady breeze which, fortunately, being from the prevailing direction, south-west, would aid them at this first stage, allowing them to hoist sails to assist the rowers. It also would carry away the sound of almost fifty oars creaking against the rowlocks.

It was an almost eerie sensation, with that flotilla of laden, high-prowed, broad-beamed and smelly fishing cobles slipping out across the great bay in the darkness. At first Ramsay was worried about the noise of all those oars creaking and splashing; but quickly he realised that there was little to fear. It was not only the slap-slap of the wavelets and the whistle of the wind; away ahead of them was a strange and continuing noise, two elements blended in it: a sort of muted thunder, above which a higher and more fluctuating sound was evident, rising and falling but never dying away. This was explained as the basic roar of the breakers on the half-mile-wide sand-bar at the bay's mouth, with the night time gabble of thousands of wild geese that made this Aberlady Bay their wintering-place and which spent the hours of darkness out at that bar, whether the tide was in or out. With all that background of sound there was little need for silence in the boats.

They could not skirt the east shore closely, on account of the shallows. In the bay, the sea was comparatively calm, but as they neared the mouth, and the noise of both water and geese grew ever louder, the wave-motion increased. Presently the boats were heaving and tossing in a turbulence of breaking, white-capped rollers, making the rowing difficult, and at the same time the great birds were beating wings on the water to rise into the air all around them, by the hundred, the thousand, honking and yelping their alarm, producing an extraordinary cacophony of affright and turmoil. It seemed strange that the creatures should choose such conditions to roost in.

Since the underlying sand-bar, which caused this disturbance of the tide, was almost half a mile wide, the boats had quite some time to endure these conditions before they won out into the open waters of the firth, where the seas were longer but a deal less steep. Now, to a more comfortable motion, the little fleet swung north-eastwards, the oarsmen settling down to steady pulling, the square sails hoisted to assist them. The noise from the bay-mouth faded away behind them.

Keeping well out from the thrusting Gullane Point, they maintained a fairly straight course for about five miles, with the breeze behind them, covering this in just an hour. Dark as it had seemed when first they set out, now their eyes, adjusted to the gloom, could see for fair distances, if less than distinctly. Which was just as well, for ahead of them now was a chain of islands, reef-guarded – Eyebroughy, Fetheray, The Lamb and Craigleith – scattered, and all a hazard for shipping. One by one these loomed up, ringed by the pale white of breakers, and were skirted, to seawards. This was a treacherous coast, where there were no havens between Aberlady and North Berwick.

Off that town, unseen although its tall conical Law-hill

might just be discerned behind, the need for care became even more essential. The Craig of Bass was only two miles ahead, with Dunbar another six miles thereafter. The English blockading fleet was known to be using North Berwick harbour as temporary local base, since they could not use Dunbar itself, the entrance thereto being immediately under the walls of the besieged castle. So enemy vessels could be looked for anywhere between the two towns; and since North Berwick's was a tidal harbour, large ships could be expected to lie off and use small boats to ferry people ashore and collect water supplies. The Scots flotilla therefore swung off, to head for the north side of the Bass, where no enemy craft were likely to linger, for good reason.

Presently they could discern the bulk of the enormous rock looming ahead, its sheer four-hundred-foot cliffs seemingly lost in the night sky. They could hear it, as well as see it, not the normal clouds of wheeling, screaming seafowl, which never ended by day and was now stilled, but a dull booming sound, which the fishermen said was the crushing of the Norse Sea rollers into the caves which penetrated that mighty stack.

As they drew nearer to this extraordinary place, the motion of the boats grew the more violent, almost alarmingly so. Not a few of the Dalwolsey men began to feel sick. Again the fishermen explained. This towering rock marked the final dominance of the land, a terrestrial fist shaken in the face of the ocean. Here the Firth of Forth gave place to the open Norse Sea, and as all fisherfolk knew, here the sea-floor dropped suddenly in vast underwater cliffs of great depths, the Bass being poised on the very edge of this. Here, then, the great ocean tides rolled in and struck against that submerged barrier of cliffs, to surge upwards in this unending turbulence. Tonight, with a south-westerly breeze, it was comparatively moderate; but in an easterly gale it had to be seen to be believed. No shipping was likely ever to lie off here.

That, to be sure, was why Ramsay had chosen this spot to wait, however uncomfortably. To say that they would lie safe in the shelter of the Bass was a contradiction in terms; but they ought to be hidden from the enemy and undisturbed save by the elements, until they ventured to make their next move.

The Luffness fishers rowed in close under the north-west face of the Bass, despite the heaving waters and the spray from breaking seas which curtained all, adding wetness to the discomforts of pitching and sickness. As they approached, sails down now and the rowing careful indeed, the place abruptly became alive. The birds, gulls, guillemots, puffins, divers, shags, cormorants and kittiwakes, which roosted in neuks and on ledges of the cliffs, suddenly became aware of the boats' presence and launched out in loud-voiced alarm. This disturbed the vast colonies of solan-geese or gannets above, and these huge birds, with their six-foot wing-span, added their harsh, croaking complaint. Everywhere the divers were plunging into the water, throwing up fountains, and larger plopping noises indicated seals leaving their seaweed-hung terraces.

Now they had showering bird-droppings to contend with, as well as all else.

The landsmen were wondering how they could possibly remain here in all this upheaval, however convenient for their ultimate purpose, when Ramsay's boat, in the lead, suddenly was pulled round to swing its high prow into an unexpected re-entrant, a cleft in the rock-face forming a V-shaped inlet, dark and loud with the booming noise. For this was the north-west entrance to the greatest cavern, from which the sound thundered, and which cut right through the stack, a dark echoing passage no less than one hundred and seventy yards long, the fishermen said, traversable by boat at low water should the seas be sufficiently calm – which it seemed was seldom indeed. Now at almost full tide, the rollers were surging in and out in a tumultuous ferment, the noise reverberating from deep within the tunnel.

There was just room for the dozen boats within the walls of that inlet, close-packed, two or three actually within the cave-mouth, but all having to be fended off the rock-faces heedfully as they rose and fell six or eight feet at every surge. But apart from this up-and-down motion they were secure enough, and hidden.

It was a matter, now, of waiting until dawn. The fishing craft from the various havens all went out each early morning to their fishing grounds, never by night. And they continued to operate whether it was peace or war, enemy occupying the land or not; indeed, with so many thousands of invading troops to be fed, the fishermen's catches were in greater demand than ever. The Dunbar boats themselves were bottled up in that harbour, unless its castle chose to let them out, which apparently it sometimes did, so that the garrison could also eat fish; but there was a nearby fishing community at Bielhaven, a mile or so to the west, on its own bay, from which most of the Dunbar men were now operating. These boats would be coming out around sun-up, and it was important for Ramsay's purpose that his own little fleet should be in position in the chosen area before they appeared, otherwise there could be confusion, questioning, unaccustomed activity and larger numbers of craft, which all might well draw the attention of the English warships and cause suspicion. Ramsay had learned all this from the Dunbar messenger who had come to Dalwolsey from Agnes. He could, of course, have sent warning of his intentions to the Bielhaven fishers, but had dared not risk this in case the secret was betrayed to the English, either deliberately by some traitor or by mere unguarded talk. So his flotilla had had to make this night-time move in order to be on the spot first, fishing, before sunrise. The Bielhaven craft would just have to fish elsewhere this day, it was to be hoped without any fuss.

Meantime, Ramsay used the waiting period to move from boat to boat, much agility required, to instruct each crew on their suitable reactions to any eventualities which might arise in the projected attempt.

The waiting seemed interminable; with the wind behind them they had made much better time than allowed for. Those who could doze did so.

At last, a faint paling of the eastern sky, plus renewed activity in the bird population, indicated dawn. A move could now be made. One by one the boats emerged from that inlet to the more broken water outside, amidst a clamour of screeching, diving seafowl. They could hoist sails again. The breeze was freshening with the new day.

Now they turned the north-east corner of the Bass, to a changed prospect and situation. There was only open sea ahead of them; and the mighty bulk of the rock sheltered them from the wind. Nevertheless, the underlying turbulence of the waters was no less.

Ramsay peered south-eastwards. Dunbar lay some six miles away in that direction, but in the half-light the land showed only as a featureless black mass, the backing Lammermuir Hills still merging with the fading night. Dunbar was not what he was looking for, however; it was the blockading

338

fleet. At first he could distinguish nothing, against the loom of the land, until a fisherman pointed out a still blacker shape, and then another and another.

As the light grew and they headed south-eastwards, the ships, dotted here and there, could be perceived fairly clearly. There seemed to be nine of them, in no sort of formation or order, the nearest perhaps three miles away. They were not at anchor, of course, at least not the neårer ones, the water being too deep. They had to beat up and down perpetually under small sail.

Now it was a matter of choosing the best area in which to start their fishing exercise. It was vital not to arouse suspicion and to seem to behave entirely normally, even though there would be more boats than usual of a morning. They spread out, therefore, over quite a wide area, but still in general movement towards Dunbar.

With Ramsay's leading craft only about a mile from the first ships, and the yellow bands of the rising sun beginning to gleam and strike glitters from the water, they commenced to put out their nets, the cobles working in pairs. Sails were down now, and the oar-work careful. The aim was to keep drifting slowly but steadily towards Dunbar harbour whilst trawling the nets. The men not on the oars put out baited lines, where they would not foul the nets, to catch mackerel.

It seemed strange, after all the careful planning and underlying tension, and actually in sight of the enemy, to just sit there quietly fishing, timing no longer vital, at least not apparently. And they did catch fish, this being an excellent area for the mackerel, the linesmen, even some of the landsmen, being fairly successful. Net-handlers asserted that they judged the nets to be doing well also.

To Ramsay's relief, their presence did not seem to be arousing any special reaction amongst the English shipmen. These, to be sure, would be used to the sight of boats fishing this area. Gradually they drew closer to the enemy vessels at their slow beating back and forth – and because of this movement the fishing craft could not ensure that they kept a good distance off. Their fears were, of course, on account of the cargoes and the extra men. All the stores and ammunition, needless to say, were covered by nets, canvas and other gear, but the cobles were bound to be lying lower in the water than was normal. And the six or seven crewmen, instead of the usual four, might be noticeable.

When presently, one of the warships did beat up quite close, Ramsay decided to take a chance, and directed his oarsmen to pull in even nearer. Within hailing distance, he cupped hands to mouth and shouted to ask whether the Englishmen would like some fresh mackerel? They would exchange good fish for, say, a cask of ale. The answering shouts were uncomplimentary, and the coble was waved away scornfully – for which its crew were thankful. But nothing untoward appeared to be suspected.

So far so good. But there was another hazard to be met. When the first of the Bielhaven boats appeared, coming out from where the Biel Water opened from that quite large bay, first two and then five more cobles emerged, having evidently waited for sun-up. What their crews thought of this quite large-scale invasion of their home waters was anybody's guess; but the Luffness and Cockenzie fishermen declared that anybody could fish in the open sea and that they quite often did frequent this area east of the Bass, which was namely for its mackerel shoals. When one of the Bielhaven craft did pass nearby, Ramsay left it to his own crew to shout pleasantries to the local men, asserting that they were too fond of their beds, that their wives would love them the better for earlier rising and bigger catches, and the like; but also to declare that the English were paying an excellent price for fish and that there were good shoals off the Bass these days. The others received these assertions in good enough part, offered some scurrilous comments of their own anent inshore, up-firth and fair-weather fishers, and then sailed on seawards.

A weight off his mind, Ramsay could concentrate his attention on the major problem, that of getting the boats ever closer to Dunbar harbour entrance without attracting suspicion. This was the crux of the matter, on which all depended. The warships would be very well aware that the harbour was kept closed by the castle, therefore any final dash thither was bound to be seen as hostile. But the harbour and castle were still fully a mile and a half off, and they could hope to approach considerably nearer without causing alarm. None of the ships were within a mile of the shoreline, and most much further out.

So they drifted on south-eastwards, not steadily, for all the cobles had instructions to beat about, make small diversions here and there, as though following fish-shoals and hopeful sand-banks, but always to maintain the general direction and not to spread too widely apart.

They passed fairly close to another English vessel, close enough to be very much aware of its cannon-mouths gaping at them; and some of Redheuch's crew, the nearest, held up fish towards the enemy, shouting their offers, again to be ignored.

That actually was the ship closest to the shore. Past it, they had clear water for a full mile. How much of that would they be allowed to cover, before the English perceived their intention?

For Ramsay, every yard thereafter, every stroke of the oars, was fraught with tension, as he assessed distances, glances darting between that last ship and the castle ahead. There flags were flying from the tower-tops, in gallant defiance, the Saltire of St Andrew, white on blue, the white lion of Dunbar on red, and the red on gold lozenges of Randolph of Moray. The besieged held out still, at least.

The dozen boats were drawing closer together now. With three-quarters of a mile still to go, Ramsay gave the signal to start hauling in the nets; these must not be allowed to delay them, and it would look natural enough, in the shallowing waters. But afterwards . . . ?

The process of net-hauling took some time – and, as it happened, most pairs of cobles had fairly good catches. All the while the boats were kept moving slowly harbour-wards. Not much more than half a mile to go.

Then, at last, there were signs of reaction, not from that nearest ship but from one further off to the east. This could be seen to be hoisting more sail and steering towards them. No doubt some sharp-eyed watch had perceived that after pulling in the nets they were still heading for the harbour, and had alerted his shipmaster. This was what Ramsay had been dreading.

He yelled to his people all around and waved an urgent arm. Immediately all pretences were dropped, fishing-lines thrown away, nets and fish abandoned. The rowers bent to their oars in earnest, starting to pull long rhythmic strokes which sent the heavy cobles surging forward.

Now it was a race. The oncoming ship, of course, could sail much faster than they could row; but with the wind

341

south-west still, she had to tack and beat. With only half a mile to cover, it was going to be touch-and-go.

Then the first cannon-shot boomed out, in dire menace. The effective range of pieces mounted on ships was not likely to be much more than two hundred yards. But any stray ball hitting one of their boats, however extreme the range, would almost certainly sink it. The ball splashed into the sea well behind their last coble, but the message was clear.

A ragged salvo crashed out, as the ship tacked to starboard and its port-side guns could be brought to bear; presumably the first shot had come from a single piece mounted in the bows. These sent up fountains still well astern, but not so far astern as the other. There was no need to urge on the rowers, at least; all knew that their lives depended on keeping ahead of those cannon-balls.

As ever, Ramsay was calculating timing and distances. When, after a brief interval, another single shot indicated that the pursuing ship was turning to the other tack and the bows temporarily brought to bear, the splash was not fifty yards behind the last of the Scots boats. They were losing this race. Moreover, the vessel they had recently passed was now in motion after them also, and in a better position as to wind. Grimly he decided that his calculations were pointless; only a miracle could save them now.

But that itself was a miscalculation. Or perhaps miracle was indeed the word and Black Agnes the divine instrument. For a louder bang than any yet smote their ears, along with the whistle of shot – this because it was from a larger cannon than any on shipboard and because the noise came down-wind – and a column of water jetted up a little way behind them to the left. Dunbar Castle's supply of powder-and-shot was not entirely finished yet, it seemed.

A ragged, panting cheer rose from the boats as men took heart. This choked off quickly however when another salvo crashed out from the English ship, setting up five spouts close by, one sufficiently so to spray them.

There was less than a quarter-mile to go now – that was evidenced by the fall of shot from the castle cannon, which would not have an effective range of much more than three hundred yards, although the spent ball could travel half as far again.

A second shot came from the outermost tower of the

fortalice, and men involuntarily ducked their heads as the ball screamed above them to plunge into the sea about one hundred yards in front of the leading ship.

Ramsay wondered whether to try to have his boats disperse somewhat, in order to present a poorer target, but decided against it, as every yard counted now and any such scattering move must delay them even a little.

The other warship now opened fire. But it was well out of range as yet, so that it contributed only to the menacing noise.

Although the boat crews waited for it apprehensively indeed, another salvo from the nearer vessel did not come, no doubt because the reloading, charging and priming of cannon took time. When a third shot from the castle registered an actual hit, even if not a vital one, on the vessel, bringing down a single sail and boom, the English shipmaster evidently decided that this pursuing of crazy Scots fishermen right under the castle walls was an unprofitable ploy, and sheered off. Ramsay, thankfully, assessed that they could reach the harbour-mouth now before the other vessel got within range.

He was faced now, however, with another worry. The great enemy army ashore must be as concerned about their approach as were the shipmen. They would have still better artillery and bombards, heavier pieces probably. He had been concentrating his attention, necessarily, on the ships and the castle; now he peered towards the harbour and its immediate hinterland. Here, behind the quays, the houses of Dunbar town thronged close, down quite steep slopes. It was difficult to distinguish details, but there was evidently considerable activity there. Would they have cannon sited in that area? If so, these would soon be within range and could constitute a still greater threat than the ships.

Then he reconsidered. Any artillery or mangonels in the harbour area would be well within range of the castle's own cannon and bombards. And since those had kept the English at bay all these months, it was unlikely that the enemy would have placed their own thereabouts, either on the quayside or amongst the houses. The same would apply to arbalests and slings. Arrows they might look for . . .

In fact, nothing of the sort eventuated, although men could be seen manning the harbour walls and thronging the street-mouths. Ramsay, judging the pressure now off, from seawards, directed his little flotilla to swing to the right and to

343

move in close under the cliff-like stack on which the outermost tower of the castle was built, where the forty-foot-high rock-face itself would serve to hide them from all folk but those directly above.

And there were folk there, above, to be sure, in plenty now, leaning over the parapets and battlements, cheering them on, exchanging their cannon's encouragement for the vocal sort. Shouting and waving, these beckoned, the boats' crews reciprocating. It was a heady moment.

Ramsay, gazing up, saw that there were two or three women there. It did not take him long to identify his sister-in-law herself, flourishing her kerchief. He shouted,

"Agnes! Agnes!"

In all the noise he did not know whether she heard him or recognised him – for of course he would seem just one fisherman amongst many, dressed as he was. But that was not important. The vital matter now was to gain access to the castle up there, with all their precious cargoes, something which was by no means obvious of attainment, as they rose and fell on the heaving tide below. He shouted again, to that effect.

Presently a very partial answer came, in the form of a rope-ladder lowered from the parapet. This, however inadequate, at least represented a means of communication. Ramsay had his own boat pulled close, rose and grasped the lowermost rungs – it was only just long enough – and made the awkward transference from plunging boat to swaying ladder. Up he climbed, barking his knuckles against the naked rock.

Eager hands aided him over the parapet's masonry. There was Black Agnes, staring.

"Sandy!" she cried, in almost a yelp. "Sandy Ramsay! You! Oh, my dear, my dear!" And she flung herself into his fishy-smelling arms.

Moved as he was, he had to cut short the gabbled incoherences, with his people waiting in agitation below.

"This is joy, Agnes," he got out. "But, see you, there is much to be done. The boats. How are they to be unloaded? We have brought you supplies, stores: food, powder and ball, wine. How to get it all up? Without attack from the harbour. Arrows. Much to unload . . ."

"You have? Powder and shot? As well as food? Oh, Sandy

344

– bless you, bless you! You have brought all that!" And she renewed her embracing.

"Yes, yes. But . . ."

"Fear nothing, we will have it all up. There is a way. Out of sight. Oh, Sandy, you are an angel of God! An answer to my prayers! My stout, brave, kind Sandy Ramsay! Our saviour here . . ."

"Scarce all that, lass!" he protested. "But where is this unloading-place . . .?"

"Come – I will show you . . ."

"A moment." He went over to lean on the parapet and shout down to the crews to wait there a little longer. The two English ships had drawn off now, keeping well out of range of the castle cannon.

Agnes led him past the single large piece of artillery on that tower-top, which had three great balls beside it but a significantly empty powder-barrel. Gesturing, she told him that those three shots fired were the last of which she had been capable, thanking heaven that they had served their purpose. She took him into the tower itself and down its turnpike stair. Through the vaulted basement chamber they reached the most seaward of the linking bridges between the rock-stacks. From a window at the centre of this, she pointed downwards.

"See yonder. That cave-mouth. And steps cut in the rock above."

He nodded, but frowned doubtfully – for the opening was more than halfway up the cliff-face, fully thirty feet above the waves.

At his expression Agnes smiled. "Even Sandy Ramsay could not climb to that," she agreed. "But there is another cave, down at sea-level. You cannot see it from here. It faces north-east. You can take your boats in there. And from it there is a passage up to that higher one, cut through the rock. Then those steps up into the main keep, by that postern-gate. A knotted rope to hold to, as hand-rail. This is where we bring our fish in, from the town boats, when there is an easterly gale. It is sheltered, you see, and hidden."

Much impressed, for he had not seen nor heard of this in his previous visits, Ramsay turned to hurry back to the other tower and then down that rope-ladder to his boats, to lead the way round west-abouts. Sure enough, there in the north-east face of the largest of the stacks, that which supported the

345

main keep of the castle, was a narrow but high fissure, forming a cavern-mouth, very much like the one on the Bass they had so recently left. Into this, with care, because of the rise and fall of the high tide, he steered his leading coble.

Inside, a ledge had been hewn into the rock, weed-hung and slippery, as landing stage, with steps leading upwards into a passage, part natural crevice, part artificial, with faint daylight from the higher opening filtering through. There was no room for all the boats in this narrow cavern, only five able to squeeze in at a time, so it was a case of hurried unloading while the others waited outside. But after all their dangers and exertions, the crews found little fault with this.

Ramsay left them to their tasks, and with Pate climbed the steps to prospect the ascent. A knotted rope fastened to the walling provided welcome assistance which men carrying heavy loads were going to require. Some forty steps up and they were at the higher cave-mouth, obviously enlarged by man, and here laden porters would have to exercise extreme care, for a misplaced step could all too easily plunge them down into the sea. The turning, to climb the second flight of stairs cut slantwise up the open rock-face, would be unnerving for those lacking a good head for heights, although here again there was a knotted rope to assist. At the top, they found Agnes waiting at the open postern door.

Pate was on his careful way down again, to superintend the unloading and porterage, when there was the boom of gunfire, and shouting from the castle parapets. The noise obviously came from landwards this time. Agnes shrugged.

"That will be Montague of Salisbury showing that he too can fire cannon, even to little effect! Each day he does this, regular as the matins-bell! If he knew that our powder was done, he could move his pieces closer . . ."

"Your powder is replenished now."

"Aye, and he will learn it, presently! Come . . ."

They went through the keep and over the other two bridges to the gatehouse-tower, the nearest to the land, and up to its parapet-walk, Agnes leading. And there, even Ramsay, accustomed to war and battle as he was, blinked. As far as eye could see, to the slopes of the Lammermuir Hills and up and down the coastal plain, the vast English army was encamped in their thousand upon thousand, a city of tents and pavilions and shelters, horse-lines by the score, baggage-wagons and their oxen, storage-dumps, cooking-fires sending up their smokes everywhere. Never had he seen so great an armed host. It seemed ridiculous that this was all arrayed against one castle, however strongly sited; but of course it was much more than that. This was the present base of English might in Scotland, the evidence of King Edward's ambitions, and the token of his determination to keep the Scots cowed while he made his attempt for the throne of France.

The cannonade had ceased already, for this was in reality only a prideful gesture to display inflexible purpose and unlimited ammunition. The enemy cannon could be discerned, lined up about four hundred yards away, just out of range of the castle's own artillery and beyond the natural creek and two protective ditches dug by Edward's own command those years before. These last were now filled in with faggots and soil, so that the enemy could cross them – but not while Agnes's guns were able to protect them.

It was not at the cannon that she pointed, however, but over to the right some way, where a low outcrop of rock, really just a projection of the coastal cliff-top, provided a certain amount of cover from fire from the castle. This was no place to site cannon behind, since it would block off the enemy aim; but that did not apply to mangonels and balista, which pitched missiles high in dropping shots and sling bombardment.

"These we have to suffer," Agnes said. "They will not reduce this hold; but can harass us. They put our cannoneers at risk, and also enable their sows to come close, to pick at our walling."

"But, the sea? The creek, here. Does that not protect you?"

"Come, look!" She drew him over to the westernmost bartisan of that gatehouse parapet and pointed over. Down there where the tide normally swirled in to flood the narrow rocky cleft between tower and land, it could no longer do so. For the cliffside beyond had been collapsed into the gap to form a rough ramp, a score of feet high and perhaps thirty yards broad, permitting a difficult but possible approach from landwards to the massive masonry which supported the western base of this gatehouse-tower.

"They did that with gunpowder, blowing up the cliff-face. By night. We could not stop them."

"And their sows come over that?"

"Yes. Each day. After the cannonade. You will see. You cannot view it from here, but they have picked a great hole just below us. In time they could win into our basement. We have wrecked many of their sows, but they always make more."

"Now you will have ample powder and ball, at least." He looked about him close by. That tower-top, its parapet, battlements and roofing, showed ample signs of the battering it had been receiving from the rocks hurled by the siege-engines, with masonry chipped, broken and dislodged. "You have suffered a pounding here, lass."

"This is our weak spot, yes." She shrugged. "At least we collect the stones they throw at us, to drop down on their accursed sows!"

She had hardly finished speaking when a harsh clanking noise sounded from the enemy lines behind that mound. Agnes grabbed his arm.

"Quickly!" she exclaimed. "They crank up a mangonel. We must hide." She hurried him round to the stair-head caphouse, its roof already gapped, all on the tower-top scurrying into shelter.

Hardly were they under cover when the crash of stone against stone resounded close by. The tower did not actually shake but there was an alarming sense of impact. They waited, and another hit registered, less violent only because evidently lower down the stonework.

"This will go on for some time," Agnes prophesied. "Until they have used up their present stock of stones. They have five engines there now. It takes time to crank up each after a throw. Say a score of shots, four each."

"You take it all notably calmly, lass!" Ramsay said admiringly.

"We have had time to get used to it. And they do not all score hits, see you. I . . ." Her next words were lost in further but very different noise, the clatter of many lesser blows against the walls, some directly above on the broken roofing, sending fragments of stone down the stairway.

"What is that, now . . .?"

"That is what we are calling bird-hail! It is slung from balista. A slingful of smaller stones hurled out of a scoop of skin. Many. They do less damage to the walling but more to

348

our folk. We have suffered much hurt from them. So we hide down here. And while we hide, the English drag forward their sows."

"So, that is their method. And the sows are the greatest danger?"

"Aye. They cover the men who come to pick and peck at our masonry beneath. It is very thick, the walling down there, near a score of feet it is said, to support the weight of this gatehouse with its portcullis drum-towers and drawbridge. But in time they will win through, and hew their way up and in."

"But you are ready for them . . ."

Another heavy crash.

"But do you not see, Sandy? Once they have dug a large hole down there, they will be protected. As inside a cave. We will not be able to get at them. So they can pack in more and more men. It is the sows that trouble me."

As the battery went on, small shot and massive rocks both, they waited, well down that twisting turnpike stairway, with occasional stones, the size of a man's fist, coming rolling down the steps to them. When at length the pounding ceased, still Agnes would not let any make the move up for a few minutes more, for she explained that the enemy were cunning and often kept a slingful of small stuff waiting still, that when the defenders appeared on the battlements again, they could face an unexpected hail of stones. However on this occasion nothing such developed, and cautiously Agnes led the way up again.

They found the parapet-walks littered with rocks, boulders, chips and rubble, but what was worse, in two places whole portions of the parapet's two-foot-thick masonry itself dislodged, stone and mortar still bonded together.

Subconsciously Ramsay kept his head down, but Black Agnes strode openly, to peer over and point. Sure enough, a strange procession was moving down into that cleft in the coastal cliff-face and across the ramp of rock and debris which part-filled it. What looked like an enormous round table was being transported by scores of men, most of whom would be unseen, hidden underneath, only those around the perimeter visible, holding up the canopy on poles. That canopy was composed apparently of layers of planking and skins of sheep and cattle, with straw between. Beneath its cover, Agnes said, the mining crews had not only picks and crowbars but iron-tipped rams on trestles, which could swing back and forth to bite and chew at both the sandstone and the mortared masonry.

"They will take a little time to get into position." She turned to some of her men. "Get those large lumps of our parapet poised to drop on them, Will," she directed. "They will serve nicely!" Other men were already rolling boulders and heaving rocks towards the edge.

Ramsay was impressed by the calm and businesslike way all, including the Countess, went about what was evidently a routine, as much as was the bombardment.

Agnes pointed again. "Yonder they come, each day, to watch the sport! Montague and his lords. Just out of arrow-shot, to be sure." A group of armoured horsemen were advancing, under assorted banners, to a point near the mangonels and trebuchets. She laughed. "Let us greet them fairly!"

She went to lean over the westernmost corner bartisan, sorely battered as it was, and whipping off the kerchief she wore slung round her neck, waved it in the air, accompanied by a loud ringing halloo, thrice repeated. Then she moved round the bartisan and along what remained of the parapet there, making a mock of clearing off the dust and debris of the bombardment with the kerchief, flourishing it, between each dusting, towards the watching horsemen.

Then cupping hands to mouth, she shouted, high and clear, "Montague! Montague! A good morning to you! Come nearer, my lord, that we may admire your handsome features!" She had a fine lusty voice, but whether Salisbury and his colleagues could hear her at that distance was doubtful.

Ramsay grinned, lost in admiration for his sister-in-law's spirit. She certainly was her father's daughter.

She moved back to where her people were preparing their own answer to their battering. "What would we do without all the excellent rocks they so kindly send us?" she wondered. "We would have nothing to give them back. Save for eating up our own towers!" She patted that larger mass of parapet masonry. "Now this, although we can scarcely spare it, we will give them ungrudgingly!"

Some of Ramsay's crewmen had now joined them on the

tower-top, and were set to the rock and boulder handling. The sow device was almost in position directly below, and some of the defenders were sniping with bows and arrows at any men showing themselves, but sparingly, for arrows were in very short supply.

"How do you drop your stones?" Ramsay asked. "One at a time, or altogether?"

"One by one, to keep them in alarm. For so long as our stones last."

"Perhaps, this once, better all at one time. With that great piece of masonry. All possible weight dropping on that cover at once."

"As you will . . ."

They instructed their men to have all in place and ready for simultaneous pushing over. This took some time. The sow was in position now, and by the nature of its operation, always exactly in the same place, so that the defenders knew just where to heap their missiles. Ramsay warned the bowmen that there would probably be targets for them in plenty soon. All ready, he was about to raise his hand when Agnes restrained him.

"Wait!" she said. She went back to her bartisan, and hallooed again. "Montague! Hear me. Beware! Beware! For your sow is about to farrow, I think! Beware!" And waving her kerchief again, she nodded to Ramsay.

With a great shout, the men in line at the parapet tensed their muscles, levered their crowbars, and heaved. Over in a fifty-foot drop went masonry, boulders, rock and stones in a single concentrated avalanche, in tons of weight.

That sow could nowise be missed. Down on to its flat top the missiles crashed, almost as one. No man-made structure of anything less than stone-vaulting could have withstood that fearful impact, however padded with straw and skins. The supports, of course, were its weakest feature, and these collapsed in splintering ruin. But not before some of the heaviest stone, particularly that great compacted slab of masonry, had smashed right through the canopy, ripping it apart.

The screaming down there rose horribly, and continued.

Most underneath that canopy were probably killed outright or crushed beyond movement. But some, around the fringes, survived and came staggering out. These the archers were waiting for, also hurlers of the smaller stones. Only a few escaped, to go stumbling back across the ramp.

Agnes was looking distinctly shaken now, and made no more calls to the enemy leadership. But, pressing her shoulder, Ramsay moved over to that bartisan.

"Salisbury!" he shouted, and hoped that he would be heard over the screaming. "You have been at Dunbar sufficiently long! I am Alexander Ramsay of Dalwolsey. Come with powder, shot and food. You will not win entry here, not now or ever. In the name of the Lady Agnes, I bid you begone!"

Whether or not they heard all that, the English horsemen turned their beasts and rode back towards their pavilions.

"You were right. About all the stones. At one time," Agnes jerked. "But . . ."

"It is war," he finished for her. "A lesson these arrogant invaders required to learn. Come, lass, we brought wine, as well as the rest. You could take a little, I think. As could I . . ."

They went downstairs together.

But Ramsay had not finished that day's work yet. After refreshment, and seeing that his men received theirs, he declared that a further demonstration of the new situation prevailing at the castle would be salutary. They had not brought so much powder that they could waste it; but some display of it right away might be profitable, pressing the lesson home on Salisbury and Arundel. A cannonade, both landward and seaward, even without ball, might be powder well spent, emphasising the message. And there was something else which they might try, something he had heard of, to drop on sows if they risked any more, or on to other close-up attackers. It was called Greek Fire, a device said to have been invented by the Greeks and used against the invading Infidels as long ago as the seventh century: gunpowder in small bottles of glass or skin, or other such, with a short-burning match or lit fuse attached, which exploded in flames, and could do much damage. They could test such a device out on the wreck of the sow below, and if it was successful, the enemy would be the more concerned.

Agnes agreed enthusiastically to all this. The supplies Ramsay had brought now being safely carried up to the castle, they made no delay, but set about their demonstrations. The English ships were still discreetly well out of range, beating to and fro, so little powder should be wasted on them, and no ball, a couple of bangs from the big north-facing cannon adequate. This was done right away, and whether the crews of the two nearest vessels perceived that there were no splashes of ball in the water, they did sheer still further off. The four pieces up on the gatehouse-tower were loaded up, and each fired a single ball in the general direction of the enemy mangonels and balista – which all fell short of course. Then they banged away most of one of the powder-barrels brought, making only a heartening noise and much smoke, but no doubt indicating that ammunition at least was no longer a problem.

All this activity brought forth no evident response from the English.

Meanwhile Agnes had been collecting bottles of glass and skin and pewter flagons and other containers to fill with powder. They used small pieces of the saltpetre-soaked rope-tow, with which the cannoneers set off their charges, to twist round splinters of wood and pack into the tops of the said containers. The length of these fuses was all-important, or they might either explode the bombs prematurely, to the defenders' danger, or too late for best effect on the enemy. So they experimented with burning unattached samples of the tow to gauge the approximate timing. These varied somewhat, but they decided that, once lit, two inches would be best, burning for about forty seconds.

Warily, preparations finished, and with warnings to all concerned, Ramsay, Redheuch and Pate went to the parapet edge with three of the devices, one small wine-skin, one glass bottle and one pewter flagon with a lid, lit their fuses and rather hastily dropped them over, to fall on the broken sow-canopy.

At first it was anticlimax. Nothing happened, except that the glass bottle broke on impact, spreading its powder without igniting; the pewter flagon bounced off on to the ground; and the skin container disappeared through the hole in the canopy.

They were eyeing each other rather ruefully when there were developments. The flagon exploded first, making a moderate report, not so loud as they would have liked, but showering fragments of the metal all around, some even soaring up near to the throwers. Then, a few seconds later, there was a more muffled but louder boom from inside the broken sow, still further shattering its canopy. But that was not all; the spilled powder thereon from the broken bottle caught fire and set the entire contraption, straw, skins and wood ablaze, in a most satisfactory conflagration – and, as Redheuch grimly commented, providing a suitable funeral pyre for the casualties inside.

The enemy could not fail to note and perceive the new hazards.

Delighted, the bombardiers made a few more missiles to hurl more or less indiscriminately. Ramsay, learning from experience, filled one of the skin bottles part-full of chips of stone before adding the powder, and approving the spray of fragments below when the thing exploded.

"I think that we have given Arundel and Salisbury sufficient to think about for one day," he confided to his hostess. "Tomorrow we shall try something else."

That evening, before the fire in the private hall in the main keep, was a cheerful occasion, with Agnes at her gayest, pointing out that she was well fed and in excellent company for the first time for weeks, singing and dancing for them and egging them on to participate. It was probably the first time that fisher-clad men had so disported themselves in any of the Earls of Dunbar's private apartments. And when, after a previously sleepless night, Redheuch and Pate excused themselves to seek their couches fairly early, Ramsay realised that he would be wise to do the same before long – and not only on account of fatigue. Black Agnes's affectionate and demonstrative nature, plus her gratitude, was such that any normal man, however loyal a husband, would be sorely tempted to go further than he should. How far his sister-in-law would have let him go, of course, he did not know. But, wisely, he did not wait to find out, there and then, especially as he informed, weary as he was, he intended an early rise in the morning, for the further education of those English earls.

In the event, by the next dawn, part-clad in borrowed armour, Ramsay and his people, with some of the castle's garrison as volunteers, were busy. Some were lubricating the chains and hinges of drawbridge and portcullis with goose-grease. When this was completed, and it took some time, still well before sunrise, very slowly and gently the bridge was lowered as quietly as possible, for the first time in weeks, and the portcullis half raised. Out the party of about fifty stole, armed, and some carrying burdens very gingerly.

Across the bridge they went, but turned down right-handed at once, into that cleft of the cliffs, deep in shadow still. Avoiding the collapsed and burned sow and its grisly corpses, they crossed the enemy-made ramp and climbed the rise beyond. This brought them out at the cliff-top, within less than one hundred yards of the outcropping mound behind which the enemy siege-engines were based. There would be an encampment for their crews and guards there, but as yet there was no sign of stirring, no morning cooking-fires lit.

Ramsay gathered his folk and whispered last-moment instructions. Then, pointing, he led the way, at a run. It was not often that that man did his attacking on foot.

They reached the mound without any alarm being raised, and split into two unequal sections, to go round each side of the fifty-yards-long rise. At its back they came on the English outpost, the balista and mangonels lined up close to the mound itself, with heaps of missiles nearby. The tents and makeshift shelters were a little way back. There were no horse-lines here, although there were wagons drawn up. If there were sentries on duty there was no evidence of them; but then, hitherto there had been no need for such.

In the circumstances, it was too easy, almost shamefully so. The attackers fell upon the little sleeping encampment without warning, cold steel smiting. There could be no real resistance. The enemy were overwhelmed and slaughtered, mostly where they lay. Some few escaped, but not many. But the silence of early morning was direly shattered now, by yells and shouting and screams – also clangings, for at the engines, Redheuch's party went to work with axes and maces, cutting and slashing, while others arranged the bombs in position, ready to ignite.

With the nearest sections of the main English camp only about a quarter-mile away, there was no time for delay, for the noise could not fail to arouse all. Blowing his horn to call off the killing, Ramsay ran back, and with Redheuch and Pate lit tinder with flint-and-steel. Then waving all their raiders away, back towards the castle, the three leaders, with Wattie Kerr and another, knelt to light the tow-matches. They had taken the precaution to give these rather longer fuses, but even so there would be no time to waste. Five bombs there were, one under each now part-wrecked machine. A shout to ensure that they lit all at the same time. Then they bolted after the others.

They were some way down towards the ramp when the first explosion sounded behind them. Then two more almost together, and then a fourth. There was no more, so presumably one bomb had failed to ignite. The runners slowed their pace somewhat, but did not linger.

By the time that they reached the drawbridge and over, the morning was loud with noise from the direction of the great camp, shouting, trumpets and horns blowing. But that was nothing to trouble them now, as the bridge was raised and the portcullis clanged shut. Agnes, waiting there, threw her arms around her brother-in-law and kissed him, before all.

Just as a rounding-off gesture, they fired a couple of shots towards the enemy from the gatehouse cannon. Then it was time for breakfast.

That night, the Luffness and Cockenzie fishermen slipped away in the dark, one by one in their boats, Ramsay and his Dalwolsey people remaining in the castle.

The days that followed were less eventful, for of course sallies like that one could not be repeated, with the English now very much on their guard. No more sows were brought to offer as targets, and although the enemy cannonading did continue, it did no damage. If they were manufacturing more balista and slings, it was not apparent.

So it was stalemate, and with winter weather approaching, the English could not but be very well aware of it.

It took ten days for matters to come to a head, ten days, and especially evenings, of close proximity between Ramsay and Agnes inevitably, wherein both were tested in their own way, but each retained respect and self-respect. The man had always admired the woman; now he grew very fond of her, but saw to it that Mariot was in no danger from her sister. And for her part, Agnes, without noticeably restraining herself, did not try him too directly. She had her strengths, that young woman, in more ways than one. The siege remained that, and little more, with some half-hearted exchange of fire each day, but no real challenges. Both sides were waiting – and basically, both knew on what they were waiting.

On the tenth day, the waiting was over. About noon, a horsed English group was reported as approaching from the

356

main encampment, under banners and pennons. This had happened before – but never with a white flag prominent amongst the others. It brought Agnes and most of her supporters up to the top of the gatehouse-tower.

A flourish, indeed a fanfare, of trumpets heralded the English leadership to just outwith cannon range. There they paused.

"They are unsure of their welcome!" Agnes said. "You shout more loudly than I do, Sandy. Tell them to come closer. If it is trickery, we have your Greek Fires."

Ramsay raised his voice. "You are safe, Englishmen, under *that* flag. We hear your trumpets. What else have we to hear?"

The party moved forward again. It could be seen by the plumed helmets, rich armour and heraldic surcoats, as well as the banners, that here were the lordly ones.

Quite close to the gatehouse drum-towers and upraised drawbridge, they drew up, and one of the knights lifted a gauntleted hand.

"I am Salisbury," he called. "We should be well acquaint by now, madam! I give you good day."

"And I return it gladly, like your missiles, my lord!" Agnes hardly had to shout now.

The Earl barked a laugh. "We have had a fair exchange, lady. Now, my lord of Arundel would speak with you. He is the Lord Edward's Governor of Scotland."

"Then he must be a sad man this day, with nothing to govern! Speak on, my lord."

A different and more abrupt voice spoke. "Countess, hear me. His Majesty the Lord Edward, King of England and of France and Lord Paramount of Scotland, requires myself, these lords and his host here, to return to England and on to France, for further and more important service there. So we leave you meantime, madam. But we will be back!"

Agnes skirled a laugh. "Indeed, my lord? We shall miss you. I wish you as good success in fair France as you have had here! Farewell!"

Arundel reined his horse around abruptly, but Salisbury was more mannerly.

"Lady, we take our reluctant departure," he called. "In sorrow that we could not come the nearer, each to each. If you keep your virtue as close as you keep your gate, then your lord, the Earl Patrick, amissing, is to be congratulated, after all!" And with that cryptic gallantry, he signed to his trumpeters.

With another prolonged fanfare, which might have signalled a famous victory, the English leadership turned and rode back to their encampment.

Agnes and Ramsay stared at each other, before dissolving into laughter.

"Who triumphs, then? Do we? Or do they?" she wondered.

He shook his head. "These English . . .!"

By evening, even the oxen-drawn cannon and the baggage-waggons were on the move; and the blockading fleet were hull-down to the south. The siege of Dunbar was over, after all the weeks.

Two days later Ramsay and his men took their leave; and in fishing boats again, since there were no horses to borrow. They made quite an emotional parting of it.

19

It was good to be back with Mariot at Dalwolsey, and for the first time really in their marriage to be able to live almost normally as man and wife, without hiding and scheming, war and battle, as daily preoccupations. It would not last, of course, all knew well; the English, if not Balliol, would be back. But meantime there was the semblance of peace.

Yet, if Ramsay and Mariot rejoiced, not all did. For famine stalked the land. The years of war, occupation and devastation, of burning and savagery and flight therefrom, men with neither time nor opportunity to till the soil, cattle being driven off, stocks destroyed, mills wrecked, now had their inevitable results. All over the southern half of the kingdom the folk were starving. Men, women and children, despite the beginning of winter, were leaving their homes in the towns and villages to scour the woods and moors for game and nuts and acorns, desperate. Because of all the hauls of English provisions captured from Hawthornden, hidden out of sight and stored away in caves and safe places, Ramsay's area was better off than most, and he busied himself with distribution. But it was going to be a grim winter.

It seemed that, whilst Ramsay was at Dunbar, so concerned was the new Regent Robert Stewart and his Council, that they had actually sent Sir William Douglas off to France, to plead with King Philip for shiploads of supplies and grain to be sent, using as pretext that the Scots, fed, would be better able to distract the English in their invasion of France. Douglas was also to see young King David, now sixteen years, and discuss the possibility of his returning to Scotland. It seemed a strange role for Will Douglas, but his fame as the Flower of Chivalry would no doubt commend him to King Philip.

Edward Plantagenet was not the man to accept the Scottish situation without some gesture. He sent Henry of Lancaster, his uncle, up to Berwick, to maintain some sort of English presence there, with Balliol; but at the same time announced that he had graciously granted the Scots a truce until the following Michaelmas, in effect for one year. This was, of course, play-acting, and circumstances, all knew, could change without warning. But at least here was a breathing-space, if a hungry one. None feared Balliol any longer.

The Steward called a parliament at Perth to decide on policy, and Ramsay, the land ostensibly now being at peace, took Mariot with him, not only for her good company but thereafter she could visit Doune, to ensure that all was in order there during her brother's continued captivity in England. So far there had been no response to the offer to exchange Moray for the Lord Robert Manners, unfortunately. She was worried about John. Considering Will Douglas's experiences in an English prison, she had reason.

That parliament was not particularly effective nor influential; but then, neither was its caller and president, the new Regent. Robert Stewart had never wanted to be Regent, and demonstrated the fact. He was indeed no leader of men, despite his resounding ancestry, a sound and likeable character but lacking in drive and initiative, even in ambition, not the man Scotland needed in this pass. He as good as announced the fact there and then, by declaring that parliament should add its authority to his personal message carried by the Knight of Liddesdale, that King David should be asked to return from France at an early date, to take over the rule and government. He was in his seventeenth year and ought no longer to need a Regent.

There were some murmurings at this, but no outright opposition. The reports about David were that he was grown into a strong and spirited youth, if somewhat headstrong. At least he might show more of leadership than did his nephew the Steward. So that matter was passed.

The military situation was then discussed. Only the two Scots citadels now remained in English hands, apart from Berwick itself; Roxburgh and Caerlaverock, this latter in a notably strong situation, islanded in loch and marshland. Bothwell, Dunnottar, Lauriston and Lochmaben had all fallen. Ramsay, who came in for much acclaim over his relief of Dunbar – with questions asked as to where was its lord, the Earl Patrick, not here present? – was suggested as the man to tackle the taking of Caerlaverock; but he declared that this was not for him. Different qualities from his were required for prolonged investment and siegery; he was a man of short, sharp actions, surprise, ambushes and the like, none of which could apply at Caerlaverock. Most agreed that only time would win them that. As for Roxburgh, it was so close to the Border with England and Berwick that it could hardly be besieged without all-out confrontation with the enemy might.

Some hot-bloods were for organising more raids into England, since this truce was purely a one-sided announcement of Edward's. But most agreed with the Chancellor, Bishop de Linton, that this would be folly in the present circumstances. Scotland desperately needed time to recover, especially with famine prevailing, not more military adventures which could only provoke retaliation. Ramsay supported that.

The problem of trying to deal with the famine and sorry state of the land took up most of the session, inevitably. It had to be a question of organisation, moving supplies, grain and cattle from the better-off to the more devastated areas, not something to arouse enthusiasm amongst the lordly ones attending the parliament. The Highlands, in especial, were great cattle-rearing country and largely untouched by war – or at least only by internecine clan-warfare – and somehow the chiefs must be persuaded to send some of their clansmen's droves south. This would not be simple to achieve, for Highland and Lowland looked on each other with suspicion and little respect, and few of the lords and lairds were on speaking terms with the chiefs.

But something must be done. The late Regent, whose estates were mainly in the North and who was much respected amongst the clans, was sadly missed in this as in other matters.

The session over, the Ramsays moved down to Doune, a mere thirty miles to the south-west. Here they found all in order, in the care of the efficient and reliable steward, now elderly, who had been Mariot's father's favourite henchman and body-servant, much in the same capacity to that Earl as was Wattie Kerr to Ramsay. He was responsible amongst other matters, for the Lord Robert Manners' security, and took no chances with his captive. Nevertheless, Manners was very comfortable, and seemed reasonably reconciled to his lot; as well he might, for he lived almost as though the lord of Doune Castle, however restricted he might be otherwise. He was disappointed, of course, to hear that there was no answer from England to the offer of his exchange for Moray, but he could not blame that on his captors. Perhaps the new truce situation would expedite matters.

They spent a couple of weeks at Doune, seeing inevitably rather more of Manners than they would have wished, but with some sympathy for his position. They arranged for quite large numbers of the Doune cattle to be sent off in droves to Stirling and Falkirk and thereabouts, compensation, in theory, to be paid by the Treasury; Doune, on the skirts of the Highland Line, was excellent cattle country. Ramsay indeed improved on the situation by making a two-day expedition northwards into the mountainous territory near the foot of Loch Tay, to the lands of one of the nearest Highland clans, that of Menzies. He knew that the chiefs of Menzies, although not their clansfolk, oddly enough were descended from the same stock as was the Lord Robert Manners, both deriving from the Norman de Meyners. The English had corrupted the name into Manners, the Scots to Mengues and then Menzies. Ramsay used this information to introduce himself to that chief, to invite him to Doune to meet his far-out kinsman, and at the same time to send cattle south into the Lowlands – at a fair price, of course. Winter feed for surplus cattle was always a problem in the Highlands, so Menzies was prepared to agree. Alexander Ramsay's fame had reached the Highlands, it appeared.

Yuletide was over, and at Dalwolsey they were looking forward to the spring and its peaceable activities, when surprising news reached the Ramsays. It came from France, via Perth, by a courier sent in a French food ship to the Regent by King Philip. He announced, amongst other matters, that in a great battle at Lille, which the French had won, two English earls had been captured – Suffolk, and none other than their old friend Salisbury. Philip, in a gesture towards Scotland, had offered their release to Edward in exchange for the Earl of Moray, and this had been accepted. Moray therefore should be home shortly.

This greatly cheered the Ramsays, and they set out on a visit to Dunbar to inform Agnes.

It was quite a strange experience for that man to be back in the sea-girt castle again in conditions of peace and normality. Agnes was in fine fettle, and embarrassingly loud in her praises of her deliverer. High spirits prevailed.

They learned that the Earl Patrick had paid a brief visit to Dunbar in early December, to inspect the premises and damage done, if not, apparently, to congratulate his wife and the garrison, and then returned to his preferred residence at Ersildoune. Mariot wondered whether perhaps he kept a mistress there? But her sister, grimacing, declared that it would be more likely to be a catamite!

John Randolph arrived back at Doune soon afterwards, and was not long in paying a visit to his sisters. He was pale, but otherwise in fairly good health, having been kept apparently in reasonably good conditions, unlike Will Douglas's experience. He thought that probably he had Sandy Ramsay to thank for that, in taking the Lord Robert Manners prisoner; for although the English authorities had not agreed to their exchange, they were well aware that ill-treatment might well bring reprisals on Manners. That, and the fact that he himself was an earl; the English were much impressed by earldoms. Anyway, he was thankful to be free again and back, and grateful to all concerned – sufficiently so to have sent Manners home, from Doune. He had been there long enough. It was good to have Moray back, for national as well as personal reasons, for he had a major influence for good on the Steward, who had always largely relied on him in major matters. So in present circumstances, the realm should benefit.

The truce still held.

Spring was truly with them, indeed the first cuckoo was calling hauntingly in the Dalwolsey woodland when the word came that Will Douglas was back, with five more French ships to land food at Perth. And not only food but arms and ammunition also – for King Philip wanted not only fed Scots but militarily-active Scots. As well, Douglas had brought news that King David would indeed return to Scotland very shortly, it was hoped in early summer. The news, when it became known generally, had a great effect up and down the land. This was, after all, the Bruce's son, and Scotland needed its king.

So a Council meeting was held at Perth to plan a suitable welcome for the returning monarch. The problem was, just when and where? The English warships were the great hazard. Some of the French supply ships sent to Scotland had been intercepted and captured. David's vessel would have to run the gauntlet. It would be safest for him to sail from a port on the French west coast, up around Ireland and into Dumbarton or another of the Clyde ports – but of course this would make a much longer voyage. However, the English armies were strongly based in North-West France, Normandy and Brittany. So it might be easier to reach a Norse Sea haven in the Low Countries, and circle widely to the east, to avoid Edward's ships. Which would be apt to mean a landfall in the North somewhere, possibly Aberdeen. Planning a reception was therefore difficult. Presumably the Regent would be sent word as to David's intentions and times.

Towards the end of May a courier did arrive from France, saying that the King was at Antwerp and his ship would sail, weather permitting, about the last day of May. It would make for the port of Montrose, in Angus, where there was a royal castle at Kincardine not far inland, which David ordered to be made ready for him and his Queen.

So there was a great haste and to-do in making arrangements at short notice. Kincardine Castle, now only a hunting-seat, had not been used since the Bruce's time, and would require considerable refurbishing. A suitably illustrious welcoming party had to be assembled up there, and adequate provisioning produced which would not shame fine folk used to lavish French hospitality. Holy Church, in the person of Bishop de Linton, stepped in here and its great abbey of Arbroath, the second richest in the land, took on the catering.

Ramsay was amongst those summoned to attend. And since the young Queen was to be there, he took Mariot with him; and at her urging, sent the suggestion to Dunbar that

Agnes should go also. There was bound to be a dearth of high-born ladies to wait on Queen Joanna, in the circumstances. Agnes, deserving a break from being chatelaine, gladly acceded. So all three headed northwards on that last day of May, picking up Moray at Doune, *en route*.

Unfortunately the weather made their long ride less enjoyable than it might have been, strong winds and blustery showers in constant succession as they made their way up through Strathearn to Perth and on into the long vale of Strathmore, by Coupar and Glamis and Forfar, eventually to reach the sea at Ulysseshaven, just south of Montrose; a journey which should have been highly scenic and attractive for unhurried travellers, but which in wet and blowy conditions was less than pleasing for horseback riding. It did not fail to occur to them, however, that conditions would be infinitely worse for their young liege-lord and his lady on shipboard out in stormy seas – a recognition which was reinforced by their first sight of the ocean at Scurdie Ness, with great white-capped rollers crashing on to the rock-bound seaboard and sending up huge clouds of spray and spume, visibility seawards limited to only a mile or two.

They rode on to Montrose town and found all ready at the harbour to receive the King's ship, but head-shakings about the weather and sailing conditions. Delay there would be inevitably, if nothing worse.

It was about a dozen miles north-eastwards, across the Howe of the Mearns, to Kincardine Castle, near Fettercairn, close under the mighty heather hills of the Mounth. They found the old, rather ramshackle place busy indeed, thronged with folk, such as it had not been in centuries, since perhaps Kenneth the Third was murdered here by the fatal Fenella. Now all was bustle and some confusion, with cleaning and tidying going on, makeshift timber buildings going up in the inner courtyard, furnishings being brought from neighbouring houses, and Arbroath Abbey servitors and monks complaining of the inadequate facilities for their purveyance. Robert Stewart greeted their arrival with heartfelt thanks, distinctly out of his depth in all this. He did not know, of course, when he would appear, nor how many people David would bring with him, to be fed and housed. And there was still much to be done at Kincardine. Why he had to choose this out-of-the-way and semi-ruinous place . . . ! There were messengers with fast horses waiting at the coast, ready to ride the moment the vessel was sighted. It was twelve miles, and they could cover the ground in not much over the hour. So that he could be back there without too long an interval. But . . .

Moray and Ramsay, and the women too, reassured him. Moray would take over here, if he so wished, and he could go to Montrose, as Regent, to welcome the monarch ashore. Black Agnes announced that she would see to all the domestic arrangements at Kincardine – she was used to managing large establishments. Mariot would go to Montrose with Robert, to take charge of the young Queen when they landed. All would be well.

So, after only a brief interval, the Steward, Mariot and Ramsay set off back southwards for the coast. The weather was improving only a little, the rain stopped, but as blustery as ever, and cold, for despite being the beginning of June, the wind was from the north-east.

They reached Montrose again in time, at least, for there had been no sightings of shipping although visibility had extended considerably. But the sea conditions were bad, with the waves pounding the shoreline thunderously, amidst a mist of spindrift; and with the wind the way it was, it was driving the seas slantwise across the harbour-mouth alarmingly, so that the local shipmen and fishers shook doubtful heads. Montrose harbour had a great and sheltered basin just inland, but its quite narrow mouth faced due east.

There had been a small royal castle here, a fort rather than a residence standing on Fort-hill; but Wallace had destroyed it the year after King Edward the First had occupied it at the time of his abasing of King John Balliol at Stracathro nearby. So the visitors now put up at the only large establishment of the town, a Dominican priory.

By evening there was still no sign of the ship – or ships, for the royal vessel might be escorted by others – so the weary travellers could retire for the night knowing that, whatever else, no shipmaster would attempt to enter a strange harbour in darkness in such conditions.

There was still nothing to be seen seawards the next morning. But just before noon a messenger arrived, in haste, the steward of Ogilvy of Benholm, a castle situated some ten miles northwards, its laird being amongst those assembled here at Montrose. He came to announce to his master that a quite large ship, flying the French colours, was beating up and down, too closely off a dangerous shore, easily seen from that castle.

Needless to say, this news set all by the ears. It was highly unlikely that there would be another large French vessel approaching this seaboard at this time. There was much shouting for men and horses. In the midst of it all, who should arrive from the south but Sir William Douglas. Ramsay had not seen him since he returned from France.

They hurried northwards along the coast road, the Steward and most of his company, by St Cyrus, Mathers and Johnshaven, Ogilvy of Benholm leading the way. At Benholm itself, perched on high ground as it was, there was no sign now of any ship. But visibility was still not good, and to the north the prospect anyway was blocked by headlands. They went down to the boat-shore, in a mist of blown spray, where fisherfolk told them that the ship had last been seen heading still further northwards, over an hour before, and far too close inshore to this dangerous reef-bound coast for safety. It might be making for Stonehaven, the next large harbour, or even for Aberdeen, fifteen miles further. But if so, it should be keeping much further offshore, with the great headland of Bervie Brow intervening.

Seriously worried now, the party rode on northwards, half-headed into the storm, Mariot the only woman.

A couple of miles on, rounding a green spur of hillside above Hallgreen, the prospect suddenly changed. Ahead was a wide bay, at the head of which a river entered, emerging from a quite deep valley, with at the mouth a small town clustering. And beyond, to form the northern horn of the bay, a mighty headland reared, rising above coastal cliffs to a peak-topped hill – Bervie Brow. The town was Inverbervie, the river the Bervie Water.

Down they rode to the town, which they found in a considerable stir, folk huddling in corners out of the wind discussing the French ship. Apparently it had come close in, as though to enter the little harbour here, in the river's mouth. But this was, of course, far too small to take a large ship, and with these cross-seas not safe even for their own fishing craft. The Frenchmen had perceived this just in time and sheered off. But with the north-east gale blowing, it had been touch-and-go as to whether they could round Bervie

Brow at sufficient distance to avoid its jutting reefs and skerries. It *had* passed from their view beyond the headland, but desperately close in; and further round, out of sight from the town, were thrusting projections, an additional hazard. A group of young fishermen had hurried off, the mile or so to the Brow, to see if the Frenchies were safely round . . .

Direly alarmed, the newcomers hastened on, to ford the river and round the bay.

They were nearing the foot of the Brow when two youths came running along the track towards them. The ship had struck, they panted. It was on the rocks they called Partan Craig, just round the headland, under the cliff. They were hurrying to get help, to try to rescue the crew . . .

Speechless now with apprehension, the riders pressed on.

Rounding the first jut of the headland on the cliff-top track, there was the great ship to be seen reared at an angle, prow up, on a long reef of rock, stern down in the water, the foremast and rigging over the side, waves breaking over the lower parts, spume drifting over all, a grievous sight. People could be seen clustered up at the bows, but there were others already on the ridge of rock below, which thrust out for perhaps one hundred yards from the cliff-foot.

How to get down there? There was no way for horses to negotiate that descent. It was not all sheer cliff but it was all very steep. At a spot where it was grass and scree, Ramsay leapt from his mount, shouting to Mariot to stay where she was, and began without pause to pick his way down the difficult slope, zigzagging and using hands as well as feet. One or two others followed him, but most rode further on looking for a better place.

Slithering and sliding, often on his bottom, somehow he got down to the shore. Fortunately the tide was two-thirds out or he could not have worked his way along to the wreck's position – although, if the tide had been full, the ship might possibly not have struck. As it was, he was quickly soaked with spray as well as from splashing through pools. Men were shouting behind him, but his attention was on the reef in front.

He could see now that the reef was in fact above water all the way to the shore, although waves were washing over it in places. People were dotted along it, slipping and stumbling and dodging the breakers. Others were swarming down the toppled mast and its gear on to the rocks.

He reached the foot of the reef and found a group of bedraggled men there, in various stages of distress, and exclaiming in French. None looked youthful enough to be his liege-lord. Ignoring them, he hurried out along the weed-hung, slippery skerry, passing others heading landwards, some all but on all fours, himself staggering and tripping on the treacherous footing and making blundering dashes between the swirls of wave-tops.

Reaching the wreck, he found youths certainly, the fisherfolk of Inverbervie, aiding people down the difficult makeshift gangway formed by the fallen mast, its sail and tangle of ropes. Amongst them was another, very differently dressed. He was in fact seeking to clamber back up the ramp to the ship again, as it were against the tide, and men were seeking to restrain him. He was shouting, in French, but the name Joan, Joan, was sufficiently clear.

None there were likely to be calling Joanna Plantagenet by her Christian name, but one.

"Sire! Sire!" Ramsay panted. "Thank God you are safe! I am Ramsay . . ."

"Joan!" the youth cried. "The Queen! She must come." He pointed, to where a small group of women huddled up in the high point of the prow. "I must get her . . ."

"Never fear, Sire, I will bring her to you. Wait you here. I will go . . ."

Clambering his way up that awkward ramp, which swayed alarmingly with the seesawing motion of the poised vessel, he gained the deck. There were four women clustered there, but only one could be called a girl. It was years since Ramsay had seen the young Queen; then she was only a child. He certainly would not have recognised this young woman, plain of face, her looks nowise enhanced by the conditions, hair plastered over her pale features, soaked and shivering with apprehension and chill, her companions in little better shape.

"Your Grace," he said. "I am Ramsay of Dalwolsey. I will take you down to the King. It is not dangerous. Come."

She shook her head, biting her quivering lip and staring at that heaving mast and its trappings.

"Never fear, Madam. It is none so difficult. We shall go slowly." He reached to take her arm.

One of the women said something encouraging in French,

and took the girl's other arm. Hesitantly, Joanna Plantagenet ventured forward to the tangle of rope, spar and canvas.

They had to wait their turn, for others were hurrying to get off the ship, and in these conditions there was nothing of deference and courtesy. Stepping up on to the wet sail-cloth and cordage, which moved beneath his feet, Ramsay hoisted the Queen almost bodily, then assisted the other women to climb also, their long wet skirts no help. Then, he in front and the women behind, they sought to guide and support the girl down the steep and unsteady gangway.

"*Mal de mer! Mal de mer!*" the woman exclaimed, pointing to Joanna.

As the ramp heaved under them, the Queen's knees gave way and she sank down on all fours, clutching at the cordage. Ramsay, about to raise her up again, recognised that she probably would be better thus, for he was keeping his own feet only with difficulty. Telling her to creep down backwards, on hands and knees, he sought to aid and guide her. The other women also decided on the same method of descent.

Down they crept, and halfway David himself came up to assist. The lower part was the less difficult.

Safe on the weed-hung rock, Ramsay left the royal pair and went back up to assist the remaining two women, who were being coaxed by an elderly man. Together they got them down, amidst cries and beseechings to the Almighty.

Back on the reef, he found that Will Douglas had arrived, with the Steward and others, and they were leading David and Joanna landward. Ramsay followed on with the other ladies. After that ramp, dodging the waves was only a minor hazard.

Ashore, with Mariot waiting there, the next problem was getting the rescued up the cliff to the horses. Fortunately, Douglas had found a somewhat easier way down, further along, than that by which Ramsay had descended, and Mariot declared that she would get the Queen up there well enough. It was slippery with the rain and spray, but they would take it heedfully.

There were now a fair number of townsfolk from Inverbervie gathered to assist in the rescue of the remaining crew of the stricken vessel, so the royal party did not linger. They tackled the steep hillside as best they could. Joanna, safe on firm land, and, with the exercise, chill receding, regained her nerve and composure somewhat, and her husband recovered his spirits quickly. By the time that they reached the horses, all were feeling a deal better, however wet and wind-blown.

It was surely the most unceremonious homecoming of royalty in Scotland's long story.

The rode back to Inverbervie, Ogilvy of Benholm hurrying ahead to organise temporary shelter and hospitality at the Carmelite monastery there.

They young monarch was now boyishly excited about their adventures, rather scornfully critical of his Queen's fearful behaviour, disparaging as to the French shipmen's ability, but loud in his praise of the Inverbervie folk who had come to the rescue. He would, he declared, make the town a royal burgh in commemoration. He obviously thought a lot of Sir William Douglas, treating him as his closest confidant; of course, he had known him in France. Queen Joanna was subdued, withdrawn, and retired to a bed in the prior's quarters, Mariot constituting herself a lady-in-waiting for the time being.

There was, of course, far too little accommodation in the monastery for all the royal party, and the small houses of the town scarcely suitable. So, it was decided that since David showed little signs of his ordeal, he and most of the company should ride on the dozen miles to Kincardine Castle that same evening, leaving the Queen and her ladies at Inverbervie, to be brought on the next day. Mariot stayed on also, and Ramsay with her, to act escort. The weather had improved considerably by the morning, although the seas were still very rough, and Joanna expressed herself as fit to make the journey.

At the castle, they were astonished to find the young King already out hunting. June was not the season for the deer, but Kincardine was famous for its deer-drives, an elaborate system of banks and re-entrants and ditches on the nearby hillsides having been established here from, some said, Pictish times, where the animals could be rounded up from the glens and moors of the hinterland and driven down by the hundred for the waiting huntsmen to slaughter *en masse*. Apparently David, who was an enthusiast of the chase, had been looking forward to this ever since he had decided to come home, and neither shipwreck, weather nor out-of-season was going to stop him now. Few of his company were so keen. All had heard that he was a headstrong, impatient and impulsive character; he was not taking long to prove it.

They learned that Robert Stewart had already thankfully

resigned his Regency, and David had taken that as a matter of course and was now giving orders right and left, in no diffident fashion. Scotland had a sovereign-lord again, although barely seventeen years, for better or for worse.

If the Steward was relieved, personally, Moray was not – and Ramsay came to share this unease. The nation admittedly needed a strong hand at the helm, but an informed and well-advised one. David Bruce could scarcely be the former, and clearly was going to require a deal of directing. He had obviously adopted Will Douglas as closest associate, but whether that was to the good or not remained to be seen.

They remained three days at Kincardine, not very satisfactory days, for the place was uncomfortable, over-crowded and lacking in amenities, the Frenchmen in particular complaining of the barbarous conditions. Then David suddenly grew tired of slaughtering deer, and to the thankfulness of most there, decided on a move south to Stirling, the main royal seat.

On the fourth morning then, after leaving instructions for the salvage of what might be possible from the wrecked ship, the move was initiated, the large cavalcade setting out with horses brought in from a wide area to mount the visitors. And quickly the monarch further demonstrated his mettle, announcing that he was not going to creep and crawl at the speed suitable for his wife and her women. With a small group, therefore, including Douglas, David rode on ahead, at a man's pace, leaving the rest to come in their own time. Since Mariot and Agnes remained with the depressed-seeming Queen, Ramsay and Moray did likewise. There was almost one hundred miles to go to Stirling. Fortunately the weather was now kind.

A new dispensation had dawned in Scotland.

20

It was not long before Ramsay had to be back in Central Scotland, for a parliament, David's first, was held at Scone, near Perth, in September. Meantime, at Dalwolsey, they had heard not a little of the King's activities – for whatever else, he was of an active disposition. From the start he had been ranging the country, showing himself to the people and to his lords, visiting towns, castles, abbeys, sitting in judgment at shire justice-eyres. Already he had made important new appointments, some of which fell to be confirmed by parliament. Bernard de Linton was too old to be chancellor, he decided, and for the first time in living memory there was put in his place a non-cleric, one Sir Thomas Charteris, little known but presumably a friend of his French days. Better known was the new Chamberlain, enjoined to put the sorry finances of the realm on their feet, no simple task; and he none other than the turncoat English priest, William Bullock, who had aided Douglas to capture Edinburgh Castle, a strange choice indeed. Douglas himself had been given the forfeited earldom of Atholl, just why was not clear, the Douglas interests all being south of Forth and Clyde.

That Scone parliament was very much David's own, with a new Chancellor unconversant with the accepted procedure, a new Chamberlain likewise, and all attending very much aware that, for the first time since the Bruce had died, the monarch himself was in charge. David, for his part, clearly expected no opposition, and had certainly come prepared to demonstrate his grasp on his realm's affairs. He declared from the throne that his kingdom was in a sorry state, hunger rife, lawlessness rampant, the treasury empty.

These must be dealt with. But first and foremost, any remaining support for the man Balliol must be rooted out, and the last trace of English occupation banished. Roxburgh Castle was still in enemy hands, to their shame, and must be recovered. And to ensure that the entire borderline with England was fully embattled, to prevent any further invasion, he was making new arrangements. The Earl of Dunbar and March would no longer act, or fail to act, as Chief Warden of the Marches. Instead, three new Wardens would be appointed, with complete powers in their own areas: the Earl of Moray to the West March, Sir William Douglas of Liddesdale to the Middle March, and Sir Alexander Ramsay of Dalwolsey to the East March. It would therefore fall to the said Sir William Douglas to recapture Roxburgh Castle, which was situated in his Middle March.

This forthright announcement was greeted with enthusiasm by most, not being involved, reserve by some, and fairly evident unease by Will Douglas. Ramsay and Moray exchanged glances. The Earl Patrick, as usual, was not present.

Taking that as accepted, David went on to do what he should have done first of all, to require parliament to confirm his appointment of the new Chancellor, Chamberlain and other officers. However doubtful some might be about the royal choice, none proposed actual rejection.

So it went on, the young King having it all his own way, all feeling that having urged him to come back from France to take up the rule, this was almost obligatory. When it came to the more humdrum business of arranging relief measures, new taxation, customs and dues and burghal contributions to the treasury, David sat back and left it to others, looking bored now. Master Bullock did most of the proposing there, and certainly sounded effective in the matter, however many scowled, especially lords whose contributions looked like being increased.

The session ended abruptly, when David declared that that was all, and without waiting for the customary valedictory flourish by the Lord Lyon King of Arms and his trumpeters, rose and hurried from the abbey refectory where the sitting was held.

Ramsay and his brother-in-law thereafter discussed it all, and of course in particular their new responsibilities as Wardens of the East and West March, neither of whom would have chosen the positions. Yet they made sense, of course, for few knew the eastern Borders and the Merse, save its own occupants, better than did Ramsay; and Moray owned large lands in the west, in Dumfries-shire and Galloway, and could call on major manpower. He would have to make his headquarters at Caerlaverock Castle, near Dumfries, the Warden's seat; but he had his own castle at Morton not far away, where he could actually dwell. Ramsay said that he thought that he would have to base himself at the castle of Foulden, on the Whiteadder in the Merse, only some six miles from Berwick, small but conveniently placed, the seat of his late kinsman, Sir William Ramsay who had died at the Berwick tournament, and who had left only a widow and child heir. There would be problems over manpower inevitably, for apart from his own Dalwolsey people, he would be largely dependent on the Homes, so strong in the Merse, and who had been used to the Earl of Dunbar and March as their overlord; and that strange man might well prove awkward, in the circumstances.

Will Douglas did not discuss *his* problems with them, or others, and indeed was one of the first to leave Scone.

Ramsay found fewer difficulties than he had anticipated at Foulden, a couple of weeks later, where he was gladly received by his cousin's widow, a motherly soul, and her twelve-year-old son. There was quite a large village here, for the quartering of his Dalwolsey men, of whom he brought about one hundred. Fortunately Lady Foulden was a Home herself, and this fact helped to pave a way for the new Warden's approaches and negotiations with the lairds of that powerful clan, whose estates so largely filled the entire area. There was another difficulty with regard to the Homes of which Ramsay was well aware, other than the question of some loyalty to Earl Patrick, and that was the fact that these Homes, living so close to the borderline, had by and large a sort of unwritten understanding with their English counterparts that they would not prey upon each other, in general circumstances – which would mean, of course, that they would not be apt to prove the most reliable supporters in any Warden's raiding over the said Border; a situation no doubt partly responsible for their earl's ambivalent attitudes also. So he did not expect too much. As it turned out, in his talks and requests to the various Home lairds, firm but tactful, little was said about their lord, whose behaviour lacked popular approval even in this his own earldom. And Ramsay's relief of the Earl's castle of Dunbar, when its owner had done nothing, told in his favour.

Foulden was only some fifty miles from Dalwolsey, and half that from Dunbar, so that it was possible to see Mariot frequently; indeed Ramsay was contemplating bringing her to Foulden for at least a prolonged visit, since there was no outbreak of any major hostilities, when another visitor put such a notion out of his head for the time being. This was none other than his sovereign-lord himself, arriving totally unannounced one winter afternoon, with only a small train.

David came in purposeful mood, having ridden from Dunbar. He was grievously disappointed with William Douglas. That man had, as commanded, made an attempt to take Roxburgh Castle, but had failed completely. It had been but a poor effort, and Douglas had given up much too readily – or so the monarch declared. This last toehold of the English on Scots soil *must* be retaken. He, Ramsay, must achieve it.

Blinking, that man sought for words, suitable words to counter a royal command.

"But . . . but, Sire, how am I to do this? It is a mighty strength. If Douglas could not do it. And now the English are warned that we are seeking to retake it. If Douglas failed, who recovered Edinburgh's castle, how can I?"

"You saved Dunbar Castle from a great English army. I have but come from there."

"That was by a device, Sire. A trick. By sea. Not a taking, only a relieving. Roxburgh is quite otherwise. At the junction of two great rivers. Cannon cannot be brought within range. Nor bombards . . ."

"Then you will have to use one of your devices, Sir Alexander! You are famed for them. Roxburgh must be purged of the English. It is a jewel in the Scottish crown. It was the seat of our royal mint. My forebear, Alexander the Third, was born there. The Good Sir James Douglas, my father's friend, took it by strategy the year before Bannockburn, therefore I sent his son to retake it now. You and Douglas are the two most notable soldiers in my realm. I do not wish to have to send to France for a commander to do it! Douglas has failed. Now you must attempt it."

Ramsay shook his head. "I do not think that Your Grace knows what you ask!"

"I know that the English took Roxburgh from the Scots. I say that the Scots can take it back! Make no more to-do, Sir Alexander. If you capture Roxburgh, you can ask of me what you will and I will grant it."

"I seek no rewards, Sire." Ramsay sighed. "I must try to obey your royal commands. But . . . I shall need time. As well as the Almighty's miracle to achieve it! For now, after Douglas's attempt, the English will expect another attempt, be on the alert. Roxburgh is only a few miles from their border. They can be reinforced in mere hours. So they must be lulled into confidence again. And I shall require much time for spying out the land, preparation . . ."

"Time, then, you shall have – but not over-long. King Philip requires proof from Scotland that we are assailing the

English on their northern borders. He does not give us all his aid for nothing! While I leave an English garrison on my soil, I cannot ask for more help. You must see it."

Ramsay bowed to the inevitable.

Thereafter, dressed in the rough clothing of an ordinary countryman, sometimes alone, sometimes with Pate and Wattie Kerr, he spent much time in the Roxburgh vicinity, which lay up Tweed just over twenty miles above Foulden. It was not difficult to haunt the area, for there was a major town just to the west of the castle, one of the original royal burghs of Scotland, with weekly markets, cattle-sales and much coming and going; and although all was dominated by the English in the castle and their men-at-arms, unarmed folk could frequent the place freely. There was a strict curfew at night, however.

The castle's site was, of course, tremendously strong, occupying a narrow neck of rocky peninsula where Tweed and Teviot joined, a long platform forty or fifty feet high, above which the curtain-walls soared for another twenty-five feet or so, those on the south side mainly actually overhanging the Teviot's course. That river had been provided with a slantwise weir or underwater dam, to channel part of its waters through a deep fosse immediately to the west of the castle, in effect cutting off the peninsula from that side also, where the town lay, the water then flowing on into the Tweed on the north side, this great ditch only crossable by the drawbridge. This was the only point where cannon and siege-engines could be brought within range; but the town itself was fortified with walls and gates, so no attack from there could be made without capturing the town first.

Ramsay did not dare visit the area too frequently in case he should be recognised or remarked upon, and sought to make himself entirely inconspicuous, sometimes using a few cattle-beasts to drove in over the Maisondieu ford to the markets, when he might peer and scan the long perimeter walling and the rocky bastions below on that south side. Weaknesses were notable by their absence.

As well as on-the-spot investigations, he sought to make a sort of study, as best he might, of how previous attempts to take the fortress had been made, only the one of which had been successful, other than by long siege and subsequent surrender. That success was the Black Douglas's triumph, of 1313, when, with a comparatively few men, he had taken the castle by surprise. He had deliberately chosen Fastern's Eve for the attack, the night before the beginning of Lent, knowing well that traditionally it was a time for feasting, drinking and general excess, the last opportunity for forty days, with drunkenness and licence almost inevitable. Using scaling-ladders, by night, his men, with black cloaks over their armour, had crept close on the north side, just how was not explained, and managed to climb the steep slopes there and then the walling, to parapet-level, overpowered the guards, such as were not too drunk to sound the alarm, and gradually won control of all save the central keep, where the Governor and his officers slept. Because the drinking-water supply, oddly enough, was outside the walls, there being no spring nor well in the rock-platform, the place's only weakness, the keep had had to yield after a few days of, as it were, internal siege.

Ramsay could scarcely try the Fastern's Eve device again, for surely nothing was more certain than that the date would see the garrison most heedfully alert of all the year; but some other occasion for feasting and celebration might be possible.

Sir Andrew Murray's assault, by outright confrontation and taking the town in a cavalry attack, had been a failure. And how Will Douglas had attempted it was not known. Ramsay had toyed with the idea of riding to Hermitage in Liddesdale to ask, but felt that he just could not go, to rub salt into the wound, and to suggest that *he* might succeed where the other had failed. In Douglas's present frame of mind, that would be too much.

So he pondered and inspected and sought a plan. Blessedly, King David left him alone meantime.

Eventually he decided on Easter Day for the attempt. It was well enough for himself, Pate and Wattie to frequent the Roxburgh area inconspicuously; but altogether otherwise for the numbers of them he would require to descend on the vicinity and expect to be unnoticed. But Easter Sunday would always see a great concourse of pilgrims attending services at Kelso Abbey, and, not wearing armour or carrying swords, his people could mingle with these, it was to be hoped, without attracting undue attention. The abbey was only a mile east of the rivers' junction. Then, by night, and with the Roxburgh garrison, it was to be hoped, also celebrating the end of the Lenten and Good Friday fast . . .

That Good Friday, then, the first move was made, small groups of men, his own Dalwolsey people, set out westwards, on foot, to make their way to Kelso by different routes across the Merse, armed only with hidden dirks and wearing no armour. Ramsay and some of his close associates did ride, on Holy Saturday, leading pack-horses laden with the gear they required, confident that they would look like merchants making for the fairs which always began on Easter Monday.

The abbey-town of Kelso was full of folk that Easter Eve, and the fifty or so men from Foulden, not congregating together, by no means stood out in the crowds. On the Sunday most of them attended one or other of the many services in the abbey chapels which, although damaged by English raiding, still functioned fairly normally. It was a wet day, which was sad for the pilgrims; but Ramsay was unsure whether to be pleased or otherwise. Rain could aid their attempts, in that it might possibly cause the castle guards to do less parading of the parapet-walks and remain under shelter; on the other hand, too much rain in the hills could cause the rivers to rise, and that could complicate his plans.

His orders were that none of his men were to leave the abbey-town until dark, which with poor weather would be early, and thereafter they were to head in twos and threes first southwards, by the causeway-ford and footbridge across Tweed, and then turn westwards up Teviot, which joined the greater river nearby. Something over a mile up they would come to the Franciscan monastic hospice of Maisondieu, for sick folk, which served both Kelso and Roxburgh. Down at the riverside from that there was a ford across to Roxburgh itself, and beside it a mill. That was their first objective. There was ample woodland nearby, where they could hide themselves.

Fortunately, unlike Roxburgh, there was no curfew at the abbey-town, nor walls and gates, so Ramsay, Pate and his horse-party were able to move out at dusk without arousing, they hoped, too much comment. They too made their way to the Maisondieu-ford mill.

The miller there was a Kerr – this was Kerr country – and Wattie had ensured that he would not make any fuss, would not allow his own and his family's sleep to be disturbed by any discreet ongoings. This was important, for he had a shallow scow-like boat, which was essential to their plans. He used it for conveying meal across Teviot, to help feed Roxburgh, drawn across the ford by horses.

They did not need his horses tonight. Ramsay's men untied the boat, loaded it up with their rope-ladders and other gear brought on horseback, and then, with ten men aboard, all it would hold, including Ramsay himself, pushed it out into midstream. But those left on land still held firmly the boat's lengthy tethering-rope, with a further length tied to it, for the craft had to remain under their control. Clutching this, the shore party moved off slowly down Teviotside eastwards, restraining the boat from being swept on in the current.

Ramsay, aboard, was of course anxious. So much could go wrong, especially in darkness. The tether-rope could get snagged on riverside alders or bushes or on sunken logs. The current could be too strong for the towing back. They might miss the weir, in the gloom – and that was vital. And if the river was indeed running too high . . .

The boat did progress satisfactorily enough, on the current, restrained by the long rope. They had almost half a mile to go, with haughland and water-meadow, cattle-dotted, flanking the river here, for the rope-holders to negotiate. From the craft the bank loomed blackly, but it was too dark and wet to distinguish their comrades at the end of the line, although they were probably not thirty yards away. Pate was in charge there, and knew exactly what was required.

Eventually a jerk stopped the boat's progress, and it swayed to and fro in the current. So Pate was holding it, at the precisely surveyed and chosen spot. The weir must be near, then. That weir diverted part of the river's flow into the great artificial fosse or ditch separating castle from town. They wanted to get into that flow, leaving the main river. The craft had its sculls, long oars, probably seldom used, and they could seek to use these here to propel the boat into the right channel, either by rowing or poling.

They heard the weir rather than saw it, the underwater dam causing a distinct slantwise disturbance and waves, easily seen in daylight. Ready for major pulling, two men to each oar, they waited. Pate was to give them a full minute after the halting of progress, before letting out the rope again.

In the event, when the boat did move on again, there was no need for the oars, for it slid into the left-hand channel of its own accord; presumably the force of the current meeting the weir produced an extra surface pull stronger than the normal flow. At any rate, they swirled on and into the dark fosse.

It was an extraordinary sensation to be riding through that artificial chasm, perhaps forty feet wide and cut in the solid rock; the castle walls, gatehouse drum-towers, no doubt full of men, could be only some fifty feet away from them. Would any be peering out, down into the fosse? Surely not. And the darkness in the gut of it was denser than ever.

Despite that darkness, Ramsay was peering ahead. For the next moments were as vital as any. Just where the fosse made a dog's-leg bend north-eastwards, to round the castle's perimeter, there was a small ledge of rock, the only one they had been able to discover when they had prospected the place time and again, from the town shore. There they must pull in and land; nowhere else would offer them a foothold. Also, if the boat went further round the bend, its tether-rope could snag and make it difficult or impossible for Pate to pull it back. In fact, Pate was still no more than one hundred and thirty yards away, they reckoned, however much more it might seem in all the tension and darkness.

As it turned out, they had little difficulty in reaching that ledge, it being right on the corner, the current carrying the unwieldy craft close to the bend. The water was lapping the very surface of it; why Ramsay had been worrying about a rise in floodwater. He was the first over the side, to hold the craft secure.

His men hurried after him, to unload the rope-ladders, grapnels and scaling-nets on to the ledge, two remaining aboard. They probably could not be seen here, right under the walling, even if a guard was looking over.

They had not got quite all the gear out when, with a jerk, the craft began to be pulled away stern-first, still with the pair aboard. Pate had somewhat misjudged his timing. However, it was not important; one man had been meant to go back anyway, to inform of the situation. They paid out now on a rope of their own attached to the prow, this to help draw the boat back in due course.

The eight of them started to move their material slantwise up, on the slippery, steep grass slope. This ledge was critical, because from it, the observers had decided that it was possible for men to clamber, at an angle, up to the actual wall-foot. On

380

this north side it was not exactly cliff, as that overhanging Teviot, but abrupt and broken grass and outcropping rock.

Slithering and sliding, somehow they dragged their ropes and grapnels up that difficult ascent. There was no hurry, at least, for it would take some time for the next boatload of men to arrive. Panting, they reached the base of the actual masonry, and whilst the men sat and rested, Ramsay went to work his way along the wall-foot, peering upwards. The parapet was some twenty-five feet above him, and every now and again along its perimeter there were projections, rounded embrasures for the defence of the walling, or machicolations for the hurling down of missiles or unpleasantness on would-be attackers – although how such attackers were to get there, other than by the route *they* had come, was not clear. Looking upwards even against the wet night sky, it was not difficult to identify two embrasures and one machicolation, now that his sight had adapted to the dark.

He went back to his seven men, and then on, with one other, down to the riverside ledge, to wait. They took up the guidance-rope.

It seemed a long time that they stood there, fearing that there had been some hitch, before they could feel movement along their rope and began to draw it in slowly. Presently the boat did appear, with Redheuch and no less than another fifteen men standing therein, more room available lacking the gear. Getting them ashore, and sending one man back, that gave Ramsay twenty-three here. It would take two more trips.

He led the newcomers up to the wall-foot.

Pate himself arrived with the next batch, with Wattie left in charge with the last group.

While they waited, he took Pate and Redheuch along the walling, to point out the three features projecting at parapet-level. It was at these points that he proposed that they should throw up the grapnels with the ladders and knotted ropes attached, where the hooks were most likely to catch on the stonework.

They waited for the last boatload impatiently, and went on waiting. They drew carefully on that tow-rope, which quickly went tight and gave no further movement. Something had gone wrong. Either the boat had caught on something, or Wattie's group were holding it back for some reason.

Ramsay decided that they should not delay longer. He had thirty-seven men with him. If he could not do what had to be done with these, the remaining fourteen would make little difference. His people were eager to be up and doing, having got thus far. And it was cold and miserable sitting there in the rainy dark, with no talking permitted.

He divided the company up into three groups of a dozen, under Redheuch, Pate and himself, and each equipped with the rope gear, moved along the wall-foot to beneath those projections. He had had his men practising throwing up grapnels, and some had become quite expert in that difficult task. Landing on the masonry the iron would inevitably make a noise, whether or not the prongs caught; so it was important that all should go up as nearly at one time as was possible. He therefore would give his favoured wheepling cry of a curlew when all should be in place and ready. They had eight grapnels, some with light ladders attached, some just knotted ropes.

Taking a deep breath, he gave the whistling signal. Eight sets of brawny arms swung, and hurled aloft their anchor-like implements.

Even from below it sounded a great clatter as the iron struck stone, but at least there was no immediate outcry from above. Men now tugged on the ropes, hoping for the essential snagging on masonry by the barbed prongs, three on each grapnel.

Of the eight, five came tumbling and clanging down again, but three remained firmly anchored – one in Ramsay's group and two in Pate's. As the throwers prepared to try again, Ramsay himself grabbed the knotted rope and went swarming up. This also they had practised at Foulden.

With knots on the rope at one-foot intervals, and using the soles of his feet against the masonry, it was not difficult to part-pull, part-walk himself up that wall, praying that the grapnel would hold. Getting over the parapet itself was the hardest of it, there barking his knuckles against the stone, dirk held between his teeth, prepared to be assaulted at once by guards. But, one leg over, and peering right and left, he saw no sign of men on that parapet-walk.

As he dropped down on to the walkway, another grapnel came soaring over, missing him by inches. Stooping, he picked it up, to anchor it firmly against the angle of his machicolation. Then he leaned over the parapet, and curlew-wheepled downwards three times – the come-on signal.

He went along the walk, to anchor other grapnels, all the time keeping glancing round for guards. None appeared.

His people were now climbing up everywhere, and soon he had most of his company on the walkway beside him. They were grinning at each other at the ease of their success, when a sibilant hiss from Pate stilled everyone. He pointed downwards, not whence they had come but into the inner courtyard of the castle. They heard before they saw, in the gloom. Men were singing in tuneless, drunken fashion. Then they could make out a pair, lurching arm-in-arm across the cobbled yard towards one of the many domestic lean-to buildings within the perimeter walling. The watchers waited, silent, until the singing died away and a door slammed.

Ramsay divided his company. A small group he sent off cautiously east-about, to circle the entire parapet-walk, to look for patrolling sentinels. The main party he led right-handed.

The twin gatehouse-towers, wherein would be the guard-rooms, flanking the drawbridge and portcullis, were only some fifty feet away. Here was where such of the garrison as were not abed would be apt to be congregated. There would be a caphouse at the head of each, giving access to this parapet-walk. In this rain, that is where the duty-men would probably be sheltering. There were not likely to be more than two, at each side.

Picking three of his people and holding the rest back, he whispered to them to move openly forward, dirks ready but laughing, singing snatches of song if they could, to enter that north-side caphouse. They should have little difficulty in dealing with anyone therein, in the circumstances; anyway, the rest would be fairly close behind them. But there must be no shouting, if possible, from them or from their victims.

Nothing loth, the three strolled on, talking aloud and slurring their words, seeking to raise a not very convincing laugh or two. The door of the caphouse was closed. When they opened it, the faint glow of a lamp showed as they went in.

Ramsay and the others now hurried forward. At the still-open door he peered in. It was to see his three men standing over a terrified-looking pair sitting at a rough table, dirks at their throats. The guards had discarded their breast-plates and helmets, which were lying on the table beside ale-flagons and beakers and a single flickering lamp. No words were being spoken, although breathing sounded heavy.

The caphouse was a small place, really only a roofed stair-head chamber. All Ramsay's people could not enter. He and two or three others moved inside, and demonstrating menacingly at the two guards, gagged them with their own neck-cloths and bound them with rope.

Ramsay did not know whether to wait there for a little, or give time for the other perimeter party to circle the walling and reach and deal with the south-side caphouse, so that they could make their ways down the stairs as nearly simultaneously as possible. But he decided against it. If, by any chance, someone should come up here from the guardrooms beneath, the alarm could be given and all put at risk. Leaving a man to watch the prisoners, he took up the lamp and, beckoning to the others to follow, opened the inner door and led the way down the twisting stairway.

Two storeys down and they came to another door, behind which they could hear voices. This undoubtedly would be a guardroom. How many there might be within there was no knowing; but it was well after midnight now and it would be unlikely that many would be awake. His own people were necessarily strung out up the turnpike stair, but all knew that there might be call for swift action now. Nodding, Ramsay opened that door quietly, and walked in.

Three men sat at a littered table, drinking. Perhaps ten more lay under blankets on benches and on the floor, around a fair-sized chamber.

Ramsay actually strolled forward, smiling, the hand holding his dirk behind his back. The men at the table glanced up, but at first did not stir. Then, as they perceived more men crowding in behind him, they did rise to their feet, staring. But by then Ramsay was close enough to leap, dirk forward now, Pate a mere step behind.

They put up no fight; they could scarcely do so, for they were not wearing their arms. Ramsay was loth to stab unarmed men, so merely brandished his dirk before their faces, Pate likewise. Some sleepers stirred and sat up, although not all, but the guardroom was quickly filled with the Dalwolsey men, and in not much more than moments the chamber was theirs. No men had to be slain, although one or two were knocked unconscious.

Scarcely able to believe their so easy success, the victors gathered all the enemy weaponry aside. Then leaving these now tied-up dozen in the care of a few of his men, Ramsay carefully opened the further door, still carrying the lamp.

As he expected, this gave access to a passage directly above the portcullis arch and leading over to a similar guardroom in the south gatehouse-tower, with defensive apertures, machi-colations, arrow-slits and the chain-gear for raising and lowering the drawbridge. Creeping quietly along this, they approached the corresponding door at the other end.

All ready, Ramsay threw it open – and, anticlimax, the chamber was in darkness and empty. Shushing, he stilled the relieved laughter.

They were deciding that they should now mount to the southern caphouse, to aid the other party, when suddenly this guardroom's far door was flung wide and in streamed Redheuch and his group, dirks drawn – to considerable hilarity all round.

Redheuch had little to report. They had found two sentinels sheltering in a turret at the extreme easternmost tip of the castle, above the river-junction, had had no difficulty in overpowering them, and then come on round the walkway to the caphouse above, which had proved to contain only one man, fast asleep.

So now the castle's on-duty guardians were all accounted for, they assessed; but of course there was still the main keep and living quarters, and all the lean-to subsidiary buildings. At this hour it could reasonably be assumed that all therein were abed. But even so, Ramsay would require as many of his men as possible to cope with the situation, and could not spare guards on their various prisoners. There were bound to be dungeons, prisons and vaulted storehouses down in the basements throughout, where they could lock up all their captives. So, moving back to the northern tower, he sent Pate and others further downstairs to explore, with a lamp, whilst they gathered their victims together.

Soon Pate was back. Yes, there was a range of stone-vaulted basements down there, sufficient to hold all the prisoners they were likely to collect. They had even found three wretched captives in one of them. So down all the disarmed guards were herded and duly locked up. Even if they shouted down there, no one was likely to hear, from those damp, semi-subterranean depths.

Now the next problem was the barracks of the castle's garrison, almost certainly situated in the lean-to buildings. And those two singers Pate had given warning of at the very start, probably could give them a lead there, for they knew approximately where these had headed, where the singing had stopped and the door slammed.

They all trooped out on to the puddled courtyard cobbles. There they had little difficulty in identifying the barrack-room, a quite long range of single-storey building, on account of the snoring emanating therefrom. They could only guess how many might be therein, possibly one hundred and more, although some of the garrison would almost certainly be quartered in the town. They found that there were two doors. Ramsay decided to leave four guards at each door, to wait, in case of anyone emerging, although this was probably unlikely. Meanwhile he would seek to deal with the main keep.

This massive oblong tower stood centrally in the court-yard, and in it would be the living-quarters of the Governor and his officers. It had a heavy iron-studded door in an arched entrance, but there would be little point in this being locked. There would almost certainly be a porter's lodge inside, but whether there would be a porter, and awake, was problematic.

Cautiously Ramsay tested the door-latch and pushed. It opened, creaking only a little. Within, there was a dark opening on the right, the porter's lodge, but a glance showed it to be empty.

Ahead, in the vaulted basement, lay the great kitchen premises. They moved, to look in. Banked-up fires gave off a glow, but there appeared to be nobody there at this hour.

The main stair brought them up to the great hall on the first floor, with its dais, tables and benches. The smouldering embers in two large fireplaces provided some light. It was the possible presence of dogs, hounds, here, which could bark and rouse; but there appeared to be none. No doubt the animals would be a nuisance in this enclosed fortress and would be kennelled in the town.

It was normal for the principal bedchambers to be on the

second floor, directly above the hall, to give the lordly ones the minimum of climbing. Lamps illuminated this wider stair. On the second-floor landing there were two doors. Which would be Sir John Musgrave's, the present Governor? One was placed closer to the outer walling, which probably indicated a smaller room. Pointing Redheuch to this one, and sending most of his men higher, Ramsay reached for the latch of the other, and quietly opened the door.

Flickering firelight greeted them, as he and Pate moved in. They saw a handsome chamber, with a great canopied bed in the centre, tapestries and hangings on the walls, cushioned window-seats and skin rugs. On the bed a man and a woman lay, asleep. The man, bearded, lay with one arm flung over the woman, both obviously naked.

The intruders tiptoed forward, while some of their people grinned from the doorway. At the bedside, Ramsay, dirk sheathed now, stooped to shake the sleeping man by the shoulder.

"Sir John Musgrave, is it?" he asked, as the other opened his eyes. He repeated the name, when the man, peering, raised himself on one elbow. The woman stirred.

"A God's name, fellow – what is this?" That came out thickly. "How dare you! Who are you? What . . . ?"

"My regrets at disturbing you, Sir John. You *are* Musgrave? I apologise for incommoding the lady. But I judge that you would wish to be informed, even at this hour. I am Sir Alexander Ramsay of Dalwolsey, and I have repossessed this castle of Roxburgh in the name of David, King of Scots."

The woman sat up as the man gobbled in astonishment, realised that her quite splendid breasts were fully exposed, and huddled down under the covers again.

Since nothing coherent was coming from her partner, Ramsay patted the man's bare shoulder. "You *are* Musgrave?" he demanded.

"I am, sirrah! As, by the Mass, you shall learn! To your cost! What . . . how are you here?"

"I told you, Sir John. I have taken over this castle. My men control all. Yours were insufficiently wakeful Now, put on some clothing. We have matters to attend to. No need further to disturb the lady."

As the other angrily sought for words, Pate leaned over to flick his dirk before Musgrave's eyes. Ramsay waved him away. But the message was sufficiently clear, especially with more men crowding at the doorway. The Governor lifted himself out of bed, not bothering to cover up his companion, who hastily hid her person as he donned a furred bed-robe which lay at the bed-foot.

"Good!" Ramsay commended. "It grieves me to be so discourteous to a fellow knight. But the situation seems to call for it. The guardrooms are both taken, the walls held, all sentinels locked in cells. None have been slain – for, to be sure, a state of truce obtains between our two realms and there should be no fighting. Therefore, I request you, Sir John, to come down with me to the main barracks of this hold, and there to command your sleeping garrison to wake and yield themselves. Peacefully, orderly and without any to-do, leaving all their arms aside, submitting quietly. This done, you and your people may leave the castle at first light, and march to the Border and into England, free men."

"And, and if I refuse, sirrah?"

"Then, I fear, there will have to be hangings. It would much sadden me, Sir John, to seem to threaten such as yourself and your officers. But, you are in the wrong, you must admit."

"Wrong? Admit? A mercy – how that?"

"Your sovereign-lord Edward has declared a state of truce with Scotland. Yet you are here still occupying a Scottish castle, a royal one, the only one still held by Englishmen. Breaking the truce. Against all law and custom. King David rightly requires Roxburgh at your hands. He graciously will overlook your fault, I am assured, so long as you now retire decently to England. You, though none other, may keep your sword. Otherwise, Sir John – you hang!"

There was a long pause, punctuated only by whimperings from the bed. Then Musgrave bowed to the inevitable, if with ill grace.

"I suggest that you don some further clothing," Ramsay suggested courteously. "The night is wet."

So, muttering, the Governor dressed, and while he was at it, Redheuch came in to announce that all was in order above and next door. The officers of the garrison had all been captured without difficulty, some with women, and all were now locked in an upper chamber, with guards on the door.

When Musgrave was ready, Ramsay led the way downstairs. They took lamps with them, and out into the wet dark.

"I advise, Sir John, that you tell your men that this is all part of the truce terms," he said. "That will ease your way, will it not?"

He got no reply.

At the lean-to barrack-range, their guards threw open one of the doors and they moved inside. The smell of unwashed, sleeping humanity was all but overpowering. None were awake, or if any were, stirred.

Ramsay beat loudly with his dirk-hilt on a wooden bench. "Hear you! Hear you, all! Wake, I say! All hear Sir John Musgrave, your Governor. Wake you!"

It took some time to rouse that long barrack-room into wakeful attention. Some of the Scots went round kicking the heavier sleepers, to help.

"Speak, you. Tell them," Ramsay directed.

Musgrave took a deep breath, despite the unpleasant atmosphere. "Hear, all," he said, and at least his voice was sufficiently loud. "I, Governor of this hold, have received . . . received orders. I am to vacate this place. We are to leave. To return to English soil. It is the truce. The truce, you understand? Between our lord King and this Scotland. We are to hand over Roxburgh to the Scots. Forthwith."

There was exclamation, surprise, obvious disbelief.

"More," Ramsay commanded. "Tell them more. Firm commands. All arms to be yielded up. No resistance. You march at dawn. Till then, all these will remain in this barrack. Your command. Tell them."

Sullenly Musgrave did as he was told.

Scarcely believing, his garrison stared, murmuring, muttering. But none actually questioned their master.

"Tell them to await your further orders. Here. Then, come."

They turned and left that bewildered barrackful, whilst the Scots went round collecting all arms and took them outside. There was no resistance.

Ramsay took Musgrave back to the keep. He was surprised to find Wattie Kerr at the door. That man explained that the last boatload had run aground at the entrance to the fosse, the rope snagging on a submerged tree-root. He was sorry. They had come on in the end, found all the grapnel-ropes hanging on the walls, and had no difficulty in gaining access to the castle at last.

There were still about three hours until daybreak. Ramsay told Musgrave to order the cooks and scullions to prepare food for all. His own people could do with it, and the garrison were going to need it on their march over the Border. No objections to this were forthcoming, at least.

Just as dawn was breaking the disarmed English were lined up in the courtyard, Musgrave himself being the only one allowed to carry a weapon. The portcullis was hoisted up and the great drawbridge over the fosse lowered.

"So we part, Sir John," Ramsay said. "My men will escort you for some way. You will be in England before noon." He shrugged. "I wish you well."

The other nodded curtly, and Redheuch, who was to lead the armed escort, pointed forward. The long and still bewildered column started on its way through the gatehouse arch, under the portcullis and over the bridge, to turn right-handed, skirt the town walls, on its roundabout road to England.

When all were gone, Ramsay ordered the drawbridge to be raised again, and set his own guards. Roxburgh Castle was back in Scots' hands.

They sat for two weeks in Roxburgh, after sending word to King David that this royal castle was now his own again, and packing off such of the English as had been billeted in the town. Ramsay always feared that there might be an English attempt from over the Border to retake the place. None developed however, and the new occupiers began to risk moving out and about, but always keeping scouting parties patrolling and on the watch. Then a royal messenger arrived from Stirling to announce David's congratulations and approval and to summon Ramsay to the royal presence. A captain and company were on their way to take over the castle. He was to leave for the north when these arrived.

In due course his old colleague Sir Alexander Seton turned up, with quite a large following, and Ramsay was glad to hand over responsibility for Roxburgh to him. Quite thankfully he set out with his people for Dalwolsey, *en route* for Stirling. At least he could see Mariot before the monarch.

He found David in highest spirits, pleased that he had got rid of the last of the English so soon after his return to his kingdom, clearly indicating that this should all have been done long before, without having to await his leadership. But he was vociferous in his praise of Alexander Ramsay, and scornful of those who had failed him in the matter previously, in especial Will Douglas. Nothing was too good for the captor of Roxburgh.

"You shall have whatsoever you ask, Sir Alexander," he declared. "What is your wish? Anything that is within my gift."

"I wish for nothing, Sire. What I did was no more than my simple duty. As one of Your Grace's Wardens of the Marches."

"Sakes, man, Douglas *could* not do it. And Moray did not. Roxburgh is in Douglas's Middle March. I swear that you should have that Middle March, as well as your own! Or, better still, you shall be Chief Warden of all the Marches, as was Dunbar. That is it!"

"Lord – no, Sire!" Ramsay quite forgot the impropriety of contradicting his liege-lord. "Not that! Never that! You cannot raise *me* above either of these – an earl of Scotland and former co-Regent, and the Flower of Chivalry himself. My friends, both. No, Sire, I beg of you."

"What, then? You are devilish hard to please, Sir Alexander Ramsay of Dalwolsey!"

"Your Grace's trust and regard are more than sufficient, Sire. And, to be sure, it was not only myself. So many others. Patrick Ramsay of Cockpen, Ramsay of Redheuch and all our men . . ."

"They shall have their reward. But you, who conceived all, devised all, led all – you *shall* have the token of my esteem, man. Since you took it, you shall be Captain of Roxburgh Castle, that none may retake it. With all the revenues of the royal burgh of Roxburgh. Aye, and as well as that, you shall be Sheriff of Teviotdale, in which Roxburgh stands, with all jurisdictions, rights, privileges and revenues thereof. That is it – Captain and Sheriff."

"No, Sire, no! Not that, either. Captain of Roxburgh, in name, if you wish, although I would not desire to be cooped up there, as its Keeper. But not, I pray you, Sheriff of Teviotdale. Will, Sir William Douglas, he is Sheriff of Teviotdale. Has been, for long. Teviotdale is Douglas country."

"Yet Douglas could not take me Roxburgh. Or *did* not! You shall have the sheriffdom."

"But . . ."

"Do not but me, Ramsay – your sovereign-lord!" the youth cried. "This is my royal wish and command. You will be Captain of Roxburgh; appoint whom you will as Keeper. And Sheriff of Teviotdale. And that is an end to it. Now you have our royal permission to retire from this audience." That was lofty.

Ramsay bowed himself out.

21

Appointing Redheuch to be Keeper of Roxburgh Castle, as his deputy, for the remainder of that spring and summer Ramsay pursued a policy of masterful inactivity as regards Teviotdale, passing his time between Foulden and Dalwolsey, and seeing no more of the King than he did of Will Douglas. There was a statutory Wardens' meeting in June, but although Moray attended from the West March, Douglas did not, sending a deputy. However, the situation began to worry Ramsay, for of course the Sheriff of Teviotdale had specific duties to perform; it was no mere honorary position, or office of profit, although it was that also. Judicial responsibilities were involved – and the Teviotdale folk, like most other Borderers, were not of the most law-abiding in the land. Word of offences, arrests and apprehensions began to accumulate, and it became something of an embarrassment. If word reached the monarch that he, Ramsay, was failing to carry out his shrieval duties, in neglect of a royal command, there could be trouble. Besides, it was wrong that men, possibly innocent, should be shut up in tolbooths and cells awaiting trial for longer than was absolutely necessary.

So, reluctantly, he sent out orders for a justice-sitting, at Hawick, to be held on a day in July.

Hawick, halfway up the long valley of the Teviot, was the largest centre of population, near to the Douglas seat of

Cavers. Thither Ramsay rode from Foulden, one warm morning, some forty miles across the Merse and by Kelso, Roxburgh and Ancrum, with only Wattie Kerr as escort. The English truce was still holding; and none, even of the most unruly Borderers, was likely to challenge Sir Alexander Ramsay, the East March Warden.

He made for the parish church, on rising ground west of the town centre, which served, as quite commonly, for the dispensation of justice as well as of religious teaching. There was quite a crowd assembled outside by the time that he arrived. Inside, he was welcomed only warily by the parish priest and sundry lairds and land-holders, undoubtedly mainly Douglases. He went to take his seat at a table placed just above the chancel steps.

There, to a full church, he addressed the company briefly, declaring that the King's Grace had appointed him as *acting* Sheriff of Teviotdale – he rather stressed that word acting – and that he had come to dispense justice to the best of his ability. He regretted any delay in coming to Hawick, but as Warden of the East March he had no lack of other duties.

He called for the first case.

This proved to be quite an awkward introduction, for the complainer was a Douglas farmer, from the Cavers property, and the defendant a Turnbull from Bedrule, further down Teviot, a much younger man. It was alleged that Turnbull had bought a roan horse from the Douglas and refused to pay for it, this because the horse had died within ten days of the purchase. The plaintiff declared that the animal had been in sound health when he sold it and any fault must lie with the Turnbull's treatment and feeding of the beast; the defendant's that the horse must have been sick beforehand, and so the sale invalid.

The case was difficult in itself, proof either way being problematical; but it was complicated, as Ramsay well realised, by the fact that the Douglases were powerful here, Hawick being one of their burghs of barony, and the Turnbulls not only a small and comparatively unimportant clan but unpopular in these parts. So the issue was going to require tact as well as justice.

Ramsay was listening to a truculent asseveration by the plaintiff that he had never sold a sick animal in his life, and never would, when the man's voice was drowned out by a disturbance outside the church, the clatter of horses' hooves and the shouting of men. The door was flung wide, and in stalked none other than Will Douglas himself, two or three of his people at his heels. He was not looking in any affable mood.

It was months since the two friends had seen each other, and not, of course, since Roxburgh. Holding up his hand to halt the proceedings, Ramsay rose to welcome Douglas.

"How good to see you, Will!" he exclaimed. "Here's a pleasant surprise. My first judging, on my first day acting Sheriff. *You* know it all, and I do not. Come you, sit here by me." And he moved along the bench behind the table.

Douglas came and sat down, without a word.

"It is kind of you to come aid and advise me, Will," Ramsay went on. "For you have sat here often, and know all the procedure. You know the folk, and I do not. I can do with your guidance."

"And you shall have it!" the other said, deliberately. And reaching down to his belt, he whipped out his dirk, and turning towards his friend, plunged it savagely down between the other man's forward-bent shoulders.

In appalled astonishment, Alexander Ramsay stared, eyes wide, mouth sagging open, sought for words, and then, in agony, slumped forward over the table, before sliding to the floor, amidst uproar in that church.

When Ramsay returned to semi-consciousness it took him some time to realise, in a welter of pain and dizziness, that he was being carried joggingly along slung over a horse's saddle, his head bumping grievously against leather. Even that much he had difficulty in establishing in his reeling mind before he sank again into oblivion.

How many times more he came to, on that nightmare journey, he did not know or care. Fuller awareness only came with more urgent agony when he was being lowered from horse to ground and thereafter being half dragged, half carried, towards some great building. He was vaguely aware of hills close all around and tall towers rearing above him, before he was taken down steps into a dark, damp chamber, thrown on to a heap of straw, and there left alone, a door clanging shut behind him.

Thankfully he relapsed into unconsciousness.

For how long it was before he came into any real awareness of his conditions, he had no notion. It could have been hours, or even days, for that matter, for he was in delirium, his mind throbbing and reeling, his body afire with pain, alternately sweating and shivering. Time meant nothing, the agony everything, insensibility bliss. In it all he did reach certain vague conclusions. He was in some small cellar, probably semi-subterranean, for it was lit, if that word could apply, by a single slit-window, set high. Sometimes faint light came from this, sometimes not. He lay on straw. As far as he could tell, there was nothing else therein but himself and the straw on the damp, earthen floor.

At some stage, his mind cleared sufficiently for him to make some calculation, not with any real interest. The ceiling above him was of wooden boards, not stone-vaulting. He vaguely remembered seeing high towers, a large castle in the hills, probably the Douglas stronghold of Hermitage in Liddesdale. But with a timber floor above, he would not be in the castle proper but probably in some courtyard outbuilding, half underground. Not that it mattered to him, nothing mattered to Alexander Ramsay save hoped for, prayed for, relief from pain and awareness.

He was aware of no visitors, no opening of that door. He was aware of no time-sequence. Sometimes there was iight from the slit-window, sometimes not, which presumably meant day and night. He was occasionally aware of a raging thirst, but not always. Sometimes he knew fierce belly-pains to add to the other bodily miseries – that could be the pangs of hunger; but if so, it scarcely concerned him. Only two matters truly concerned him – his desperate need for Mariot and his longing for oblivion.

As time passed, such consciousness as came to him tended to be unconnected with that dismal, dark cell. He was far away, in better places, sometimes in his childhood and youth, but most often with Mariot, seeing her beside him, speaking with her, holding her, and not in misery or fear but happy. In these interludes he was unconcerned with all the war and fighting and struggle which had made up so much of his life of late years. There were admittedly still grievous periods when he surfaced to desperate pain, gnawing hunger, violent sickness; but these grew ever less frequent, the less to be dreaded, in that strange other-life in which he was now living.

In time, only one conscious activity, tiny as it was, linked him with that cell. His fingers, groping around him, had been encountering hard little rolling objects which some detached part of his reeling wits recognised to be grains of corn, wheat or oats, amongst the straw, on the earthen floor. These he would put to his mouth and swallow, if he could, not in any eager fashion but almost automatically, as in response to those grinding hunger-pains. How and why these seeds of grain should be there he neither wondered nor cared.

How long it took Ramsay finally to replace this strange, disjointed and uncertain form of reality by the true, eventual and eternal reality which awaits all, there was no knowing, the process being as fitful as it was gradual, and in truth unimportant – for what is time here, minutes, hours, days, in the face of eternity?

His release came then, unheralded, like a thief in the night, and Alexander Ramsay rode on to the fulfilment he had been destined for all along, and where one day, love would ensure that Mariot Randolph joined him.

AUTHOR'S NOTE

Accounts vary, as historical versions are apt to do, but most say that it took the wounded Ramsay seventeen days to die at Hermitage Castle, some claiming that those grains of corn, falling through planking seams from a granary above that cell, delayed the eventual demise, unfortunately or otherwise.

What made William Douglas do what he did, is one of the mysteries of history. Historians are inclined to state the bald fact of it, and leave it at that; but the novelist must at least seek for reasons. Douglas was, of course, a man of strong passions, pride and temper; but to murder his friend and fellow-hero in such fashion surely demands some sort of explanation, to be acceptable.

My own theory is that he was, to some extent, a changed man after his period of captivity in England, with the experiences of being marched in chains down through that country, to be mocked at and spat upon, then to be immured in some castle dungeon for months on end, this grievously affecting his attitudes and behaviour thereafter. His eventual unexplained release and return to Scotland at least postulates that he in the end came to some sort of deal with his English captors, a deal of which, at heart, he was utterly ashamed, but which he had to live with thereafter, and which soured his life, freedom bought at too high a cost. Perhaps his agreement was not to attack the English in warfare thereafter – although Edward Balliol, whom they were now abandoning, could be a different matter. Roxburgh Castle was held by the English forces, in their King's name, not by Balliol.

Modern psychiatrists have a theory they call cognitive dissonance, a state in which the victim of a dire injury and threat can in fact come into a strange and almost sympathetic relationship with his oppressors – as has been illustrated not infrequently of late with innocent hostages and their hijackers. Perhaps the famous Flower of Chivalry was a victim of cognitive dissonance? Who knows?

At any rate, while no doubt Douglas paid for his infamous deed in the surely inevitable torture of mind and conscience, he paid some years later in more dramatic fashion. For he was ambushed in Ettrick Forest and slain as a traitor by his own nephew and namesake, who became the first Earl of Douglas, sire of an illustrious line.

So ended the lives of the two men who did most to save the Scotland of Bruce's son, chivalry withered in its flowering.

As to wife and children, history is silent. Whether Alexander Ramsay left a direct heir is uncertain. Some sources claim that he was succeeded by his son, another Sir William Ramsay, some by his brother of that name, some by a nephew; and the long line of the Ramsays of Dalwolsey, or Dalhousie as it is now called, still flourishes in Scotland, as the Earls thereof. But whatever he left in the matter of heir, he left an imperishable record of gallantry, daring and sheer initiative, for all generations to acclaim.

N.T.
Aberlady, 1988

NIGEL TRANTER

DRUID SACRIFICE

King Arthur's niece, sister to Gawain and daughter of King Loth: Thanea was high-born and privileged.

But when, as a devout Christian, she objected first to the druidical practice of human sacrifice and then refused to marry the man her pagan father had picked out for her, her execution was ordered.

Then, after a miraculous survivial, she was cast adrift in an oarless coracle as a sacrifice to the sea-god.

Yet, again, she was saved, cast up on the Fife coast and rescued by the monks of St Serf . . .

The life of Thanea, and of her son, St Mungo, the founder and patron saint of Glasgow, is a dramatic, action-packed story from the early centuries of Scotland's history.

MORE NIGEL TRANTER TITLES AVAILABLE FROM HODDER AND STOUGHTON PAPERBACKS

All these books are available at your local bookshop or newsagent, or can be ordered direct from the publisher. Just tick the titles you want and fill in the form below.

Prices and availability subject to change without notice.

HODDER AND STOUGHTON PAPERBACKS, P O Box 11, Falmouth, Cornwall.

Please send cheque or postal order for the value of the book, and add the following for postage and packing.

UK including BFPO – £1.00 for one book, plus 50p for the second book, and 30p for each additional book ordered up to a £3.00 maximum.

OVERSEAS INCLUDING EIRE – £2.00 for the first book, plus £1.00 for the second book, and 50p for each additional book ordered.

OR Please debit this amount from my Access/Visa Card (delete as appropriate).

Card Number ☐☐☐☐☐☐☐☐☐☐☐☐☐☐☐☐

AMOUNT £ ....

EXPIRY DATE ....

SIGNED ....

NAME ....

ADDRESS ....